"It's not like I don't know your world, Jay."

"I don't want it to touch you." He brushed his fingers over the brace around her neck, his eyes softening with regret and apology. "If this happened because of me . . ."

She took his hand and held it tight, waiting for his gaze to meet hers. "This is not your fault. It's not my brothers' fault. If someone targeted me, it's because you guys are a threat to them and that means you're close to taking them down. That's necessary and important. Worth a good scare and a few bruises."

But was it worth facing for the rest of her life?

"It could have been so much worse," Jay whispered, his deep voice thick with emotion she didn't expect.

Her heart warmed and expanded in her chest.

By Jennifer Ryan

Montana Heat Series
TEMPTED BY LOVE
MONTANA HEAT: TRUE TO YOU
MONTANA HEAT: ESCAPE TO YOU
MONTANA HEAT: PROTECTED BY LOVE (novella)

Montana Men Series
HIS COWBOY HEART
HER RENEGADE RANCHER
STONE COLD COWBOY
HER LUCKY COWBOY
WHEN IT'S RIGHT
AT WOLF RANCH

The McBrides Series
DYLAN'S REDEMPTION
FALLING FOR OWEN
THE RETURN OF BRODY MCBRIDE

The Hunted Series
EVERYTHING SHE WANTED
CHASING MORGAN
THE RIGHT BRIDE
LUCKY LIKE US
SAVED BY THE RANCHER

Short Stories
CLOSE TO PERFECT
(appears in SNOWBOUND AT CHRISTMAS)
CAN'T WAIT
(appears in ALL I WANT FOR CHRISTMAS IS A COWBOY)
WAITING FOR YOU
(appears in CONFESSIONS OF A SECRET ADMIRER)

JENNIFER RYAN

TEMPTED BY LOVE

A MONTANA HEAT NOVEL

AVONBOOKS

An Imprint of HarperCollins*Publishers*

Excerpt from *Dirty Little Secret* copyright © 2019 by Jennifer Ryan.

TEMPTED BY LOVE. Copyright © 2018 by Jennifer Ryan. All rights reserved. Printed in the United States of America. No part of this book may be used or reproduced in any manner whatsoever without written permission except in the case of brief quotations embodied in critical articles and reviews. For information, address HarperCollins Publishers, 195 Broadway, New York, NY 10007.

First Avon Books mass market printing: September 2018
First Avon Books hardcover printing: August 2018

Print Edition ISBN: 978-0-06-264529-6
Digital Edition ISBN: 978-0-06-264530-2

Cover design by Nadine Badalaty
Cover photographs by Michael Frost Photography (man); © namein-fame/iStock/Getty Images (background image); © 1Photodiva/iStock/Getty Images (barn)

Avon, Avon & logo, and Avon Books & logo are registered trademarks of HarperCollins Publishers in the United States of America and other countries.

HarperCollins is a registered trademark of HarperCollins Publishers in the United States of America and other countries.

FIRST EDITION

18 19 20 21 22   QGM   10 9 8 7 6 5 4 3 2 1

TEMPTED BY LOVE

A MONTANA HEAT NOVEL

CHAPTER ONE

Walk away.
Now!
The other way.
Stop walking!
Turn around before it's too late!

Jay ignored the commands in his head, too tempted by some other, deeper part of him and the beauty staring into her glass at the bar to override good sense and self-preservation.

She's your two best friends' sister!!!

Even that didn't halt his steps.

Since she arrived yesterday at the lodge for both her brothers' weddings, every time Alina drew his eye—far too often for his comfort considering his connection to her brothers—she seemed happy, vibrant even.

So why the sadness in her eyes?

Caden married Mia just hours ago. Family and friends, like him, celebrated the couple's nuptials after the lovely garden ceremony with dinner and dancing. Alina enjoyed herself through all of it, socializing with her parents, brothers, and other family. The friendship between her and Caden's wife, Mia, and Beck's fiancée, Ashley, seemed genuine and growing closer.

As the party ended and everyone went back to their rooms to rest before Beck and Ashley's wedding tomorrow, he'd snuck out onto the terrace to take yet another work call. He never expected to come back in and find Alina alone, and looking lonely, at the bar.

He should go up to his room and leave her be. A smart man would, but he took a seat beside her, waved a signal to the bartender to bring him what she was having, then tried to wipe that forlorn look off her beautiful face. "You're not losing your brothers, you're gaining two sisters. As I see it, they've got those guys wrapped around their little fingers, so it's three to two against your brothers now." The stupid statement earned him a halfhearted smile.

"Actually, I'm the only girl and the youngest, so I'm pretty much a spoiled brat and already get everything I want." Her lips turned down into another thoughtful frown. "Mostly."

Jay nodded his thanks to the bartender for the double whiskey. "Well, spoiled is one thing, brat is another."

Alina pinched her lips into an adorable pout. "I don't know how they did it. Those two." She shook her head. "I mean, seriously. I thought they'd be single forever, or at least take another ten years before figuring out work wasn't more important than having a life."

He had a couple years on her oldest brother, Caden, and nearly ten years on her. She probably thought him ancient. He still hadn't taken the plunge, or even come close.

"But somehow in the midst of the chaos that is their lives, they each found the perfect person. I can't even find a guy who can manage to show up on time, put his phone down for a real conversation, and doesn't think a text is as good as a phone call."

"Any guy who thinks he's got something better to do than talk to you isn't worth your time."

Alina rolled her eyes at that bland platitude.

Jay had ignored the beeps and pings coming from his cell phone since he sat down, alerting him that even if he was taking a few days' vacation the bad guys weren't. His work continued—and demanded his attention—even this late at night.

Right now, the dark-haired beauty sitting next to him had his full attention.

He sipped his drink, surprised by the smooth warmth of it instead of the burn down his throat he expected. Alina had great taste in whiskey. He'd had a couple of beers and toasted the happy couple with champagne at the reception, but now wished he'd been drinking with Alina the whole day. She liked the good stuff.

"Trust me, there will come a time when a guy takes one look at you and he'll know what I know, what you already know, that you're a woman worth holding on to." The outstanding whiskey hadn't loosened his tongue enough to make him spill that truth.

He wanted her to know it.

Her head came up and her gaze finally left the drink she'd been staring at for the last five minutes and met his. Her head tipped to the side as she studied his face and looked deep into his eyes. "How do you know? We've barely spent any time together."

"I've been to dozens of birthdays, holidays, and dinner parties with your brothers. We've done the small talk thing on many occasions. But I've really gotten to know you through your brothers. They talk about you all the time. For all their teasing and grumpy attitudes when you tell them what to do, they adore you. They're so proud of you for all your accomplishments. You graduated top of your class, earned your bachelor's degree in three years, completed the Pharm.D program with honors."

Her eyes widened with shock that he knew that much about her.

"How's the new job? Is your boss still giving you trouble?"

Caden and Beck both appreciated the married man who had taken Alina under his wing at work, but grumbled about his overly affectionate way with Alina.

If they saw Jay with her now, they'd send him up to his room. Alone. In their eyes, no one was good enough for their sister. He got a kick out of hearing how they gave every guy she'd ever brought around a thorough once-over and stern warning. The guy who could stand up to them just might be the guy who kept her.

Jay didn't move. He liked her company.

"You mean, is he still 'in love' with me?" Thanks to the air quotes, he didn't think she believed her boss was really in love with her, just harmlessly infatuated.

"Who isn't in love with you?" he teased and earned another sweet smile. "You charm everyone around you with your friendliness with those you know and open acceptance of newcomers."

"Yet we've barely shared more than pleasant chitchat."

True. "In my line of work, observation is key."

Her blue-gray eyes sharpened on him. "And you've been watching me."

Busted. He couldn't deny it.

From the moment he arrived and joined the wedding festivities, he'd been unable to do anything else. All of a sudden, she drew him like a flame in the night. He didn't know why. She was the same attractive woman he'd seen before, but something changed inside him when he spotted her laughing with her soon-to-be sisters-in-law in the lobby. To him, she glowed brighter than the brides-to-be. Her laugh punched him in the gut and lightened his mood all at the same time. He'd wanted in on the joke and to laugh with her. He couldn't remember the last time he laughed like that.

He sipped his drink and tried to tell himself he didn't see the interest in her eyes he'd seen in many other women's sultry looks. He failed at convincing himself because Alina looked more like a desirable woman tonight than his buddies' baby sister.

He needed to rein in the growing desire to reach out and touch her to see if her golden skin was as soft as it looked.

Maybe he'd had one too many drinks. The whiskey loosened his tongue and cracked open the door on his libido. He'd vowed to stay single until he could devote more than one night here and there with many nights in between to a woman. It wasn't fair to leave any woman to wonder if he'd fallen off the face of the earth or just got buried under paperwork.

His job had become his life. And just like Alina, he wondered if the kind of friendship, love, and connection Caden and Beck had found would ever be his.

"Don't worry, Alina, you've got plenty of time to settle down. Enjoy this next part of your life now that you're done with school and finally living your life the way you want. You've got a great job, friends, and a family who supports you. The perfect guy will come along."

She might have time, but he was creeping ever closer to his forties and that dreaded point where people wondered what the hell was wrong with him that he hadn't found someone to share his life. He hadn't even had a long-time girlfriend in the last few years. He didn't trust anyone and was always looking for their angle. In his experience, nobody liked that, especially a woman he was trying to date.

This past year, he'd felt time slipping by along with the dreams he'd had for the wife, kids, and home he'd always thought he'd have someday.

His somedays were running out faster than he'd ever imagined.

Reading the change in his mood, Alina settled her hand over his on the bar. The warmth of her skin sank into him and spread like a living thing through his system.

The sadness faded from her eyes as that sultry look she gave him earlier took over again. "My brothers both said they never saw Mia and Ashley coming. Maybe we should stop looking for love and enjoy the company we're with. Love will either find us, or not."

"I've had a lot of not. It can be fun, too." For a little while, because it never lasted.

Alina picked up her drink, but kept her other hand over his.

He took his glass in his free hand and clinked it with hers. "To the most beautiful company I've had in a long time."

Alina tossed back the last big swallow. He did the same. The warmth from the whiskey spreading through his system was nothing compared to the heat in her eyes.

The next round led to two more as conversation easily flowed. At some point, he turned on the stool toward her and her gorgeous legs ended up between his. They shared some embarrassing but funny stories about their lives. He told her about one particularly strange breakup that had her reaching out and placing her hand on his face. "She seriously broke up with you because your smile is just a tad lopsided?" The frown didn't match the mirth in her bright eyes.

"You should have seen her place. Don't ask me why I noticed, but every switch plate in her house had the screw heads with the lines perfectly vertical to match the up and down switches. Attention to detail is one thing, but that's just bizarre. Seriously, who has the time to do that? Everything was straight lines, pictures and knick-knacks perfectly centered, everything symmetrical."

"Except your face."

He thought it had more to do with him being late to every date or canceling altogether because of work.

Alina brushed her thumb over his lips and burst out laughing.

He wanted her to dip that thumb in his mouth so he could suck it and turn that sweet giggle into a seductive moan.

"That is the craziest reason *ever* to break up with such a handsome man."

"You think I'm handsome?"

She tipped her drink to her lips, then brought it down just enough to stare at him over the rim. "You know you're gorgeous." She took a sip, then gave him a sexy grin. "Even with your crooked smile."

"Doesn't matter. I don't use it much."

She set her glass down and leaned in. The silly moment turned serious. "You should. It looks good on you."

He found himself leaning in to kiss her, but pulled back when he remembered he'd sat down to cheer up a friend—who was strictly hands-off if he wanted to live the next time he saw Caden and Beck.

"Worst breakup?" he asked to get them back to having fun and to cool the heat building between them.

"Well, it's not a breakup, but one guy didn't know how to take no for an answer."

Jay narrowed his eyes, angry some guy came on to her and didn't keep his hands to himself.

She read the look and waved her hands back and forth in front of him. "It's not like that. He just didn't know when to quit. He asked me out practically every day at school. He was inventive, if not silly."

"Silly put you off. You're smart, hardworking, honest. You want a guy who—"

"Isn't a perpetual child," she finished for him. "We were in college. I wanted maturity. He wanted to play high school pranks."

That intrigued him. "Like what?"

"We had to dissect a cadaver."

He scrunched his nose in distaste. "You did that?"

"Not my favorite, but yes. So, I opened his chest and discovered the heart missing. The joker popped up on the other side of the table and held the heart out to me and said, 'My heart belongs to you.'"

Jay groaned and rolled his eyes. "Ah, that's bad. Terrible." He laughed with Alina and it felt damn good to let loose for once.

"Corny as hell and the perfect example of what I'd been dealing with with that guy. Totally not serious about anything."

"And you turned him down flat again."

"I spread the cadaver's chest wide, looked inside, and said, 'Yep, some guys don't have a heart.'"

Jay feigned being wounded and touched his hand to his chest. "Hey, we all have hearts. It's just some of us don't know how to use them." He dropped his hand back to his thigh.

"Are you sure?" Alina leaned in, put her hand on his chest, and the sweet smell of her and a shock of electricity shot through him. His heart stopped for a second, then triple-timed it against his ribs.

For a moment, time stopped. Their gazes locked and held for one second, two, three. He fell into the depths of longing in her eyes and nearly lost himself. With their faces inches apart, he leaned in so close he smelled the whiskey on her lips and felt her shallow breath warm his skin.

A millisecond from losing his mind and kissing her, the overhead lights went out. They broke apart like the band pulling them together snapped. The lights around the back of the bar, highlighting the bottles of booze, bathed them in a soft glow.

"It's twenty minutes past closing," the bartender announced with a knowing grin.

Alina reached for the check, but Jay snapped it up.

"My treat. I can't remember a better evening." He truly meant it.

Their eyes locked.

"Thank you."

"You're welcome."

Lost in Alina and the feelings he shouldn't have clouding his mind and making his heart beat in that strange rhythm that seemed to keep time to whatever it was about her that drew him in deeper and deeper by the moment, he forgot to sign the check until the bartender cleared his throat.

He left the guy a huge tip for giving him the extra twenty minutes with this beautiful woman.

Self-preservation kicked in. He took the hand she'd used to touch him time and again over the last few hours, stood, and brought her off the stool. "Time to go." He didn't know what else to say, but he needed to get out of there before things went too far.

They left the empty bar. God knows if anyone from the wedding party had come in or if they'd had the place to themselves the whole time. He both cared and didn't give a damn if anyone saw them. He'd blow it off as two friends passing the time if it got back to Caden and Beck.

He held Alina's soft hand. She used her free one to punch the button for the elevator. Tipsy—okay, drunk— she swayed on her four-inch heels. He steadied her with an arm around her shoulders as they walked into the elevator. She hit the button for the fourth floor. The cozy lodge Caden and Beck rented out for the weddings wasn't huge, but it boasted some of the nicest rustic-chic rooms for those who wanted an elegant country retreat.

They stood at the back of the elevator, side by side, leaning against the wall, hands clasped tight. He'd see her to her room like a gentleman. Then he'd go back down to his room and sleep alone like every other night since God-knows-how-long-now.

Alina tilted her head to the side and glanced up at him, her blue-gray eyes soft and alluring. "I don't want tonight to end."

Neither do I.

The part of his brain that told him this wasn't a good idea got drowned out by the buzz of lust that swept through him.

Don't do this!

You're crazy!

Ignoring that voice and overrated reason, he leaned forward, hit the button for the third floor, and drew Alina around in front of him. "My room's closer." Those were the last words he got out before he finally satisfied his curiosity and the demand of his body and kissed her.

The second his lips touched hers, fire shot through him. He cupped her face, pulled her up to her toes, and sank his tongue deep into her mouth. Her hands slipped into his jacket, around his sides, and up his back. Her body pressed to his and her belly rubbed against his hard cock.

She moaned. He let loose and kissed her again.

The elevator doors opened with a soft ding. She backed out the door. He had no choice but to follow if he wanted to keep tasting her sweet mouth.

She put her hand on his chest and pushed, breaking

the kiss. "Which room?" She looked down the hallway in one direction, then the other.

It took him a second to get his bearings, but once he did, he took her hand and practically dragged her down the hall to his room.

She traipsed after him giggling.

At his door, he put his finger to his lips. "Shh. Someone will see us."

"You mean hear us." She laughed again.

He shook his whiskey-soaked head, put the key card in the lock, and shoved the door open and Alina inside. She backed up through the sitting area toward the bedroom, kicking off one of her shoes along the way. He pushed the door shut at his back and stalked her, feeling very much like the animal inside of him that wanted to be unleashed to get his hands on her.

She stopped at the foot of the bed, turned, dropped her sparkling purse, and stared at him over her shoulder, silently and provocatively inviting him to slide the zipper down the back of her killer dress. He'd get to it. First, he stopped behind her with his chest pressed to her back and slid his hands over her shoulders, down her arms in a soft sweep of fingertips, then dipped his hands under her arms and around her sides and up her belly and ribs to cup her full breasts. Her hands went up and reached over the back of his neck until her fingers combed through his hair.

Her hard nipples pressed into his palms as he squeezed her breasts and kissed a trail down her neck to the curve of her shoulder. Every taste of her skin, the rock of her rump against his hard cock, the intoxicating scent of her, made him want her more with each passing second.

Impatient to see all of her, he unzipped the satin dress. He shucked off his jacket and threw it aside. The tie he'd loosened at the bar followed. She dropped the front of the dress down her arms and pushed it over her hips with an ass wiggle that made his dick twitch with anticipation. She kicked the pool of blue away along with her other shoe. He undid his shirt cuffs and several more buttons down the front, then reached back and pulled the whole thing over his head and sent it sailing to the floor.

Alina turned to him and stared at his bare chest, lust and admiration in her eyes. He held back the impulse to flex. Barely. His gaze roamed down her beautiful face to her lace-covered breasts. She reached behind her, undid the bra clasp, and tossed the thing, smiling mischievously when he growled low in his throat and moved toward her again, wanting to get his hands and mouth on those pink-tipped breasts begging for his attention.

She backed up and fell on the bed, her breasts bouncing as she scooted back. He almost laughed, but the sight of all that creamy skin, soft curves, and her welcoming smile tightened his chest and shut off his brain to speech because all he wanted to do was devour.

The gorgeous goddess lay on the white blanket, a shapely silhouette of golden skin.

Like gravity, she pulled him in.

He drew closer, leaned over, planted his hands on either side of her hips, and kissed her belly, his bottom lip grazing her dark blue panties. She sighed and melted into the bed. He licked his way up to her belly button and circled it with his tongue before traveling back down, taking the lace in his teeth and tugging the panties down her gorgeous legs. She drew her legs up and to the side, raised her arms to her head, and raked her fingers through her long, dark hair, spreading it over the white bed. Stunned by her beauty, his heart slammed into his ribs. His mind lost all thought but one. Sexy perfection.

He stood at the end of the bed with her panties hanging from his mouth and undid the belt at his waist and kicked off his shoes. Her eyes smoldered as she watched him undo the button, slide the zipper down, slip his hands inside his boxer briefs at his sides, and push his pants and underwear down his legs all at once. Socks went flying a split second before he stood before her naked, his cock standing up, hard as rock. Her eyes blazed. He tugged the panties out of his mouth and rubbed them down his chest, over his dick, and tossed them away.

Her hips rocked back into the white cloud of blankets, then up. An invitation if he'd ever seen one. He crawled up the bed and Alina and laid his body over hers. She cradled him between her thighs and rubbed her slick center against his aching cock. He wanted this one moment to feel her against him, skin to skin, soft to his hard, before he got the condom.

He sank down and kissed her softly, then pressed back up on his hands and stared down at her in the soft light coming through the window sheers from the hotel garden lights glowing outside.

She took his breath away. "You are so beautiful."

"I want to touch you."

Those bold words should have warned him how the night would go. He was unprepared for the onslaught of sensations—fire and need—she'd evoke with every brush of her hands, press of her lips, lick of her tongue, and stroke of her body against his. She held nothing back. She gave everything. Accepted all he poured into making love to her. The immense pleasures they shared forged some kind of bond that had her eagerly responding to him every time he woke her in the night, greedy for more, and needing to make every last second of their time together mean something because somewhere in the back of his mind he knew something this amazing wouldn't last.

CHAPTER TWO

Jay woke up with the last woman in the world he should have in his bed. The pounding in his head was nothing compared to the thrashing he'd take from the two men he worked with if they found out he'd slept with their sister.

Well, they hadn't done much sleeping.

Not helping.

This might be the stupidest thing he'd ever done, especially since he was here to attend both those men's weddings. But he had to admit the beauty sleeping in his arms felt damn good. Intoxicated by more than the whiskey they'd shared last night, he gently brushed his fingers over her soft skin, inhaled her sweet, orange-blossom scent, and rubbed his chin against her silky dark hair. She snuggled closer, her face nestled against his neck, her breath whispering over his chest. Her hand lay over his heart, which seemed to be a bit out of rhythm this morning. He tried to dismiss it as part of his raging hangover, but a part of him attributed it to the woman pressed down his whole side with one leg draped over his thigh, her small foot pressed to his other calf.

She held him like she owned him. Not such a bad thought, especially after the amazing night they shared. He could blame the alcohol for the wild, hungry, unforgettable sex that was still replaying in his mind and hardening one particular body part he thought down for the count after rising to the occasion three times last night. But again, some part of him gave all the credit to the sweet, sexy, kind, giving woman he should have said good-night to at the bar.

It might turn into a curse if her brothers found out about this. Though he didn't know how he'd keep it a secret when he definitely wanted to see Alina again.

And they had Beck's wedding to get through today.

Worry about it later.

That's exactly how he'd been dealing with his personal life.

Just like with a hangover, this morning he needed a little hair of the dog to make him feel better. Instead of reaching for a drink, he leaned down, tilted Alina's chin, and kissed her awake. That same zip of fire rushed through him with an undercurrent of something he couldn't name but felt all the same. She melted into him, her warm body pressing closer to his. He lost himself in her for a minute, then wrapped her in his arms and held her close. "Morning."

Her whole body stiffened a second before she broke free from his arms, planted her hands on his chest, and pushed herself up to glance at the clock. He didn't mind when she obstructed his view of everything with her perfect, pink-tipped breasts in his face. All thoughts about getting up and ordering breakfast fled his mind as the blood drained from his head and headed south.

"It's nearly ten."

He hooked his arm around her middle and flipped her over so she landed on the bed a split second before he covered her body with his. He leaned down and kissed her again. "Morning."

She stared up at him, wide-eyed and nervous. "Hi. Uh, I'm late. I have to go."

He rocked his aching cock against her center. "Are you sure?"

Her eyes dilated and softened. Her body melted beneath his. But instead of giving in to the desire he saw in her eyes, she planted her hands on his shoulders, shoved him off her, and rolled up and out of bed. Her feet hit the floor, but she swayed and pressed a hand to her head.

Yeah, they'd had a lot to drink last night.

He moved to the edge of the bed, gripped her hips, and held her steady. "Slow down, sweetheart."

She shook her head, the wild mass of dark hair cascaded over her shoulders and around her pale face. "Don't call me that." Her gaze locked on her reflection in the mirror over the dresser.

He thought she looked adorably rumpled and well-loved after last night. The shock in her eyes made it clear she didn't agree.

She raked her fingers through her tangled hair. Her gaze dropped to his. "What have I done?"

"I can give you the blow-by-blow. I'm still thinking about how well you did that last night. And then there's that thing you did with your hips—"

He hoped to see her smile.

Instead, she clamped her hand over his mouth. "Stop talking." She pressed her fingers to the side of her head.

"I'll order coffee. Drink some water, it'll help with the hangover until breakfast arrives."

Her eyebrows drew together. "I can't stay here."

"Why not?"

"This was a bad idea."

He didn't like the panic in her eyes. "Maybe, but it was your idea."

That panic rose to outright terror when she glanced down at her naked body. He had to admit, it held most of his attention. She snatched up the sheet to cover herself and ended up exposing his naked lap and morning wood standing proud, begging for her attention, especially now that her eyes locked on it. It twitched with the bolt of lust that pounded through him.

She stepped out of his reach and backed up two more steps. "This was a mistake." She bent and snatched up her maid-of-honor dress and the silky panties he'd taken off her with his teeth last night. She found her lace bra under his slacks and rushed into the bathroom.

He didn't like her running away or the tight feeling it left in his chest, but he knew what he had to do even if he didn't like it.

He abandoned all hope last night would carry through to the end of the weekend. He'd hoped they could smile at each other in the light of day, sober and happy for the time they spent together. A part of him hoped there might be something more.

What?

He didn't know, but the disappointment filling him made him wonder what he'd expected.

"Dumbshit." This didn't end any other way than her walking out the door and both of them forgetting it ever happened. He worked with her brothers. He barely did anything but work. Young, beautiful, she wanted to go out and have fun. He barely had time to sleep most days.

And he was making excuses to ease the rejection that stung more than it should.

She was Alina, his best friends' sister. He was Agent Bennett, the guy who should have kept his head last night for both of them. Enough said.

So he'd be the responsible one and get her out of here without anyone the wiser. Maybe one day, she'd look back on this with fond memories and not that wash of embarrassment and regret he'd seen in her eyes.

He found her purse under the bed, checked the room

number on her key, put it back, and set the bag on the bed where she'd see it. He grabbed one strappy heel off the nightstand, the other from under the coffee table between the leather club chairs by the fireplace. He squashed the idea of making love to her on the soft rug in front of it tonight. He set her shoes at the end of the bed and listened to the water running in the sink while he dragged on a pair of jeans and a black tee. He had time to get ready for Beck's wedding later. Right now, he needed to scout out where everyone was and if he could get Alina to her room unseen.

Shoes on, he walked right out of his room like he didn't have a care in the world. No one in the hall, he made his way to the stairs, passing one of the open alcoves that opened up and looked out over the lobby. Several wedding guests, Alina's parents, her aunt, and Mia's aunt were in the lobby and restaurant below.

He didn't spot Caden or Beck. Caden was probably still in bed with his bride. Beck was probably getting ready for his wedding in a few short hours.

Jay pushed through the heavy door to the stairwell and jogged up the flight of stairs to the fourth floor. He peeked through the small glass panel in the middle of the door and sighed with relief to see the hallway clear and Alina's room one door down.

With everyone occupied with breakfast below or in their rooms waiting for the festivities later this afternoon, he made it back without being seen. He walked in and found Alina slipping her second shoe on. With her hair brushed back, tangle free, and her face scrubbed clean, she looked young and fresh and so damn innocent compared to him even if she was wearing a wrinkled dress.

"Agent Bennett . . ."

He cocked up one eyebrow. "Seriously? Miss Cooke."

"Okay, that was ridiculous."

"It's bullshit, *Alina*." He emphasized her name because damnit he knew every inch of her and hearing that *Agent Bennett* in that formal tone grated every last nerve. He'd woken up feeling . . . happy. The feeling felt strange because he'd gotten used to content. He wanted more of that surge of bliss that filled him when he'd woken up with this particular beauty in his arms.

Clearly not going to happen, his emotions sank past content to weary resignation.

She raked her fingers through her long hair. "I'm sorry, Jay. This is the last thing I expected to happen."

"Me, too. Believe me." While he had a lot of regrets locked away in his soul, this wasn't one of them. Memories of her he'd pull out and savor for a long time to come. Unforgettable, Alina, and what they shared last night, took up residence in the front of his mind and hunkered down for a long stay. He didn't mind. He had too many bad things from his job that often peeked out and demanded his attention. Now, he had something really worth ruminating about day and night.

An odd look came over Alina. One he couldn't read, and he'd made a close study of her the last twenty-four hours. "I have to go."

"I already scouted it out. Your parents, the aunts, and most of the other guests are downstairs in the atrium and restaurant. Your brothers are probably in their rooms, Caden with his bride, Beck getting ready for later today. Hug the wall and they won't see you walking past the overlooks. Take the stairs up to the next floor. There's a small window in the exit door. Make sure no one is in the hallway before you step out. Your door is very close. No one should see you."

"I guess you've got practice sneaking women out of your room."

The flippant, bitter remark stung and left a painful

pinch in his chest. "They usually stay for more, and I'm happy to give it to them," he shot back. Though none of them ever stayed long, they didn't sneak out in the morning like nothing happened and they didn't want to be seen with him.

Maybe that last part wasn't fair, but he didn't like her making him feel that way. He got they needed to be discreet. He thought they'd be in on it together. This felt very much like she wanted to erase last night and him from her life.

She stood perfectly still, her face blank, but her mind working behind her gray eyes that hinted toward blue unlike her two brothers. He couldn't imagine what she was thinking, but she shifted from one foot to the next like she couldn't wait to get out of here.

He gave her an out because the need to touch her again grew with every second she stayed. "You're late, sweetheart. Better get going before someone misses you."

He missed her already and didn't like it one damn bit.

Her full lips pressed together a split second before she turned for the door. If she meant to say something, she thought better of it. Unable to watch her leave, he turned to the windows and stared out at nothing but another lonely day and empty bed ahead of him.

The door opened. He felt her hesitate and prayed she changed her mind and came back to him. For what, he didn't know. She wasn't for him. He stuffed his hands in his pockets so he didn't turn and reach for her in some vain attempt to hold on to something neither of them were willing to bring into the light of day. He had no intention of ruining Beck's wedding by giving him a reason to kill Jay today of all days.

When the door closed and the emptiness of the room suffocated him, he told himself it was over, maybe not easy, but done. For the best. Right?

CHAPTER THREE

Alina stood on the terrace, the sun bright overhead. Her brothers smacked each other on the back in greeting as Beck waited for Ashley to come downstairs and promise to be his wife for the rest of her life. Mia had made that same promise to Caden yesterday. He looked damn proud of himself and well satisfied after a long night in the honeymoon suite. The smile on his face, the happiness dancing in his eyes, made her little green monster rear its ugly head again.

She mentally socked him back into his hole where he belonged because she was happy for her brothers. They deserved to be this every-dream-came-true happy.

Okay, so last night after everyone left the reception she'd let loose the self-pity she'd kept hidden behind an Oscar-worthy smile all day. She'd always thought she'd get married long before her workaholic brothers. The simple plan turned out to be not so simple. Leave her high school days in the rearview mirror where they belonged along with the high school sweetheart she liked but didn't want to keep forever. Attend college, hook up with a few cute guys, have some fun, gain some experience and perspective in life and love, but stay focused on the future. Grad school was where she planned to find the perfect someone: educated, motivated, kind, gorgeous, and oh-so-in-love with her. They'd build the foundation for their relationship as she finished her Pharm.D. She'd get the perfect job, they'd get married, and live happily-ever-after.

The first two items she checked off the list no problem. Desperate to leave high school and be on her own, she loved college and meeting new people. She found her drive to be the best. Her circle of girlfriends was easy to maintain but dates became few and far between. Nights out with friends gave way to long hours studying.

Now she had the job she mostly loved, worked long hours as a partner in the business, and went home to her empty rented one-bedroom. Thanks to her scholarships, she'd been able to use the money her parents saved up for college plus a sizeable loan to buy into the business. In a few years, she'd have it paid off and make a more than decent living with a lifelong career ahead of her.

Yay?

Lately life felt very unsatisfying. She'd accomplished everything she'd set her mind to but the one thing she really wanted: a husband and partner to share it all with.

She wanted a family. Children. Yeah, she still had time, but she wanted it now while she was young enough that she didn't have to play beat the biological clock.

Her brothers always cautioned her to be patient. But her caution in letting people, men in particular, get close to her landed her right here, where her brothers were both about to be happily married and she was single and exactly what that word implied. Alone.

You weren't alone last night.

Agent Bennett.

She needed to stop thinking of him that way.

Jay found her looking for the meaning of life in the bottom of her whiskey glass and cheered her up. She'd always thought of him as her brothers' work partner. DEA. Tough. Quiet. Driven. Another workaholic who carried the weight of all the bad things he saw in the worst of society on his broad shoulders and lurking in the darkness she saw in his eyes. Strength inside and out and a barrier around him that warned not to get too close.

But last night he'd dropped that mistrust learned on the job. She'd seen the man who found himself at his buddies' weddings and wondered why he didn't have that for himself. After all, her brothers were younger than him. Yet love and a wife eluded him. That common thread tied a bond between them that felt so strong last night she hadn't wanted to lose it. Yes, she'd had a lot to drink, but she'd still had enough mental faculties to know exactly what she wanted: to get her hands on the muscles that bunched beneath his pristine white dress shirt. He'd been so perfectly put together in his suit, his dark hair flawlessly styled, all she'd wanted to do was mess him up.

And let's face it, the heat in his gaze had burned away all her inhibitions.

No man had ever looked at her with that kind of hunger and need so clear and direct.

He'd fought it and tried to be the good guy and walk her to her door. But the possessive hold he'd kept on her hand made her feel even more wanted. And protected. Safe.

A triple threat to any woman's heart.

And so she'd leaped, telling him exactly what she wanted: to be with him, because despite how little they really knew about each other, she trusted him. Partly because her brothers trusted him to watch their backs on the job, but mostly because something inside her instinctively knew he'd never hurt her.

But she'd hurt him this morning by acting like a complete idiot and letting all the consequences of sleeping with him crowd her mind and make her take a huge protective step back before things got too complicated and messy.

In reality, she'd wanted to wallow in his arms in that rumpled bed, drown in the need in his eyes, and glut herself touching him and making love while both of them let the world slip away to just the two of them.

And those overwhelming feelings filled her up to bursting and scared her because she'd never experienced anything that all-consuming and powerful, so she'd run this morning when she'd wanted to be as free as she'd been in his arms last night.

She wanted to blame the alcohol, make excuses that it could never work because he worked with her brothers, and told herself he was too old for her and not in the same place in his life as her. But all of that sounded like a lot of bullshit just like he'd said to her when she'd tried to turn back the clock and go back to thinking about him as Agent Bennett, not Jay. The man who made her go up in flames again and again in his arms and held her like he didn't want to let her go.

She'd seen it in his eyes a split second before he turned his back and stared out the window, his hands deep in his pockets like he couldn't trust himself not to touch her again. Like if he kept looking at her, he'd come after her.

It thrilled her, and yet she'd still walked out the door, too afraid to discount all the reasons why it wasn't a good idea and acknowledge all the reasons why it felt so right.

"Alina!" Beck glared down at her.

"Huh? What?"

"Can you take Adam upstairs and tell Ashley it's time and to hurry the hell up?"

"I can, but you might consider starting off your marriage without ordering your bride to 'hurry the hell up.'"

"I spent the night without her and haven't seen her yet today. I want her here now."

Alina tilted her head and smiled. "That's barbarically sweet."

Beck grunted. "She said today, one o'clock she'd be my wife. Let's get this done."

She gave Beck a smart-ass salute. "As you wish."

She turned to go, but Beck caught her arm. "Hey, are you okay? You look kind of tired. Didn't you sleep last night?"

Barely. But the couple of hours she did get were really great, especially when she woke up warm and wrapped around Jay's strong body. "I'm fine."

Not really. Truth be told, she regretted how she'd acted this morning. Last night probably shouldn't have happened, but she wanted more at the same time.

It was all still too fresh in her mind.

She definitely didn't want Beck seeing that she was hiding something from him. The man could ferret out secrets with one long survey of her face and all she couldn't hide in her eyes. To keep him from looking too closely, she took Adam's hand and led him across the terrace to the open doors leading into the hotel.

"I hope she's ready," Adam said.

Alina wasn't ready to see Jay, but he appeared in the doors and stopped short and stared at her for one long moment. His gaze didn't drop, but he took in every inch of her just as she did the same to him. Gone were the casual jeans and tee he'd worn this morning. The suit fit him to perfection and highlighted his lean, toned frame and wide shoulders. He looked every bit the man in control she'd met in the past. The man who took charge in his job let her take the lead last night and this morning. Though he'd ruled her body last night, she'd dictated what would happen and if it would happen.

While the look in his eyes clearly said he wanted her, he'd let her go this morning because he knew, just like she did, that this could never work. What they shared between the sheets didn't translate to day-to-day life. They had nothing in common. More things separated them and stood between them than pulled them together.

Still, a wave of heat washed through her body. Memories of last night heated her cheeks and made her breasts grow heavy. Her nipples peaked behind the silky dress that hugged her curves and in this moment made her feel completely naked. No doubt, Jay remembered every square inch of her and recognized the desire she couldn't hide.

"Jay," Caden called from behind her.

He stepped out the door to meet with her brother. As he passed, close enough to brush his arm against her shoulder, he whispered, "Beautiful," then continued on like they didn't know each other intimately.

What did she expect? She'd walked out on him, making it clear that what happened last night ended.

That's not what you really want.

"Aunt Alina, come on." Adam tugged her hand to get her moving again, but all she wanted to do was go after Jay and . . .

What?

She let Adam hit the button for the elevator and lead her to his mother's room. After all Ashley and Beck had been through to get to this day, she especially loved that they had Adam to share it with them. Ashley may have saved Adam from a madman, but Adam had brought a joy and healing to Ashley and Beck these last months. They had become a family the day Beck saved Ashley from freezing to death after her daring escape. But today, that family would become official. They had everything.

The ache in her stomach intensified as she thought about what she'd walked out on this morning. Wishful thinking that the possibility of what could be might have turned to reality if she'd stayed played with her mind and worse, her heart.

Mia stood outside Ashley's door. "Hey, you two." Her beautiful new sister-in-law smiled with a carefree gleam in her eyes. What did she have to worry about today? She'd married the man of her dreams last night and she and Caden had a bright and happy future ahead of them.

The hangover headache pounded back to life behind her eyes with all the swirling thoughts about love, weddings, what her brothers had and she wanted. "Marriage looks good on you."

Mia beamed. "I can't believe Caden and I are finally married."

Adam used the key card his father gave him to open the door.

Mia's gaze swept over her. "I'm not the only one glowing this morning. Did you hit the spa last night?"

"No." Something better. The same thing that made Mia's smile so bright today. Though thinking of her with Caden . . . yuck! And double *yuck*! She switched that blip of a mental picture and tuned back into her night with Jay and the incredible vision of him pressed up on his hands, his hips locked to hers, and the smoldering look in his eyes as he stared down at her.

"You should treat yourself."

She'd definitely treated herself last night when she gave in to impulse and followed Jay to his room like a wolf on the hunt. He'd treated her to a night filled with fantasies come true. Which she indulged in until she woke up this morning and, instead of acting like a sophisticated woman, ended up having a mini panic attack. She'd hurt the man she'd crawled all over during the night, and made an undignified run for it without so much as a "good morning" over coffee. Maybe if she'd gotten her caffeine jolt she could have handled things better. She owed him an apology but didn't know if she had the nerve to deliver it.

Mia touched her hand to Alina's back and gave a little push to send her into the suite. Ashley greeted them, standing in her beautiful gown looking every bit the gorgeous, Oscar-winning movie star.

It took some time to get past being starstruck every time she saw Ashley, but now that they'd gotten to know each other, Alina only thought of her as Ashley, the woman who'd taken her broken brother and made him whole again.

For that alone, she'd love Ashley the rest of her life. But having a new friend, two of them, sisters she'd always wanted, added something to her life she never expected. A camaraderie she'd never shared with her brothers because they didn't get it. Sure, she was close to Caden and Beck, but sometimes they made her feel like an alien from another planet because they didn't relate to her worries and problems. When she talked to them, all they did was tell her how to fix it, or offer to fix it for her. Ashley and Mia listened. Sometimes, that's all she needed, someone to let her spill her guts and say, "You'll figure it out." Because she was perfectly capable of dealing with her problems.

Most of the time better than she handled waking up with Jay this morning.

Why couldn't she get him off her mind?

Because she hated acting the fool. Not because she missed him. Not because she wanted to get to know him better. Definitely not. Because then her brothers would find out and the last thing she needed was them stepping in and telling her what a bad idea it was to date *him*.

Of course, they said that about every guy who came into her life no matter how innocent the relationship.

Maybe she should sic them on her business partner and get Dr. Grabby-Hands to back off.

Mia hugged Ashley, then held her at arm's length. "Oh my, you're gorgeous."

Ashley admired Mia in her pretty burgundy matron-of-honor gown. "You're beautiful, Mrs. Cooke."

Mia beamed her a wide grin, pleased to hear her new name.

"Mommy, you're so pretty." Adam hugged Ashley's legs.

Ashley brushed her hands over his golden hair, not caring one bit if he wrinkled her dress. "You're so handsome." Adorable in his tiny black tux, he smiled up at her.

"Daddy can't wait any longer. He said, 'Hurry it up.'"

Adam so easily let the past go and settled in to being with Ashley and Beck and accepting them as his new mother and father. He spoke to his birth father, Scott, once a month.

"Beck is impatient to get this done." Alina shook her head. "Once those guys set their minds to something, they want to get it over with immediately."

"Caden sure did look relieved when you said, 'I do,' yesterday," Ashley pointed out to Mia.

"Like I'd say no to that man." Mia's bright smile matched the happiness in her eyes. The joy matched that in Ashley's smile. They'd found their true happiness.

Alina wanted some of that for herself.

You had it last night.

And if she tried to keep it, she'd have to accept what came with it. Lots of nights alone. Broken promises because of work obligations. And the one thing that tore at her all the time. The memory of sitting by Beck's hospital bed wondering if he'd survive his gunshot wounds after a drug bust went terribly bad. The fear clawed at her even now, thinking of those hours and days when he'd been critical. And after he got out of the hospital, the weeks he'd been sunk in pain and depression so deep she couldn't reach him.

Ashley did. Somehow, she'd broken through his walls and found the courage to face life with Beck.

Alina didn't want to live every day wondering if the man she loved would go off to work one day and never come home. It scared her too much to see her brothers face danger every day.

She and Jay had fun last night, but the only thing she faced right now was the hangover sapping her energy and souring her stomach. Tomorrow she'd go back to work and Jay would go back to taking down bad guys. They'd go their separate ways. She didn't have to watch him put his life on the line, though she admired him for doing it. She wouldn't hold her breath, waiting for something terrible to happen, because eventually it would. Her brothers' lives had taught her that.

"Let's not keep Beck waiting." Ashley's sweet voice pulled her out of her head and those dark thoughts. Ashley bent and looked at Adam. "Do you have the rings?"

Adam pulled them out of his coat pocket. "I got this, Mom."

So confident. He got that from Beck. Alina wished she tossed caution to the wind more often and brought out her cocky side. Her brothers had mastered that while she'd learned from their many close calls to stay away from the wild side.

Ashley kissed Adam on the cheek, took his hand, and they all walked out of the suite. Mia rushed ahead to tell the gathered guests to take their seats in the garden. Adam ran for Beck at the end of the aisle to let his father know Mom was on the way.

"Thank you for all your help with the wedding preparations, Alina."

Alina turned from the open terrace doors, told herself she wasn't looking for one particular face among the guests, and smiled at her soon-to-be sister. "The wedding coordinator did most of the work."

"But I enjoyed doing it with you. It gave us a chance to get to know each other better."

Alina smiled but remained distracted by the guests taking their seats outside.

"And since I've gotten to know you, I can see something is bothering you. Did one of your brothers upset you?"

"If it was Caden, I'll talk to him," Mia volunteered.

"Not at all. They've been too preoccupied with the wedding."

Ashley touched Alina's arm. "Is that it? Are you feeling left out?"

Kinda. But not in the way Ashley meant. She felt left out of love.

And this was Ashley's big day, not Alina's Pity Party.

Alina gave her a hug. "Thanks for worrying about me, but I'm fine. I'm over-the-moon happy for you and Beck." She smiled at Mia. "And you and Caden."

"It may sound cliché but it will happen for you someday." Ashley's bright optimism gave Alina hope.

The music played outside. "It's happening for you right now." Alina took her place behind Mia and accepted the lovely bouquet of white roses the florist handed her. Mia made her way down the aisle. Alina waited her turn and spotted Beck impatiently waiting at the front, his eyes locked on the space behind her where Ashley waited just out of sight. Love and hope shone in his eyes. A love she'd seen grow these last many months.

The wedding coordinator signaled her to go. Alina turned to Ashley first. "Thank you for making my brother so happy. I love you. Welcome to the family."

Ashley's eyes glistened with unshed tears. "Thank you, Alina. That means so much to me. I love you, too."

Alina walked out the door feeling better, knowing she did have love in her life. And one day, she'd find her true love.

Of all the many guests staring at her as she walked down the aisle, one drew her eye but she turned away. There might be fire between them but Alina wasn't about to get burned by a man who felt right but was all wrong.

CHAPTER FOUR

Jay wanted to wring Alina's pretty neck, kiss her, and drag her back to his bed all at the same time. Instead, he took another sip of his beer. No more whiskey. He'd save the high-priced champagne for toasting the bride and groom dancing together under a massive crystal chandelier surrounded by their family and friends. They looked so damn happy.

They deserved that kind of happiness.

And he was beginning to think he'd done something to piss off the fates and the universe so that every woman who came into his life found it so easy to walk right back out of it. Of course, he'd done a poor job of making them want to stay. He'd certainly never found himself thinking about buying a diamond ring and making a promise for forever. Hell, he couldn't even promise he'd show up for a date. But somehow Caden and Beck managed to make it work. They found women who understood them and the life they lived and how their work was more than a job.

He didn't immediately understand why he'd woken up with Alina feeling so right until she walked out the door and closed it on them. A part of him felt like she could be one of those rare women who understood those things about him because she'd seen the impact of the job on her brothers. She understood the work and the men who did it. And maybe that was exactly why she'd left. She didn't want any part of delving deeper into that world with him.

How much of it had to do with what he did for a living, and that he worked with her brothers? How much of it had to do with him in particular?

He'd never know because she'd made it clear their paths were never to meet again. She'd practically run away every time they got within ten feet of each other today. She went out of her way not to look at him all through the meal. He couldn't seem to keep his eyes off her.

This wedding couldn't end soon enough. He'd go home, back to work, and forget this weekend ever happened.

"What'd she say to piss you off?" Beck slapped him on the shoulder with those damning words. If Beck picked up on . . . whatever the hell was going on between him and Alina . . . and found out he got drunk with his sister, then slept with her, Jay was a dead man. Admittedly, he didn't get much sleep. Which if pointed out to Beck would only result in an even more torturous death.

Which made him think fast to play this off. "Ashley's an angel, and definitely heaven-sent seeing as how she'd need divine grace to reform you."

"Nice try, but I've seen you glare at my sister about five times now. So what gives?"

Shit. Better to take the blame than lay it at Beck's sister's feet. "I stuck my foot in my mouth, said something stupid, and fumbled the apology."

"She put you in your place, did she?"

Yeah, on the other side of the door and out of her life and memory. "She's got a way about her. It was stupid." He should have walked away from the bar instead of taking a seat next to her. Short of that, he should have seen her safely to her room last night, said good-night, and gone back to his bed alone. Like most nights. A series of dumb decisions. He shouldn't be surprised it turned to shit this morning. "I'll stay out of her way. Don't worry about it, man."

"She can hold her own."

Relieved Beck intended to drop it, he turned the conversation to why he was really here. "Congratulations, Beck. I don't think I've ever seen you happier."

"It's strange. We've been together for months. I always knew she was mine, but the second she said 'I do,' I felt the connection between us roar out, 'She's mine!'"

Why the hell isn't Alina mine?

He squashed that thought and the possessive beast that showed up out of nowhere this morning and wouldn't go back to his lair and hibernate.

"Weird but true," Beck went on. "Anyway, I need a favor."

"Sure. Anything."

"Alina is taking Adam for a few days while Ashley and I are on our honeymoon, but Alina has this thing on Wednesday. I had a sitter lined up to take him that night, but it just fell through. Mind babysitting my kid instead of a bunch of drug dealers that night?"

"Pizza, ice cream, and cartoons. I'm in. It'll be a hell of a better night than most."

"You need a woman."

I had the perfect one last night. "You and Caden took the best ones."

Beck and he stared at Caden and Mia wrapped in each other's arms swaying on the dance floor. Ashley danced with Beck's dad. Alina twirled Adam around, dodging the cupcake in his hand as he clutched it and took a bite.

"It changes everything." Beck's adoring gaze followed his bride across the dance floor.

For the lucky ones. Jay didn't seem to be one of them. "Anyway, thanks for taking care of Adam. Do you want me to work out the details between you?"

Jay didn't want Beck to think there was a good reason for him and Alina not to have a simple conversation about pickup and drop-off for a babysitting gig. "I'll set things up with her. Go get your wife. Looks like it's time to cut the cake before your son steals another cupcake."

Sure enough, Adam tried to pull Alina back to the cake table. Alina laughed and tried to coax the little guy away. Adam finally gave up and swung back to Alina, running right into her legs with his white cream-smeared face. Alina's eyes went wide with shock, then resignation when she saw the mess on her beautiful red dress. Adam looked up at her with a wobbly bottom lip and apology in his eyes. Alina cupped his chin and smiled down at him with her lips pressed together, then said, "It's okay. Accidents happen."

Jay read the words on her lips and thought about last night. No accident, but, yeah, sometimes things happen. And it's okay. The mess can be wiped clean.

He'd do that now and set them back to being, if nothing else, acquaintances who smiled politely, exchanged pleasantries, shared babysitting duties, and never let on that they'd spent one wild night in each other's arms.

He'd learn to live with it.

And start now. He went around the bar, ignored the side-eye from the bartender, wet a towel at the sink, and rushed over to Alina. Beck used a napkin to wipe Adam's face and hands.

Jay handed the wet towel to Alina. "Try this." Their fingers touched and it evoked a thousand memories from last night.

Alina's breath hitched. She covered by gently wiping the largest lumps of frosting from her dress, then using a clean corner to wipe the smears. "Thank you." She spoke the words bent over and staring at her lap, wiping nonexistent frosting away.

Jay didn't say anything with Beck standing right there with Adam in his arms.

"Sorry, sis." Beck poked his finger into Adam's belly. "What do you say?"

"Sorry."

Alina smiled for her brother and nephew. "It's okay."

"Looks like Ashley is ready to cut the cake." Beck glanced back at the three-tier wedding cake and his bride smiling for him.

"Go. I'm fine." Alina shooed him away with her hands, the dirty, wet rag swinging. She still didn't look at Jay.

"Jay can take Adam on Wednesday."

Alina's gaze finally swung to him but she didn't say anything.

"We'll work it out. Go, your bride is waiting for you." Jay cocked his head toward Ashley, waiting patiently with the wedding coordinator, who checked her watch.

Jay waited for Beck to walk out of earshot. He didn't look at Alina when he handed her his phone. "Put your number in there. I'll text you for the pickup and drop-off times. Oh, and your address."

Alina tapped all the information into his cell, then sent herself a text. He tried not to make it obvious he watched her every move, noticing her slender fingers, the swell of her breasts pressing against the top of her gown, the incredible way she smelled. Sweet and exotic.

"Now I have your number."

"You had my number last night."

Her gaze snapped to his. "What is that supposed to mean?"

He stuffed his hands in his pockets and sighed. "Nothing."

"I think you meant something."

"You didn't want to hear it this morning, it won't make a difference now. You made up your mind."

"What is it you think I think?"

"That this is a bad idea." He couldn't really disagree when Beck kept checking them out despite helping Adam pick another cupcake from the assortment stacked on a rack next to the big cake.

She didn't say anything. He took his phone from her hand hanging at her side and walked away. They didn't have anything left to say to each other on that subject. He skipped the cake and opted for another beer at the bar. He kept his back to the room and everyone having a good time dancing and celebrating the happy couple.

Two hours and three beers later he made his way up to his room and flopped on the perfectly made bed with his back against the headboard. He stared at the black TV and listened to the silence, fighting the memories of him and Alina wrecking the bed that felt as empty as his heart.

He didn't regret last night. In fact, doing it all over again nearly had him running to Alina. But his friendships with Caden and Beck mattered. They were like brothers to him. He didn't want to disappoint or piss them off. This could affect the trust and bond they'd forged working side by side in the trenches.

But Alina was a grown woman with her own mind. She'd been all-in last night. And he'd reveled in the way she gave herself over to him with complete abandon. So much so, he wanted more. A lot more.

She may have had second thoughts this morning, but there'd been that moment when she stared at him before she walked out and wanted to say something but held it back. He'd caught her looking at him throughout the reception and thought he'd seen a glimpse of the same look in her eyes that he felt inside. That what happened between them may have been impulsive, but doing it again was a temptation worth repeating.

Wishful thinking?

No one had to know.

It'd be their secret.

You hate secrets.

But he really wanted her and more of that happy feeling he found last night and woke up with this morning.

He wanted her like he'd never wanted anything in his life. If he didn't do something, try, he'd regret it.

"Shit." He rolled off the bed and headed for the door. He didn't often give in to impulse or subject himself to the potential for utter humiliation, but tonight he threw caution to the wind again and headed to Alina's room. He knocked on the door and it opened seconds later. Alina stood there with a glass of champagne in her hand wearing the hotel bathrobe loosely tied at her waist. He swept his gaze over her beautiful face, scrubbed clean of makeup, the swell of her breasts in the opening of the robe, and all the way down her gorgeous legs to her bare feet and sheer-pink painted toes.

She didn't say anything, so he did. "I have a bad idea."

She pushed the door wider, grabbed his shirt and tie in her free hand, and yanked him into the room. He took that as a *"yes!"* and bent, grabbed her by the ass, hauled her up so she wrapped her legs around his waist, and kissed her, igniting the fire between them all over again.

He carried her toward the bed, their lips locked, his hands sinking down past the hem of the robe to her bare bottom. He squeezed the two globes in his palms and grinded her against his aching cock. She moaned into his mouth and he took the kiss deeper. His knees hit the edge of the bed but he didn't put her down. He slid one hand past the swell of her bottom and found her center.

"You're so damn wet for me." He slid one finger, then two, deep into her slick core.

Her legs locked tighter around him as she rocked against his hand. She placed one hand on his face and kissed him hard and deep.

He wanted his mouth on another part of her, leaned forward, and set her on the bed, breaking the fiery kiss. The robe gaped open at her breasts, just hiding her pink nipples from his view. He grabbed both sides, spread it wide, and bared her naked body to him. He remembered every curve and plane, but she still took his breath away.

"God, you're beautiful."

She downed the last swallow of champagne, tossed the empty glass over the edge of the bed, hooked her hand at the back of his neck as he leaned over her, and pulled him in for another searing kiss. He pressed her down into the mattress, then laid a trail of kisses down her neck, chest, and belly to the very tempting prize he desperately wanted to sink into and lose himself in her warmth, locked in her arms.

Instead, he tasted heaven and earned the very satisfying reward of his name tumbling from her lips on a deep groan. He hooked his arms under and around her thighs, drawing her legs over his shoulders. He buried his face between her legs, licked her soft folds, then sank into her, taking her up to the peak but not letting her fall over the edge. He kept her right there, lingering over the task, and drawing out every sweet sigh and greedy groan for mercy. He gave it to her, driving one finger deep and sucking her clit. She shattered against his lips and a wave of pure satisfaction and lust shot through him.

He eased away, kissing his way down her thigh and gently setting her legs back on the bed. He stood and reached for his tie.

Alina stared up at him, her half-mast eyes sultry and filled with satisfaction. "That was a very good bad idea."

He pulled his loosened tie over his head. "Just good?"

"Amazing." She sighed out the word, her eyes locked on his chest as he undid shirt buttons.

He dropped his shirt and coat all at once down his back and attacked the belt, button, and zipper at his waist. He managed to grab the condoms out of his wallet before he dropped his pants and boxers. He'd kicked off his shoes at some point during loving Alina into the puddle of bliss before him on the bed. He slipped off the last of his clothes and stared down at her.

"I have another bad idea." He put one knee on the bed and leaned forward with one hand planted next to her hips.

She rolled out of the robe and onto her belly before he could cover her with his body. She glanced over her shoulder, and drew her long, dark hair away from her face and held it in her hand. The seductive smile held his attention. "You shouldn't have to come up with all the bad ideas." She spread her legs wide, giving him a tempting view of her sweet ass and the glistening invitation that said, "Fill me," clear as day.

He rolled on the condom, crawled up the bed behind her, covered her body, his chest to her back, and thrust into her to the hilt, nudging her forward a few inches before she pressed back into him. He stilled, seated deep inside her hot body, and whispered in her ear, "Excellent bad idea."

She rocked her hips forward, then back into him and he lost all control and took temptation all the way to mind-blowing climax.

They settled into the quiet. He held her close with her back curled into his chest, his face buried in her hair, his arm locked under her breasts, his hand curled around her side. Her heartbeat vibrated against his palm as her breathing evened out and he enjoyed the feel of her against him.

He didn't sleep. He didn't want to miss a moment of this.

When she spoke, her words were soft and unsure. "We shouldn't do this again."

"I've got another bad idea left in me." He rolled her onto her back, shifted over her, and showed her in slow, long strokes of his body, against and in her, that some bad ideas should be repeated over and over again.

Exhaustion claimed her while she lay tucked at his side, the single lamplight casting a soft glow over her beautiful face. He looked his fill, soaked up every second she was in his arms, then reluctantly slipped from the bed before the morning light touched the sky and she turned her back on him again and crushed the heart she'd somehow taken from him without him even trying to hold on to it.

He stood by the door, looked back at her sleeping in the bed, her hand lying where he'd been beside her, and whispered, "I wish every bad idea I ever had was as good as being with you."

Tempted to slide back into bed and make love to her again, he forced himself to remember this was always meant to end. In a few hours, he'd drive home and go back to work, she'd attend the family-only breakfast before Beck and Caden left on their honeymoons and she returned to her life.

Although it should surprise him how much he wanted her in his life, it didn't. Not after all they'd shared.

But his life and hers didn't connect. Except on Wednesday when he picked up Adam for the night.

Even if they couldn't keep doing *this*, he couldn't wait to see her again. Just one more time.

CHAPTER FIVE

Alina pulled into the lot behind the medical building where she worked in the pharmacy. She cut the engine and stared at the brick wall, lost in thoughts about this past weekend and the man who refused to get the hell out of her head.

Day and night, she thought about him.

The all-too-familiar flush of heat that rushed through her, both welcome and unwanted all at the same time, reminded her of how she felt when he looked at her, touched her, and simply held her.

But that was over now. He'd gotten her back for walking out on him and left her sleeping alone in her hotel bed that felt even more massive and lonely without him in it.

Damn the man.

Okay, yes, she'd deserved it after the way she acted, but when he'd come to her room after Beck's wedding, she'd thought maybe there was a chance to turn a one-night stand into something more.

Nope. The empty bed and no goodbye said it all. He'd gotten what he wanted—okay, so had she—and walked away before things got complicated. And messy. She didn't even want to think about what her brothers would say if they found out she hooked up with their friend.

Despite knowing very little about him, she liked him.

She liked that she let loose around him. She didn't watch what she said, or hold back taking what she wanted. A couple times she'd actually begged him for more. As greedy as her, he'd given it to her with a tilt to his lips that hinted at a satisfied smile, though it didn't come easy and looked rather rusty. The why came easy enough. His job. The things he did and saw day in and day out working with people at their most desperate and vulnerable. Add in the dangerous ones out to kill or be killed over the drugs and money that flowed no matter how hard the DEA tried to stop it. The constant battle took its toll.

She saw it in her brothers. She saw it in the weariness in Jay's whiskey eyes.

She saw a lot more. In the dark, she'd found herself staring at a man who, asleep in her arms, found a peace she didn't see in him any other time. It did something strange to her heart to see him so at ease with her. She'd reached out and traced her fingers along the lines flaring out from the corners of his eyes, down his cheek, past the gray threaded through his dark hair at his temples to the stubble just starting to appear on his strong jaw. In the quiet, he leaned into her touch and held her tighter. She'd snuggled in and found her own peace and a feeling she couldn't identify but felt very much like the thing she'd been searching for without really knowing it.

Something she thought she had, but never felt quite like that any other time.

Contentment. Like she and everything in her life was exactly right in that moment.

And she let it go.

She let him go.

Without a word. Without a fight.

And now she was without.

Alone again.

It sucked.

She didn't like this empty feeling gnawing at her gut and turning her chest into a heavy hollowness that made it difficult to breathe in moments like this when she let her mind wander into daydreams about what could be when she knew that door had closed.

She'd closed it.

He'd done the same after one more bad idea that felt so right.

As goodbyes went, it was pretty spectacular.

None of her other relationships had ended quite so well.

The metal back door to the pharmacy swung open and bounced off the door stopper inches from the metal railing. She expected to see Mandi, the pharmacy tech, coming out to dispose of the cardboard boxes in the recycling bin. Instead, two twenty-something men walked out but turned back to speak to whoever remained concealed by the open door.

One of the guys, in jeans and a too big black zip-up hoody hiding his face, hung back. The other, dressed nearly identically, though he had chains hanging in a wide loop from the front of his hip to his back pocket, pointed a finger at whoever stood behind the door. A tattoo she couldn't identify darkened his forearm and disappeared beneath the pushed-up sleeve of his black sweatshirt. The jabbing of his finger toward the unseen person punctuated the anger in the guy's stance and whatever he said that had the other guy bouncing on his toes with his hands fisted at his sides like he wanted to fight but held back. For now at least. The energy surrounding those men seemed charged and ready to spark.

Tattoo guy finished whatever he had to say, dropped his menacing pointy finger, balled his fists at his sides, and leaned forward in a challenge to the person he tried to intimidate. If Alina stood behind that door, she'd be frightened and want desperately to get rid of the menacing man. He turned to leave and in that split second, he caught her staring from inside her car. His dark eyes held her gaze for a moment. The second he turned to leave, she let out the breath she'd been holding.

He rushed with his friend to a truck parked down by the neighboring building. The back door slammed shut, making her jump. Once the men were on their way, she slipped from her car, checking to be sure they didn't change their minds and come back, then headed into work.

The back door was locked, as it should be, so she found the key on her ring and inserted it into the first of three locks. Because they received deliveries through this door, she glanced up at the overhead camera knowing her partner, Dr. Noel Evans, watched on the monitors behind the counter. She waved, wondering if he'd been the one talking to those men and why.

Two more locks and she walked into the back room that was mostly just an open space with shelves of cleaning supplies, boxes of over-the-counter medications, and first aid products. There was a private restroom for staff. She unlocked her locker, stowed her purse, and traded her lightweight summer cardigan for her white coat with her name embroidered in blue. Dr. Alina Cooke. She'd worked hard to get here. She'd secured her future with a job she liked and would provide a good living for her and the family she hoped to have soon.

She passed the office and used her key card to enter the main pharmacy where they dispensed prescriptions. Noel helped Mrs. Cafferty at the counter with her monthly rheumatoid arthritis prescriptions. Alina went over and stood next to Noel.

"How are you today, Mrs. Cafferty?" Alina took one of her hands, careful not to move her swollen knuckles, and held it between her own. "Did the pharmaceutical company come through with your drug discount?"

"Noel took care of it. Without his help, I don't know what I would have done."

Noel placed his hand over their joined ones. "Now that you're taking the medication regularly, your symptoms should decrease and you'll be more comfortable."

Yes. And thank God, because Mrs. Cafferty endured endless pain having to forego her overpriced medication on her limited income just so she could eat and keep the heat on. While pain medication masked aching soreness, her arthritis grew worse. The new medication could take months to start working but would make a real impact into easing her disease.

Noel finished ringing up the purchase.

"Don't skip doses to spread out the medication."

Mrs. Cafferty had done that for weeks until the last of her meds ran out, which also made them less effective.

"Take it as prescribed. If anything changes with your discount or you're not getting the relief you need, you come back and we'll see what else we can do. We'll work with your doctor to find the right cocktail to make you better."

"You got yourself a sweet one here." Mrs. Cafferty patted Alina's hand, then took her bag from Noel.

He swung his arm around Alina's shoulder and pulled her close to his side. "I sure did. Together, we'll keep all our customers in good health."

Alina tried to hide her discomfort. Noel seemed to be one of those touchy-feely people. He shook hands with customers, offered a comforting touch to the shoulder or squeeze of the hand when someone seemed upset or agitated, and hugged those he'd known for years.

She'd been Noel's partner a few months. In that time Noel had treated her as a respected colleague. He'd shown her the ropes and expressed how happy he was to have a new friend and someone to share the burden of the operation. As time went on, the simple gestures increased in frequency and intimacy. Still, he seemed to know there was a line and went right up to it, but never crossed it.

Or maybe she allowed him to move that line a little at a time. And now she found herself embraced in a possessive kind of hug that seemed friendly but also a bit too much because he held it instead of letting her go right away.

She stepped aside, waved goodbye to Mrs. Cafferty, and went to the counter where they filled prescriptions and looked through the stack of orders.

"Anything wrong?" Noel stood beside her and finished counting out pills for a prescription he'd started working on before waiting on Mrs. Cafferty.

She deflected. "Who were those guys out back?"

Noel stilled for a moment, the stick in his hand held between two pills and the rest spread out on the board. He didn't look at her, but slid the two pills to the right into the trough to be dumped into the prescription bottle once he had the allotted amount. "What guys?"

"Black boots and hoodies, jeans. Early twenties. Took off in a beat-up red-and-white truck."

Noel nodded, then smiled, though it didn't reach his eyes, and his hand shook. "Must be Mandi's boyfriend. I thought I heard them fighting before she left out the front for a coffee run."

Alina didn't know Mandi had a new boyfriend, let alone one she was fighting with. Though Mandi-with-an-*i*, purple hair, multiple piercings, and a blue butterfly tattoo on her neck liked tough guys with attitude, Alina didn't think she'd stand for a guy pointing at her like that and yelling in her face.

Not Alina's business. People fell for each other for all

kinds of reasons and managed to stay together despite arguments and obstacles.

Noel lost count of the pills and started over, darting looks at her as he went.

She wondered why. "Are you okay? You seem distracted."

Noel leaned against his palms on the counter and hung his head.

"Is it Lee?"

Noel's wife had been battling a second occurrence of ovarian cancer for the last three months.

"The doctor told us yesterday the tumor hasn't shrunk. She's going back for more tests to see if the cancer has spread to her other organs. She starts a new round of chemotherapy day after next."

Sympathy swelled in Alina's heart. Alina placed her hand on Noel's shoulder. "I'm so sorry. The last round was really difficult for her."

"I don't know if she can keep this up."

Lee suffered from the side effects from the treatment. They left her fatigued, sick, and without an appetite, but she'd endured and gotten through it.

"She's a fighter. She won't give up. She's got you and the girls."

Noel's grown daughters were away at college. One in grad school, the other studying nursing. Noel and Lee's pride and joy. And part of the reason Noel took on a business partner. He needed someone to be here when he took time away to be with his ailing wife. Mounting medical and college bills made it a necessity.

Noel turned and wrapped her in a hug, holding her close. Too close. Too intimate with his cheek pressed to her hair. She wanted to offer comfort, but found herself pushing him back with her hands on his chest. He captured one hand and held it against his heart.

"It's so good to have a friend like you." His gaze held hers. His filled with sincerity mixed with what she hoped wasn't desire, but felt very much like a longing for something more than friendship.

The bell over the front door dinged.

"I brought you a caramel macchiato." Mandi stopped in her tracks and stared at Alina and Noel standing close and looking like they were more than friends.

Alina's first instinct was to pull her hand free and step back like two people caught doing something they shouldn't. But she held her ground. She didn't want to give Mandi or Noel the wrong idea.

"I'm very sorry to hear about Lee. If there is anything *she* needs, just let me know." A gentle reminder to stay focused on his wife never hurt.

Noel released her and tried for a smile. "Thank you, Alina. I can always count on you." He nodded to Mandi. "I think I'll take my lunch break."

"We've got you covered," Mandi assured him, her gaze bouncing between them.

Noel left the pills he'd been counting for Alina to finish and walked out the front door, looking even more troubled.

"Everything all right?" Mandi handed her the coffee.

"Thanks. He's worried about Lee and this new round of chemo."

"Probably about the bills, too."

Alina took a sip of the much-needed caffeine. "No doubt." Alina had her own bills to pay. Lucky for her, nothing so far had interfered in her three-year plan to get out from under her school and the partnership debt. Once she was free and clear, she'd make enough to live a very comfortable life. So long as she lived within her means and tucked away a little bit each month for emergencies.

That's you, Alina, ever cautious and careful.

The tedium her life had become made her want to break out and do something wild. Or maybe that side trip to Crazy Town with Jay over the weekend made her want to return.

Not going to happen. That kind of wild held too much risk. The last thing she wanted to do was get involved with a guy like him. Someone just like her brothers, who spent all their time on the job or thinking about the job.

Let's face it, they never really left it.

Well, she had to admit, her brothers had found a better balance with Ashley and Mia in their lives. That didn't mean Jay wanted a committed relationship. At his age, he'd never been married and had no kids. Seemed obvious he didn't want either.

Mandi touched her shoulder. "Hey, I lost you."

Alina shook herself out of more thoughts about Jay. "Sorry. It's been a long few days with the wedding and taking care of Adam."

"How is he doing with his mom and dad gone?"

"They call in the morning and at night before he goes to bed. He loves staying with me. And I've tried to keep him to his routine as much as possible. He's at day camp now. His babysitter will pick him up and take him to my place."

"Don't you have that community center drug program tonight?"

"Yeah." All she really wanted to do was go home, color dinosaurs with Adam, read him bedtime stories, and snuggle her nephew as much as possible before his parents came home from their honeymoon.

The tingle in her belly warned she also wanted to see Jay again. A little too much. More than she wanted to want to see him.

"You okay? You seem off, too. Sad."

Sad? Maybe.

Mandi waved hello to a customer walking in the door. "I get it. Seeing your brothers get married, the happy couples, makes you want to tap into whatever love mojo they found. Seems to me, dating gets harder and harder the older we get."

Alina nodded her agreement and used the opening. "Sorry to hear about your fight with your new boyfriend."

Mandi's eyes filled with confusion. "How did you hear about that?"

"I saw—"

"Yo, Mandi." A guy with wild curly brown hair yelled over the door ding and held up a purple sweater that matched Mandi's hair. "You forgot this."

Mandi used her badge to rush through the side door into the main store. She launched herself into the guy wearing baggy jeans and a red work polo. She kissed him hard and fast, then stepped back. "Thank you, sweet."

The guy's baby face cheeks flushed. "See you after work?"

"I'll be waiting."

"Korean barbecue and Warcraft?"

"Old-school. You got it, sweet." Mandi hugged him.

The guy's smile notched up to megawatt. He stepped back, stared at Mandi for one long moment, then turned and left, though it was clear he wanted to stay with her.

Mandi glanced over at Alina. "Isn't he adorable?"

"Yes. And not what I expected."

"He's a total nerd. Works at the electronics store across the street next to the coffee shop. We hit it off playing Warcraft online. It's a game," she added for Alina's benefit because Alina was totally clueless. "I had no idea we'd crossed paths like a hundred times. He'd waited on me at the store a couple of times and I never really noticed him. Then we started this private chat and it went on and on for hours and days. He's the best. Won tournaments and cash prizes. He's this total badass in the gaming world." The smile and pride in her eyes said how much she adored him. "It's weird, huh, you meet someone a couple of times but don't really see them, then you do and there's this connection like a blast that opens up your heart and your life."

Alina understood all too well. She'd crossed paths with Jay on several occasions but never really took notice or gave him any mind. Until she did and found something there she hadn't seen but unexpectedly latched on to her and made her take notice.

"You two look really happy together."

"I've never met anyone like him. He's smart and kind and sweet as can be. I used to think guys like him were weak, but he's not. He's got this dedication and drive. But you know what I love most about him? He pays attention to the little things. What I like to eat. Things I like to do. What I say and how I feel. He cares."

And right before her eyes Mandi took on that same look she'd seen in Beck and Caden when they fell hard and fast in love.

"Anyway, the tiff we had last night was nothing. I got a little jealous that this gamer skank tried to move in on him. We sorted it out." In bed, based on the sultry gleam in Mandi's eyes.

Wait. The fight happened last night. And Mandi's boyfriend wasn't the man at the back door.

So who were the two guys arguing with Noel?

Why did he lie about it?

CHAPTER SIX

"**Y**ou never said your new partner was a sweet little honey. You tap that, Doc?" Brian sucked on his cigarette, then blew out a stream of smoke all while giving Noel that snide smile.

"She's not a part of this." Noel didn't want to be a part of it either, but he'd set the ball in motion when these two dipshits tried to rob him a second time. Noel had come up with a foolproof plan to make some decent side money with the drugs at his disposal, but he lacked a street connection. So instead of handing over the drugs during the robbery and calling the cops, he'd made them an offer. Instead of a one-time score, he'd supply them with a steady stream for a hefty cut.

The plan worked better than expected. The drug money and partnership with Alina helped keep his head above water with the endless college tuition and medical bills. But Alina posed a problem he thought he could mitigate with careful management of the pharmacy accounts. He hadn't anticipated she'd ever see Brian and Davy. He certainly didn't want them to focus on her.

With the money she brought into the business and his ability to spend more time with his wife when she needed him, he didn't need the headache or risk of continuing this dangerous endeavor. But there seemed no way of getting out of it now, not without considerable leverage or money. He had neither. They had him by the balls. When he tried to slow things down, keep their partnership on the down-low, Brian showed up like he did today and squeezed to remind him what happened if Noel didn't go along with the plan.

Brian's eyes narrowed with menace. "She saw us. She can tie *us* to *you*."

"She doesn't know anything. She thinks you're the new guy in Mandi's life."

"I'd tap that." Davy, Brian's number two, raised an eyebrow and nodded, a leering grin on his pimpled face.

"Both of you are going to stay away from Mandi and Alina and the store. We can't take the chance of being seen together. The last thing we want is people asking questions about our association."

Brian stepped close. "Then get your shit together, Doc, and give me that list."

"It's too soon after the last time. We need to wait, or the cops will find the link."

"Supply and demand, Doc. We've got a demand you need to supply." Brian flicked his cigarette to the pavement. "If you won't do it, maybe I don't need you. Your pretty little partner should be easier to convince and control." Brian made a rude gesture, holding his fisted hands out at waist level and pumping his hips like he was fucking her.

Noel lost it and grabbed Brian by the front of his shirt. "You touch her, this all goes away."

Brian slammed his hands into Noel's chest. He lost his grip and fell backward and onto his ass on the ground. Brian stood over him and pointed a finger in his face. "You've got more to lose than any of us. This is a simple arrangement. Don't make it hard."

Noel rolled up to his feet and glared at Brian. "Then don't be stupid." If he let Brian walk all over him, this would unravel and he'd lose everything. "You knew going in this would take patience. It wouldn't be a big score but a steady stream. You'll get what you need when I tell you it's time."

"You've got two days. I'm not a patient man." Brian waved at Davy to get into the beat-up truck. Brian started the engine and revved it. He leaned out the window, his arm draped down the scarred door. "She's already seen us with you. That's a problem I don't need." Brian sped off, sending a cloud of dust up in the empty parking lot outside a deserted antique store on the outskirts of town.

Noel stood immobilized, not believing the threat underlying Brian's parting shot.

Brian wouldn't do anything stupid. They had too much to lose. Noel had to believe Brian wouldn't go after Alina, but the fear of being wrong sent a blaze of acid eating his insides.

Sweet Alina. Yes, she always asked after his wife, but her concern for him, *his* well-being, touched him deeply.

If something happened to Alina . . . he couldn't bear thinking about it.

CHAPTER SEVEN

The last few days dragged as Jay looked forward to seeing Alina again. Something about her tugged at him. The want to see her had turned into a gnawing need. Memories of her took up all his limited free time and then some the last few days. He couldn't concentrate on anything but her.

He didn't get it. The smart and logical thing meant staying away. But his brain kept circling back to her, and the desire to see her again increased with every passing second.

If he could pinpoint the one thing about her that drew him in, maybe he could let it go, but it seemed to be the sum of so many things he knew about her and the millions of things he didn't but wanted to discover.

Alina was a complication he didn't need but wanted in his life all the same.

He had no idea if she wanted to see him again. They'd spent two amazing nights together. She had to feel some kind of connection to him, right?

Go find out if there's something there. He'd been sitting outside her condo for nearly five minutes staring at the tan building with white trim. She had the end unit with a wide garden area bordering her patio enclosed by a short lattice fence.

Shit security if you asked him. Anyone could hop that

flimsy barrier that offered little privacy and break the glass sliding door and be inside her house in seconds. They could be in and out in minutes. With the back exit to her complex diagonally across from her place, the getaway car could speed away before any of her neighbors noticed because her place blocked their view.

He couldn't help it. Security, knowing the ins and outs of a place, potential threats; those things came as natural as breathing.

You're procrastinating.

The clock read five-thirty straight up. Right on time, even if he arrived early. He slipped out of his car and walked up the short path to her front door tucked along the side of her place, facing her neighbors. Anyone could blitz attack her here and no one from the street or other homes would see.

He shook his head and knocked.

"Jay!" Adam yelled inside.

"It's open," Alina called.

Sure enough, the door wasn't locked. He walked right in and glared at the beauty pulling her purse strap up her shoulder. "Are you crazy?"

She stopped fussing with her bag and stared at him. "Excuse me?"

"You leave your door wide open. Anyone could walk right in."

"I left it open, so *you* could walk right in."

"You've got no security here."

Alina rolled her eyes. "Believe me, I know. My brothers have said as much in a million different ways."

Jay planted his hands on his hips. "Why don't you do something about it?"

"Because no one in the complex has ever been robbed. It's a safe neighborhood. The facility has a security guard who patrols the place."

"One guy for a place this big. All the bad guys need to do is post a lookout to keep an eye on him and rob every place on the opposite side of where he's patrolling."

"If I ever want to take up a life of crime, I'll keep that in mind."

Jay dropped his gaze to Adam standing between him and Alina, his head bouncing back and forth as they talked.

Adam's gaze found him. He waited for Jay's reply to Alina's ornery comment. Jay knew better than to keep this up, especially when she'd already had the argument with her brothers.

"Hi." Adam held up his hands to be picked up.

Jay scooped up the little boy and held him close. "Ready to have some fun?"

Adam's eyes beamed with excitement. "Yes. Pizza."

"First thing on the list, buddy. I missed lunch. I'm starving."

"Why'd you miss lunch?" Alina cocked her head to the side as her gaze dropped from his face and scanned all the way to his feet, then back up.

He liked that she worried something might have happened to him. "I'm okay, Alina. With your brothers out, I'm covering for both of them which adds up to a lot more paperwork and a meeting with an informant that wasn't happy to see me instead of Beck."

"Everything turned out okay, though?"

"Great." He lied to protect her from the hard truth that he'd been slammed into a wall with a gun pointed at his head before Jay could identify himself to the shit-head low-level drug dealer Beck used as an informant. Jay took it in stride. Beck warned him the guy tended to act like big shit, but was all bluster. To give the guy an ego boost, he hadn't laid the dumbass out flat when he caught his attack out of the corner of his eye. The second

Jay jabbed him in the gut with his elbow, he buckled under and backed off. Good thing he expected Jay, or he might have actually found the balls to pull the trigger. Jay believed the gun was all for show, but he never underestimated anyone who thought they had something to prove.

Alina didn't need to know. He didn't want to give her another reason not to want to see him.

"If you're swamped, I can pick Adam up later at your place instead of you keeping him for the night."

Jay shook his head. "I'm looking forward to some guy time." He poked Adam in the tummy and made him laugh. "Where are you going anyway? A date?" Since he came to take the kid, it seemed the easiest way to find out if he had competition.

Alina frowned. "The last date ended with the guy asking me to pay my share of our coffee order, then telling me he had his van outside if I wanted to spend a little more time with him before I headed home."

"What the f . . . hell?"

Alina smiled at his almost swearing in front of Adam. "Careful."

"What kind of men are you dating?"

"None right now. For obvious reasons. His profile said he was a marketing executive. Turns out he worked at a copy place and got fired a few weeks before our date. Hence the reason our six o'clock date was coffee and not drinks."

"Couldn't afford to buy you a glass of wine," Jay guessed.

"He didn't have the decency to buy my coffee. He took the half muffin I didn't finish when he left."

Jay couldn't help the laugh. "Oh man. That's not right."

"I hate liars. He admitted to using the app to hook

up. When I told him that's not what I was looking for, he said, 'What a waste of time and a grade A . . .' bottom?"

Jay tried to hold back the laugh, but when Alina chuckled over the disastrous date, he joined in with her. "I can attest to his loss."

The smile on her lips slipped, but her eyes warmed, which encouraged him to do what he'd spent the better part of the last few days mulling over, only to come to one conclusion: he didn't want this thing between them to end. Her brothers would definitely kill him for hooking up with their sister, but the chances of that decreased if he dated her with the intention of truly getting to know her better. Because two nights wasn't enough. He wanted more. Of everything.

He'd prove to her and her brothers that he could be a good guy. He wanted to be for Alina.

"Let me make up for all mankind and take you out on a proper date. You name the day and where you want to go, and I'll prove to you at least one guy doesn't suck."

The heat in her eyes turned molten. "If memory serves, yes, you do."

He took a step closer. "Happy to do it again."

They stared at each other for a long moment until Adam called out, "Pizza."

Jay fought to tuck away the raging desire burning through him. For now. Damn hard to do when Alina wore a pretty, short-sleeved black knit shirt that molded to her breasts and trim body, with a wide, silky, black skirt that flared out and swished back and forth with every tiny movement.

"About that date?" He wasn't leaving without one.

It took her a second to decide with one side of her mouth scrunched in a thoughtful pout that drove him crazy wild to kiss her. "Sunday?"

"That works," he confirmed. He'd have to shift some things around, but he'd make it work.

"McGee's downtown at seven?"

Beer and burgers. His kind of place. Definitely his preferred kind of date. "I'll pick you up at six-thirty."

"I can meet you there."

He shook his head. "Proper date. I pick you up, we eat, share some conversation and laughs, I see you back to your door."

And by the look in her eyes, he'd have her in her bed one more time.

Sunday seemed like a long few days to endure to get to, but being alone with Alina again was worth the wait.

Jay bounced Adam in his arms. "We should be off. Where are you going?" She still hadn't answered him on that front.

"I'm giving a talk on prescription drug abuse at the community center for parents of at-risk teens."

"Wow. You should have told me. I'd have come with you, given the DEA perspective and all."

"I grilled Beck and Caden for information to add to my speech." She pressed her hand to her belly. "Still, I'm nervous. Public speaking isn't really my thing. I hope they ask a lot of questions. Making it a conversation makes it more comfortable."

"You'll do great."

"I wish Noel hadn't pushed it on me, but he wants me to become more active in the community." She waved him toward the door. "Sorry to rush, but I don't want to be late."

"What time does your thing end?"

"I'm not the only speaker, so it goes to eight-thirty. Noel told me to expect people to want to chat afterward, more of a one-on-one thing, so I hope to get out of there by nine. Why?"

"Call me when you get home, so I know you're safe. You can tell me how it went."

"Jay, that's not necessary."

"It is to me. Downtown late at night, not the kind of place for a single woman to be alone. Call me, or I'll call you."

"I'm perfectly capable on my own, you know. I don't need another worried brother."

Jay closed the distance between them and kissed her before she knew his intention. Their lips met and he held the kiss until he had her attention and she leaned into him. He kept the kiss tame—for Adam's sake—and pulled back just enough to look her in the eye. "I'm not your brother."

Dazed, she shook her head. "Nope." The *p* popped out of her mouth. "Definitely not." She pushed him back, keeping her hands on his chest, and backed him toward the door. "Gotta go. I'll call you later."

"That's my girl."

She stopped and dropped her hands. "This is still a bad idea."

He cupped her cheek in his palm. Her soft hair brushed his skin. He wanted to sink his fingers into the dark, silky mass but held back. They didn't have time for all he wanted right now.

"We're amazing at bad ideas. All I'm asking for is a chance to see if there's more than heat between us. I want a chance to know you better, because I want there to be more between us." He'd never been that open and honest with another woman. With Alina, it came naturally.

Alina pressed her cheek to his palm. "I want to get to know you better, too."

"Pizza," Adam demanded.

Jay shared a smile and laugh with Alina, reluctantly

released her, and picked up the race car duffel bag by the door. "You and me, buddy, and a pepperoni pizza."

"Bacon."

Jay hugged Adam close. "Even better."

Alina followed him and Adam out the front door carrying Adam's car seat. He walked down the path to the parking area. He unlocked the door with his key fob and waited while Alina secured the booster seat. He tossed the duffel on the empty seat and set Adam inside and buckled him. A soft poke to the belly made Adam laugh. Jay loved the bright, carefree sound of it.

He closed the car door and turned to Alina. "Your place has shit security. I don't like it."

"My security is not your concern. I can take care of myself."

"In a very short time, you have become my concern."

Alina held her hands out wide, then let them fall to her sides. "Jay, I don't know what to say to that."

"That you'll call and get a security system installed in your place. You'll ask the property manager to install another light at this end of the lot. Tell him it's for your security and your neighbors. Get them on board if the manager balks. Or I'll talk to him and convince him."

She took his fisted hand, unfolded his fingers, and linked her hand with his. "You're sweet. I know you mean well—"

"I mean what I say. Do it, or I'll do it for you." He cut off any spunky retort from her lips with a searing kiss. He didn't understand where all this protect-my-woman caveman attitude came from, but he couldn't contain it when it came to her.

Why look for threats where there were none? She didn't live the kind of life he did. She wasn't like the people he dealt with at work.

She led a simple, quiet life.

And he wanted to keep it that way. He never wanted the darker side of life to touch her.

He gave in to need and took the kiss deeper, sliding his tongue along hers, tasting the temptation that always swept through him when he had her this close. He wished they were going out, that instead of some hotel room, she'd be in *his* bed tonight.

"Pizza," Adam called from inside the SUV.

Jay broke the kiss and pressed his forehead to Alina's. She kept her eyes closed and sighed.

"He's single-minded in his wants. I can think of a hundred things I'd like to do with you."

Alina's eyes flew open. "This is crazy."

"I'm okay with that." He kissed her softly. "Call me later." He stared at her for one long moment, then made himself climb into his SUV. He looked over his shoulder at Adam. "Where are we going?"

"Pizza!" they shouted in unison.

Jay smiled out the passenger window at Alina. She laughed and shook her head as he pulled out. He kept his eyes on her in the rearview mirror. She watched them drive away. The happy, confused look on her face made his chest tingle.

The two of them together might not sound like a good idea, but it felt too right to walk away. He didn't like sneaking around, but it did add a thrill and a level of danger that made it all the more exciting.

He set aside the possibility of discovery and the repercussions when her brothers returned from their honeymoons.

Right now, he'd enjoy the fact that he had a date with Alina on Sunday and another chance to kiss her into doing wild and crazy things with him again.

CHAPTER EIGHT

Alina breathed a sigh of relief when the last group of people left the community center. She'd worried about her speech and conveying the information while still showing compassion. She never expected talking with parents and friends of people addicted to prescription drugs to be so personal and sad. So many lives affected. So many stories with the threads of lies, heartbreak, worry, sadness, feeling useless, frustration, expectation, disappointment, and hope running through them.

She was glad to discuss the prescription drug abuse epidemic, but meeting the families cranked up her compassion while leaving her drained and wanting to help even more.

Maybe she could put together a program to present at local middle and high schools to kids and parents. After all, many of the young people found the drugs in their parents' medicine cabinets.

The DEA held an annual Drug Take Back Day. She'd talk to Caden and Beck and see if she could sponsor an event in town at the pharmacy.

Jay would be a great speaker. It wouldn't hurt to ask. With his direct manner and air of authority, he'd get the kids' attention. He'd keep their attention with his wit and humor, just like the way he teased and played with Adam. He liked kids.

Yes, he took Adam to help her and Beck out, but the guys were close. They covered for each other at work and in their private lives. They hung out because they weren't just colleagues, they were friends.

Which made dating Jay tricky. She didn't want to jeopardize his relationship with Caden and Beck. And the other guys on their team. If one went against the bro-code, the others might cut him out. In their line of work, they needed to function as a team. Animosity and rivalry could be a threat they didn't need on the job facing an even deadlier threat from the cartels and local drug dealers, suppliers, and producers.

The nightmare of Beck shot and lying near death in a hospital bed with tubes and wires coming off him blazed to life in her mind. Jay's face replaced Beck's and her heart clenched tight.

She looked forward to their date, but was she doomed to a life of bone-chilling worry and heartbreak? She enjoyed his company, the off-the-charts sex, and the easy way she felt around him. While he might make time for her now, he'd been so dedicated to his job, he'd never gotten married. At his age, she'd expect at least one ex-wife.

If he didn't want a wife and kids, then whatever they were doing together was going nowhere. At least not where she wanted a relationship to go. And the relationship she imagined wasn't the reality of life with a DEA agent who spent most of his time in the field, not sitting behind a desk.

She liked Jay. A lot. Maybe more than she should without really knowing him. But wasn't that a precursor to knowing the relationship could be something more than what they'd already shared?

She vowed to spend more time on their date talking to him than kissing him.

Though she really liked kissing him.

"Thanks for everything." June, the event coordinator, walked out with her.

Alina pulled her purse strap up on her shoulder. "You're welcome. I'll call you next week about doing this again and expanding the content."

June beamed with her bright smile. "I appreciate your enthusiasm."

"It tends to get away from me sometimes." Like when she jumped into bed that first night with Jay. And planning to immerse herself in the county's drug crisis. "This is a worthy cause that needs all the attention I can give it." So was sleeping with Jay, though she needed to make up her mind about what she really wanted with him. Obviously, she couldn't get him off her mind.

Alina waited for June to lock up.

"Drive safe." June waved goodbye and headed left to her car on the other side of the empty lot.

Alina took a moment to breathe in the cool night air and appreciate the glimmering stars overhead. She loved nights like this. Quiet. A soft breeze. The enormity of the night sky making her feel like there was so much more out there to discover.

And some things here she should open herself up to and enjoy.

She needed to call Jay.

Dutifully, she'd wait until she got home safe and sound.

The short walk to her car gave her time to find her keys buried at the bottom of her bag. She hit the button on her key fob and the doors unlocked. A car engine started on the street behind her. She didn't pay it any attention, though she did think about walking across the street to see if the frozen yogurt shop was still open, but changed her mind. She'd save her treat for a job well done tonight for a glass of wine at home while she called Jay.

She slipped behind the wheel and pulled out of the lot and onto the quiet street. Not much happening in this part of downtown on a Wednesday night. The south end restaurants and bars bustled, but down here, most of the shops closed early. She thought about stopping again, but dismissed it when a dark SUV pulled out behind her. Close. Too close for her to abruptly slow and make it into the lot next to the shop.

The car behind her backed off, but followed her down the two-lane street. Alina turned on the radio and let the day go. She wondered if Adam enjoyed pizza and movie night with Jay. He missed his mom and dad. They'd be home this weekend. She had a few more precious days with her nephew all to herself.

She made the turn toward home, singing along to Billy Currington's "Do I Make You Wanna." Jay definitely made her want to "let her hair down" and "act just like you don't care now." So she bounced to the beat and sang along, thinking *yes, I wanna with Jay.*

Maybe she could have a sleepover with him and Adam.

Bright headlights blinded her in the rearview mirror a split second before a car slammed into her back end. Her head whipped forward, then back as the car lurched. She checked her initial reaction to slam on the brakes, but she did take her foot off the gas. As her car slowed, the car behind her hit again. Metal crunched and tires squealed as the car pushed hers into a spin. The car overturned, locking the seat belt against her chest and shoulder as she went upside down, the airbag hit her in the face, glass shattered and sprayed across her, then her head whipped from one side to the other as the car rolled and landed back on its tires and rocked to a stop.

Dizzy, streetlights and the stars spun in her blurry vision a few seconds, then everything went dark.

CHAPTER NINE

Jay checked the time on his watch again. Alina promised she'd call when she got home. The event ended at eight-thirty. He'd given her until nine before the first inkling of worry wound its way into his tight stomach. At nearly ten-thirty and four unanswered calls, he paced his living room and tried not to let his dark thoughts spin out of control.

Maybe her phone battery died.

Maybe she went out for coffee to talk to someone who attended the seminar.

Better not be another guy. He didn't want to think about her laughing and talking and . . . and nothing. She wouldn't go off with some guy she didn't know. Well, okay, she'd gone off with him. But she knew him. Kinda. And since she was seeing him, she wouldn't start seeing someone else. Not when they had a date planned.

Not when she'd promised to call him tonight.

He made one more circuit past the dining room, down the hall to check on Adam sleeping peacefully in the spare room, and back to the living room that felt like the walls were closing in on him. Ready to put himself out of his misery, he scrolled through his contacts for a local PD guy he worked with on a task force a while back. He'd check accident reports before he started calling hospitals.

Or went extreme and contacted her brothers with his worries.

His phone rang with a Billings Clinic number. His stomach dropped and his heart stopped.

"Bennett." He barely got the word past his clogged throat.

"Agent Bennett, this is nurse Andy at Billings Clinic Hospital. Alina Cooke asked me to contact you."

A dozen nightmares flashed through his mind and stopped his heart. He barely choked out, "Is Alina okay?"

"Yes. She's been in a car accident. Her injuries are varied but not severe. She asked if you could pick her up. She should be ready for release soon."

He had a million questions, but the only things that mattered right now were that she was alive, okay, and he needed to see her with his own two eyes before his heart started beating right again.

"Tell her I'm on my way."

"She's in cubicle four in the emergency room."

"Thank you for calling." He hung up and hit the speed dial for his mom. Someone had to stay with Adam. He didn't want to wake him up and scare him in the middle of the night. Alina's condition might not be serious enough to keep her overnight at the hospital, but he didn't know the extent of her injuries and didn't want to traumatize Adam if he saw his aunt looking anything less than perfect.

"Hi, monkey. What you doin' callin' so late?"

Jay dismissed the nickname she'd never given up calling him since he was a baby. "I need you to come over and watch a friend of mine's kid."

"Is it a girlfriend's kid?"

"No." The last thing he needed right now was her meddling in his love life. He'd kept that to himself since he was a teenager. He didn't want to start sharing now.

Not to her. But he was about to bring home a woman who meant more to him than . . . anything right now. He needed to get to her. "Get here fast. Someone's in trouble and I need to get on the road."

At minimum, the drive into Billings from his place would take half an hour breaking every speed law along the way. Which he would and use his badge if that was what it took to get to her as soon as possible.

"I need a minute to dress, monkey, but I'm on my way."

With her just across the property in the guest cottage, she'd be here in less than ten minutes. Which gave him time to check on Adam one last time, grab a mug of instant coffee—not his favorite, but it worked in a pinch—unlock his gun from the safe, clip on his badge, and snag his car keys off the hook on his way to the door. He opened it just as his mother glided up the path wearing one of her favored floral scarf skirts. The silky material danced around her legs as she walked. The dark pink flowers on the skirt matched the simple T-shirt and her painted toes. The rhinestone flip-flops completed her bold outfit. That was Mom.

"Where you headed, monkey?"

"Hospital. A friend got in a car accident."

"Is *she* okay?"

Way to ask a double question, Mom. "*She* is fine." *I hope.* "I'm watching her nephew tonight. Beck's son."

"He still on his honeymoon with his movie star wife?"

"Yeah. Adam is asleep. I don't know how long I'll be."

"Happy to help as long as you need me, monkey." She tilted her head.

He bussed her cheek with a quick peck and headed for his SUV.

"Hope your girl is okay."

He wanted to say, "She's not mine," to get his mother off his back, but couldn't make the words come out of his mouth. Not when the gnawing ache in his belly and pressing need to get to Alina overwhelmed everything else.

The long drive usually gave him time to relax and think, but tonight it amped his anxiety. The dark roads leading into Billings seemed longer. Every light in town seemed to be red. He blew through a few when there were no cars in sight. Parking his car in the lot instead of leaving it outside the Emergency doors took time he didn't want to waste, especially when his patience wore out halfway to town.

He'd been to this emergency room on numerous occasions after he'd been injured on the job, to see coworkers who'd been hurt, and to question suspects. He'd never felt this kind of insistent need to be sure someone was really as okay as the nurse assured him on the phone. He had to see her with his own eyes, so he bypassed the reception desk and jogged down the corridor past busy nurses and doctors tending to other patients, threw back the curtain at cubicle four, and stopped in his tracks when he saw Alina lying with her eyes closed on the gurney. The bright red scrape and bruise on her cheek, white neck brace, tangled mass of hair, and sling on her left arm told him she'd been through the wringer.

With a heavy heart, he went to her. Afraid to touch her, but needing the contact all the same, he placed his hand lightly on her stomach, the other at the top of her head, and leaned down and kissed her on the forehead.

"Jay." She sighed out his name but didn't open her eyes.

He kissed her on the head again and pressed his forehead to hers. "Are you okay?"

Her eyes opened and the pain dulled her normally bright blue-gray eyes. "I will be. Right now, I'm one big throbbing ache."

"What happened?"

"I don't really know. The police think someone targeted me."

Jay pulled back, planted his hands on either side of her shoulders, and leaned over her. "What? Why?"

"I'm not sure. I left the community center and a big SUV pulled out on the main road behind me. I didn't think anything of it. They followed me, but at a distance. I thought we were just going in the same direction. I was singing to the radio and thinking about getting home and calling you. I thought I might go to your place and have a sleepover with you and Adam."

Jay softly brushed his thumb over her chin, then leaned down and swept his lips over hers. "Looks like you get your wish. I'm taking you home with me."

Her lips trembled and her eyes glassed over. "Good. Because now that you're here, I realize I'm still a little shook up."

He cupped her cheek and held her face. "You're safe now, Alina. I swear, we'll find out who did this to you."

"That's just it, I have no idea who would want to hurt me."

"We'll figure it out. How did you get hurt?"

"It happened so fast. One second they're several car lengths back, just driving along like me, and the next they're speeding up and hitting the back of my car. It stunned me. I tried to think what to do, but before I did anything, they hit me again, kind of on one side, pushing my car into a spin. I rolled once."

Jay stepped back with the blow those words evoked in him. "You rolled the car?"

"Yes. It landed back on its tires with a violent bounce side to side. That's how I hurt my neck and shoulder." She pulled the paper gown down to show him the bruises from the seat belt.

"Damn, sweetheart, that looks really bad."

"The doctor said it will look worse in a couple of days. Nothing is broken. I've got whiplash. The airbag hit me in the face. It could have been so much w-worse." She broke down and tears cascaded down her cheeks.

He leaned in close, his cheek pressed to hers, and held her in a light hug. "Don't cry, baby. You're okay. I'm going to take you home, tuck you into bed, you'll be safe with me."

Her fingers combed through the back of his hair and held on. "They wanted to keep me overnight. I need to get out of here. I have to get out of here." The terror in her voice inflamed the protective streak growing inside him. She didn't know who did this to her or why but feared they'd come back to finish the job. "I'm sorry to drag you into this. If my brothers were home . . ."

"I'm here, sweetheart. I'll take care of you and get to the bottom of this. I'll talk to the cops, see what they found at the scene." No need to wake Caden and Beck on their honeymoons in the middle of the night. With the different time zones, he'd be waking them in the wee morning hours with little to no information. He'd call them in the morning.

"I'm sorry. I know you're covering for them at work, helping out with Adam tonight, and now you have to deal with this."

He pushed up and stared down at her. Her gaze dropped away from his. "Alina, look at me." He waited for her to do so. "Work is work. Watching Adam is a favor for a friend. You needing me here because you want me to comfort you, that's between us. I'm glad you called me. I can't stand to see you like this. Whoever did this to you will pay. I won't let them get away with it."

"How are you feeling, Alina?" A nurse came up behind him.

"Ready to go."

"I see your ride arrived." The nurse gave him the once-over, his gaze landing on the badge and gun at Jay's waist. "Your very own police escort home."

"I'm DEA. Is she ready to go?"

The nurse held up a white paper bag. "Your meds." He handed them to Jay, then checked Alina's chart. "We gave her pain medication an hour ago. She can take one to two pills in three hours if she needs them. Every four to six hours as needed for the next several days. Keep the neck brace on for at last five days to give your neck time to heal, then take it slow. No sudden movements. Ice several times a day for your neck and shoulder. After a couple days, you can alternate ice and heat."

"I've got it." Alina pushed up. Jay helped her sit and swing her legs over the edge of the bed.

"There's a refill on your prescription if you need it."

"Thank you."

The efficient nurse consulted the tablet one last time to be sure he'd covered everything. "Do you need a doctor's note for work?"

Alina tried to shake her head, then hissed in a breath when the movement hurt. "No. I'll take tomorrow off and see how I feel from there."

The nurse rolled the wheelchair he'd left nearby into the cubicle, close to the bed.

Alina slid off the mattress. The small movement stiffened her frame. Jay held on to her arm to steady her and helped her slowly sit down in the wheelchair.

"I'll run out and pull my car around."

Alina held his hand in her trembling one for a moment before she reluctantly let him go. The fear and hesitation in her amped the rage in him. Someone took this vibrant, fun, outgoing, and independent woman and made her afraid to be alone. They made her feel vulnerable.

They'd pay for that.

Jay wouldn't stop until he had them behind bars and knew exactly why they'd go after her.

He worried this may be some sort of retaliation for a case Caden or Beck worked, but couldn't know for sure. It didn't feel like a threat from the cartel. For one, they'd have stayed at the scene and put a bullet in Alina's head to be sure she was dead if they wanted to send a message.

The sickening thought stopped his heart.

If Caden or Beck worried someone was coming after them, they'd have said something. This, coming out of the blue with no warning, took dangerous to a whole new level.

He needed to contact Caden and Beck and find out if they could shine some light on a reason for this threat and violence.

He hated to interrupt their honeymoons, but they needed to know about Alina. Jay needed to know what he was up against and if this was an ongoing threat and he needed to get round-the-clock protection for Alina and the rest of the Cooke family.

He'd get Alina home and settled, then make some calls. First to the cops to see what they got from the accident scene.

He checked the parking lot for anything or anyone suspicious, got his SUV, and pulled it around to the front of the ER. Alina sat slumped in the wheelchair. The nurse beside her held a plastic bag of Alina's possessions, hospitalization papers, and meds. Alina's feet were bare.

He jumped out and ran around the car. The nurse stowed Alina's things in the backseat. He took Alina's hand and pulled her up. She walked right into his chest and wrapped her good arm around him. He held her close, pressed his cheek to her head, and thanked God she was going to be all right.

"Feel better, Alina." The nurse pushed the wheelchair away.

Alina held on for another moment before she stepped back and looked up at him. "Thank you for coming. I know that what we have has been totally . . . impulsive—"

"What we have means I'm here in the middle of the night and ready to take care of you and give you whatever you need right now."

She leaned in and pressed her forehead to his chest. "I need to sleep, but I don't want to be alone."

"You're not. You won't be." He nudged her toward his car and helped her get settled in the seat and buckled. "Rest. Let me worry about the accident and what happens next."

"My brothers are not going to like this."

"I'm not thrilled about it either." Understatement of the year. He wanted to rage. He wanted to get his hands on whoever did this to her.

He closed the door and climbed in on the driver's side. Her eyes drooped as he pulled out of the lot. By the time he hit the first light, she slept. He kept his hand on her thigh to reassure her she wasn't alone. He kept the radio on low to give her a sense of peace and where she was while he drove them out of the city and to his place.

He didn't often bring a woman to his home. Mostly because he liked his peace and quiet and the solitude he needed. But his mother also lived on the property and the last thing he wanted was for her to jump to conclusions and involve herself in his personal life.

Nope, not going there. Her opinion was the last one he needed when it came to relationships.

He had no qualms about bringing Alina home with him. He didn't care what his mother thought or said. He wanted Alina with him and in his bed tonight.

He didn't think too hard or long about how nice it

would be to have her there every night. Yes for the fantastic sex, but his heart spoke up for the first time in a long time and told him it had more to do with the panic he'd felt when he'd learned she'd been in an accident. The protective streak told him not to let her out of his sight—ever—and the tenderness that rose up every time he looked at her and the injuries she'd sustained said more than words that she mattered. A lot.

He wanted to hold her and make it all go away.

The law enforcement side of him wanted to hunt down those responsible for causing her one second of pain. The man wanted to make them pay and hurt a thousand times more than Alina hurt right now.

You're falling fast and hard.

It kind of felt like flying: exhilarating and terrifying all at the same time.

CHAPTER TEN

Alina woke to quiet and a thousand stars shining in the big sky outside the windshield. She tilted her shoulders toward the side window and light spilling into the yard from the gorgeous ranch-style house with a wide porch, stone walkway bordered by lush plants and flowers, and nothing but dark land on either side of the house.

"Where are we?"

Jay's warm hand squeezed her thigh. "My place. You slept the whole way."

She rubbed at her tired eyes. "Sorry."

"Don't be. Your meds must have kicked in."

She cautiously rolled her sore shoulders. The pain level had decreased considerably, though her head felt thick and slow.

"That's one huge house. I love the stone." Gray stone accentuated white clapboard. Huge boulders sat amidst the garden shrubs. "Those doors are amazing." Carved wood with leaded glass.

"I bought them at a salvage place and refinished them."

She sighed. "They're gorgeous."

"How about we go in?"

"Sure." She didn't move, just stared at the house.

"Something wrong?"

Her lips pressed together before she spoke. "No. It's just, I never expected this."

"What? That I live in a house?"

"This place is a home."

"Yeah. It's my home." He didn't get it. Or maybe he did and didn't want to admit she saw far more than walls and a roof.

"I'll bet you put your stamp on all of it, like the path that leads up to the porch and those doors that welcome you in with the light shining through the glass. This isn't some bachelor pad. This place says, 'Welcome home.'"

He held back a smile. "I think your meds muddled your mind."

"Blow it off if you like. All I'm saying is, this place says more about you than all I've learned from sleeping with you."

"We didn't do a lot of sleeping."

She shook her head, winced with the piercing pain, and silently reminded herself to stop moving so much. He obviously didn't want to open up to her.

Sleeping with him didn't mean she got in his head. Or his heart.

At least it seemed that's what he wanted her to believe until he did the unexpected and opened up.

"I finished this place just over two years ago. Completely renovated every room. Myself. It took forever because I work a lot. And yes, I did it because I wanted this place to be home. Not just a place I lived. Or slept for a couple of hours in between work. When I'm here, I don't know, I'm at ease. It's the place I want to be and the embodiment of what I want for my future."

He wanted to live here the rest of his life with his wife and a family. He'd built it, now all he had to do was fill it with those missing pieces. The missing pieces she had in her life, too.

Yep, the drugs emboldened her mind to let loose her deepest thoughts and desires and opened her up to making comparisons and finding common ground with a man she barely knew and probably couldn't keep.

"And sweetheart, if my house surprised you, then this will blow your mind. You and me in bed, that's a kind of sharing I've never had with anyone else. Telling you this, letting you in on the fact you get to me, that's new for me, too."

Wow. Could he be any more adorable? Those honest words meant more to her than anything, because *who* said that? No one had ever been that open with her, but she'd wanted this for a long time: a guy who cared enough to lay it all out there.

As much as she'd wanted it, it scared her. "This is all new for me. I like you, Jay."

He smiled that smile that only came when he let his guard down. "I like you, too, sweetheart. More than I probably should."

"Want to show me the inside of the house before I pass out on you again?"

"I'll show you the house tomorrow. Tonight, all you need to see is my bed."

She raised an eyebrow at that, which earned her another of those charming smiles.

"You need to get some sleep. Adam's in the guest room. So you and me, we're sharing a bed again."

"Are you sure? I'm not really up for—"

He laid his hand on her thigh. Heat spread through her. "Give me some credit, Alina. After what happened tonight, I want you close. I want to make you feel good in a different way."

She put her hand over his and squeezed. "Good, because if you'd let me finish I'd have said that I don't have it in me to make love to you the way I want to, but I desperately want to be wrapped around you."

Jay slid close, hooked his hand at the back of her

head, and gently drew her in for a kiss that held all the hunger he kept in check and the tenderness the moment deserved because they'd shared some truths tonight and set aside their reservations about them being anything more than what they were right now.

He pulled back. She leaned in, trying to hold on to the tingly, peaceful way he made her feel when her mind was still spinning out of control with the replay of the crash and what it meant.

"Come on, sweetheart, before I forget you're tired and hurt and having you in the front seat of my car is a bad idea."

"Bad ideas are our specialty."

He reached out and brushed his thumb over her bottom lip. "You're the best bad idea I ever had."

She leaned into his palm. "That first morning, I thought it best to file what happened under insane-things-I-do-when-drunk-and-lonely. We had so many reasons to say, 'That was fun, let's move on.' I never expected you to be like this."

"This is me with you. I like being this me. It's the most real I've felt with anyone in a long time. I hated letting you go that morning, but I thought it best, considering."

"I didn't want to leave. But I did, considering. I'm not the girl who sleeps with guys on the first date. Or no date, just 'Let's get it on.' The things we did together . . . most of that was a first, too. And all of it felt so right, it scared me. Because you're you. And I'm me. And I don't know how we fit together when . . ."

"Yeah, your brothers are going to kill me. We barely know each other. I'm older than Caden. My job sucks up my life. After watching what your brothers have been through, I'm sure you never saw yourself with a DEA agent. I tend to date women who don't expect much or want anything more than a good time." He frowned and shook his head. "You want and deserve a commitment and a promise of a future. I don't know if I can give you that the way you want it."

Honesty. The one thing she always wanted in a relationship. He gave it to her straight.

"With my job and background, I don't trust easily."

That got her attention. "What do you mean, your background?"

He stared past her toward the house. "We'll talk about it another time. Come on, you're fading fast." He slipped out of the car without another word. Apparently the sharing portion of the evening had ended.

When he opened her door, he'd closed up and put a barrier between them. He helped her out, grabbed her plastic bag of personal items the hospital collected from her, put his hand around her waist to keep her steady and close, and walked her up the path to the front door.

They entered into a wide foyer that opened to a huge family room and the kitchen beyond. Old wood doors to her right similar to the front doors led into an office. A hallway farther down probably led to the bedrooms. She didn't know how many, but she wanted to find his and crash. In his arms.

She barely had the energy to take in the comfortable furnishings, black-and-white photographs of horses on the walls, and dark hardwood floors. A blonde woman—must be Jay's mom who came to watch Adam—rose from the leather sofa in front of a stone fireplace, the TV over the chunky wood mantel playing one of those housewives reality TV shows that wasn't anything like the lives of any of her married friends.

"You're back." The woman used the remote to turn off the TV, then turned to them. Her gaze landed on Alina and the smile and welcome in her eyes died.

"Like father like son," she mumbled, but clear enough for Alina to hear.

The remark made Jay release her and turn to his mother, his back to Alina like he shielded her from the woman and whatever that comment meant. "Thanks for watching Adam. You can go."

"Aren't you going to introduce me to your *friend*?"

The tension in Jay made Alina even edgier. The easygoing, open guy in the SUV turned into in-charge-agent-man right in front of her eyes.

It took Jay a full ten seconds before he stepped aside and shifted so she and his mother were facing each other. "Mom, this is Adam's aunt Alina. Alina, my mother, Heather."

"Pleased to meet you," Alina said.

"Too young and pretty. Just the way they like them."

"Mom." The warning in Jay's voice didn't stop Heather from surveying Alina from head to toe. Despite the "pretty" comment, Heather made it clear she found nothing worthy about Alina.

Granted, she didn't look her best in the paper shirt over her wrinkled skirt, neck brace, and arm sling. Tangled hair, bruises on her face, makeup smeared, the list made her cringe, but she didn't deserve the judgmental glare. And wasn't going to stand here mentally fading, physically exhausted, and holding on to her composure by a thread and take this shit.

"Where's the bed, honey?"

One side of Jay's mouth tilted up slightly at her bold question and endearment. "Down the hall, hook a left at the bathroom, last door at the end."

Alina turned to go, but stopped short at Heather's next comment.

"Another waitress who works hard on her back?"

Alina turned and pinned Heather with her angry gaze.

"No, actually, it's Doctor Cooke. And your opinion of waitresses and your son is deplorable. I may not know your son well, or what is going on here, but I know he's a good and decent man and neither of us deserves the shots you're firing." Alina walked to Jay, took her bag of stuff, and placed her hand on his chest and stared up at him, telling him without words she meant it.

CHAPTER ELEVEN

Jay watched Alina walk away, or at least down the hall to his room. He couldn't believe what she'd said or how she'd stood up for herself and him. Most of the time, he and others dismissed his mother's tendency to say exactly what she thought without thinking about how others took it. They chose to ignore her instead of starting a fight.

"Are you going to let her speak to me, your mother, like that?"

"*You* were out of line with that crack about her on her back."

"Well, she is in your bed."

Exactly where he wanted her. But his mother didn't need to know how badly he wanted her there. "You took one look at her and turned her into the woman Dad married."

"I'd think after what happened you'd have better sense. No wonder you never bring any of your women home to meet me."

"Yeah, because tonight went so well."

"They're naïve girls with no idea what they're getting themselves into with your work and life."

"You don't even know her." He raked his fingers through his hair. Sometimes he forgot his sweet mother had a sour center that came out when she felt threatened or less than adored. "Alina is a respected pharmacist and the sister of my best friends. She's not some hookup." They had hooked up, but she was more than that. Had been since the moment he kissed her in that elevator.

Naïve. Hardly. She knew his life. She'd lived it with her brothers. Which didn't necessarily make it a positive. In fact, if what happened tonight tied to a DEA case, it was definitely a negative and she'd want as far away from him as possible.

Right now, though, he needed to deal with the problem in front of him. "Someone ran her off the road tonight, and you ran over her with your bullshit hurt, lack of sympathy, and that unwarranted comment that men date younger women sometimes. I don't care how old she is. I like her because of who she is and how she makes me feel. I'm not Dad. She's not your rival."

"You have no idea what I went through with your father."

"Oh please. I'm tired of dancing around this subject with you. You hurt him. He left you. You live your life dejected, covering up your unhappiness with your righteous indignation when we both know you had an affair with his best friend to make him jealous. When it didn't work, he lost his friend of forty years, you lost your husband, the guy you were sleeping with but didn't care one lick about, and my respect."

"He was never home."

No, he wasn't. Jay often resented him for it, too. All the things his dad missed or didn't show up to wore on their relationship. But he respected his father for standing up for something he believed in. He worked hard in the sheriff's department and took his job seriously. Protect and serve meant something to him and he'd instilled that commitment to helping others in Jay.

"When he was home, you didn't make things easy." Yes, he had resentments for his mother, too, who wanted her husband's undivided attention but went about trying to get it the wrong way every time.

"I put up with a lot. Was it so much to ask that he want to do the things I liked when he was home?"

"He did the best he could." Jay had seen that, even when he got upset that his father didn't always have time to do everything Jay wanted. But his dad carved out time when he could to spend with Jay. They'd go off on a long ride. Just them and the horses and the landscape. They'd share long silences and talks about nothing and everything.

"Where have I heard that before?"

In every argument his parents shared that ended in slamming doors. His mother retreated to their empty room. His father went back to work. Nothing resolved. Both of them wanting something the other couldn't give.

His father did the best he could.

His mother did the best she could.

It wasn't enough for either of them.

Both of them had tried to bend in their ways, but in the end, the whole thing broke.

He wondered if this thing with Alina would lead him down the same path of bitterness and breakup because of his job. He didn't want to disappoint, hurt, or lose Alina, but he'd seen firsthand what responsibility, obligation, duty, and distance did to a relationship when those things were focused on work and not the person you cared about most.

Then again, his two buddies had just married women who understood and accepted all those things.

Alina had been through some tough times with her brothers. Was she willing to go through them with him?

That was the million-dollar question. And for the first time, he wanted a woman, her, to step up and say, *yeah, you're worth it.*

Exactly like his father had probably hoped his mother would do.

Beck worked undercover. Infinitely more dangerous than Jay's job. Not that he didn't face danger, it just wasn't a daily thing. Alina would see that as they spent more time together.

Although he wasn't in the thick of things all the time, work still demanded his attention.

His phone buzzed with another email. They never seemed to stop. He checked his messages, relieved to see the case file for Alina's accident had been sent as promised by the officer he'd contacted while Alina slept on the ride home. He'd go over it as soon as he got Alina settled for the night.

His mother stood tall and fisted her hands at her sides. "Let me guess, you have to go back to work. You're going to leave that poor girl all alone tonight."

Jay rolled his eyes. "Now *I* have whiplash from the way you change your tune. A moment ago, you made it clear you don't like her because she's too young for me, now you're chastising me for not staying to take care of her."

"I want you to be better than him."

"I'm not better or worse. I. Am. Not. Him." Jay sucked in a breath and let it out to calm himself before this turned ugly. "Thank you for watching Adam. I appreciate that you came over so late. Now, if you'll excuse me, I need to make sure Alina has everything she needs and gets some rest."

His mother tilted her head and studied him. "You really care about her."

"Good night, Mom."

She leaned up and kissed his cheek. Head down, she started to walk away, but he reached out, took her hand, and gave it a squeeze. Her gaze swung up to him and they exchanged a look that said, "Let's forget the whole thing." For now anyway. The seesaw of their relationship evened out. Sometimes, like tonight, it tipped up and down but they never really got anywhere but on the same ride.

With things between him and his mom back in balance, he locked the door behind her and headed back to his room and Alina. He hoped she hadn't heard that whole mess. She'd gotten a good dose of family drama in the short exchange she had with his mom.

Would, or could, the two ever be friends? Maybe if his mother didn't see her past every time she looked at Alina.

This is why I don't bring women home.

Probably why he never kept any of them either. He feared his parents' doomed relationship would become his reality. Stupid. He wasn't his father. He knew when to set work aside and focus on his personal life.

Liar. When's the last time you did that?

That little voice of reason needed a beat-down.

Okay, maybe he needed to be better at balancing his life.

He had more important things to do than analyze the whys behind what he did or didn't do. Right now, Alina needed him. And damn if he didn't need her, too.

Work would always need him, but he needed something for himself.

And she was here with him, and he would do everything he could for as long as he could hold on to her.

He spotted Alina in Adam's room, standing by the bed, staring at him. She leaned down and kissed his forehead and softly brushed his hair. The bruises along her cheek and under her eye stood out even darker against her too pale skin. She stood and turned to Jay, her eyes sad to match the slight frown.

"You heard all that," he whispered as she walked out of Adam's room and past him. He pulled Adam's door closed and followed Alina to his room.

"I'm sorry my presence stirred up old wounds for you and your mother."

"We like to stir up the ghosts and let them out of the closet every once in a while. Our relationship is usually good, but occasionally she looks at me and sees my dad. She can't help it really, I look just like him."

"I saw the pictures in the hallway. You were a cute kid. I love the one with you dressed like a cop for Halloween standing beside your father decked out in his uniform."

"Law enforcement is in the blood. His father was a cop. Great Grandpa was military police."

"Wow. So, you always wanted to be a cop?"

"Mostly. When I was five I swore I was going to be a firefighter. At eight it was a fighter pilot. Then in high school, six friends thought it'd be cool to smoke some dope. They didn't know it was laced with PCP. One of the girls had an undiagnosed heart condition. She went into respiratory failure and stopped breathing. A few of the others were out of their minds, hallucinating. One of the guys freaked out, pushed everyone into his car along with the girl who wasn't breathing, and tried to drive to the hospital from the school football field. About two miles total. At night with little traffic, he might have made it, except he was high, speeding, and ran a stoplight he said looked like dancing devils with pitchforks. He T-boned another car. The mother of two died on impact. No one in my friend's car wore their seat belt. He and the front seat passenger went through the windshield. The driver lived for two days. The other guy died at the scene. The girl who stopped breathing never took another breath. The three in the backseat with her on their laps sustained minor injuries. One of them ended up in the psych ward for twenty days because of the drugs and what happened. One became an alcoholic. One, my best friend, someone I considered a brother, and would have been with me at the movies that fateful night if I hadn't come down with the flu, committed suicide on the anniversary of the accident."

"Jesus, Jay."

The guilt still punched him in the gut when he allowed himself to remember. "I knew them all and watched their destruction from one stupid mistake that led to another and more and I knew what I wanted to be: the guy who keeps that shit out of the hands of stupid teenagers who think getting high is no big deal. What could happen, right?"

"I'm so sorry, Jay. That must have been a very terrible time in your life."

"Yeah, and it happened when my mom and dad split up for good."

"Not many people can come back from cheating. Once the trust is broken . . ." Alina shook her head.

"Exactly. Mom expected Dad to forgive her and vow his undying love and change who and what he was. Instead, he divorced her, found someone else, and had another family."

"Let me guess, a younger woman."

"Yeah. She adored my dad every day until he dropped dead of a heart attack, leaving two grieving women and sons behind."

"You have a brother?"

"Kevin Jr. He's a sophomore in high school. Plays baseball. Straight-A student."

"Are you close?"

"I go to all his games. We have a standing bros weekend every third weekend of the month."

"That's sweet."

"Dad died when he was just a baby. He never got to know him the way I did. If he can't have his dad, at least he has a big brother who cares. Plus, when Kevin was younger, that one weekend a month gave his mom the break she needed, being a single parent and all. She remarried when Kevin was in sixth grade. He likes his stepdad, but he tends to talk to me more."

"Well, you're the cool big brother with a gun and a badge."

Jay laughed under his breath. "I guess. I'm not his mom or dad. I give him things straight."

"You're a good guy, Jay."

"Sometimes." He ran his hand over the back of his neck and tight muscles. "Now you know why she said what she said to you. In her mind, Dad left her for a younger woman and a new family. Things were more complicated than that. For me, none of the how or whys mattered. My dad died too young, but he was happy in the end."

"That's all we can hope for, right? That we die happy and loved."

"Yeah." Jay went to his dresser and pulled out a clean tee. "Bathroom's through there if you want to wash up. You can wear this and crawl in bed."

Alina hesitated, then touched the sling. "I could use some help. Everything hurts when I move."

Jay went to her and untied the back of the paper shirt. He pulled one side down her good arm, then held her arm in the sling still, pulled the sling free and off her along with the stiff shirt. "Damn, sweetheart." He stared at the bruises blooming down her shoulder and across her chest from the seat belt locking against her. Instinct made him lean in and kiss her soft skin above the bruises at her shoulder. She went still at his touch.

He followed the line of bruises down her bare chest, then went back to her tempting lips and kissed her softly. He held the press of his lips to hers for a long moment. He cupped her face and stared down into her eyes. "I'm so glad you're all right."

Tears welled in her eyes.

"Don't cry. It kills me to see tears in your eyes."

He didn't know what to do about the tears, but he could take care of her before she dropped from exhaustion. Getting the T-shirt on made her gasp with every tiny movement. His gut tied in knots with every pained sound but he got the job done, including sliding the skirt down her legs and putting the sling back on her arm. He helped her lie down in his bed. The second her head hit the pillow, her eyes closed. He leaned down and kissed her again, then pressed up on his hands and stared down at her.

"You look good in my shirt and my bed."

Her eyes opened to half-mast. "Thanks for letting me crash here tonight."

"Let's not talk about crashing anymore. Every time I think about what could have happened . . ." He pressed his lips to her forehead and tried to erase the nightmares from his mind.

"Stay with me." The plea in her voice made his heart ache.

"I gotta do one thing, then I'll be back."

She grabbed hold of his arm and held tight. "Telling my brothers can wait for the morning. *I* can't wait for you to hold me. Please," she added on a ragged breath. "Just until I fall asleep."

"As long as you want, sweetheart." He quickly removed his clothes down to his boxer briefs, turned off the light, and crawled under the covers. With her neck in the brace, he didn't want to move her too much, so he slid close to her side, draped his arm over her hips, his other up and over her head, and brushed his fingers lightly through her hair as he laid his head on his bicep and nuzzled his nose into her hair. "How's this?"

"Perfect," she whispered and settled into complete relaxation.

His mind went back to what he'd said to her and what it meant. Yes, he'd hold her as long as she wanted to-night, but deep inside he knew he wanted to hold on to her a lot longer.

Maybe forever.

And that thought led to a lot of possibilities and complications better left to think about later, because right now he wanted to lose himself in this sweet moment with her lying in his arms in his bed before he had to call her brothers, tell them what happened, and potentially let them know how involved he was with Alina.

I'm in deep.

CHAPTER TWELVE

Alina wished for more sleep, but the sliver of light coming through the slit in the drapes blinded her and the ache in her whole body throbbed in time to her heart. She didn't dare move. Her stiff neck felt locked in place. The flare of pain in her chest every time she breathed promised the splatter of bruises from the seat belt would be a vivid reminder of the car accident for days to come.

The pills were on the nightstand. All she had to do was roll to her side and grab them, but that seemed like a recipe for more pain, so she remained still and focused on the room and the empty spot beside her. Her hazy mind conjured a memory of Jay leaning over her in the early morning hours, softly kissing her and telling her to go back to sleep. His presence in the night kept the nightmares at bay, but the terror she faced last night when that car hit her and she realized the driver meant to harm her trembled through her again.

She hoped the police found the person responsible. She wanted to dismiss it as some random drunk driver, but with the work her brothers did, she had to face the fact that this could be some kind of retaliation.

Why come after her? Why not go after them?

Jay walked in the bedroom door with the phone to his ear. She met his steady, worried gaze.

Being with him makes me a target.

Maybe not this time, but if they stayed together, in the future. She didn't delude herself into thinking that his life wouldn't impact hers. She'd seen it with Caden and Beck. Both of them had cartel members coming after them for retribution, and their wives had gotten caught in the mess.

"She's up. Hold on." Jay came to her, held the phone away, leaned down and kissed her, then stared into her eyes. "You need some pain meds."

"And coffee."

He held the phone out to her. "This is for you. I told them what happened. We're working on it."

Alina rolled her eyes because smacking him for calling her brothers wasn't an option until she had those pain meds. She took the phone, stuck her tongue out at Jay, childish though it may be, and said, "I'm fine."

"What the hell, Alina?" "Why didn't you call us?" her brothers said over each other. Of course Jay got them both on the line at once.

She rolled her eyes, just about the only thing that didn't hurt. "Did I mention, I'm fine?"

"Jay filled us in on the crash and what the cops put in the accident report. We'll go over it and start digging," Beck promised.

"You know you're DEA, right? Not the cops. It was just an accident." She really, really wanted it to be just an accident.

"Someone hits you once, it's an accident. Twice is a threat." Leave it to Caden to spell it out in blunt terms and shatter the lies she told herself and wanted to believe because they were easier than the truth.

She took a breath and held tight to the phone, hoping to erase the tremble in her hand. Jay stood over her, watching her every move, noting all the little signs she couldn't hide that the fear hadn't dissipated.

"Who would want to hurt me?" If she knew who,

she'd know how to protect herself, who to watch out for and why.

"Neither Caden or I have had any recent death threats or run-ins that would warrant this kind of retaliation. It could be an older case and someone is out of jail and out to get their pound of flesh."

"Beck, if that was the case, why come after me?"

"We're out of town with our wives, so you're the only target there to go after," Caden suggested, though he didn't sound convinced.

"It doesn't feel right. If this was cartel related, why the car accident? Why not a drive-by shooting? Why not get out of the car and put a bullet in my head to be sure I was dead and you got the message?"

Jay's face paled. He sat on the edge of the bed and rubbed his hand across his jaw. He pulled her hand toward him and put the phone on speaker. "She's got a point. Though this could have been a warning."

"For what? Caden and I both backed off our cases or closed them before we left. Nothing we had going triggers even a possibility of something like this happening." Beck paused for a beat, then asked, "What about you, Jay? Could someone have seen you with Alina and thought to get back at you by going after her? She's not with you, but they wouldn't know that."

Jay stared at her, his eyes filled with trepidation. He opened his mouth to say something, but she shook her head, warning him not to tell Beck and Caden they were together. Sort of. Maybe.

His eyes narrowed. "I picked Adam up at her place yesterday. Someone could have seen us together, but I didn't spot a tail or see anything unusual at her place, except that security sucks."

"Yeah, we need to do something about that," Caden agreed.

"I'm perfectly capable of taking care of myself, thank you very much."

"Your car was totaled last night and you could have died. Granted, not your fault, but we need more information and to assess the situation and see if there is an ongoing threat." Beck was right, but she didn't need to tell him that. He'd only issue more orders or lock her in a room until they solved this. Not going to happen.

"You should stay at Jay's place until we sort this out," Caden suggested.

"I won't let her out of my sight," Jay assured them before she protested.

"And what about Adam? If I'm the target, shouldn't we leave Adam in DEA protective custody?" She glared at Jay. "We don't want whoever came after me, if that is what this is, to discover Adam is here."

"They'd have seen Adam yesterday," Jay pointed out.

"You're the target. Most people, even the cartel, wouldn't go after a kid." Caden didn't inspire her to believe this had just been an isolated incident. "If this person is going after a woman, they're serious."

"I can't stay here."

Jay cocked up one eyebrow.

"I have to go to work. I've got a business to run. Jay has his work. Adam is supposed to be at day camp."

"Alina." She hated when Beck used that tone with her. "Your safety is more important. Caden and I can be home by tomorrow."

"Hell, no. You are not cutting your honeymoons short. I will not have my sisters-in-law hating me for spoiling your vacations. Lord knows, the way you two work, you won't take another for the next ten years."

"Alina." This time Caden took that tone, saying so much with just her name.

"I said no. I'll stay with Jay and take today off work."

"You'll take tomorrow off, too. This is your weekend off anyway, right?" Of course Beck remembered her schedule since she had agreed to watch Adam. "We'll be back Saturday night."

The order to take tomorrow off work grated. Even more when Jay nodded for her to agree. "Fine. But if nothing comes of this and the police and Jay have no evidence that I was targeted, then I'm going back to work on Monday."

"Jay, make sure she has a shadow at all times," Beck ordered.

"Already in the works."

"Thanks, man." Relief infused Caden's gratitude. "Call us if anything else happens. Text any updates on the case."

"Will do, but I've got this," Jay assured them. "Enjoy the rest of your vacations."

"Good luck keeping Alina locked down." Beck finished that smart-ass comment with, "Feel better, sis."

Jay ended the call and stared down at her. "I had to tell them."

"It could have waited until they came home."

He shook his head. "Not if someone is after you because of them."

"Or you," she pointed out.

"I really don't get this. We put our heads together. No one has threatened us. Lately." The qualifier illustrated the danger they faced and how the balance between the good guys and bad shifted. Sometimes in a moment. "Running you off the road feels random, yet targeted."

"I want to say it was an accident, but I believe they followed me and waited for the right moment to hit me. But they didn't finish the job, so it doesn't feel like a drug hit."

His frown deepened. "I hate that you're thinking this way."

"It's not like I don't know your world, Jay."

"I don't want it to touch you." He brushed his fingers over the brace around her neck, his eyes softening with regret and apology. "If this happened because of me . . ."

She took his hand and held it tight, waiting for his gaze to meet hers. "This is not your fault. It's not my brothers' fault. If someone targeted me, it's because you guys are a threat to them and that means you're close to taking them down. That's necessary and important. Worth a good scare and a few bruises."

But was it worth facing for the rest of her life?

"It could have been so much worse," Jay whispered, his deep voice thick with emotion she didn't expect.

Her heart warmed and expanded in her chest, making it hard to breathe past the lump in her throat. Because it was her nature, she tried to make Jay feel better, even if she had her reservations about the ongoing threat, something she had to face now and possibly in the future if she stayed with him.

"I'm fine. Really, I am. You, Caden, and Beck will all work to uncover the who and why. I wouldn't want to be that guy. If he wanted to send a message, all he did was put three determined expert agents on his ass."

Jay leaned down and pressed his forehead to hers. "I get my hands on him, he'll wish he was never born."

The sweet sentiment behind the deadly threat sank into her heart and glowed bright and warm in her chest.

They had a date this Sunday, but Jay never signed up for her to stay here the next few days.

Jay felt the shift in her, sat up, and stared down at her. "What is it?"

"You told my brothers you'd keep an eye on me, but that doesn't mean I need to stay here. Give me about ten minutes to figure out how to get out of bed, another fifteen to get Adam up and ready to go, then you can take us to my place." She pinched the T-shirt he let her borrow last night. "I'll return this once I change clothes at my place."

He glared down at her. "All done?"

"Uh, yeah."

"Great. Today, you can wear my shirt and anything else you need. You will lie around and rest, watching whatever you want on TV. I will feed you, by which I mean I'll order you anything you want from the pizza place and deli I pay dearly to get delivery out here." The embarrassed boyish grin made her smile.

"I take it you don't cook."

"Some. In dire circumstances. But I wasn't expecting company, so the fridge is kind of bare. Unless you want cereal. I bought some for Adam, since I planned to feed him before day camp. He's staying home today, too."

Home. She didn't delude herself that he meant anything by it. After last night, her heart wanted to latch onto something good with the possibility of great. But she needed to stop that train of thought in its tracks and center herself in reality, not fairy tale. The call with her brothers this morning and Jay's fear this had something to do with them or him brought the danger in Jay's life too close to home.

She spent far too much time worrying about her brothers. Did she really want to spend a lifetime with a man who put his life on the line every day? Would they have a lifetime? Was the possibility of a lifetime together worth the danger?

Would she regret letting a chance at happy go?

She and Jay had started this thing between them by enjoying the moment and not thinking about what came next. If she spent all her time wondering about what might happen, would she miss out on more of those wonderful moments with him?

Not just the sex, mind-blowing as it was, but moments

like they shared this morning when he opened up to her about nearly losing her. Or the way he crawled into bed with her last night and just his presence alone comforted her and chased away the nightmares of what she'd been through.

Last night she'd been looking forward to their date on Sunday. This morning she woke up to the reality of being a part of Jay's life.

"I lost you, sweetheart. What's wrong? Is the pain too much?"

"Yeah." True enough, but the swirling thoughts and emotions left her confused and dazed and a little scared. The pain would fade. She wasn't so sure the pinch of regret would cease if she walked away from Jay now before she got in too deep and things got too dangerous for her and her heart.

Jay walked into the adjoining bathroom, ran the water, and came back with a filled glass for her to take the pain meds the doctor prescribed at the ER. Jay handed her the bottle from the bedside table. She read the label.

"What's with the frown?" Jay sat on the bed beside her.

She pulled back one side of her mouth in dismay. "This is Dilaudid."

"You were in a lot of pain last night. The tension in your body, the way you're holding perfectly still, and the pain I see in your eyes tells me it's not any better. You need that."

She took one of the pills out and downed it with the water Jay handed her. "I just think the doctor could have prescribed something less powerful than this. It's not like I broke a bone or had surgery."

"I think he just wanted to be sure you were comfortable. You can barely move your neck. Every breath you take must hurt like hell with your bruised ribs."

She shook the nearly full bottle of pills up and down.

"All that is true, but he gave me a ten-day supply. People become addicted to powerful pain meds like this in less time than that."

"Are you worried about taking them?"

"I'm more concerned that doctors hand out prescriptions like this when less powerful drugs taken for a shorter period of time would get someone injured like me through the worst of the pain the first few days until the body heals enough and the pain subsides."

Jay nodded toward the bottle. "It's part of the reason those pills go for big bucks on the street."

"It's why ordinary people who have never or rarely taken drugs end up dependent."

"I've busted soccer moms buying pills with their kids strapped into car seats in the back of their minivans." He didn't hide the disgust in his eyes.

"Now that's just sad." Her heart broke for those poor kids—and the moms who probably wanted to be everything their kids deserved but found themselves sucked into addiction.

"I see sad every day. But nothing is harder than seeing the innocent people who are affected by drugs." He sighed and his gaze dropped to the floor. "If what happened to you is because of me, I'm really sorry. You have no idea how much. I'd never want anything I do to come back on you. I know your brothers feel the same way."

Unable to get up just yet, she placed her hand on his knee because she needed to comfort him in some way. She needed the contact. She needed to remember that he really wasn't responsible just because he did a very necessary job that he loved.

"This is not your fault. Bad men do bad things. You're one of the good guys. So before you start taking responsibility, let's wait and find out what really happened. For all we know, it was an accident or some asshole went all road rage on my ass because I was daydreaming about the way you like to kiss your way down my thigh and driving too slow."

The under-the-breath chuckle didn't light up his eyes. "You don't believe that."

"I don't not believe it either. I don't know what to think."

"Any new details come back to you?"

The replay went through her mind again. She wanted to stop it, but couldn't. The fear washed through her with a cold chill as she relived the jarring surprise when he hit her the first time. The realization that he was coming back for more set off another bolt of terror. When the car rolled, she'd feared it was over. Then the car stopped and she jolted back into place in her seat and the world spun . . . and a light flashed.

She stared up at Jay who held her trembling hand protected in his warm ones. "He took a picture."

Jay rocked back with the news. "Are you sure?"

"I saw the flash right before I passed out. He's just a dark figure sitting in the front seat of the car with the phone held up. And the flash goes off. I'm sure. He took a picture."

"Why? He didn't send it to your brothers or me as a threat. The DEA hasn't gotten anything."

"Maybe for insurance purposes?"

The ridiculous suggestion made Jay glare. "He fled the scene of a major accident."

"He freaked and fled?"

Jay growled. Actually growled. "I don't want to talk to you anymore. Not until the drugs wear off, because they have obviously muddled your mind. I'm going to check on Adam and get you some coffee."

"My hero." She desperately needed a caffeine kick, and despite Jay's comment about the drugs wearing off, she needed them to kick in soon to stave off the throbbing pain. And after her conversations last night with those affected by prescription drug abuse and the doctor prescribing her a highly addictive painkiller, she needed to think about how best she could serve her community and help keep dangerous prescription drugs off the streets and out of the hands of vulnerable people.

CHAPTER THIRTEEN

The squeal of high-pitched laughter drew her to the kitchen along with the smell of coffee. Jay left her lying in bed and hadn't yet returned with the promised caffeine fix. She wouldn't mind staying there for the rest of the day, but she wanted to see Adam, call in sick to work, figure out a plan to get some clothes from her house, and get the ball rolling with her insurance company for the car accident. She needed a new car. But she'd start with a rental for now.

She didn't remember much of the house beyond the spacious entry, but she found the rest of the place as clean, neat, and orderly as Jay's bedroom. All the wood furniture gleamed as shiny as the wood floors. Jay kept the decorations and color scheme simple. Off-white area rugs anchored the rich, brown leather sofas in the living room and the farmhouse table in the dining room. Wrought-iron chandeliers and table lamps gave the place a rustic feel, but the simple clean lines in the furnishings gave a contemporary feel without making the place seem sterile. The rich wood added warmth. And so did the small touches, like the horse photographs on the walls, the massive stone fireplace with the chunky mantel covered in family photos, silver candlestick holders, and white ceramic pots filled with fake greenery that looked like a live mounding plant. On the dining room table sat a bowl of red apples she'd bet were made of wood but looked edible.

"Hey, you should have stayed in bed." Jay stood in the kitchen doorway, his hands braced on either side of the doorframe. He looked good enough to lick in worn jeans and a black T-shirt that stretched across his wide chest and around his biceps.

"I would have if you delivered the promised coffee."

"Sorry, I got sidetracked with Adam and a bowl of Lucky Charms."

That made her smile. "It gave me a chance to see the house." She pointed to the dining room on the right. "That antique mirror over the buffet is gorgeous." Distressed by time and use, the flaws and black spots gave the simple oval mirror character, which complemented the black metal frame worn to silver on part of the edges. "Did you take the photographs?"

"My mother."

"They're great. Your horses?"

He pointed to the chestnut in the entry. "Scooby. My childhood pal. I lost him about ten years ago." He waved his hand toward the white horse standing in front of a dark barren tree in a snow-covered field. "Blizzard. She's out back in the pasture with Willa. Adam wants to feed them apples after breakfast."

"Sounds good." She went to him, hooked her hand around the back of his neck, and brought him down for a kiss because she couldn't move her neck. He came willingly, brushing his lips over hers, then sinking in for a long press of his mouth to hers, his eyes still open and staring into hers.

She placed her palm on his face and swept her thumb over his cheek. "Thank you."

"No thanks necessary. I don't need a reason to kiss you." He finally released the doorframe and wrapped his arms around her back in a loose hug.

"No, thank you for last night, for taking care of me, letting me borrow your clothes, holding me through the nightmares, just being you."

"You look good in my clothes." He smiled and stared down between them at the too-long T-shirt and the pair of cutoff sweats that, even tied at her waist, still hung low on her hips and draped to her shins.

"I look like an elf in your clothes, but they're comfortable and smell like you."

His eyes smoldered. "You make it hard to remember you're hurt, the kid's in the kitchen, and I can't take you back to bed right now."

She laid her forehead against his chin and pressed her aching body to his rock-hard one.

Jay combed his fingers through her long hair to the back of her neck and held her close. "You okay, sweetheart?"

"Yes. And no. I'm still off after last night."

"It's understandable. Plus, you haven't had your coffee." The teasing in his voice made her grin.

She pushed back and stared up at him, appreciating his attempt to lighten her mood and that not everything between them had to be about sleeping together. He'd been a real friend last night. And so much more when he turned on that tender side and spoke from his heart. She didn't mind the protective streak either. Much. Though she had a feeling he'd try to dictate her movements over the next few days, if not longer, and they'd butt heads about it for sure.

He took her hand and led her into the kitchen. Adam sat at the breakfast bar off the marble island staring down at Jay's cell phone. He moved his finger over the screen, his face scrunched, gaze serious.

She went to him, kissed him on top of the head, and glanced at the screen. "Frogger?" The old-school game held Adam's attention as he tried to move his frog across a river of logs and turtles.

"Aw, man! I lost again." Adam took a huge bite of cereal and started over.

Jay handed her a mug of coffee and held up a loaf of multigrain bread. "I can make you toast and eggs."

"You're sweeter than you look."

He shook his head, fighting back another grin, then went to the fridge to get the eggs. He moved with intention and precision. The job made him purposeful. He remained aware of her and Adam behind him, glancing over his shoulder from time to time, even giving her a questioning eyebrow raise when she continued to stare. She just smiled sweetly and enjoyed the view. Tight ass, broad back, strong arms, and big, competent hands.

Her purse lay on the breakfast table. Jay must have brought it in from his car early this morning. She snagged it and sat at the bar beside Adam. Her phone only had ten percent left on the battery, but it would be enough to call in to work.

The phone barely rang when Noel picked up. "Are you okay?"

The desperation in his voice froze her in place and stopped her heart for a few beats. "Uh, I'm fine."

Jay turned from the stove and gave her an are-you-serious face.

"Actually, I was in a car accident last night. How did you know something was wrong?"

Jay pinned her in his intense gaze.

"Uh, well, y-you're ten minutes late for work. You're never late." True, but ten minutes didn't warrant the amped concern in Noel's voice.

"I'm really sorry, but I won't be in today."

Jay's eyebrow shot up again.

"I won't be in tomorrow either," she added before Jay made another face at her.

"How badly were you hurt?"

"I actually got off lucky with just some scratches, bruises, and a sprained neck."

"Oh God, I'm so sorry." The depth of emotion touched her but also seemed over the top.

"Are you sure you don't need me there so you can be with Lee?" This time she didn't even look up to see what kind of face Jay made at her.

"No." The word snapped out too quickly, like he wanted to keep her away from the store. "You need to rest. I can take care of things here. Don't worry, I will take care of them." Odd wording, but she let it go, chalking it up to the stress Noel was under with his ailing wife and covering for her.

"If you're sure."

"Stay home. It's for the best. When you come back, I'll have everything back to normal."

"I'm not sure what you mean."

"Oh, sorry, I'm distracted. My mind is all over the place this morning with everything going on."

"Noel, if it's too much for you . . ."

"I can't believe you got hurt. I can fix this. I will. Take care. Be safe. I'll see you Monday."

She dropped her hand from her ear and stared at the phone, wondering what the hell happened. Noel didn't sound like himself. He wasn't making sense.

"I think the meds are messing with my mind."

Jay set her plate of food in front of her and laid his hand on her shoulder. "What's wrong?"

"Nothing. It's probably just me."

"But?"

"It's almost like he knew something happened."

Jay tensed beside her; everything about him went on alert. "What do you mean?"

"Granted, I'm not usually late to work, but when he answered, he seemed overly upset that I didn't show up on time. As if the only reason I'd be late was because something terrible happened."

"Something did happen."

"Yes, but why assume the worst?" She tried to reason it out in her mind and came up with the only answer that made any kind of sense. "His wife has cancer. He tries to hide how much he worries about her and what might happen. I guess he's transferred that concern to me as well."

Jay's eyes squinted. "He's as concerned about you as he is his *wife*. Something you want to share about that?"

Damn investigator radar for the details people leave out. "You're annoying sometimes, you know that?"

Unfazed, he gave her shoulder a soft squeeze. "Spill it."

"He's kind of got a thing for me. We're partners in the business. We spend a lot of time together. He's lonely." That got another eyebrow raise. "His wife is sick. His girls are away at college. He's kind of alone and looking for . . . I don't know, companionship."

"Uh-huh."

She didn't like that "Uh-huh" one bit.

"Just because your wife is sick doesn't give you the excuse to go looking for love somewhere else. She needs him. He should be with her."

She liked his when-things-get-tough-you-stick-together attitude. She admired that about him. "I agree. I'm just saying that he's dealing with her stuff and his own. I get the sense he feels like all the attention is on her—rightfully so—but he wants to be taken care of, too."

"I'll just bet he wants you to take care of him."

She held her hand out flat toward Adam happily shoveling Lucky Charms into his mouth in between video game levels. "Watch it. I like Noel. He's built a successful business and gave me a shot when I had little experience."

"He needed the money you brought to the table." Of

course Jay knew the background. Her brothers probably told him during some long stakeout.

She didn't like his unintended allegation that she'd get involved with Noel—a married man. She didn't think he really believed that, but let his jealousy show that he didn't like Noel getting too close to her. "I keep things professional."

"Let me guess, he sometimes crosses the line."

"I've made it clear, we're friends, but he can be overly familiar. That makes things uncomfortable for me. He's never crossed the line, but he sometimes goes right up to it. I don't even think he realizes it."

"Yes. He does." As a guy, Jay knew how they thought and acted.

She didn't want to argue. She shouldn't keep making excuses for Noel's bad behavior either. "I believe in promises and vows. I would never do anything to jeopardize a relationship, especially when it's vulnerable. Lee is sick. Noel is trying to cope and looking for understanding and comfort."

"If he tries to find it with you again and won't take no for an answer, I'll be happy to drive the point home that you're not interested."

She tried to laugh it off, but Jay held her gaze, his serious and intent.

"Right?" Jay asked.

It took her a second to figure out what he meant. "No. I'm not interested in him. He's practically old enough to be my father. His oldest daughter is only four years younger than me."

"You don't seem to mind older guys," he pointed out.

She shook her head. "You are the only 'older guy' I've dated and Noel has several years on you. Look, I get it, the age thing reminds you of what happened with your parents and how that embittered your mom. I have older brothers. I know what they were like and what they liked when they were younger. I liked a lot of the same things you all probably liked. I thought a lot of their friends were hot. Back then, most definitely inappropriate. Now, I don't see it as a big deal, and I don't think you really do either."

"So, we're dating?" The humor in his eyes didn't mask the seriousness in his tone.

She shook her head. "That's what you pulled out of there."

He waited for her answer.

"We have a date this weekend. So long as nobody tries to . . ."—she glanced at Adam—"you know." For Adam's sake, she left off, *tries to kill me.* "I'm looking forward to a little normal between us." They'd hooked up a few times. That seemed too casual for what they shared but she couldn't come up with a better description. Because of her "accident," she was staying here for a few days. That didn't make them dating. Did it?

Jay leaned on his forearms on the counter and stared over at her, none too happy-looking about her response. "Your brothers are a bigger concern than our age difference. But we are seeing each other. Exclusively. No pharmacists on the side."

"I'm not an on-the-side kind of girl. For me, or the guy I'm *seeing*." After what his parents went through, she didn't think he was the cheating or seeing-multiple-women-at-the-same-time kind of guy either.

"I barely have time to *see* you, sweetheart."

It seemed both of them couldn't quite decide what *seeing* and *dating* really meant for them at this point. The physical part of their relationship seemed so easy. The emotional stuff, their wants and desires for everything else, they still needed to work out.

This time she gave him the scrunched annoyed face.

He leaned in and kissed her softly, pulled back just an

inch, stared into her eyes, and whispered, "You're all I want." He sealed that promise with another soft kiss that in its simplicity left her feeling the warmth and sincerity of the perfect moment through her whole being.

He brushed his thumb down the side of her face and gave her one of his not-so-straight smiles. "Eat your breakfast, sweetheart."

She stared down at her lightly toasted bread and over-medium eggs. "How did you know how I like my eggs?"

"That's what you ordered the first morning of the wedding weekend."

She glanced over at him. "You remembered that?"

"I remember all kinds of little things about you. I seem to be storing them up."

"Can we go feed the horses now?" Adam pushed his empty bowl away, set the phone down, and blinked a few times from staring at the screen too long.

"Sure." Jay pushed off the counter, handed her the fork beside her plate, and ordered, "Eat. I'll take the kid for a walk to work off all that sugar he just ate."

"You sure you don't need your walker, grandpa?" she teased just to emphasize the age thing really didn't matter.

He leaned into her ear, his big hand clamped onto her thigh, right near her hip, his fingers splayed wide. If he dipped his hand just a little, he'd touch the fire burning in her. "You know I don't need a walker or even a little blue pill to show you just how young and fit I am. But if you need a reminder of the *hours* we spent together, say the word and I'm yours."

Adam grabbed Jay by the arm and tugged. "Come on, Jay, you promised."

"I always keep my promises," he answered Adam, but said the words to her. An echo of what she'd said to him about believing in promises and vows. He kissed her on the forehead. "We'll be back soon. You need anything, hit the call button on that panel." He pointed to the intercom system by the back door. "I'll hear you over the speakers in the stables."

"I'll be fine. After breakfast, I think I'll take a shower and figure out what needs to be done next."

"Take it slow and easy."

"The pain med is kicking in. The more I move, the looser I feel."

"Come on." Adam tugged harder on Jay's arm, though now it had turned into more of a game than anything as Jay didn't budge an inch and Adam giggled and pulled with all his might.

Jay finally let Adam drag him toward the back door, but stopped when his phone pinged with a text message. Alina picked it up from the counter where Adam left it and held it out for Jay, but pulled it back close when she spotted the name that flashed on the screen in the alert.

"Who is Ginger?"

Jay snatched the phone from her, unlocked it, and read the message, absently saying, "Stripper name."

"What's a stripper?" Adam asked.

Jay didn't respond. Alina didn't know what to say or think about a stripper texting Jay.

"Care to share?" she asked Jay, waiting for him to stop typing a mile a minute and answer her.

"Code name for King while he's undercover." Jay finally looked up at her, then a smile split his face. "Why? Jealous?"

"If King's undercover as a stripper, I won't judge. It's all in the line of duty, right?"

Jay's eyes danced with delight. He didn't buy her lame cover one bit.

"What's a stripper?" Adam asked again.

Jay distracted him. "Get an apple out of the fridge for Willa and Blizzard."

Adam dashed to the fridge eager to get the apple and go see the horses.

Jay sent off another text.

"Is everything okay? If you have to leave, we'll be fine here alone."

Jay studied his phone, but answered her. "You will not be left alone even if I have to go, but I don't. King's just checking in, giving me an update."

"You look worried."

"I'm always worried about my guys. King's just out of jail and taking on a major assignment. He's already made contact with his target but things with his mark are . . . complex."

"How so?"

Jay didn't answer at first, then he smiled. "Women complicate everything."

She rolled her eyes. "Get out."

Jay took Adam's hand and opened the back door. "Kicked out of my own house."

"I can't even go back to mine."

Jay let Adam walk ahead and turned back to her. "I will find whoever hurt you and make sure they never do it again. In the meantime, for what it's worth, I like having you here." He closed the door behind him.

She sat at the counter with her perfect breakfast in his lovely home. "I like being here." Maybe too much. Because though they'd shared a bed, they hadn't shared much else. As close as she felt to him, she still didn't believe this thing between them would really go anywhere.

But the longer she spent with him, the more she wanted it to.

CHAPTER FOURTEEN

Jay stared at his black home office window, seeing nothing but his reflection in the glass, his mind on the call that left him with nothing but unanswered questions.

He focused on the beautiful woman behind him and not his dark thoughts about what happened to her. She stood with her hand on him, her face slightly tilted down, dark hair falling over her shoulders, a slight smile on her rosy lips.

They looked good together. It both intrigued and concerned him. He wanted her with an intensity he'd never imagined possible. Lust for a beautiful woman came easily. But his feelings for Alina ran deep, like a river disappearing into a mountain, filling his cavernous heart. Uncharted territory. Scary. But every time he shined a light on it, it reflected through him, brightening his soul.

With the way he lived his life, working more than living, threats around every corner, sometimes coming too close, he didn't know if it was fair or if he could hold on to her. But he wanted to more than he wanted to admit, because losing her meant more days alone, but now he'd really know what it was to be lonely for someone.

She gave him a reason to want to tip the seesaw of his life from work to personal and find a balance that made him happier. And kept Alina by his side. Because he found himself thinking about the future where he had someone to come home to, a reason to let the never-ending paperwork wait a little longer, the long, drawn-out missions that kept him gone for days go to someone else so he could attend Little League, soccer games, and ballet recitals.

The bruises and scrapes on her face, the brace around her neck, the stiffness in her body, reminded him how close he'd come to losing her. That desperate-to-get-to-her feeling rushed through him again even though she stood inches from him.

What would he feel if he actually lost her?

"Jay, are you okay?"

No, he wasn't okay. For the first time in his life, he wasn't sure how to get what he wanted, if he could make it happen, or how to make it happen. For a guy who'd gone after everything—school, training, the job—with single-minded determination and gotten everything he wanted, this uncertainty about Alina unsettled him more than he expected.

He wanted to tell himself it didn't matter that much. Whatever happened, happened. But lying, especially to himself, wasn't his deal. He didn't know how it happened, but she mattered more to him than anything. And keeping her safe, making her happy, had become his number one priority.

He took her hand from his shoulder and kissed her palm, then pressed it to his cheek. He wasn't okay, but couldn't tell her that, so he deflected. "Is Adam down for the night?"

Alina pulled her hand free and spun his chair so he no longer looked at their reflection but up into her earnest face. "He's asleep. Now, what's wrong?"

Smart woman. He should have known she wouldn't let him get away without answering her. Plus, he should have anticipated she'd read him better than most since he had no trouble letting down his guard around her.

"I was just thinking about us."

"And that upsets you?"

He shook his head and tried to make her understand even if the things running through his mind didn't make a whole lot of sense to him either. "The cops found the car that ran you off the road."

"Great. Do they have a suspect?"

To his utter disgust, they had nothing worth a damn. "No. The car had been reported stolen this morning when the owner woke up and discovered it missing from the driveway. The cops located it with the GPS tracker. It had been abandoned behind a strip mall about six blocks from where the accident occurred. No prints. They wiped the inside clean." Which to him seemed more calculated and professional than some random accident that scared the unknown driver into ditching the car so he wouldn't get caught. "Nothing left behind but the damage from the accident."

"Okay."

"There have been no threats to your brothers or me. No one has contacted us or the DEA claiming responsibility." The frustration building inside him came out with his tight words. "There's no chatter on the streets about someone trying to take you out for retribution for . . . whatever. As far as we know, no one in your life is angry with you and wants to hurt you."

"Jay, sometimes the simplest answer is the right answer. Someone stole the car, took it for a joyride, and got a bug up their butt and hit me."

"That was an eighty-thousand-dollar car. It takes skill to jack an SUV with all the bells and whistles. They'd have done so to take it to a chop shop and earn some cash. Not to joyride and . . . what? See what it's like to nearly kill someone for the hell of it!" His heart thrashed in his chest, blood pounded through his veins, along with his rising anger and frustration.

"Shh." She touched her fingertips to his lips to stop him from yelling even more. "You'll wake Adam."

He pulled her hand away, stood, and walked to the tall windows, still seeing his reflection and not the dark night. He didn't like the desperate look in his eyes. "Damnit, Alina, don't you get it?"

She placed her free hand on his back and rubbed it up to his shoulder. "Someone stole the car so they could hurt me, ditch it, and not get caught."

The words spelled out his worst nightmare. Not some random act, but a cold, calculated attempt to kill her.

Why?

Because of him?

The thought tightened the knots in his stomach and clenched his heart so hard it hurt to breathe. With no outlet to take out his aggression, he let his fury fly with the fist he sent into the window frame. The pain in his hand was nothing compared to the rage still consuming him.

Alina took her hand from him and stepped back. He felt the loss of her touch like a dying man in the desert misses water. Then she surprised him, spinning him around, hooking her arm around his neck, pressing her body against his a split second before her mouth landed on his and she kissed him. Not sweet or soft or even hungry, but with a purpose to make him pay attention to all she said without a single word.

She had his attention. And possession of him with her arm wrapped around his neck. Chest-to-chest and hip-to-hip, she gave herself over to him and still managed to convey that she had no intention of letting him go.

She slowed the kiss, then brushed light kisses against his lips, one after the other, as his breathing steadied and his muscles loosened but he didn't let go his hold on her either.

Foreheads pressed together, their eyes closed, she sighed out his name. "This is not your fault. I know you will find out who did this and why. You will stop them. And no matter what happens, I know, with you, I'm safe."

His eyes flew open and he stared into the crystal-clear granite of hers and knew those words held the strength and conviction he saw in the blue-gray depths of her eyes. Somehow he'd earned her trust despite the fact she'd been hurt and what they'd shared up until now had been a series of lust-fueled encounters with an underlying current of what could be if they only gave in to their deepest desire to connect with that kind of passion on another level.

"I want . . ." He didn't know how to put it into words. "So much. I want you to be safe. I want this to not be so complicated. I want you. Do you get that?"

Her hand slid from his hair to the side of his face. She held him still and stared into his eyes. "It's not complicated. I want you, too." The decision made shown in her eyes.

She'd been struggling with the same questions and misgivings he had about starting a relationship, but somehow it had not only started but they were in the thick of it and committed to each other.

He never expected it to happen like this.

"I thought relationships started off slow and built into something unbreakable and lasting. That feelings grew stronger over time. I never thought it would burst inside of me like this and just be."

Her words knocked him off-kilter but righted everything inside him at the same time. She didn't say it outright, but that had been a straight-up declaration of love.

And now, nothing about *them* scared him.

Everything became clear. He didn't need to do anything, say anything, make some kind of magic happen. "It just is between us."

The same kind of relief her words gave him softened her eyes as his words sank in for her.

For a split second he was like, *Okay, we're on the same page, now what?* Then she smiled at him and her whole face lit up and that new feeling living inside him took over and he kissed her. He fell back on what brought them together and let that spark ignite a fire.

Before, he focused on the need to have her. Now he wanted to show her how much she meant to him because acknowledging it had set something free in him that he needed to share with her.

It seemed like one move, undoing her bra and pulling it, the sling, and her shirt off over her head. Her pained squeak and the bruises across her chest reminded him to be gentle and that taking her on his office floor wasn't the best idea. He tossed away the bra, sling, and shirt, kept kissing her, dipped and slid his hands around her bottom and picked her up off her feet. She followed his lead and wrapped her legs around his waist. He walked out of the office with her wrapped around him. He couldn't see where he was going, didn't need to, since he knew the house so well. He followed his need and the hallway down to his room, kicked the door closed, hoping the noise didn't wake Adam, and laid her out on his bed, trailing kisses down her chest and belly as he stood and pulled her pants and panties off her legs.

He made his clothes disappear as fast as her eyes traveled down his body as he exposed more and more flesh. The desire there heated his skin before he even touched her. He barely remembered to grab the condom before he joined her on the bed. She sat up to kiss him, their tongues dancing the way their bodies demanded to move.

She pushed at his shoulder to make him roll to his back. He barely got the condom on in time before she straddled his lap and sank down on him, his name nothing but a sigh of relief and a plea for more. He gave it to her. He'd give her everything to make her happy and keep her in his arms. And so he let her set the pace, slow and easy in concession to her still sore body, but intense in their need to draw out every touch, kiss, and slide of their bodies together. She rode him, giving him free rein to touch her soft skin, worship one breast and the other with his mouth and tongue until her body tightened and her breath came out on soft little moans that drove him wild.

He hooked his arm around her hips, held her close, and rolled her to her back, making sure he didn't jostle her too much. She sank into the mattress and he thrust deep into her. Hands on his hips, she pulled him in again and again. He held himself over her, stared down at her beautiful face, eyes closed, lips slightly parted as she sighed. He rocked his hips to hers, creating that sweet friction she needed. Her breath caught, body tensed, and her hot core clamped around his hard cock as she quaked. The second she started coming down, he thrust hard and deep and spilled himself inside her, setting off another round of aftershocks that made her hands clamp down on his ass and her nails bite into his skin. The sweet pain made his dick twitch inside of her and she rocked her hips into him again, prolonging the most explosive orgasm he'd ever experienced.

He stayed just like that, locked in her body and the intensity of being joined with her until his arms shook and he let loose his tight muscles and settled on top of her. He managed to keep his forearms braced just enough to not crush or push on her bruised ribs.

The hands on his ass smoothed over his skin and up his back in hypnotic brushes up and down his spine and over his hips until they came up, she wrapped her arms around his middle, and held on tight.

He turned his head into her hair and kissed her just under her ear, then whispered a truth he couldn't hold inside anymore. "You are everything I ever wanted."

She turned and looked at him. "You're not what I expected and better than I thought possible."

He settled on the bed beside her, left her on her back for her injured neck, wrapped her up close, leaned his head against hers, inhaled the scent of his shampoo in her hair, and hoped that this night was what every night with her would be like from now into forever.

Hours later in the dead of night, he should have hoped that work wouldn't tear him out of their bed. Instead, he answered the call disturbing the quiet night and Alina's sleep.

"Are you okay?"

"We have a problem." King, his undercover agent, had nerves of steel. The ominous tone to his words made Jay roll out of bed when all he wanted to do was stay there with the woman who came into his life unexpectedly and filled the missing piece in his world.

She wasn't going anywhere if he had anything to say about it, but he had a feeling he was on his way to take care of whatever problem crept up in King's case.

Normally he didn't think twice about diving into a case and putting it all on the line, but as he stood staring down at Alina in his bed, he found he'd rather be there with her than anywhere else. The danger he faced going after drug dealers seemed even more real and ominous because it could take him from her. But he couldn't give up his work because of what might happen.

She'd be here when he got back.

God that sounds good.

And now he had a very good reason to make sure he made it back.

CHAPTER FIFTEEN

Jay hated leaving a beautiful woman alone in his bed in the wee hours of the morning. He'd wanted to stay with Alina, but the late-night call from King couldn't be ignored. He didn't like leaving another agent at his house to watch over Alina and Adam. The protective streak inside him tightened his gut and made him worry.

If he wasn't the one protecting her, she wasn't safe enough.

Irrational, but that's how he felt.

The agent with her was trained and competent. Jay wouldn't have asked for his help otherwise or left Alina and Adam in his care if he couldn't handle a dangerous situation if it should arise. The rational part of his brain told him no one would find her at his place. That didn't stop his brain from spawning a million nightmares and scenarios of whoever went after her before coming back to finish the job.

He shook off the chill that ran up his spine that had nothing to do with the predawn temps outside the non-descript sedan he drove to meet King. The sun barely cracked the dark night on the horizon as he made his way down the main drag and spotted the strip mall with the dog groomer shop King and he agreed to use as their meeting point should the need arise. According to King, this couldn't wait, so Jay had foregone sleep and making love to Alina one more time. This better be worth missing both those things and the bad coffee he'd picked up at an all-night gas station minimart on the outskirts of town.

He cut the lights before the turnoff, pulled into the lot behind the shop, and parked beside King's beat-up truck.

Jay, wearing a black jacket and ski cap on his head to ward off the cold and conceal his looks, got out and carried the two carryout cups of coffee. He set one cup on the truck roof, opened the door, handed one cup to King, retrieved the other, and climbed inside. He closed the door on the cold breeze, sat back, and stared out the window.

On a yawn, he said, "It's damn early to call me out here. I hope you have something good."

King handed over a note enclosed in a plastic bag. "Print it. See if you get a hit in the system."

Jay read the note.

if you want to live stay away from Cara

He rolled his eyes. "You brought me here for this. Iceman's warning you away."

King shook his head. "He warned me in person. Right after he made me keep my mouth shut about Manny Castillo's death."

"Why would he care if you said anything about that dirtbag?"

"Because Manny tried to manipulate Cara into marrying him. He thought the two of them could take over for their fathers one day and run the show. When Cara discovered his plan, she wanted out. He cut off her finger and made her think he was ransoming her back to her father."

The brutality the cartels resorted to didn't surprise

Jay anymore, but he hated that that cruelty had been inflicted on a woman. It made him think about Alina.

King's hand fisted around the steering wheel. "Instead, he was just a sick fuck trying to prove to her that her father didn't care about her."

Jay actually followed all that convoluted cartel, family loyalty bullshit. "What the fuck!"

"Exactly. I always knew Iceman set up that raid and Manny's takedown." King went undercover to take down Iceman after Iceman set up the DEA, King, to take out a rival to the Guzman cartel. Manny Castillo. "I never knew why."

Jay put the pieces together. "To get revenge for his daughter." Iceman wanted Manny to pay but couldn't go after Manny himself, not without starting a bloody war between the cartels.

"He pays her a couple thousand every month. She thinks Manny is paying her off for what he did to her. A means to keep the truce between the two cartels. Really, it's Iceman's way of looking out for her."

"So they are close. He didn't turn his back on her."

"They aren't close. Cara despises him. Iceman does everything he can to keep her out of his world even though he can't help checking on her."

Jay held up the plastic bag. "Hence the note."

King shook his head. "Not him. Not his style. If he wanted me to stay clear of her, I'd be gone. He wouldn't stand by, spying on us in the middle of the night."

That sent Jay's eyebrow and his interest up. "What were you two doing in the middle of the night?" He'd sent King undercover to get close to Cara, but not to cross a line that put him and the operation in jeopardy.

King barely contained a growl of frustration. "I was doing my job. Getting close to her. Getting her to open up and trust me."

King wouldn't look at him, which probably meant King was getting too close to Cara. It could work to their advantage, or blow up in their faces if she really worked with her father.

"And does she trust you?"

"Yes. But it's as fragile as a flake of ash."

Same as everything in this line of work. Nothing was ever certain. On the surface everything looked like one thing, then in a blink of an eye changed to something else.

"You knew going in she wouldn't be easy to get close to."

"If I didn't believe she wasn't involved with her father and his crew, I'd think her paranoia was tied to keeping their business under wraps and her out of jail. But it goes deeper than that. She's never had anyone to count on. No one to keep her safe and protected and make her happy. She's never come first for anyone. She's been on her own practically her whole life."

"Use that to get close to her. Prove to her that you will keep her safe, that you care about her." Jay left "Don't sleep with her" unspoken. Despite King's obvious bond to her, he didn't need the reminder from Jay. King needed to convince Cara to give up her father and his operation for this mission to succeed. If King couldn't do that, Jay would pull him out.

"So is she an asset or a waste of time and we should go after Iceman directly?"

King took his time answering. "She knows the only way she'll ever be safe is if her father is dead. In jail might be her preference, but it still makes her a target. Especially because he can't seem to stay away from her. I think I can nudge her to our side and get her to actively try to take him down. Right now, she stays out of his business and only acts on things when she inadvertently finds out about them."

"Like her calling in the produce truck full of drugs."

King got that information day one undercover. If he was getting closer to Cara, this whole thing might be over soon. And Jay could get his ass home to Alina where he really wanted to be.

"Right. That will probably end now that Tim's father got busted during the raid on that truck and is now behind bars. She's lost her link to the operation through them. Iceman isn't stupid enough to give her any means to cause him more problems."

"Turn her against her father and do it quick. We're getting intel he's got something big planned."

King leaned back and sighed. "I feel like we're spinning our wheels."

"Nature of the game, man. We take down one, another pops up. But getting Iceman will seriously impair drug distribution in the state in a major way." And be a huge coup for the DEA and King and Jay's careers.

"I don't know if Cara will do what we need her to do. For all her strength and determination, she's got a soft heart. Deep down, she loves her father and understands that his staying away from her is for her benefit as much as she believes he's a deadbeat dad who doesn't give a shit about her."

"Sounds like he's both. The question is, does she believe the man who deals drugs for a living and wrecks lives, including hers, deserves to be taken down once and for all?"

King stared out the window, his gaze intense. "I don't know how Trigger played this game day in and day out." Guilt and reservations filled King's eyes.

Trigger had spent years working undercover.

"At a cost. To him and others."

King raked his fingers through his hair. "I feel so damn guilty for lying to her. She's a good person. She's not doing anything wrong. In fact, she's such an upstanding citizen she calls in drug raids on her own father."

"She took you in thinking you're an ex-con and gave you a job." Jay stated the truth, but the underlying message came through: Cara got to King.

King wasn't like Trigger. He couldn't keep things all business.

"Listen, King . . ." He used his real name instead of Flash, the name he used for this undercover operation, to remind King of who and what he was: a DEA agent, here to take down the bad guys. "Trigger didn't like using innocent people either. It weighed on him. That's why he always tried to turn someone involved. They got away with their part or reduced charges and Trigger got the goods on whoever we were taking down. So if you don't think you can turn Cara completely against her father, then find another way."

King's eyes lit with understanding and excitement for a new mission. He desperately wanted to do this without involving Cara.

Jay's nudge to do that if he could eased some of the tension in King.

Jay needed King focused on the job and ultimate goal. Now that he was, Jay slipped out of the truck with the suspicious note, leaving King to go back to work on the case.

Jay spent the long drive back to the office down south analyzing the situation. His strong suit, finding all the ways to handle any given situation, possible solutions and scenarios. His analytical mind served him well. Most of the time, he found more than one way to handle the circumstances.

But as his mind pulled him back to Alina and what was happening between them, he found only one way to handle her brothers, his best friends. Directly. If they continued to hide the way they felt about each other, it would only be worse when Caden and Beck found out. Like him, they wanted to protect Alina and keep her as far away from the world they lived in as DEA agents as possible. Look what happened to her. Someone might have targeted her because of the job they did.

But if he wanted to keep her, he had no way to keep her out of it.

And that tied his gut in knots far worse than the thought of facing her brothers and letting them know he was in a relationship with their sister. He could handle a beat-down if Caden and Beck wanted to go there, but he couldn't handle Alina getting hurt again.

He'd do anything to keep that from happening, but couldn't bring himself to let her go.

He needed to find the threat and eliminate it.

CHAPTER SIXTEEN

Alina settled down in the front seat of her armed bodyguard's car and finally took a moment to enjoy the late afternoon sun on her face, the beautiful landscape stretching out on both sides of the two-lane road, and memories of her and Jay making love last night.

Thoughts of him were never far from her mind. Hard not to think about him when she spent most of the day surrounded by his things, living in his house.

She shut that line of thinking down. She didn't live there. He'd just given her a safe place to stay while he and the police investigated the accident.

She had to think of it as nothing more than an accident, because the thought of someone targeting her, for whatever reason, terrified her to the point she wanted to run. But she had nowhere to go and didn't know who she was hiding from anyway.

Noel sent her four texts today and called twice to be sure she was okay and not in too much pain. It felt intrusive and possessive in a way. Like he didn't think she could take care of herself, or she'd break because something terrible happened to her. A friend would check up once, twice, hear in her voice and words that she was fine and just needed time to recover. Six times seemed like he didn't believe her capable of coping.

Jay called twice and kept things casual but direct.

"Feeling better?"

"Yep. Took a shower this morning. It made my sore muscles ache, but the hot water also made me feel better. Pain meds are clouding my mind. I seem to remember you kissing me goodbye in the dead of night and ordering me to not go anywhere without my bodyguard and to stay away from him at the same time." She grinned at the memory and discovering that Jay had a streak of jealousy where she was concerned. She had to admit, her bodyguard, DEA agent Dave, just Dave, was handsome and nice, but he wasn't Jay.

And that realization hit her square in the chest. All of a sudden, handsome men had become just other guys.

Jay didn't respond to her pointing out his green monster. *"I gotta get back to work."* He paused for just a second, then added, *"I can't wait to see you tonight."*

He hung up on her. She didn't mind. Much. They were both still figuring this thing out. Confessions in the dark aside, they still had to figure out how to be with each other in normal, everyday life when they weren't tearing each other's clothes off in a rush of lust and need. Though she loved that part, the real intimacy of sharing their lives scared her. She didn't want to mess up what they had now. Because it was pretty great and had the potential to be spectacular.

She didn't want to squander a chance at phenomenal. Not after she'd had mediocre disguised as happy moments.

She didn't regret those experiences; she scolded herself for settling for them when it hadn't felt right. Not like it did with Jay.

Of course, those experiences led her here and made her appreciate so much more what she'd found with Jay and within herself. She had the capacity to feel this deeply about someone. To have that reciprocated was a gift. One she'd seen her brothers get in their lives and had envied. Their happiness had made her jealous. Now, all she wanted was more of Jay.

"Did Jay tell you what time he'd be home tonight?"

Dave shook his head, his eyes on the road and scanning the mirrors to be sure no one followed them. It took them twice as long to run their errand to her place to get her and Adam more clothes and supplies for their stay at Jay's place. They'd had to circle and zigzag her neighborhood before Dave decided no one followed them or watched her place and they could go in.

"He'll probably check in again soon." Dave took the turnoff for Jay's driveway that wound away from the main road enough to make the property feel secluded but still had easy access for Jay to make the long drive into work.

She had no idea what took Jay away in the dead of night. She worried about him, too, today. Was he in danger?

Beck had spent years in constant danger undercover. Caden went on dangerous raids all the time. Jay was in charge. Did he spend his days at the office giving orders, or was he right beside his guys?

Right beside his guys, she answered her own question. Jay wouldn't let others handle things or do anything he wouldn't do himself. He couldn't even let the cops handle the car accident. He had to be involved.

His dedication and devotion to his guys made her admire him, but it also made her worry about what life with him would be like. Easy enough to imagine, she lived it with her brothers. The constant worry, wondering if any minute she'd get that devastating call that they'd been hurt or killed. But because of that, she'd always valued the time they spent together. She tried to enjoy it and soak up all the good memories with them because she never knew if that was the last time she'd see them.

Maybe living that way with Jay would be stressful, but so worth it if they committed to living their lives like it could be taken away at any time.

Not a great thought, but living present in their lives had to be better than passively wandering through each day thinking there was always tomorrow and missing out on truly being in the moment.

Her mind went back to her and Jay and when they were first together, both of them thinking it a one-time thing they had to make perfect and last. They'd given themselves over to each other and the moment and it turned out to be such a gift. A memory to cherish.

They pulled into the drive in front of the house dappled in shade from the large trees. Again, she got that sense of comfort. Until she spotted the woman scowling on the front porch. While the house might say welcome, Jay's mother had made it clear she didn't want Alina in her son's life.

"Wait in the car. Let me check things out before we go in." Ever vigilant, Dave's gaze scoped out every shadow and potential hiding spot around them.

"I don't think that's necessary. Heather Bennett is on the porch. I'm sure if there was some kind of danger, she'd be aware of it."

"Still. Let me take a look. Otherwise Bennett will kill me."

"Can I play Frogger on your phone?" Adam asked from the backseat as he yawned, waking up from his nap after the long ride.

She'd downloaded the game onto her phone this morning after Adam woke up, discovered Jay went to work and took his phone, and he pouted and asked her every three minutes, "When will Jay be home?"

She hoped soon because she didn't want to spend too long alone with his mom.

Adam greedily stole the phone from her hand as she passed it back. Dave slipped from the car and made a circuit around the house, saying something to Heather as he passed from the front to the back. She waited on the porch, her arms crossed at her chest, eyes glued on Alina.

It took Dave an interminably long time to circle the house and make his way from room to room inside before he waved the all clear.

Dave grabbed their bags from the backseat. She put her hand on Adam's shoulder and led him up the path to the front door. With his head bent, eyes glued on the screen, he didn't pay one bit of attention to where he was going.

Alina sent Adam through the door, hoping he found his way to the couch without stumbling into anything.

"All this space to run wild and you let him play those games."

"He likes them."

Heather shook her head in disgust. "He'll be addicted to that device and never play outside."

"I'm the aunt, not the mother. It's my prerogative to spoil him. Besides, your son is the one who hooked him on the game." Alina took a calming breath and tried to be nice. "Jay had to go to work. Is there something I can help you with?"

"I know he left in the middle of the night."

Alina tried not to read anything in her know-it-all tone, but she got the impression Heather wanted to tell her that she'd never keep him away from work and in her bed for long. Or maybe she was projecting her inner thoughts and doubts on Heather's words.

"I thought Adam might like to help me feed the horses. I take care of things here when Jay is away."

As in Alina had no business being here while Jay was at work.

"I'm sure Adam would love to help you. He can't seem to get enough of the horses. He'll work up a good appetite." Evening closed in and she needed to get dinner prepped and cooking.

Heather tossed a lock of golden hair over her shoulder. "I'll take care of dinner as soon as we're done with the horses."

As if Alina couldn't handle either job. Well, she grew up on the family ranch feeding horses and cows at the crack of dawn. She'd shoveled her fair share of horse shit and she didn't need any more from this woman about her abilities on the ranch or in the kitchen.

Heather snapped out, "There's no Restaurant Run or Diner to Door around here."

"Jay's got some steaks in the freezer and a grill out back."

Heather folded her arms at her chest. "And nothing much else in the house to eat. I'll take care of dinner."

"Jay's been kind enough to allow me to stay here during this difficult time. I'd like to do my part."

"You mean because someone tried to kill you." Heather seemed to want to add herself to the list.

"Yes."

"He's got enough trouble in his life. He doesn't need you adding more."

Alina sighed. "It's still not clear whether or not my accident had anything to do with someone associating me with Jay."

"Why? How long have you two been seeing each other?"

She'd walked right into that one. No way in hell she discussed her relationship with Jay's mother. For all the honesty she and Jay shared in bed both spoken by word and with their bodies, they still hadn't figured out how to translate any of it into them day to day.

"Jay suspects that someone saw us together when he picked up Adam at my place. They may have assumed . . ."

"Yeah, well, it won't last. None of them last once they discover he's got another love that takes all his time."

Alina had enough. "I'm not one of *them*. My brothers are DEA agents. I know the time, dedication, sacrifice, and heart it takes to do the job. If nothing else, I understand Jay in a way that none of *them* ever did, because I've seen firsthand the triumph they felt with the success of a big case and the devastation when things went wrong."

Alina could only guess at the memories that clouded Heather's eyes. Some from Jay's work. Others from her husband working for the sheriff's department. She wanted to project her experience and ultimate outcome on Alina. But it didn't have to be that way. Alina didn't have to resent Jay for doing his job. Jay could find a balance that worked for both of them. Right?

"I've known Jay for a time, but we've never really been friends. After what happened to me the other night, he was a very good friend. To me. And to my brothers for looking out for me while they're away. I appreciate all he's done to keep me and Adam safe. I understand you're looking out for him. I am, too."

She and Jay had been honest with each other. That's the best she could do to set up their relationship on solid ground. It was a hell of a lot better than spending weeks flirting, dancing around each other, trying to figure the other one out without actually being direct and open because they were too busy guarding against rejection and hurt.

She and Jay had already acknowledged to each other the obstacles in their path, their reservations about this thing working, and decided they wanted to go forward because the feelings between them were too strong to ignore, the pull too forceful to fight.

Together, everything felt right. Apart, they only longed to be with each other.

She couldn't explain it and didn't want to even try just to appease Heather. All she wanted was a chance to see if she and Jay could build a lasting future. And that was between them, and no one else's business.

"I'll tell Adam you need his help. Dinner will be ready soon." She walked past Heather to the open door.

"He needs someone willing to make him the priority, because his life will dominate theirs."

She turned back and looked Heather in the eye. "We all need someone who lets us be us and accepts and understands and compromises when it's necessary."

"You're too young to know it takes a hell of a lot more than that to keep a relationship together."

Yeah, it takes a hell of a lot more than cheating on your husband to get his attention. She kept that nasty comment to herself. Arguing with Jay's mom wouldn't do her or him any good. She'd let her actions speak for themselves, because that's what would show Heather and her and Jay that their relationship worked.

And work it would be with Heather's disapproval and her brothers' overprotective, overbearing interference.

Heather's frown deepened. "Acceptance and understanding and compromise break down when the other person is never around."

Yeah, that's when relationships fell apart, or could be built up stronger when both people put the work in to keep it together. Because that's the thing about relationships, you have to work on them. Sometimes it was just minor repairs. Other times a full-on rehab. If you let it all fall apart and rot away, sometimes there wasn't enough left to salvage.

She'd learned that watching her parents and brothers and in her own relationships. Though she'd been focused on school, she'd attempted a couple relationships in the hopes of building a home when the other person wanted an apartment. She wanted something permanent. They'd wanted something they could get out of easily and move on to something newer and more their style.

Sucky analogy, but she didn't want to be someone's temporary place to crash. She wanted to be someone's home.

Jay had built the house. He needed someone who wanted to stay and make it a home.

She wanted a chance to see if they both fit here without everyone else in their lives interfering.

"Heather, your argument is that this won't work because I'm too young for him and he'll never be around. It kind of makes him out to be the bad guy, and he's not."

"Of course not."

"So if you want him to be happy, you might encourage the one woman he's brought here to see what a good man he is and that doing his job doesn't mean he cares less about me." She'd have to remind herself of that as they moved forward. Especially on those nights he faced danger and she slept alone wondering if he'd come back to her.

Heather eyed her, one side of her mouth twitching. Maybe to hide a smile, or simply to not frown and cause lines. But then she surprised Alina with, "You might be all right."

Alina gave Heather a nod that she'd take it and walked into the house. She may not have convinced Heather she was the right woman for Jay, but she'd gotten her to concede to back off and give Alina a chance.

CHAPTER SEVENTEEN

Jay pulled into the drive after a long day of chasing down leads, trying to get forensics to hurry the hell up and print the note King gave him, and find one tiny speck of evidence of who hit Alina's car. He came up empty on all counts. Frustrated and annoyed, even the drive home hadn't eased his mind or the tension aching in his shoulders. But one look at his lit-up house and knowing Alina was inside waiting for him loosened all the knots and made it easier for him to, if not let go of, then at least push to the back burner what he didn't get accomplished today.

Alina was still in danger. Maybe. And that maybe unsettled him.

Fear ate at his gut that something might happen to her. It fed his raging desire to find the bastards who hurt her and eliminate them.

He slipped from the SUV, checked the drive and distant property for any sign he'd been followed, spotted nothing, and made his way up the walkway.

Dave popped out from around the corner of the house and met him on the porch. "Everything's quiet here. Your girl's cooking up something that smells amazing. Your mom, on the other hand, is stirring up trouble. She doesn't like your girl."

Great. Just what he needed, his mother sticking her nose in his relationship. "What happened?"

"I didn't hear all of it, but the gist seemed to be her age and your job add up to disaster so she should get the hell out now."

Jay huffed out his frustration.

Dave slapped him on the shoulder. "For what it's worth, you can have a life outside of the job. Caden and Beck do. I don't see why you can't work it out with their sister."

Dave had promised to keep quiet about Jay and Alina until they made their relationship public. "Maybe we can, if they don't kill me first."

"She held her own against your mom. She's taken over your kitchen and the barbecue. That's a good sign."

"I have her under guard at my house. It's not like she can leave." Something in Dave's eyes alerted him to trouble. "What?"

"I, uh, took her to her place today to get her things."

"You what? Anyone could have ambushed you there." A rush of unwarranted panic shot through his system. "What the fuck were you thinking?"

"That I know what I'm doing."

Jay couldn't deny that. It's why he'd handpicked Dave to protect Alina.

"I had the local cops sit on her place before we got there. If there'd been even a hint of a threat, I'd have aborted and brought her back here. Even you admit the car accident doesn't scream cartel. They'd have shot her in the head and been done with it. Maybe you're too close to this to see that." Dave really meant he was too close to *her* to think objectively.

Probably.

Jay nodded, because Dave spoke the frustrating truth.

"I take it you have no new information."

Jay sighed. "Absolutely, fucking nothing."

Dave cocked his head toward the door. "Then go have

'I invited your mother to have dinner with us. I hope t's okay."

And just like that she showed him that she fit here h him. She forgave his mother's rude comments the er night and whatever they got into today.

"Sounds good." Though he'd much rather have a iet, unobtrusive evening with Alina.

"Dinner's ready. Take a seat at the table. I'll call your om and Adam in for dinner."

"I can help."

She shook her head. "You've had a long day. Sit. .elax."

And that felt nice, too. To be taken care of, rather than xpected to take on more after a long day.

He sat at the table he usually forgot he had while he stood in the kitchen grazing on whatever he could find in the fridge and cupboards. He let the quiet peace in his house surround him. He listened to Alina call down to the barn, then rattle around the kitchen plating up the food. The aromatic smell made his stomach grumble. He took a sip of beer, stared at the place settings around im, and wondered what it would be like to sit down ev- ry night for dinner with Alina and a family, listening to eir news, decompressing from a long day at work with ople who loved him.

Wait. Nope, not going there. Sleeping with her didn't an . . . But the punch to the gut feeling of dread he felt en he got the call from the hospital meant something. hey'd barely begun this relationship. Hell, her broth- idn't even know about them. They'd spent a couple ectacular nights together, but he hadn't even taken a proper date. Her brothers might kill him for the ut maybe they'd understand if he could turn this real relationship.

t's what he wanted. More of this. But with every-

dinner. Joey's here for the night shift and walking the property. He'll check in later. I'm out of here."

"See you tomorrow."

Dave waved a salute and headed to his car parked be- hind the barn.

Jay walked into the house and stopped short in the en- try, inhaling the scent of a home-cooked meal. The dining table was set for four. The fridge closed in the kitchen a second before Alina stepped out holding a bottle of his favorite beer and looking tempting as sin, her hair fall- ing in soft waves past her shoulders, a sultry smile on her lips and lighting up her eyes.

"Welcome home."

He dropped his messenger bag at his feet, hooked his arm around her waist, pulled her body against his, and dove in for a kiss he needed like a heroin addict needs his next fix.

She tasted sweet and a little tart, like a good white wine. He dove in for more and found himself lost in memories of them tangled in the sheets and around each other. He wanted to drag her to his room and lay her out in his bed and spend the rest of the night feasting on her, but a buzzer went off in the kitchen reminding him she'd prepared dinner. For him. It touched him deeply and spawned a lifetime of dreams of him coming home to her just like this.

Adam was around here somewhere. They weren't alone, but he wanted desperately to spend some quality one-on-one time with her.

He kissed her one last time, long and deep with a sul- triness that he hoped left a mark on her and made her want everything he wanted later.

He reluctantly broke the kiss and stared down into her pretty blue-gray eyes and softly traced her bruised cheek with his thumb as his fingers slid into her silky hair. "How are you?" He dipped his gaze to the brace around her neck. She'd taken off the sling.

"I'm fine. Much better actually." Her eyes narrowed and studied his face. "How are you?"

He didn't have the words to tell her what it did to him to come home and find her here waiting for him with a meal and her welcoming smile. "I'm much better, too." Better than he'd been ten seconds ago. Better than he'd been in a long time.

"Is something wrong?"

"Everything is right." That ambiguous answer only sparked confusion in her eyes. "I'm happy to see you. Though I can't believe you talked Dave into going to your place when I told you to stay put."

"Adam and I needed clothes."

"I would have picked them up for you on my way home."

"That's completely out of your way. You left in the middle of the night and worked more than a full day, plus you spent hours on the phone and at your computer after dinner last night."

"That's the job." He wanted that to be clear. His job wasn't nine to five. It was all the time.

"I know." She handed him the beer.

He took a long pull. She picked up his bag and set it beside the door to his office. He watched her, watching him. "What is it?"

"This is strange, right?" Her gaze slid from him to the set dining table, the kitchen beyond him, and down the hall toward the room they'd shared last night.

"I was actually enjoying coming home to a beautiful woman and a home-cooked meal. It's been so long since I walked in the door to someone waiting for me, I can't remember the last time it happened."

"It's not even a little weird having me here in your house?"

"Don't take this the wrong way, but technica staying here, not living here. Maybe that makes bit better, but . . ." He didn't know if he could, c say the rest. Not when this whole thing felt ten new and yeah, scary.

She wrapped her arms around her middle. "B

The abrasions on her face, the brace around he the bruises across her shoulder and chest he c see now but were burned into his memory, rem him why she needed to stay at his place. "But I'm napp you're here and safe." True enough, but he'd copped ou on admitting the real truth: he wanted her to stay. Fo how long, he didn't know. He didn't have a deadline fo her to go. He simply wanted her to be here with him so he could hold on to the comfort and joy he felt when he walked in the door and saw her standing there waiting for him.

Most of the moments in his life he'd like to forg He saw a lot of horrible crap on the job. But that tal picture and the way he felt when he walked door tonight he'd pull out and savor every time he something good to remind him his life was fill more than the destruction and devastation he fac on at work.

"I am safe here with you."

He wanted to believe she meant more tha and the DEA agents watching his place a her feel safe. He wanted her to trust and c He wanted it more than he'd ever wanted else.

I'm falling fast. Maybe he should hi this thing down.

thing going on, how did he turn this into what he wanted? What he hoped Alina wanted.

She walked out of the kitchen with a platter of thick steaks and a big bowl of mashed potatoes and set them on the table in front of him.

"Do you want to go out with me?"

She stared at the food she cooked, then glanced at him and raised an eyebrow. "Now?"

He shook his head, trying to corral his swirling thoughts and make sense. "No. I mean on a date."

"Are you okay?"

"Yeah, why?"

"Because I already agreed to a date with you. Remember? Sunday. Burgers and beer and more getting-to-know-you talk."

Jay's mom and Adam came in through the back door and joined him at the table.

His mother glanced from Alina to him and gave him a nod that included a slight smile. Whatever those two got into earlier had turned the tide on his mother's pessimism about Alina being here and in his life. He didn't need her approval, but it did make things easier.

He hoped Alina's brothers were just as easy to bring around.

"Hey, monkey, how was your day?"

Adam climbed into the seat beside him, picked up his fork, and stabbed a steak on the platter and plopped it onto his plate with a satisfied grin. No way the kid got even halfway through that big piece of meat, but let him give it a go.

Jay selected his own steak. "Not as productive as I'd like, but fine."

"Nothing new on Alina's accident, I take it."

He shook his head and smiled at Adam who scooped up a huge blob of mashed potatoes and dumped them next to his steak. He used the wood spoon to carve out a hole in the middle. Alina came to the table with a bowl and ladle and filled the hole to overflowing with gravy.

Adam's face nearly split with a wide grin as he watched the gravy drip over the edges of the potatoes. "Lava." He swiped his finger over the side of his "volcano" and licked it clean.

Jay chuckled. "Use a fork, buddy."

Alina spooned two helpings of green beans onto his plate. Adam looked up, one eye squinted, his mouth turned down into a disapproving frown. "Ah, come on, Auntie."

"Vegetables, or no chocolate cake."

Adam stabbed two green beans and popped them into his mouth.

Jay rubbed his hand over Adam's shoulder. "Smart man."

Alina went to the kitchen and brought back two glasses of wine and the bottle. She handed one of the glasses across the table to his mother.

"I'm so glad you like the Pinot Grigio."

Alina lifted her glass in salute to his mother.

The new camaraderie set off his suspicions about his mother's motives for suddenly embracing Alina.

Now who's being cynical?

Apparently he came by it naturally. So he eyed his mother. "You brought the wine?"

His mother gave him an I'm-not-a-horrible-person look. "She cooked. I brought the wine."

Jay took the first bite of his perfectly cooked medium rare steak and let his eyes roll back in his head as the garlic butter melted on his tongue and the hint of pepper gave it just the right amount of bite. "Oh man, that's good."

Alina laughed under her breath. "I'm glad you like

it. That's an impressive barbecue setup you've got out back."

"I may not be a good cook, but I can grill."

"Which explains the number of steaks, chicken thighs, and pork chops in the freezer."

"I'm hoping you can do something equally amazing with some of those tomorrow night."

Alina gave him one of those dazzling smiles. "You really are enjoying this."

He laid his hand over hers on the table. "Yes, I am."

"Are you his girlfriend?" Adam asked, licking potatoes off his lips.

Alina's hand stiffened under his. She didn't answer right away.

"What do you think, Adam? You think she should be my girlfriend?"

Adam studied his aunt. "She's really nice and has a lot of chocolate."

Jay locked eyes with Alina and couldn't hide the smile tugging at his lips. "Everything I ever wanted in a girlfriend." He really wanted to know what she thought about what he said, but his phone rang and drew his attention away from her and the fun.

His phone sat beside his plate. Caller ID read King, so he snatched up the phone and flipped his internal switch to work mode once again. "What's up?" He didn't identify himself in case someone on King's side overheard their conversation.

Everyone at the table went silent. Alina nodded for Adam to finish his dinner. His mother stared at him, then Alina, gauging her reaction to him taking the call at the dinner table. Alina seemed to take it in stride.

"Sorry, man, I thought I'd kill some time while I staked out a potential lead. She's on the move. Gotta go." King had his full attention.

"What lead?" He stood and went into the kitchen.

His mother's words behind him irritated him. "Get used to it. Work always comes first."

Alina didn't respond to his mother. At least not with words and he couldn't see her face to tell if the call bothered her.

King filled him in on the new development. "Cara's friend and waitress. Tandy's been meeting with one of Iceman's men."

He'd told King if he couldn't turn Cara to their side to take Iceman down to find another way. Tandy might be the inside person they needed to finally arrest Iceman.

"I think she's dealing for him."

"Do you need backup?" Jay started forming a plan in his head.

"I got this. Talk to you later. She's on the move."

Jay was used to things moving fast and situations changing on a dime.

King sucked in a breath. "What the fuck?"

"What's happening?" Jay went back on alert, ready to move if King needed help.

"She didn't get in her car. She's headed for the truck stop across the street."

"Headed for dinner? Looking for company?" Good assumptions given the time and the fact Tandy lived over the coffee shop King worked undercover at in the middle of nowhere.

"Maybe. I'm headed that way to see which one she's on the hunt for, or if she's looking for some kind of trouble."

"Who's watching Cara?" Jay wanted to remind King of his true purpose there: getting Cara to give them information to take down her father, Iceman.

"She's at home waiting for me to tell her if her best friend is stabbing her in the back." Resentment filled

King's words, but Jay's job was to keep King on task and focused on the goal.

"You sure she won't tip off Tandy?"

"Loyalty is more important to Cara than anything. If Tandy is involved with Iceman, it will crush her." King didn't want Cara to get hurt. He didn't usually work undercover and seemed to be having trouble keeping his feelings out of this assignment.

"You're getting close to Cara." If King got too close to Cara and couldn't do the job, Jay would have to pull him out and find another way to get Iceman.

"That's the job, right?"

Get close to the mark, earn their trust, and use whatever they gave you to get the target. So far, Cara hadn't given King what they needed. Now he was after Tandy. A good call? Jay wasn't sure, but he'd give King leeway to find out. "It is. You have to get close to people to get them to trust you. Just be sure your mission is clear."

"Cara's too conflicted about her feelings for her father. Turning her against him seems easy, but it's not. As you suggested, I found another route to get to Iceman. I'm going to follow it and see if it leads me to his end. That's the mission. That's the job. So let me do it my way."

"Never said you were doing it wrong. Just making sure you're thinking with the right head."

Flash hung up on him. Jay dropped his phone on the counter, planted his hands on the edge, and hung his head between his shoulders. Jay couldn't fault King for falling for the wrong person, if that's what was happening. And wrong wasn't quite right. Cara and King together might be great. Under different circumstances. If Cara wasn't the daughter of a notorious lieutenant in one of the deadliest drug cartels and King wasn't a DEA agent assigned to take him down.

Which made Jay think of him and Alina. He wanted a

wife and family now. She'd just started her professional life and probably wasn't ready to settle down for a quiet life with a man who spent far more time working than enjoying life.

His mostly full plate appeared on the counter in front of him. Alina's hand ran up his back to his shoulder.

"Eat before you have to go."

"I don't have to leave." This time. "But that could change at any moment."

She stood beside him, reached out and placed her hand on his face, and made him turn toward her. She locked gazes with him, no animosity or censure in her eyes. "Then you should eat and enjoy the evening while you can."

He turned, cupped her beautiful face in his hands, leaned down, and kissed her forehead, wishing he had the words to tell her how much her understanding meant to him. And how much he hoped that understanding didn't turn to resentment if they really did make a go at a relationship together.

She hadn't commented on the whole girlfriend thing. It didn't seem right to bring it up now and push for everything he wanted. Not when she'd just gotten another glimpse of what his day-to-day life was like. Calls in the middle of the night and during dinner. Him leaving on a moment's notice. The shift in his moods. He'd been smiling and laughing at the dinner table with her, Adam, and his mother and now his mind was on King and whatever danger he might be facing. He'd be on edge until King called back with an update.

Until then, he'd put his worries on the back burner and hold Alina close while he could.

Sensing his need for her, she stepped into him, wrapped her arms around his back, laid her head on his shoulder, and held him. She didn't say anything, just stood in his arms and held on as long as he needed her.

The answer to that might be forever, she felt that good in his arms.

Which meant he had some things to figure out, like how to hold on to her and not drive her away with his work and chaotic life.

"It's okay, Jay. I do understand."

He didn't know what to say, so he held her away, stared down into her sincere eyes, sank his fingers into her silky hair, held her head, and hoped she saw in his eyes all he didn't know how to say. It boiled down to one thing: hold on.

As if she read his mind, her hands gripped his sides. A silent signal that she wouldn't let go.

He wanted to believe it, but had been disappointed in the past. And for the first time in a long time, he really didn't want to blow it.

"Auntie, can I have chocolate cake now?" Adam walked in with his mostly cleaned plate.

Alina placed her hand on Jay's chest and gave him one last long look, then turned her attention to Adam. "Sure, honey."

Jay's mother walked in behind Adam. "Everything okay?"

"Fine." He took his plate and put it in the microwave, set the timer, then hit START, sending the plate spinning. "Alina, did you finish your dinner?"

"Not yet."

"Bring your plate. I'll heat it up. We'll finish while the monster devours his cake."

Alina sliced a thick chunk from the fudge-covered chocolate cake and set it on a paper plate.

Adam's eyes went round with anticipation. He took

the plate with a "Thank you," and headed back to the table.

The microwave dinged. Jay took his plate out and replaced it with Alina's.

She grabbed the bottle of pain meds from the shelf next to the stove and popped a pill in her mouth.

"I thought you said you were feeling better."

Alina set the bottle back on the shelf and turned to him. "All the cooking and moving around made my shoulder and neck sore again." She tilted her head and stared into the distance, thinking.

"What is it?"

She shook her head. "Nothing."

"Alina?"

She scrunched her mouth, then admitted, "I should have waited another hour to take the pill. I felt it wearing off and the stiffness and pain coming back and . . ."

"And you felt you needed it. It's okay. It's only been a day. I'm surprised you're doing as well as you are, but you need to take it easy and give yourself time to heal. Do too much and you'll make it worse and need more of those."

Her lips tilted in a pinched half smile. "You're right. I'll be more careful."

She went to the cupboard, then fridge, and poured two glasses of iced tea. "No more wine with the meds." She handed him one glass. "In case you have to leave later."

Yeah, he rarely got to have more than one beer. Not that he needed more, but it would be nice to not have to think about leaving in the middle of the night like he did all the time.

Alina took her plate and his. "Come on. Let's eat." She walked out of the kitchen, just as his mom walked back in.

"It's not going to change, you know."

Jay didn't want to ask, but did so anyway. "What?"

"The calls, the late-night and all-night stakeouts and raids, the constant interruptions and demands on your time. It's the job. I know that. It seems she does, too. But it doesn't change the fact that she'll bear the brunt of keeping you together because when you're gone you've got all that work stuff to occupy your mind and time and all she'll have is loneliness and unfulfilled wishes for company."

It wasn't a lie, but it wasn't the whole truth either.

"It's not all on her. I'm part of the equation that makes up us. Her happiness matters to me. If I want to keep her, I'll have to give her a reason to stay."

"There are lots of reasons to stay. Love. Money. Kids. It's better than truly being alone. But it doesn't make the day-to-day any easier to bear."

"It wasn't all bad for you and Dad. I remember the good times. I remember you guys laughing and having fun together."

"Sometimes we did, but those times became fewer and fewer as the years went on."

"Maybe he let work consume him. Maybe you let resentment push you further away."

"I tried to keep us together."

Jay pressed his lips together to keep from snapping at her that having an affair wasn't the way to hold on to someone you supposedly loved. It was retaliation. It was mean. It was not a way to mend fences, but a means to tear them down.

"Alina and I aren't you and Dad. Stop telling her I'm not worth the effort. Stop telling me I'm so self-centered I'll never be able to give someone the care and kindness they deserve."

"I'm not saying that at all."

"Aren't you? You've made it clear that you think so

long as I'm DEA I'll never be good enough to marry and have a family with because I simply won't be here to do it. I'll be too busy doing my job and not loving them. That's not how things work. That's not how *I* do things. I am capable of being a DEA agent and a good man. Dad was, too. Your unhappiness wasn't solely because of his job. You should ask yourself why he wanted to stay at work rather than come home."

"You blame me." The surprise in her voice didn't match the guilt in her eyes.

"You were both at fault. That's what you don't seem to get. For all he did to you, you gave it back. You both gave up and that's when it fell apart. You don't think I'll even try, so I should just give it up before it ever starts to be something. Well, Alina and I are already something. We're figuring it out together. So long as we do that and keep things honest between us, then there's no reason to think it will all fall apart because I have to go to work when it's inconvenient."

"Jay, honey, all I'm saying is this is all new and moving fast. She, better than most, seems to get your life. I see that. But don't take for granted that she gets it and it won't be hard and resentments won't build despite that."

Jay sighed. "Mom, I love you, but pack up your cynicism and go home. I can't take any more tonight."

"I just want you to be happy."

"Great. I'm happy. I intend to stay happy and a little support and understanding would go a long way to keeping me that way. You not trying to run off my girlfriend would be really great." The sarcasm only made his mom frown.

"I didn't try to run her off."

"No, you went out of your way to point out all the reasons I'm wrong for her, she's wrong for me, and this will never work. Last time I checked, no one asked you."

"Fine."

"Fine. Thanks for feeding the horses."

"I'm always here for you."

He refrained from rolling his eyes again. "I appreciate the help." And yeah, it had nothing to do with the fact she lived here rent-free in exchange for helping him with the horses when he had to work. He should have saved himself the trouble and hired someone. Instead, he'd moved her to his place to keep an eye on things and to make life easier for her.

No good deed . . .

"How long is she staying?"

He eyed his mother, wondering where she was going with this.

"So I know if I need to continue to care for the horses or if my services are no longer needed."

"Your insecurity is showing." He hugged the frown and anger off her face, set her away from him, then stared down at her, trying to hold on to his patience while his dinner got cold again. "I need *your* help."

His mother found her manners and said goodbye to Alina and Adam, then walked out the front door, giving him room to breathe again.

He took his seat at the table and sighed out his frustration.

"Adam, please go get ready for your bath. I'll be there in just a minute."

Jay poked his fork around in his cold potatoes.

Alina put her hand over his on the table. "She loves you. She wants you to be happy, and in her mind that means you don't make the mistake she made."

"So I should never fall in love?"

"In her mind, marrying someone in law enforcement means divorce and heartbreak."

"Then she should be worried about you, not me." He

thought about how that sounded. "Not that we're getting married or . . . you know what I mean."

Alina's soft smile and breathy laugh made the butter-flies in his belly flutter.

"She thinks that your job will end your relationship and you'll be unhappy."

"I'm not exactly happy with only work in my life. Can I at least be happy for a while before it all gets fucked up?" He tossed the fork down and sat back in his seat, frustrated.

Alina stood, closed the distance, and fell into his lap. She wrapped one arm around his neck and settled into his chest. "How about we see how long we can be happy before we fuck it up?"

Half a smile tugged at his lips. He stared down at her and shook his head. "She doesn't get to you, does she?"

"A little bit. But if all I'm looking for is the bad stuff, I'll miss out on the good stuff."

"Like this." He leaned in and pressed his lips to hers, letting the kiss go on and on until his muscles went loose and he lost himself in the taste and temptation of her.

She leaned back in his arms and stared up at him. "That's worth the interruption during dinner."

"How about me leaving in the middle of the night?"

"What we're going to do once Adam goes to bed is promise enough to make me want to wait for you to come back."

He kissed her again, hard with an edge of despera-tion. "Go put that boy to bed. I'll do the dishes and meet you in bed. I'll show you how worth it waiting for me is."

CHAPTER EIGHTEEN

After two books that turned into three, one sing-along of "Let It Go" from *Frozen*, and a ten-minute video chat good-night with Beck and Ashley, Alina finally got Adam to bed. Jay wasn't waiting for her in their room. She found him in the office, going through his emails. The second he saw her, he closed his laptop, stood, and came to her, picking her right up off her feet in a hug that brought her face-to-face with him. He kissed her the whole way down the hall to their room. They undressed each other without a word. The quiet intensity between them drew them together to fill the silence with something deeper than words.

They spoke with the soft brush of fingertips over skin, sweet kisses that grew into an urgent need to taste every tempting curve and hollow. Gentle hands became greedy. And close wasn't close enough until they became one, their bodies moving together, hands clasped, hearts pressed together, and all that passion burst like a firework, the sparks twinkling inside of them as they snuggled close and drifted into contented sleep until they woke in each other's arms this morning, both of them unable to help smiling at each other because they were happy.

Jay made her breakfast. She didn't complain or even care when he took a phone call that lasted half an hour.

She enjoyed her meal and time with her nephew. The morning went by with an ease that felt like they'd spent countless mornings together.

Jay's concern for her healing injuries touched her.

Alina lounged on the couch, reading one of Jay's mystery novels, wallowing in self-indulgence as she ate a slice of chocolate cake and sipped her tea. This was her kind of relaxing, made even sweeter because Jay had spent the night and this morning pampering her.

He wanted her to rest, so he took Adam horseback-riding in the pasture out back, giving her time to sit in the quiet, read, or take a nap. Whatever made her happy.

She was happy here. With him.

Being here felt so natural and comfortable.

And if his mother, her brothers, and the outside world didn't intrude, she'd be happy to stay right here with him. Well, maybe not right here on the couch but in his bed, those big hands moving over her, his body stroking hers into a fever pitch that had her melting into him as they set fire to the sheets.

They were great at that part. Admittedly, this morning had been really great, too. But she really needed to remember that, although one part of their relationship worked well, the rest was still uncharted territory for them.

The door swung open. Jay walked in with a giggling Adam tucked under one arm like a wiggling piglet and the phone to his ear. The serious look in his eyes and set of his mouth didn't jibe with the way he plunked Adam on his feet, tickled him in the belly, and brushed his fingers over Adam's golden hair.

"I'm grabbing my stuff and headed out the door right now." Jay gave her a cursory look, then went into his office, unlocked the tall safe, and pulled out his gun. He grabbed his badge off the desk and strapped both things to his hip while he listened to whoever was talking to him on the phone.

"I'll get the team together. We'll surround the truck stop and begin surveillance. You stay on Tandy. I'll let you know when we get there. We'll coordinate as we gather intel and figure out what she's got going besides dealing in the parking lot."

Jay listened for another few seconds. "I'll have the note analyzed with the other. We should have something soon." Jay grabbed his coat off the rack by the door.

"I think he has to go," Adam said.

Yeah, she got that, but she didn't like the serious look on his face. Or that he went back to the safe, grabbed two more ammunition clips, and stuffed them in his pocket before closing the safe and making sure it was locked so Adam—or anyone else—couldn't get into the other guns stored in there.

"Dad looks just like that sometimes. Something big must be going on." Even at Adam's young age, he understood the severity of what Beck and Jay did for a living.

She wrapped her hands at Adam's chest and pulled him back into her thighs and held him close. "He'll be okay. He's trained just like your dad to arrest the bad guys."

Jay stared at both of them. "I'm on my way. Call me on the road if anything else comes up before we get there." He hung up and stared at her for one long moment. His gaze dipped from her down to Adam and back up again. "This has been a strange couple of days. You know?"

Yes. A glimpse at life with them as a couple with a child. But nothing was normal about this situation as most people knew it. She was here for her protection. Adam wasn't their child. And Jay had to leave, gun locked and loaded, to take down a drug dealer.

She didn't know what to say. This was their life. Not some ideal most people didn't live up to in the first place. All they could do was live each day as they came. Today, she spent the morning blissfully happy doing ordinary things with Jay and Adam. Now he had to go do his job.

She didn't want him to go. She feared something happening to him. But he needed to go because he believed in what he did for a living and for other people. So she did the hard thing, knowing tomorrow wasn't promised to anyone. She'd hold on to the wonderful memories they made together and let him do what he needed to do.

"Be safe. We'll be here when you get back."

He closed the distance, put one hand on Adam's head, the other on her face, leaned in, and kissed her softly. He backed away just enough to look her in the eye. "You make it hard to go."

She glanced sideways at the wide-open living room and dining room. "You make me want to stay."

He growled deep in his throat and narrowed his eyes. He kissed her hard and fast, then bent low to Adam. "You get two scoops of ice cream after dinner if you make sure she doesn't leave the property this time."

Adam gave him a thumbs-up.

Jay brushed his fingers through Adam's hair, stood, and pointed a finger at her. "Stay put."

"Come home in one piece," she ordered right back.

One more quick kiss and he was out the door, taking her heart with him. Until he came back, she'd miss him and worry and carry the strange weight that settled in her chest. She didn't want to think it meant something bad might happen, but the real possibility put a lump in her throat.

Adam grabbed onto her wrists at his chest, leaned forward, and swung himself side to side as she held him.

"Let's go wash your hands and get a snack."

"When will Mom and Dad be home? You said today."

"Not until late tonight. After you go to bed. They'll be here first thing in the morning to pick you up."

"Okaaay." Adam sighed out the word, more than ready to see his parents and go home to his own room and toys.

"Want to watch *Frozen* again?"

"Olaf!"

She loved that adorable snowman, too. He'd put a smile back on Adam's face.

With Beck home tomorrow and back to work on Monday, maybe Jay wouldn't have to spend so much time working with King on his case and he'd stay closer to home. She couldn't count on that. He worked cases all over the state just like her brothers. The only thing she could count on dating a DEA agent was that nothing would be predictable or normal. Dates would get rescheduled and interrupted. He'd be gone for hours, days, even weeks at a time, depending on the case. She needed to be prepared to face the reality of Jay's life and how it impacted hers.

She'd have work, friends, and her own interests to fill the time. And she'd have Jay.

Then again, Beck might kill him if Adam spilled the beans about Jay kissing her.

So many things to worry about.

She didn't care what Beck, Jay's mother, or anyone else thought about her seeing Jay. They liked each other. Everyone else could just get over it.

First, she should get over it and enjoy it.

"Okay, starting now."

"Now, what?"

She hooked her hands under Adam's arms, lifted him in the air, regretted doing so the second her bruised ribs protested, but spun him around anyway. "Fun!"

"Yay!"

Yay was right. She wasn't going to spend the night worrying about her relationship with Jay, what other people might think, or that he was out there possibly facing life and death.

She'd spend the evening playing with her nephew, and once she had him tucked in for the night, she'd dig in to her research on prescription drug addiction and start working on her proposal to the DEA to set up a drug take-back program in town.

She had things to do. She didn't need to check her phone to see if Jay called. But she did grab her phone from her purse and kept it close. Just in case.

CHAPTER NINETEEN

Jay didn't have time to think about the scene at his house, saying goodbye to Alina, seeing her there with Adam, what it made him feel, knowing she'd be there when he got home. But that was temporary, and he didn't have time to think about that either.

You make me want to stay.

Those words rang in his head, but he had to push them aside and focus on the job ahead even if he wanted to focus on his personal life. It had needed some attention for a long time. He finally had a reason to make it a priority. He had a woman he couldn't get out of his mind—and had made her way into his heart.

With Beck and Ashley's return, Adam would go home. He'd have to face his best friend and confess that he'd been seeing Alina. But first he wanted to take her on a date, find a rhythm that worked for them, and let their relationship turn into whatever it would be for them before more people got involved.

His mother was enough to handle.

Beck and Caden looking out for their sister and warning her away from him wouldn't help at all.

Maybe they'd surprise him and accept that their sister wanted to date him. A fellow DEA agent with a chaotic life. Yeah, right. And hell would freeze over.

His gut twisted at the thought of losing his shot with Alina.

He'd work damn hard to make their date as memorable and amazing as their nights together.

One problem at a time. First, he needed to coordinate the surveillance at the truck stop King suspected was being used to traffic drugs. Work distracted him from the nagging feeling inside that what he and Alina said to each other when he left meant more than the few words they shared.

They seemed to say a hell of a lot without words. Before memories of making love to Alina last night stole his concentration, he called the office and got an update on the agents he'd ordered to assemble for tonight's mission.

By the time he met the team, went over the plan for the night, and took up his position at the back of the truck stop lot, he had his mind in the game. He'd get this done and go home. To Alina. The thought held a lot of appeal. Maybe too much. The last thing he wanted to do was rush and make a mistake.

Mistakes put lives at risk.

Work first. Personal stuff later.

He scanned the rows of big rigs, the diner doing a brisk business, and the light traffic on the main road headed out of the little town he'd sent King to for his undercover mission. He listened to the other agents check in over the com in his ear. Everyone was in place and ready to go on King's go. All they needed was for the star of the show to make a move. From Jay's position, he couldn't see the coffee shop across the street or Tandy's apartment over it.

For the last several hours he'd organized the agents and gone over the plan from every angle. He needed to be sure he'd covered everything, but there was still so much unknown about the players.

His phone vibrated with an incoming call. He checked the ID, excited to see the labs number. "What do you have for me?"

The tech got down to business. "Both notes you gave us have the same prints."

At least he didn't have more than one person threatening King. "The FBI flagged the same prints for several threatening letters to government officials. The ATF contacted us about prints found on bomb parts at a farm and several drug lab bombings."

"Do they have a name to go with the prints?"

"No, but this guy is big-time wanted by multiple agencies."

"Send me all the information. I'll talk to my undercover agent and see if we can narrow down the suspects."

Jay hung up on the lab and made the call to King.

"Flash."

"Bennett. I just got the information back on the notes you received."

"About time."

Jay put King on speaker and scrolled through the information the lab tech emailed him. "ATF has the same prints on bomb parts recovered at a ranch and several drug lab bombings. The FBI has threatening letters against the governor and other state representatives."

King swore. "The explosion at the ranch, is it a property owned by Manny Castillo, or at least some shell corporation under the Castillo cartel? DEA confiscated the property after a drug raid." The urgency in King's voice pushed Jay to look up the information. Not easy to do on his phone, scanning through pages and pages of information.

He found the address and the deed to the property. "Yes. How do you know that?"

"Because Cara and Manny were supposed to live

there together, but after she discovered he'd lied to her and she tried to leave him, that's when he chopped off her finger. She managed to escape, but he went after her again."

"Why isn't this information in any of your reports?"

"What is in my reports is that I believed Iceman tipped off the DEA about that meeting between him and Castillo in order to get us, me, to take Manny out for him, so that he could hold on to the truce between the cartels and blame Manny's death on us." King evaded answering directly.

"Do you have proof of that now?"

"Cara's story about what happened to her confirmed it for me. Her father wanted revenge, plain and simple, and he used me to get it."

"Then he blew up the ranch?" Jay didn't think that made much sense. His prints weren't on the bomb parts, but someone else could have made the bomb and Iceman used it.

"Her uncle. Iceman's brother. Cara made an offhand comment about him spouting off in front of city hall about government intrusion in people's lives. I didn't think much of it, except that the old guy who lived in the woods behind her house was an eccentric old coot."

"More like Unabomber-in-the-making if he's our guy." This new development added another dangerous level to their mission. Not only did they need to take Iceman down, they needed to find a guy willing to obliterate people and property. It also meant Jay needed to call in the ATF. Another complication he didn't need. Not in the middle of an operation already in progress.

"He's got a still on the property where he's making moonshine. Once this thing with Iceman ended, I planned to shut him down. Now I'm wondering if all his secrecy, homemade alarm systems, and living off the grid means he's hiding something a lot more dangerous than high-proof hooch."

"Judging by the number of threats he's issued over the years and the escalation to bombing the farm after the DEA seized the property, I'd say we need to consider him armed and dangerous."

They needed to get this guy in custody immediately. "I'll send a team out to pick him up."

"No. Not yet."

Jay didn't want to wait and risk lives.

"Cara's out there with him tonight. You send a team, he's liable to take her hostage."

That's the last thing Jay wanted.

"Let's finish this with Iceman and Tandy tonight. Once we've got them in custody, we'll make sure Cara is safe, then go in and get her uncle. Right now, all we have is speculation that he's behind the notes."

True, but the evidence spoke of someone not dealing from a full deck. "It makes sense if he wants to keep her away from you, her father, and safe." No telling how far Cara's uncle Otis was willing to go to make that happen.

"Then we want the same thing for her, and I want to do this right. So far all he's done is threaten people and blow up some empty buildings. I don't want to push him to do something desperate, especially if Cara is with him."

Jay wanted to move on this ASAP, but they were sitting on Tandy waiting for her to make a move. They had no evidence of an immediate threat from Cara's uncle. If he called in the ATF right now, he'd have to pull resources from this op and potentially put agents at risk without proper backup. The last thing he wanted to do was give Iceman a means to sneak through the trap they'd set tonight. "Agreed." They'd handle one bad guy at a time. But that meant he wouldn't get home anytime soon.

He wouldn't see Alina's smile or get to kiss her until he finished this growing assignment. He was used to things changing on the fly, but it took him by surprise to feel the regret and building desire to end it quick so he could go home.

"Tandy's on the move."

And so it begins. "I'll alert the team. We'll make plans for Cara's uncle later." He hung up on King and used his com. "Suspect on the move." Jay adjusted his bulletproof vest, pulled the mask over his head to conceal his identity, and hunkered down next to one of the semis parked at the back of the lot, the driver fast asleep in the cab, none the wiser for the number of agents surrounding him.

"She crossed the street and approached a blue Ford truck. She's speaking to the driver. We've got an exchange for drugs and money." Agent Alvarado gave the play-by-play for those agents out of sight of the front of the lot.

They already knew she was dealing. They wanted to see what else she was doing out here. "Send the truck tag to the local police on standby and have them pick up the driver away from here." He'd spent over an hour with the local police coordinating this operation. He hoped they stuck to their word and didn't show up here and bust his case.

"Suspect's headed to the parked rigs," Agent Alvarado announced.

Tandy sashayed up to the mark King saw her with last night and climbed into the rig like she didn't have a care in the world.

Agent Alvarado filled them in on the situation. "We've got her for another count of dealing." The line went silent, probably because Tandy was putting the moves on the driver.

Was he in on whatever was about to happen? None of them knew for sure. They'd sort it out once they busted

Tandy and whoever else showed up tonight. Their best hope was that Iceman showed his face and they took him down once and for all.

"The suspect and driver are going at it in the front seat." The boredom in Agent Alvarado's voice made Jay smile. Some things lost their curiosity over time. When part of your job made you the voyeur in other people's lives, nothing surprised or affected you after a while.

"Truck's coming," one of the other agents whispered over the com.

Alvarado chimed in again. "Suspect just pulled the driver into the sleeping compartment. They're out of sight."

So Tandy's job was to distract the driver. Why?

The incoming truck maneuvered into position behind the rig with its back end at the roll-up door on the trailer. Four guys jumped out of the extended cab truck. One guy opened the trailer. The others began pulling crates off the back of the truck and loading them into the tractor-trailer.

He'd bet the guy up front with Tandy didn't even know what the hell was going on.

Jay had seen enough. They had them dead to rights. "Ready on three."

"Abort," King said into his com. "Let it play out."

They were nearly done loading the truck. If they drove away . . . "They'll get away," Jay responded.

"Second truck approaching," another agent said.

King's original thought that they'd been using the big rigs to distribute the drugs across the state and country turned into an even more complex operation. "Stay back. They're not done loading the truck. If I'm right, these are the incoming shipments for Iceman's crew."

"You don't think he's shipping this stuff out?" Jay asked.

"Check out the plates on the vehicles that have arrived so far."

From Jay's position, he couldn't see the truck plates.

"One California, one Arizona," Agent Alvarado supplied. A second later, he added, "Texas just showed up."

King broke down the complex operation. "Pick up the drugs from Mexico from those states and drive them up here to Montana. Let's get those plates to highway patrol and get them tracking the vehicles on their return trips and see if we can't cut off the supply chain from making yet another return run up here. Maybe they'll lead us to where the drugs are coming into the country in those states."

Their little operation just expanded to three more states.

Jay scrambled to coordinate everything using his phone, issuing orders to another agent to start contacting highway patrol to get on those trucks and notify each state's police all while still listening to his men on the coms.

As the guys from the last truck closed up the trailer and took off, King said, "Under twenty-five minutes."

Fast. Efficient. The whole thing impressed Jay. If these guys ran a legitimate business, they'd make a killing. Instead they were just killing people with the poison they loaded into that truck. "Any sign of Tandy?"

"Not yet, but I suspect she's got the timing down right and will pop her head out any minute." King had done it: he found another way to take down Iceman that didn't involve Cara, who they originally suspected of working with her father.

This had to be a huge relief to King, who seemed reluctant to use Cara but had had no choice.

King wanted to take Tandy down himself. Tandy wasn't a significant enough of a bust. They wanted Iceman. If she agreed to give them information, they'd cut her a deal. Let the little fish go and reel in the shark.

"Team One, stay on the rig. Don't let it out of your sight. Let's see where it leads us next. Team Two, we're on Tandy." Jay worked his way around the rigs and met up with Agent Alvarado at the front of the lot.

Tandy climbed down from the truck, sent one more smile up to the driver, slammed the door, and sauntered back across the lot toward the truck stop diner where Iceman's guy discreetly stuffed a fat wad of bills into her purse. And just like that, she waved goodbye and walked right out of the diner and headed across the street and back to her place.

Jay exchanged a "Wow" look with Agent Alvarado about their brazen activities. They didn't even try to hide what they were doing.

Why would they? The drivers who stopped here didn't stay long and kept mostly to themselves. They had a schedule to keep and didn't want to get involved in something that didn't involve them.

Jay got back on the com. "Daryl and Tom, take Iceman's man on his way out of the diner." He and Agent Alvarado followed Tandy back to her place and met King at the bottom of Tandy's stairs.

King pulled on a DEA jacket, leaving it open in front so Tandy would see his badge. He pulled his gun and held it at his side as he made his way up the stairs. Jay let him take the lead and followed him up, gun in hand, ready to serve the warrant he'd obtained earlier today.

At the door, King pulled the mask over his face to protect his identity in case they didn't get Iceman tonight and he needed to remain undercover with Cara. He pounded on the door with the side of his fist and shouted, "DEA, search warrant. Open up!"

A glass thumped on the floor a few seconds before

Tandy opened the door a couple of inches to peek out at them.

King shoved the door open with his shoulder, planted his hand on Tandy's chest, and shoved her backward into the small apartment and right into the thin wall separating the living room from her tiny kitchen. She gasped when her head hit the wall with a *thunk*. He grabbed her shoulder and turned her around to face the wall, then cuffed her.

"What the hell is going on?"

"You're under arrest." Agent Alvarado held up the wad of cash and ten or so bags of drugs from her purse. "We've got you for possession with intent to sell, dealing in the lot across the street, prostitution, and drug trafficking."

"No." Tandy shook her head. "I'm not trafficking. I was just having a bit of fun. Someone must have put that money and drugs in my purse." Tears streaked down Tandy's cheeks, no more real or true than the words coming out of her mouth. "This can't be happening. He's supposed to watch my back, not set me up."

"The guy hanging out in the diner, hitting on the waitress and downing beers like they're water?" Jay laughed. "The only back he's watching is hers. He wasn't watching you, but we were. You've got quite the scheme going. I bet that driver has no idea his empty trailer is now full to the brim with crates of drugs."

King took Tandy by the arm and led her to the leather sofa. Too nice for someone who lived on tips. Agent Alvarado had upended her designer bag on the coffee table. Little things in the house showed how Tandy was living beyond her means if she wanted anyone to believe she was nothing more than a waitress. The name-brand purses that weren't knockoffs, the expensive makeup, jewelry, computer on the desk in the corner, and the tablet lying on the back of the sofa showed that Tandy liked nice things.

King gave her a nudge to get her to sit. "Stop the fake tears, the bullshit, and start talking."

She stared up at him, trying to look past the mask and recognize what little she could see of his face. "Do I know you?"

Jay prayed King hadn't blown his cover. King purposely dropped his voice an octave when he spoke. He didn't answer, but went to the open door, put his back to it, kept her pinned in his gaze, and gave Jay the lead.

He started with the basics. "How long have you been working the truck stop for Iceman and his crew?"

"I'm not. It's just a means to supplement my income."

"Are you selling in the coffee shop, too?" He needed to be sure Cara wasn't in on the drug business with her father even if it made King want to throttle him.

"No. I'm forbidden from selling in the coffee shop. If he found out—" Tandy snapped her mouth shut.

King broke in. "We know you work for Iceman. His guy comes into the coffee shop, you leave out the back, pick up the drugs for him and the information for which truck to hit. Right?"

Jay eyed King, silently telling King to let him handle it before he blew his cover and ended his involvement in this case.

Tandy sighed and spilled her guts about selling sex and drugs to the truckers. How she betrayed Cara by working for Iceman.

"You're going to jail for a long time." Jay leaned down and made sure Tandy understood her choices were limited. "Unless you help us out. Then maybe we can see about helping you out."

"He'll kill me."

Jay pressed her again. "Help us put him behind bars and he won't get the chance."

Tandy's eyes filled with incredulity. "You really think you can get close to him. No way. He's gotten out of worse and killed others who seemed out of reach."

"Do yourself a favor, talk now, or you'll never see the light of day outside of a cell again," King pushed. Maybe it would coax her out of her fear of Iceman with her fear of losing what she considered a damn good life here with Cara and her little enterprises.

Jay tried a different track. "Where is the driver taking those drugs?"

"How should I know?"

"Is the driver in on the operation?"

"No. Teddy doesn't know anything. Don't you hurt him. He's a good man. He's got a wife and kids to support and he works hard." Tandy praised the man who paid her to fuck him in the back of his rig all the while telling her about his loving wife and kids.

It didn't really surprise Jay, which only confirmed that his life was so far from normal.

King took up the questioning again. "So you distract the driver, the men load up the truck, then he drives it to where he's supposed to deliver the empty trailer and pick up a loaded one?"

"I guess so." Tandy shrugged. She wasn't interested in anything more than her small part in things and getting paid.

Jay took King's question and played it out. "Once the driver delivers to the warehouse, he'll take the loaded trailer on his next run, and someone from Iceman's crew will pick up their loaded trailer and take it to wherever they're stashing their supply."

"That would be my guess. I bet the other team will see the whole exchange and contact us soon with a location."

Jay nodded in total agreement. It made sense. They were in for a long night tracking that shipment.

Tandy leaned forward, a hopeful look in her eyes, despite the fact her hands were handcuffed behind her. "So you'll let me go. I'm not part of all that."

Jay shook his head in dismay that Tandy just didn't get it. "Agent Alvarado will take you in." He exchanged a nod with Agent Alvarado who silently acknowledged the order and that he'd take Tandy into custody and process her.

"What about my deal?"

Jay laid it out for Tandy. "We know what's going on based on what we witnessed tonight. Our team will pick up the driver and follow the trailer wherever Iceman's crew takes it. We'll get him there. Unless you have information on Iceman or Cara, you're of no use to us."

"Little-miss-do-gooder doesn't know anything. She's too busy passing judgment on all of us just trying to get by and get better. She works day in and day out for shit money. Her father could use that place and make her rich, but she turns her back on her own flesh and blood and scorns him when all he wants to do is help her have a better life than selling donuts and coffee to truckers and soccer moms with book clubs. She could make a fortune. We all could, but she's content to wake up at the crack of dawn and break her back and thinks that food on the table and a roof over your head is enough to call it a good life."

"It's an honest life," King pointed out, respect in his voice for the woman who didn't let the money and power tempt her. She turned out to be exactly what she appeared to be in the reports, a woman who lived a simple life and found satisfaction helping others by giving them a hand up when they fell on hard times.

Tandy's anger came out as reality set in. "It's a fucked life filled with hard work and nothing to show for it. I've got money saved. I'm not going to wither and die here alone like her."

King glanced down the stairs and sucked in a surprised breath. Jay stared past him and spotted Cara standing there, stock-still, tears running down her cheeks, recognition in her sad eyes.

No telling how long she'd been there. Long enough to hear the disdain and disregard for all she'd done to help Tandy and give her a decent life. One Tandy threw in her face.

King turned to go to her, but she held up a hand to stop him from coming closer, backed down the stairs, the tears falling in a cascade down her too-pale cheeks, made even more sallow by the yellow porch light. "Don't," she choked out. "You lied."

Jay cursed. She made him even though King still wore the mask. The DEA jacket outed him.

Cara's feet hit the pavement; she spun around and ran for the truck idling in the lot.

King ran down the stairs. Jay followed. They needed to stop Cara before she alerted Iceman the DEA was after him.

Cara jumped into the passenger seat. A man, Jay presumed her uncle, came out on the other side and pointed a gun right at King's head. "Stop right there, son."

King stopped in his tracks with his hands held out to the sides. Jay stood on the stairs above him with his gun trained on the older man, ready to take him down. "DEA. Drop it."

Cara's uncle shook his head. The gun in his hand never wavered. He never took his gaze away from King.

"Stay away from her. You've done enough damage. It's over. After tonight, no one will ever hurt her again." He slid back into the front seat, slammed the door, and drove off in the blink of an eye.

King spun around and pleaded, "Don't shoot. You might hit her."

Jay didn't have a clean shot and lowered his weapon and walked down the stairs to join him. "If they tip off Iceman, we could lose him or walk right into a trap."

"We need to go after them. We have to get her back."

Jay reached for his phone to call in backup and get the local cops to intercept the truck.

Out of nowhere, a wall of heat and a blast of pain picked him up off his feet and tossed him several yards and dumped him in a heap on the pavement and everything went black.

CHAPTER TWENTY

Jay came awake in increments. First the ringing in his ears. Then the pain throbbing in his head in time to his heart. And the overwhelming need to see Alina, hold her, tell her . . . everything . . . before it was too late.

His head felt like it might split clean open. If he didn't survive this, who would take care of Alina and make sure whoever tried to kill her paid for it?

It took his mind a minute to answer that question with her brothers, but it should be him.

He needed to keep her safe. He needed to protect her.

He needed her here with him right now.

If she were here, he'd be okay.

He could barely move but managed to pull his phone from his pocket. It didn't surprise him her name came up first in his Favorites list. They'd kept in touch a lot these last few days. After they got together at the wedding he'd wanted to call her all the time. He should have.

JAY: I wish you were here

JAY: Explosion head hurts

JAY: need to see you

JAY: hope I see you again

JAY: should have told you I love you

JAY: I never said that

JAY: I should have said it

JAY: maybe it's too late or I have time
JAY: stay put I want you safe have to prote

His brain overloaded and switched off.

He came awake again to the sound of sirens, wiped his hand over his stinging forehead, and pulled his bloody fingers away from the wound. The sirens grew louder as the ringing in his ears subsided so all he heard was the high-pitched fire trucks and police vehicles and the throbbing of his heart like a bass drum echoing in his head.

The reason for the pain, spinning stars overhead, and blood running down his raging head hit him. A bomb. He rolled his head to the side and spotted King sprawled on his stomach ten feet away and fought the wave of nausea that soured his gut and sent searing acid up his throat before he swallowed it back.

It took him two tries to push himself up to sitting. His phone fell off his chest and landed on the ground between his legs. He didn't remember taking it out.

The all-encompassing pain in his body narrowed to his splitting head, left shoulder, and right calf. He reached over his chest and swept his fingers toward his back along the edge of his bulletproof vest, feeling a sharp pain when his fingertips hit wood. He pinched the piece between his index and middle finger and pulled hard to get the inch-thick piece out of his back. Blood soaked his shirt. He couldn't see it, but he bet his vest took a few more hits when the building exploded into a mass of fire and shards of wood and glass.

Jay pulled another, thicker, piece of wood out of the back of his calf. More blood ran down his leg. Other nicks, scratches, and gouges peppered his legs and arms. He felt like a pincushion. He should probably look at them to see if any needed immediate attention, like his shoulder and leg, but he needed to check on King.

"You alive, King?"

King rolled over and sat up with his legs out in front of him and held his head in his hands. "Fuck."

That about summed it up.

Emergency vehicles poured into the lot as his phone rang. He checked caller ID. Alina. God, he wanted to hear her voice.

Firemen, cops, and paramedics poured out of the vehicles and went to work attacking the fire and securing the scene.

Jay hated to do it, but he ignored the call that mattered more to him than anything else; he needed to get his head together and make sure King was okay. He needed to contact the other agents still tracking the truck. And worst of all, he needed to contact his superiors and let them know they'd just lost a man. Agent Alvarado and Tandy had been inside that building when it exploded. No way they survived the blast. The building had practically been leveled.

A police officer squatted in front of them. "You guys okay?"

Jay took the wad of gauze a paramedic handed him and pressed it to the oozing wound on his forehead and tried to wipe some of the blood from his face. "We're rattled but good. We had an agent inside, second floor, and a woman in custody." Jay stared up at what little remained of the building and shook his head, his sour gut tightening with dread and remorse that he couldn't save them.

The paramedic stuffed a gauze pad under his shirt over his shoulder and pressed hard on the wound. Jay bit back a groan as pain exploded through his shoulder and back.

His phone dinged with a string of text messages. He pulled them up and stared at the messages he didn't remember sending to Alina.

Oh shit! What had he done? Did he really say . . . yep, he did. He waited for the denial, the need to take it back, his mind to figure out a way to play it off as nothing. But it was something.

ALINA: Answer the phone!!!
ALINA: What happened?
ALINA: Are you okay?
ALINA: ANSWER ME!!!!!!

That was a lot of exclamation point yelling.

The paramedic ripped open his pant leg, pressed another pad over his seeping wound and rolled some gauze around his leg and tied it tight to stop the bleeding soaking his black cargos.

He tried to focus and rattled off Agent Alvarado's and Tandy's information to the police officer. King sat quietly beside him, letting the other paramedic tend to his own wounds, enduring the flashing light in his eyes and checking out of the back of his head, all without much participation from King.

The paramedic touched King's shoulder to be sure he had his attention. "Looks like you've got a concussion."

"No shit."

"Ambulance just arrived. We'll transport you to the hospital and get you checked out for any other internal injuries. A doctor will stitch your arm and clean these other cuts and scrapes."

Jay needed the same attention, but he was in charge. He was responsible for King, Agent Alvarado, Tandy, and all the other members of his team still doing their jobs.

"They'll do a scan to see how bad the concussion is. You'll probably stay a couple days," the paramedic rambled on.

King shook his head, planted his bloody, road rash-scraped hands on the ground, and pushed himself up. His legs wobbled under him until he stood tall and balance returned. Mostly. He swayed.

The paramedic held him steady by the arm. "You need to stay seated until they get you loaded on a gurney and take you to the hospital. It'll only be a minute."

King shook off the fireman paramedic and waved off the ambulance guys. "I've got work to do."

"You've got a head injury," Jay reminded him before the paramedic could point out the same thing.

"She's in danger. I need to get to her." King didn't need to say who or why. The desperation in his voice felt as deep as Jay's need to see Alina. He hated to keep her waiting after the string of random but telling texts he'd sent her. He hated putting her through hell. He didn't want to think that this might be the very thing that ended it all.

"We've got an APB out on Otis Potter and his truck," the officer interjected. "We'll find him."

The desperate look on King's face said it all. He needed to find Cara and make sure her uncle didn't do something stupid. Jay stared at the blaze the fire department fought to extinguish that had taken Agent Alvarado and Tandy. Well, something stupider.

The man wasn't right in the head.

Jay stood, not so steady on his feet. "Thanks for the help, guys. We'll leave the scene to you," he said to the officer, and handed over his business card. He didn't have the strength or heart to even try to stop King from going after Cara. "Keep me posted. I want to know when you recover Agent Alvarado's and Tandy's bodies. The DEA will notify the agent's family. I'll have another agent here soon to oversee everything."

The officer took the card and nodded.

"Come on, King, let's get moving."

They walked across the street to the gas station and the back corner where King had stashed his truck.

They both slowly climbed into the cab. King dug the keys out of his pocket, making the scrapes on his hand bleed even more.

Jay checked his dinging, cracked phone, swiped the screen, and read the incoming text messages. "Iceman's men picked up the loaded trailer. We're following."

King started the truck, but didn't pull out of the lot. He dug the heels of his hands into his eye sockets and rubbed his eyes, then stared out the windshield at the destruction across the street.

"Why the fuck did he blow the place? He has to know how much she loves it. Where the hell is he taking her? She won't be on board for any plan that involves killing her best friend, even if Tandy betrayed her."

Jay sent off a string of texts to his team, telling them to stick close and not lose that truck. It was the only lead they had to find Iceman and hopefully Cara. "My best guess, based on the fact he destroyed that ranch she and Castillo planned to live on, is he's getting rid of everyone he thinks hurt her. It's not the first place he's blown up. Several rival cartel bombings have been attributed to Iceman's crew."

"Fuck. Iceman and her uncle are working together."

"After he did this tonight, looks that way."

King pulled out onto the main road and headed in the same direction Cara and her uncle took. "Do we have eyes on Iceman?"

"Haven't in weeks. Not since your talk with him at Cara's place."

King smacked his bloody hand on the steering wheel. "Fuck. He knows who I am."

Jay turned to King. "How do you know?"

"Why else would he keep out of sight for so long?"

"How would he find that out?"

King raked his scraped fingers through his hair and winced when he hit the goose-egg-shaped lump on the back of his head. "I told him."

"You what?" Jay couldn't believe King spoke that freely to their target.

"I told him I knew Manny Castillo was dead. He must have guessed a guy with one conviction and barely any ties to the drug world probably didn't know that information offhand."

Jay got it. "You knew a little too much."

"I think so. He may not know I'm DEA, but he probably guessed I'm a cop."

Jay's brain still processed everything slower than normal. Plus, part of his mind was still on Alina as he stared down at the new text from her.

ALINA: Please tell me you're okay. I need you to be okay.
JAY: I'm okay
JAY: I swear

"Does Cara's uncle know?"

JAY: I'll call you when I can

King swore under his breath. "He found out tonight when Cara caught me here with DEA emblazoned across my chest."

"How did she recognize you behind the mask?"

King didn't take his eyes from the road, but something came over him that had him looking inside and to whatever he and Cara shared.

Jay didn't want to know, but he suspected King and Cara had grown much closer than was wise when King had a job to do and was using Cara to do it. The desperation and resignation in King's eyes said he understood that whatever they had was on the line. Cara knew he'd lied to her.

Jay's phone went off again. Not Alina, but the team updating him again. "The truck ended up at an auto body shop. It's a thirty-thousand-square-foot building." Jay let his head fall back as he thought about the daunting task ahead of them.

"Gonna be hard to surround something so big with only five guys on the team that followed the truck."

"They've called in backup already."

The last thing Jay wanted was a shootout with Iceman's crew. He'd lost one man tonight. He'd nearly been killed along with King. He didn't want to lose anyone else.

"Surrounding buildings?"

Jay read the incoming information on his phone. "Mostly empty or small businesses closed for the night. Nothing with a line of sight into the second-story windows."

"Iceman chose wisely. Snipers can't take a shot at him if he gets caught in there."

"If he goes out the back, there's a huge junkyard to help him evade and escape through."

"Any sign of Cara and her uncle?"

Jay typed out his replies. "I just sent a text telling the team to be on the lookout for them."

Jay loaded up directions to the auto shop on his map app and set his phone on the dashboard for King to follow.

King pushed the truck as fast as he could take it down one street, around a corner that sent Jay leaning into the door, and down into an industrial district.

"Slow down. It's dark and the way you're squinting tells me your vision isn't all that clear yet."

"I'm fine."

Jay's phone dinged with another text message. "Backup just arrived at the auto shop."

"Good. They can take down whoever is inside and recover the drugs."

Jay read the next three messages. "Not good. Cara and her uncle drove inside the building. Several minutes later, eight armed men fled out the back."

King pushed the pedal to the floor and took the next turn with the tires squealing. "Contact the team. Tell them I want a rifle ready. He's not walking out of there alive if he hurts Cara."

The texts and bad news just kept coming. "It gets worse. The team surrounded the building, but are sticking back."

"Why?"

"The guys they caught running out the back said Iceman told them to run because the place is rigged to blow."

"He's going to take them all out." Dread filled King's voice. If he could make the truck go light speed, he would to get to Cara.

King's hands tightened around the steering wheel. "I'm getting in there."

Jay understood King's need to protect Cara. He felt the same way about protecting Alina from whoever tried to kill her. Well, shit. Didn't that just say so much? If he recognized how King felt about Cara, why didn't he acknowledge it for what it was inside himself?

Still, he needed to reel King in and make him think straight. "King, it's suicide. He's out of his mind. He's going to blow the place sky-high."

"Not with her inside of it. I will get him to let her go. Deep down, he doesn't really want to hurt her. He wants to protect her. Right now, he thinks the only way he can is to kill her."

Jay had dealt with people out of their minds, their

thinking clouded by drugs or convoluted by extreme circumstances and trauma. "Do you hear yourself? That's crazy talk. That's exactly what he is." And talking him out of his beliefs might be futile at this point. Not when he'd gone this far to get Cara and Iceman alone. "He'll blow the place the second he sees you."

Jay stared at the sheer number of vehicles clogging up the street outside Anderson Automotive.

"Then we need to distract him so he doesn't know I'm coming." King pulled the truck in next to the DEA's armored vehicle. A tactical team stood beside it going over plans to infiltrate the building or figure out a way to get a sniper into a position with line of sight to take out Cara's uncle and Iceman if necessary.

He knew the men, had worked with them on several occasions, and trusted them to give him an assessment of the situation. Once up to speed, Jay could help form a tactical plan that didn't involve sending King to his death.

King jumped out of the truck the second he killed the engine. Unsteady on his feet, he slapped his hand on the hood, catching himself before his knees buckled. He may not be a hundred percent, but right now his focus was on getting to Cara and making sure she made it out of that building alive.

Jay climbed out of the truck at a much slower pace. His vision blurred, then refocused. Every step sent a blast of pain through his injured calf. He tried to keep his arm still and the searing pain in his shoulder at bay.

"King. You look like shit," Cruz, the team leader, said the minute they joined the group.

"I feel like it. What's the plan?"

"With the potential for another bomb like the one you just survived, we can't get close to the building. We're about to make contact via phone, but from what I've been told, this guy isn't in the talking mood."

Jay considered all the angles and the lives of the men around him. Any plan they came up with had to take into account that Cara's uncle wanted King dead and had already tried to kill him once. As much as King wanted in that building to save Cara, Jay didn't want to give the guy another shot at him, but controlling King in his state of mind might not be so easy.

He believed in King's abilities. And though driven by his personal needs, King would do the right thing.

"Bomb squad and a hostage negotiator just arrived." Jay gave King a once-over, finding him still unsteady on his feet, his eyes clouded with pain, though his determination hadn't waned. "Let them handle this." Jay had to try to keep King thinking straight, but he didn't delude himself into believing King would follow his orders. Not in this case. Not with Cara inside that building with a death sentence hanging over her head if they didn't handle this the right way.

King nodded his agreement, even though he probably had no intention of sitting back and doing nothing. In King's place, Jay would do the same thing.

Controlled chaos reigned around them.

Jay let King simmer and focused on the discussion between Cruz, the bomb squad leader, and the negotiator. They batted around one idea after the other, but in the end, the negotiator didn't deliver encouraging news.

"Extremists like this are tricky. They hold on to their ideas even when confronted with logic and reason. Compromise is difficult when they are deeply rooted in their beliefs."

Jay didn't believe the negotiator, or anyone, would deter Otis from carrying out his deadly plan.

Jay left the negotiator and Cruz to work out a plan for what they hoped to accomplish with the first call and when to send in the tactical team, if at all because of the bombs, if and when Otis refused to cooperate. He caught King behind the tactical vehicle, sneaking in to grab some gear. "You know I can't sanction you going in there."

"Damn it, Jay, I love her. I'm not leaving her in there to die alone." King never used his first name on the job, but this wasn't just any job to King. This was personal. "I'm going in whether you like it or not."

Jay's phone pinged, not dinged, with another text, signaling this one wasn't business, but personal. Jay turned the phone over and quickly read the message.

ALINA: Call me back NOW!!!!!!!!!!

He'd had no right to text her that message earlier and then leave her hanging. He hated that his job had to come first. But King was about to put his life on the line and Jay needed to be ready to back him up. Because that's what friends do. And first and foremost, they were friends, even if Jay was the boss.

King tilted his head and eyed Jay and the way he tried to hide the phone and the embarrassment heating his face. "Why are you getting text messages from Alina?"

Jay swore. No sense lying. Not when King was so deeply personally involved in this case. And he'd just been caught. "After the bomb and nearly dying tonight, I texted her a message better said face-to-face." Jay looked away, not wanting to give anything more away.

King clamped his hand on Jay's shoulder. "I get it, man. That bomb made so many things clear to me. Like what and who are important to me."

Intense situations tended to do that. He appreciated King's support, though he expected King to warn him away from Alina because she was Caden and Trigger's sister.

"As much as I'd love to call my family, Cara is in

there facing everything bad in her life. Whatever I have to do, I'm getting her out of that building alive." King squeezed Jay's arm. "Call Alina, then you can say you never saw me sneak away."

Jay leaned in past him and grabbed a bulletproof vest out of the tactical vehicle. "Put that on and take this." Jay pulled his gun from his back and handed it over to King. "You're the best shot we have—take them down."

King pulled the vest over his head. He winced with pain when the vest brushed the lump on the back of his head. His movements were slow and deliberate. The pain obvious in every line on King's face.

Jay helped pull the vest into place and secured the side straps as King tucked the gun between the vest and his stomach. "I'm barely on my feet after that bomb nearly blew us to hell. I don't know how you're still standing with that head injury."

King glanced at the gash on Jay's forehead, reminding him that they were in the same condition. Sheer will and waning adrenaline kept them both from giving in to the pain and exhaustion.

Jay tapped King on the chest. "Don't get killed."

King eyed the vehicles and men surrounding the building. "Tell everyone out here not to shoot when I send her out."

Jay grabbed King's arm and held him still. "You mean when you come out with her."

"However it goes down."

Jay didn't like King's fatalist attitude. He didn't like sending his friend into a situation where he believed he wasn't coming out, because he'd sacrifice everything for Cara.

Jay felt the same way about Alina.

This time when Jay's phone rang, he answered it and the need to hear her voice.

CHAPTER TWENTY-ONE

Alina stood in the open door and tried to hold it together. With her gut tied in knots and her heart in her throat, she didn't know how much longer she could pretend she was okay.

"If you want me to stay, I will." Beck stood on Jay's porch, sticking back to talk to her while Ashley loaded Adam into their car. They'd returned from their honeymoon and decided that it didn't matter how late it was, they wanted to see Adam and take him home with them.

Sweet, but with Jay in trouble of some kind and her unable to reach him, all she wanted was for her brother to leave so she could try Jay again without Beck knowing how desperate she was to hear Jay's voice. And why.

"I'm perfectly safe here. They've found nothing about the car crash that leads to an ongoing threat. I've got a guard. I'll actually feel better knowing Adam is away from me and with you just in case someone is targeting me."

"You know we'll find out and keep you safe. Come home with me."

She shook her head. "You just got back. After all you, Ashley, and Adam have been through, I don't want to bring more trouble to your door. I'm fine here."

Beck's usual intense vibe amped up and deepened his frown. "I'm not so sure the trouble didn't find you because of me."

"If it did, it's not your fault. I understand the game and how hard you guys play to win." Like tonight, Jay put his life on the line to take down a drug dealer. She had no idea what happened, but he'd had to keep his focus on the job instead of talking to her after he'd sent those text messages.

Something dire made him send those messages and kept him from contacting her again. What, she didn't know, but a thousand tragic nightmares filled her mind.

As much as she wanted to get Beck on the phone to the DEA and find out what happened, she didn't want her brother's first hours home to suck him back into work before he even had time to unpack. That wasn't fair. She needed to believe in Jay and his abilities and those of the men he worked with to keep him safe. Men like her brothers.

She had to have faith.

Though the longer her phone remained silent, the more her confidence waned.

Beck studied her harder. The man was a human lie detector and adept at ferreting out secrets. "Is something else bothering you?"

She tried to stay calm. She didn't want to lie so stuck as close to the truth as possible. "Jay's helping King tonight. I've heard a little about the case. I hope everything goes their way."

"Jay's got the experience and tactical mind to make it go their way. You don't need to worry."

She couldn't stop worrying after his texts. Nothing was a given in their line of work. Taking down one of the top lieutenants in a drug cartel meant facing life and death because those guys didn't go down without a fight.

Beck's gaze sharpened on her face. "You really are worried." He touched her shoulder. "Sis, I know he went above and beyond for you after the accident. I appreciate it more than I can say. If you want, I'll call the office and see if I can get an update on what's going on."

She shook her head. "I'm sure he's fine. He's been really good to me and Adam. When you and Caden are on the job, I worry, but I've never been this in on what you guys do. I guess knowing what he's doing, what he's facing, it kind of puts your job and what you go through into perspective even more and brings it up close and personal."

"Caden and I always come back, right?"

She hugged Beck, and it eased her heart. "I don't think I told you how happy I am for you and Ashley."

Beck rubbed her back. "You did. But don't think Caden and I didn't notice something seemed off with you. What's going on? Does it have to do with your accident?"

She leaned back and pressed her lips together for a moment. "No." It had everything to do with Jay, but she'd keep that to herself a little longer. At least until she and Jay had a minute to settle into this thing between them that seemed to get more intense with every passing day. She needed time to think, breathe, and just be with him. She really wanted him to be standing in front of her right now instead of Beck. "Seeing you and Caden so happy on your wedding day, it just made me want that even more for myself."

Beck hooked his hand around her shoulder and held her tight. "You'll find it." He gave her a rare smile. "Try to get some sleep."

"Drive carefully."

"I will. I'll check in with work tomorrow, see what's going on with King and Jay, but I know they've got things under control. It's tough waiting, but when they're in the thick of it, it's best to let them focus and get the job done."

"I'm sure he's fine." *I pray he's okay.*

Beck studied her face, but didn't say anything before he turned and walked down the porch steps toward his car. "We'll figure out your situation in the next couple of days. We'll get you home as soon as possible."

She waved Beck off and closed the door on the house that felt more and more like home. If only the man who lived here was with her right now.

She stood in the foyer, staring at Jay's office. She saw the baseball he and Adam played with lying on his desk, the neat stack of folders, the pens in a mason jar, the books on the shelves alongside framed photos of Jay, family, and friends. She hadn't noticed the one of him with her brothers and a few other men from the DEA, standing behind a table stacked with drugs. Must have been a big bust for them.

She couldn't deal with the quiet and being surrounded by reminders of him. She pulled her too-silent phone from her pocket and called him again, hoping he answered, but expecting his voice mail yet again. Even the sound of his voice right now might be enough to soothe her overactive imagination.

"I'm okay, sweetheart." Jay's strong and steady voice eased her aching heart.

The endearment sent tears to her eyes. Intense emotions she couldn't even decipher clogged her throat. "I . . . I . . . Are you really okay?"

"Please don't cry. I'm in the thick of it here. I still have so much to do, but if you cry, I don't know . . . I can't get to you right now."

She sucked in a ragged breath, wiped her eyes with one hand, then raked her fingers through her hair and held the top away from her face and tried to contain her emotions. "I'm not crying. Of course, I'm not crying. I just needed to hear your voice. And you're fine, and I'm okay. So okay. Everything is okay."

"It is now that I've heard your voice." The weariness in his killed her.

"Will it be over soon?"

"I don't know. King's just walked into a trap I hope he can get out of. If not . . ." Desperation filled Jay's words but underneath ran his confidence in King.

"He'll make it out." The best she could do right now was support him. "You said there was an explosion. Are you hurt?" The five seconds of silence sent a bolt of panic through her system. "Jay? Are. You. Hurt?"

"I'm on my feet, but I won't lie, as soon as this is over, I'll probably need to go to the hospital."

Panic turned to terror and amped her heart rate to hummingbird speed. Instinct took over and she started searching for her purse and keys to a car she didn't have anymore. "I'll call . . ." What the hell was the guard's name? "The guy into the house. He'll bring me to you." She rushed from the kitchen toward the front door. "Where?"

"Shots fired," someone in the background shouted.

"Stay put, Alina. I'll call you later. I . . . I have stuff to say, but it has to wait. I'm sorry." He hung up on her without telling her where he was or what hospital they'd take him to or why he needed to go in the first place.

"'I'm on my feet.' The damn man hangs up on me and that's all he says." She flung the front door open, took a second to remember who was watching her tonight, and yelled, "Joey, we're leaving!"

She stood on the porch barely able to contain the urge to stomp her foot with impatience. About to yell for him again, she opened her mouth but snapped it shut when Joey ran around the corner of the house.

"Hey, are you okay?"

She rushed down the steps. "No. We need to go."

"Where?"

"I don't really know for sure, but you're going to find out for me."

Joey ran his hand over his dark hair. "Uh, I'm supposed to protect you. Here."

"Either drive me where I want to go, or I'll go wake up Jay's mother and make her take me. Either way, we're leaving." She jumped down the steps from the porch and headed for Joey's SUV, calling over her shoulder, "It's useless to argue. We're going to see Jay."

Joey ran after her. "He's on a case. You can't just go see him."

"He's been injured and will be taken to the hospital soon. I will be there when he gets there."

Joey unlocked the doors with his key fob. He climbed in behind the wheel. She sat in the passenger seat and pulled her seat belt on, though it rubbed against her bruises and made her shoulder and chest throb with pain.

"I know you can get the name of the hospital from work."

Joey eyed her, scrunched his mouth into a perturbed half frown, then started the engine. "I thought this gig would be easy. He's going to kill me. You know that, right?"

"You can tell him I threatened you."

"With what?" Joey shook his head, but drove down the driveway anyway. "I could take you out with one hand."

"You've got a long drive to come up with something both good and plausible he'll believe."

CHAPTER TWENTY-TWO

Every bruise and sore muscle throbbed, but it was nothing compared to the ache in her heart. She should move, shift to a more comfortable position, but that required energy Alina just didn't have after spending the night in the uncomfortable chair beside Jay's hospital bed.

She'd beat him here, but hadn't been allowed to see him until the doctors had completed their exams, run their tests, stitched and bandaged him up, and settled him in the room exhausted and out for the night. Then, and only then, did they allow her in for what they said was a brief visit. She'd simply refused to leave. With a DEA agent watching the door, they didn't see the harm and withdrew from the battle she was ready to fight if they tried to have her removed.

It took her a moment to realize Jay's eyes were open. She'd been staring at him so long, her vision had become blurry with fatigue.

She'd propped her legs on the bed beside Jay. He reached out and rubbed her knee, her sock-covered feet tucked in his armpit. His still groggy but sharp gaze swept over her. "Are you okay?"

After the sleepless night she'd had, not so much. Sweet that he cared, especially with him lying prone and unconscious for hours.

She gripped the chair arms and pulled herself up

straight, easing her feet to the floor and straight into her sneakers. She took a moment to tug them on, holding back the groan as her achy body protested the movement.

"Alina?"

She tamped down the unwarranted anger rolling in her gut, stood, and leaned over him. His eyes were clear if not wary. She kissed his forehead next to the bandage covering his stitched gash, leaned back, touched her hand to his face, and stared down at him. "How do you feel?"

She felt a million times better, seeing him awake and alert. And even as that relief washed through her, last night's fear flared to life, too, bringing with it the nightmare of what happened to him. What could happen to him in the future.

He gripped her arms and held her still. "Better seeing you here."

Alina's cell buzzed on the blankets with yet another text, the fourth in the last hour. She barely glanced at it.

"What's that about?"

Alina rolled her eyes. "Noel. Checking on me. Again." Since the accident, he'd become obsessed with making sure she was okay. Like a gnat buzzing at her ear, she wanted to swat him away and be left alone.

"Is that what has you so upset?"

"No. I'm *upset* because last night I got this disturbing text that you'd been blown up, then those texts stopped coming, and I waited and waited and waited in frantic desperation to hear from you."

His eyes clouded with regret. "Alina."

"When I finally do speak to you, you tell me you need to go to the hospital but you can't because you're still working but you're on your feet." She slipped from his grasp and stood over him, raking her fingers through her hair. "You're still standing!" The incredulous tone made him wince.

"I'm sorry, sweetheart. I shouldn't have reached out to you—"

She fisted her hands at her sides. "Shut up."

His eyes went wide, then resignation set in. "You're angry."

She shook her head because the anger only hid the deeper feeling that sent her running here to his bedside. Fear. All-out terror that she'd lose him. Tears welled in her eyes. Tears she hadn't allowed herself to shed last night.

He grabbed hold of her arms again. "Oh God, don't cry. I don't know what to do if you cry."

She sucked in a ragged breath. "You scared me."

His frown didn't deter her.

"I did this with Beck not even a year ago. Sat by his bed, hoping he'd wake up and be okay."

Jay shook his head and rubbed his hands up her arms and back down to soothe her. "This isn't that serious."

"This time." The desperate text message he'd sent her, the details of what Jay had been through last night that Joey got for her as she waited to see Jay, it all came in a rush of fear that made her heart thrash against her sore ribs. "Someone tried to blow you up."

He pulled his hands away and clasped them over his stomach like he needed to restrain himself from touching her. "I admit, it was a close call. One I don't want to repeat, believe me." He touched his head and winced, then stared down at his bandaged leg propped on a pillow. "In the back of my mind, I knew you didn't want any part of this. Though I have to admit, I thought maybe . . ."

The sadness in his eyes tore at her heart. She sat with her hip propped on the bed next to his injured leg. "What?"

He didn't reach to touch her again and she hated it so much her insides felt like claws raking her soul raw.

"You've worried about your brothers all these years. Last night, I guess it finally clicked that being with me really does mean sometimes bad things happen. This is what it would be like for years to come if you and I . . ." He shook his head, unable to finish that statement. "I can't tell you what it means to me that you came, but I understand you don't want to stay."

The anger came back with a swift kick to her exhausted system. "That blast really rattled your brain."

"I wouldn't recommend it." He pressed the heel of his hand to the side of his head.

"Do you need me to get the nurse?"

He shook his head before she finished speaking. "It's down to a dull throb, nothing more. Don't worry about me, sweetheart."

She placed her hand on his chest. "I want to worry about you."

His eyes lit with surprise and his hand covered hers.

She tried to sort out her feelings to find what was real. "This thing between us has been one adrenaline rush after the next. Sneaking around at the wedding. You racing to my bedside after the car crash and protecting me. Now I'm running to be with you after someone tried to blow you to bits." The thought stopped her heart. "And I ask myself, are we just reacting to what's happening around us?"

He shook his head but didn't say anything because in his mind he thought she didn't want him. As he was. Who he was.

"It's so much more than that, right?"

Anticipation filled his eyes. "It is for me."

She placed her free hand over his on top of hers. "You said something to me last night. Though, because of the circumstances, I won't hold you to it. And with everything else going on, it made something clear to me."

"What?" The hope in his eyes and voice, the way he leaned in, softened her even more.

"As . . . open as I've been with you in one respect, I've been guarded and reluctant to get deeper into a relationship with you because I didn't want to find myself exactly where we are." She glanced around the hospital room and stared at him lying in the bed.

Jay gripped her hand tighter. "But? I'm really hoping there's a but in there."

"But . . . when I thought the worst happened to you . . ." She nearly choked on those words.

Jay nodded, his lips drawn into a frown as he silently let her know he'd felt the same way when he rushed to her in the hospital.

"I thought I lost you," she whispered, emotion clogging her throat. "And then I heard your voice on the phone and I knew I didn't want to miss . . . anything with you."

His fingertip touched her chin to make her stop staring at his chest and look him in the eye. "Do you mean that?"

"Yes."

He brushed the tears from her cheek with the pad of his thumb. "About that thing I said that you don't want to hold me to."

She shook her head. "You were in an extreme circumstance, emotions running high. We'll just forget it."

"You should hold me to it. I had my own moment of clarity and had to tell you the truth. If that was the end, I needed you to know."

"Jay . . ."

"I can't forget about it. It's kind of a living thing inside of me now. But I will allow us time to . . . I don't know . . . spend time together doing normal things."

She touched her fingers to his lips to shut him up. "It's Sunday. Date night. I would love to sit across a candlelit table and share a meal with you. We'll go to Mia's place. No, Mia and the aunts will be there. Someplace no one knows us so we can be alone."

Jay smiled for the first time since he'd woken up. "Anywhere you want, sweetheart."

She stood, though Jay didn't release her hand. "I'll go see what time they're springing you. We'll go home, rest, make a reservation, then have a quiet evening together."

Before she'd even finished that sentence, his smile dimmed with whatever he didn't want to tell her.

"What?"

"I want to spend the day with you and take you out to dinner. I do. More than anything."

"But?"

He didn't say anything as his gaze fell away.

She narrowed her eyes. "You're going back to work."

"It's my case. There's a lot of cleanup and follow-up. Once I check on King, I need to get with my team and"—his lips pressed together, his eyes rolled—"there's a lot left to do."

"You have a major head injury. Until they stitched you up, there was a hole in your leg and shoulder. You're covered in cuts and bruises from *an explosion*. You're in the hospital." She barely restrained the urge to stomp her foot.

"Only for observation."

She cocked one eyebrow up for that inane argument. "Seriously? After what happened last night, you've earned a few days off."

"Alina, I'm in charge of this case. I'm responsible. This is my life."

"Yes, and yesterday you almost lost it." The tremble in her voice made Jay's eyes fill with misery. She raked her fingers through her hair and sucked in a steadying breath. Losing her shit wouldn't help. Letting her emotions reign and saying something she didn't really mean would only make things harder on him, her, and the relationship they were both trying to get on solid ground. "I'm sorry."

"You don't need to be sorry for how you feel. I've disappointed you. You're worried, which I appreciate more than I can say."

She sat on the edge of the bed again. "I'm worried because I care, Jay." She pressed her hand to his chest. "I'm upset because I don't want anything to happen to you. What happened last night and with Beck all those months ago . . . it scares me and makes my heart hurt." She sighed. "As much as I know what I'm signing up for, a part of me doesn't know if I can give you the support you need to do what you need to do. I want to be that strong. It's easy to be brave when nothing is happening. Not so much when I see you hurt and you want me to let you put yourself in harm's way again. There's a very big part of me that just wants to hold on to you and keep you safe. I don't want to hold my breath and pray every time you go to work."

Jay stared at her for a long moment. "Do you trust me?"

"Yes." She didn't even need to think about it.

"Then, when these feelings come up, like now, remind yourself that I know what I'm doing. I'm good at what I do. That the decisions I make are to keep my team and myself safe." He took her hand. "And that more than anything, I want to come back to you. I will do everything in my power to make that happen. I never had that in my life, Alina. You have to know I don't want to lose it or you."

She leaned down, planted her hands on either side of his head, and kissed him softly. "It's been a rough couple of days. My head's a little off and my emotions are raw."

"But your heart and mine are in the same place. We

both want each other to be safe. We both want more of this." He drew her down for another soft kiss.

She sank into him, letting the warmth spread through her and wash away the last of the cold fear she'd felt last night. The kiss deepened, turning that warmth into a five-alarm fire. He cupped her face, rose up to sitting, taking the pressure off her sore shoulder and neck as she bent over him, then took the kiss deeper. His arms wrapped around her and he held her safe and protected in his strong arms.

Jay broke the kiss and pressed his forehead to hers. His arms squeezed her tighter to his chest. "This is what I needed last night. You in my arms, making everything better."

She rubbed her hand up and down his back, her fingers grazing his bare skin where the hospital gown gaped. "This is what I should have done the minute you woke up."

"Next time," he teased, but truth rang in that statement. He may very well end up in the hospital again.

She leaned back and eyed him, letting him see her annoyance. "Reality sucks sometimes. But you're right, I need to be prepared. And find a way to not think about it every second of the day and make myself crazy."

"If it helps, I like that you're crazy about me."

She rolled her eyes, took his face, and gave him another kiss to stop him from saying anything else sappy but sweet. Deep down, she loved it. And him. But she was letting that settle in before they went headlong down that road without getting this relationship on solid ground with a lot less drama and extreme circumstances and more sharing the day-to-day, ups and downs, and simple things that turned into lasting memories.

A quick knock sounded on the door. They split apart, not wanting to get caught making out by the nurse. Jay gently lay back on the pillows, his body still sore and tense from the blast. She remained seated on the bed and turned to the door and waited. It didn't open right away, but when it did, she understood why Joey had given them the warning.

Beck strolled in, his gaze raking over her, then darting to Jay and back to her again. She couldn't read anything in her brother's eyes and didn't want to go there right now.

"What are you doing here, sis?" Beck gave her a soft hug, stood back, and studied her face. "You should be home resting."

"I'm fine. I'm perfectly capable of making my own decisions and knowing what I want." She hoped her brother remembered that when he found out about her and Jay. She'd tell him soon. "Since you're here and Jay's going back to work, I'm headed home now."

Beck's gaze bounced from her to Jay and back. "When did you get here?"

Yeah, she'd turned up the flame on Beck's suspicions, but now wasn't the time to talk about them when Beck and Jay had work to do. "A while ago." She stood and leaned over Jay to give him a friendly hug. His awkward pat made her smile. They'd just been fused together in a hotter-than-hell kiss and now he didn't know how to touch her in front of her brother. "Don't overdo it. You need to watch that leg and rest if your head starts throbbing again."

"I'll take it easy."

She shook her head. "Taking it easy would mean going home and resting like you should."

"I won't be back until tomorrow, but make yourself at home."

The warmth in his voice told her more than those words. He really wanted her to think of it as home. But they weren't there yet. "Since there's no evidence of an immediate threat and you won't be there anyway, I'm going home to my place. Joey can take the couch," she added to appease Jay and her brother. "First, I need to rent a car since mine was totaled. I'll buy a new one when the insurance pays out." Before either of them protested, she gave Jay's arm one last squeeze. She needed to trust him and leave so he could get back to doing what he needed to do.

Beck didn't smile when she touched his arm in goodbye. She didn't expect him to. He rarely smiled, except for his new bride. His eyes bore into her back as she left and met Joey in the hallway.

JAY WATCHED THE door close behind Alina and bit back the urge to call out to her and order her to stay at his house. He wanted her there when he got home, but that was unfair to expect. Although, after all they'd been through, the way he felt so deeply, it just felt right.

Plus, he didn't want anything to happen to her. He didn't want her out of his sight.

Irrational. Like the way she felt about letting him go back to work. Neither of them could control what happened next.

Beck broke into his muddled thoughts. "She seems a little pissed at you for nearly dying."

"Something like that," Jay said before he caught himself and shut the hell up.

Beck smiled down at him.

Jay tried to change the subject. "What are you doing here? You're not supposed to be back to work until tomorrow."

"Today, tomorrow, what difference does it make? You and King had a lot of excitement. I wanted to check on both of you. I spoke with Cara about King and what happened last night. You took a pretty big hit with that blast."

"I'm fine. The head's a dull ache, thanks to the meds.

I'll probably limp for a while, but the leg isn't that bad. I'll get by."

"But will you get back into Alina's good graces?"

Jay finally met Beck's narrowed gaze, noting the hint of amusement in his eyes. "You know."

"That you're sleeping with my sister?"

Jay gave up. He didn't like hiding things from his best friend. "It's a hell of a lot more than that." He hoped Beck didn't take a swing at him. Jay was in no shape to defend himself.

Beck frowned. "Damn. I could tell at the wedding you two had something going, the attraction between you was there, but I didn't think it had gone that far."

If Jay's brain was working on all cylinders, he wouldn't have walked into that verbal trap he should have expected from Beck. The man worked undercover and ferreted out secrets for a living.

"Is this where you warn me away? Because I can save you the breath. No. I will not stop seeing her."

Beck's eyebrow shot up at Jay's definitive tone.

"What she and I have . . . it's different than anything I've ever had. I value your friendship and want to keep working closely with you, but, no. I won't give her up. I can't."

Beck stuffed his hands in his pockets and rocked back and forth on his heels. "She's in love with you."

Jay wanted to believe that. He wanted to think that was enough to keep them together. "How do you know?"

"Pretty clear after her car accident. She didn't call our parents. She didn't call our aunt. She called you to pick her up from the hospital. She wanted you."

He hadn't really thought about it like that.

"Does Caden know, too?"

"He caught a vibe between you two. We talked about it at the wedding."

"So what's it going to be? Shot and buried in the mountains? A beat-down for touching your sister? You going to lay out all my faults and sins for Alina and turn her against me?"

Beck's gaze grew darker.

"I get that she's your sister and you want to protect her."

"And you're my friend. Someone I respect and trust with my life. Do I think the two of you are a good idea? I don't know. It seems sudden. I can't imagine what you have in common. Then again, I never looked for similarities between you two."

"I like her. A lot. She's smart and funny. Kind. Generous. She's confident and accomplished. She's amazing."

"And she understands your life in a way most other women wouldn't because she's my sister and has lived with what Caden and I do for a long time now."

"She understands, but if you'd been here earlier, you'd know she's not thrilled about it."

"That's just it, Jay, she was here. For you. I'll bet the second I left last night, she came straight here."

Jay nodded. It meant so much to him, he couldn't even put the depth of his appreciation and need for her into words.

"You need someone like her, who knows the danger and, despite that, is willing to go all in. She needs a guy who is ready to give her what she wants. Something I think you've wanted for a long time, too."

"What's that?"

Beck knew both of them. Jay wanted his take.

"She has such a big heart. She takes care of everyone in the family, but what she really wants is a family of her own. Maybe you didn't see it at the wedding, as happy as she was for Caden and me, she wanted to be the one saying 'I do' to the guy she'd promise forever to and mean it with everything she is. If you're not in it for that, if you don't see the incredible value in that, then, yes, I'm warning you off."

He'd seen exactly what Beck described. It's what had drawn him to her at the bar. "Everything she feels is in her eyes. When I woke up, she was sitting beside my bed. The relief I saw in her dwarfed the anger that came later."

"You scared her."

"I scared myself. I nearly died and all I could think about was that I finally had a chance to be with someone I really cared about and wanted a future with and it was gone before it ever got started."

Beck's eyes went wide. "You love her."

"It's so much more than that. I need her, otherwise what the hell am I doing with my life?" Loving her was bigger than taking down bad guys. "I can't promise her there won't be another scare like the one I gave her last night."

"None of us can," Beck admitted.

"But I can promise her to do my best to come home to her, to love her with everything I am, to be the best I can be for her."

Beck stared at him for a moment, then nodded like he'd come to some decision. "I'll talk to Caden. We'll stand back and let you two figure it out."

Jay breathed a sigh of relief. "Thanks." With her brothers on the sidelines, he didn't have to fight them to be with Alina. But he still needed to work on settling Alina into his life and making her see that she was important and a priority.

He'd done a poor job of that today. She didn't want him to go back to work so soon after what happened, but he needed to tie up this case, so he could focus on her. And uncover who tried to kill her and make them pay.

CHAPTER TWENTY-THREE

Sweat trickled down Alina's back. She pulled the bar down behind her head three more times to finish her set. She hated working out but silently admitted she felt better for it. If not for that, she'd be back at her place drinking another cup of coffee and enjoying the donuts Dave brought this morning when he relieved Joey from guard duty.

Dave stood by her apartment complex's gym door and watched everyone coming and going while she finished. She released the bar and stretched her shoulders and neck. She'd taken off the brace this morning and hoped to work out the remaining stiffness with some light weights. She wasn't at peak performance, but her muscles and the tension in her body had loosened. She felt more like herself today than she had since the accident.

A beep alerting her to a text interrupted the podcast she listened to each morning that gave the highlights of local news. It kind of felt like someone reading her the newspaper. She kept up on what happened in her community while she got her workout in. Multitasking at its best.

She checked her phone messages.

JAY: Almost done here be back this afternoon

She smiled and her belly fluttered with anticipation. Jay had checked in with her every few hours since she left him at the hospital yesterday morning. She'd stopped by his place, picked up all her stuff, then gone home and slept in her own bed, only to toss and turn searching in the night for the man who should be beside her. How she got used to sleeping with him after one night, she didn't know. But it felt damn good to have him there and not out facing whatever danger came his way next.

Before she texted Jay back, the announcer on the podcast reported, *There have been three more break-ins where thieves target medicine cabinets and small valuables. Police believe the burglars' intent is to take prescription drugs to resell on the streets for a huge profit. The three break-ins add to the home burglaries that have increased by nearly 30 percent in the last six months and are up 47 percent from last year overall.*

Wow. She needed to look into those burglaries and use that information in her next community talk.

No one was home during these break-ins; however, two people have lost their lives after suffering head injuries when robbers struck the homeowners in order to subdue them while they stole valuables from the house.

Good Lord, that was terrible.

Someone tapped her shoulder. Taken off guard, she jumped and spun around ready to defend herself.

Dave held his hands up in surrender when she shrieked.

She sucked in a ragged breath and scolded herself for overreacting. The podcast reporter droned on about the weather forecast for the next seven days. She pulled her earbuds out and gave Dave a sheepish grin. "Sorry."

"I didn't mean to scare you. I feel even worse after your reaction that I have to tell you, they're pulling me off guard duty."

"Really?" A rush of panic swept through her before she tamped it down and reminded herself the accident had been just that, nothing more.

"Caden, Beck, and Jay put their heads together with the local cops. There's nothing tying the accident to a DEA case and a threat against them."

"That's what I told them."

"The accident is still suspicious. The cops will continue to work the case. Jay wants you to remain vigilant. Don't go anywhere alone if you can help it. Check in with him and your brothers so they know you're okay. If anything else happens, you feel like you're being followed, something seems off about a situation, call for help immediately."

"Is this your way of leaving me feeling safe?"

Dave blushed and tried not to stare at her in her sports bra. His eyes had nearly popped out of his head when she walked out of her bedroom to hit the gym in her bike shorts, midriff exposed, along with her legs that he couldn't stop staring at. At first she thought to skip the gym if he thought she looked that good, but then she'd giggled and walked right past him. She wondered what Jay would say if he knew his trusted buddy had spent the last half hour staring at her ass while she did squats, lifted weights, and did a sprint on the treadmill.

"You are safe. No one has made another attempt to harm you. The DEA, your brothers, nor Jay have received any kind of message threatening them or you."

She held out her hand to shake. "Thank you for everything. I really appreciate it."

Dave took her hand. "They wouldn't pull me off if they thought for a minute something might happen to you."

She smiled. "Believe me, I know." The overprotective lot of them went to the dark side because of the work they did and the evil they saw men do all the time.

Sad.

"If you're ready, I'll walk you back to your place before I head out."

"Thank you, I'd like that." She snatched up her towel from the weight bench, wiped it down, then followed Dave out of the building and along the path back to her apartment. He waited for her to unlock the door.

"You take care. Oh, and get some security for this place. A child could break in."

She chuckled under her breath. "I'll get to it."

"Sooner rather than later if you're going to be seeing Jay." Dave gave her another sheepish grin and waved goodbye.

She walked into her place and shut the door firmly behind her. "So, the cat's out of the bag." She took two steps toward her bedroom, then turned back. The accident still rattled her. The replay went through her mind at odd moments. She saw the SUV casually following her for miles, then all of a sudden, it lurched forward and hit her. Did the driver have some kind of emergency and stomp on the gas? Did an animal dash across the street and he tried to avoid it and hit her instead? Either scenario seemed plausible. But that ominous chill that it was more personal she always felt when she thought about the accident shivered up her spine and froze her bones.

She locked the door and put the security chain in place.

"You can't be too careful." She'd talk to Jay about a security system. Until then, she'd be vigilant. Her confidence may be shaken, but she wasn't going to let the accident make her paranoid and keep her from doing what she used to do without any thought to someone out there who wanted to hurt her.

CHAPTER TWENTY-FOUR

Jay finally found the time to do what Alina asked him to do at the hospital. He left work early to take care of himself. After dealing with the ATF about the bombing and additional C4 found at Cara's property, he'd secured the drugs found at the auto shop where King took down Cara's uncle. He put King on paid administrative leave while they finished the paperwork and review of the case and the shootings. King needed time to heal, clear his head, and find a way to get Cara back.

Jay smiled to himself. King had it bad. Jay knew the feeling.

The smile on his face grew the minute he stepped into the pharmacy and spotted Alina at the counter talking to a young woman holding a groggy toddler. Alina spotted him and her smile widened, too. He hobbled his way to the far side of the counter, waiting for her to finish.

Alina held her finger up to him. "I'll be with you in just a second." She turned back to the mom with the dark circles under her eyes. "Make sure you give her the medication for the full ten days. Otherwise it may not be effective."

"Yucky medicine."

Alina patted the toddler's little hand. "Not this time, sweetie. I made it orange. Just like you like, right?"

The toddler nodded but never picked up her golden head from her mother's shoulder.

"Thanks, Alina." The mom hitched the kid up a little higher as her weight sagged the mom's shoulders.

"Use the dropper in the bag. She'll be feeling better in no time. If the ear hurts or she can't sleep, try filling a water bottle with warm water and have her lie on it. That should help ease the pain. You can always give her a little infant acetaminophen." Alina pulled an orange lollipop from her coat pocket and held it out to the little girl who snatched it before her mom could take it from her.

Alina and the mother laughed when the little girl ripped off the plastic wrap and tossed it, sticking the pop in her mouth and smiling around it.

Jay leaned over to retrieve the discarded wrapper from the floor. He groaned when he stood up.

"Police." The little girl pointed to his badge and gun, then raised her finger to his head. "Ouchie."

Jay touched the spot just beneath the stitches in his head. He'd gotten rid of the ridiculous bandage around his head yesterday. "It doesn't hurt anymore. I took my medicine. If you do, too, you'll feel better."

The mom smiled and carried the little one out the door. At the last second, the girl waved to him over her mother's shoulder.

"Flirt," Alina teased.

He turned to her and his heart tripped over itself. "I want one of those."

Alina produced a red lollipop from her coat pocket and held it out to him.

He shook his head. "No. A little girl. Or boy. Both."

Alina's eyes went wide as saucers. "Really?"

He laughed. "Does that surprise you so much?"

"Yes. No. I don't know." Her lips pressed together before she stumbled over any more words. "If you took me on a proper date and we shared these kinds of things, I'd know more about you."

"Okay. Go to lunch with me."

"What?"

He took her hand across the counter, smiled even more when her hand trembled in his at the contact, then looked her in the eye. "Would you like to go to lunch with me?"

"You're not working?"

"I took the rest of the afternoon off to take you to lunch. I know it's kind of late, but I hoped you hadn't eaten yet." He checked his watch. "It's almost two. If you ate, how about an early dinner? I'll come back and pick you up in a couple of hours, but I can't promise I won't get called back to work."

"Um, I can't leave just yet. Noel is out. Mandi should be back from her break in about five minutes."

"So for the moment, we're alone?"

She nodded. He tugged her hand to make her lean over the counter, then he kissed her softly, letting her know how much he missed her. He eased away and fell back on his heels, pulling his aching calf.

Alina noticed his wince. "What's wrong?"

"I've been walking a lot today. My leg hurts."

"Did you pull the stitches?"

"No. It's just swollen and throbs like a sonofabitch."

Alina released his hand, walked to the door that separated the pharmacy shelves from the store, and came out and around to meet him. She took his hand again and guided him to the chairs they had lined against the wall.

"Sit. Pull up your jeans while I get an ice pack." She went to one of the rows of medical supplies, found what she wanted, and tore open the package as she walked back to him. She kneeled by his bandaged leg, cracked the instant ice pack, gently laid it against his calf, then tugged his jeans back over it to hold it in place.

She pulled the chair beside him out, turned it, and put it in front of him. He thought she'd sit. Instead, she propped his foot on it. "I have a few orders to fill before Noel returns. Relax. Don't answer your phone. We are going to lunch."

"Can I answer emails while I'm sitting on my ass freezing to death?"

She rolled her eyes. "If you want to."

"I want to pull you into my lap and kiss you senseless."

She brushed her hand over his hair. He leaned into her soft touch, feeling better already after a long day.

"That is my favorite thing to do, but I'm at work and anyone could walk in the door."

He tugged the edge of her white doctor's coat. "This whole professional thing is kind of a turn-on."

She laughed. "Maybe I'll wear it and nothing else for you tonight if you don't go back to work."

"Now that's all I'm going to picture every time I think about you."

She tilted her head up and laughed. Her hair spilled down her back. As he looked up at her with her face flushed and that wonderful joy coming out of her, he forgot to breathe. "God, you're beautiful."

She stepped close. He leaned his head against her ribs and breast. His body tightened with need at the same time everything eased inside of him. Her fingers brushed through his hair. He closed his eyes and savored the feel of her against him.

She gently laid his head back against the wall and stared down at him. "Rest. I won't be long."

His stomach grumbled. He hadn't eaten since late yesterday.

She giggled under her breath, went to the snack aisle, found him a pack of peanuts, and brought it to him. "Eat this." She leaned down and kissed him softly.

"You keep spoiling me like this, I might bump up the sandwich I planned to buy you for lunch to a burger."

"Ooh, maybe I'll work my way up to pizza."

"If you're a good girl."

And there was that laugh, her smile, and the lightness in his chest that erased even more of the tension he'd been carrying around the last two days.

"You keep smiling at me like that, making me feel like this, I think there's a steak in your future."

She shook her head and touched his face with her fingertips. "I'm really glad you're here."

"Nowhere I want to be more." He adjusted the ice pack on his leg before he got frostbite.

"Keep that on." She went back to the door to the back area, punched in a code, then went through to the long prep counter where she filled prescriptions, bagged them, and attached information pamphlets. Several customers came in to pick up their medication or buy other items from the store. Alina was polite, friendly, and efficient.

The front door dinged again. A young woman rushed in, purple hair tied on top of her head in wild disarray, blue butterfly tattoo on her neck, and thick black eyeliner highlighting her striking green eyes. She stopped short a few feet from him and backtracked several steps. "Whoa. Is something going on?"

"He's mine," Alina called out.

Purple-haired girl tilted her head. "Huh. I don't see the family resemblance."

"Boyfriend, not her brother," Jay supplied, hoping he hadn't overstepped.

The smile on Alina's face turned into a laugh when purple-haired girl gaped at Alina.

"When did this happen? Why don't I know about it? How come you don't make him sit in the lobby all the time so we can stare at him?" The very appreciative sweep of her gaze over him left him feeling both desirable and like a piece of meat.

"Mandi." The mild censure in Alina's voice didn't stop Mandi from ogling him for another uncomfortable moment. "Mandi," Alina shouted. "Meet Special Agent Jay Bennett. He works with my brothers."

"And he's yours," Mandi added with a teasing lilt to her voice. "You are so lucky."

"Hey, you have a super cute geek who adores you."

"Nothing beats tough guy with a badge, gun, and all those muscles."

Alina leaned over the counter and stared at him. "I know, right? And he left work early to take me to lunch."

Mandi sighed. "And he's nice, too."

Alina smiled. "It's awful, isn't it?"

"I hate you." She obviously didn't mean it and held her hand out to him. "Nice to meet you. While you seem really great, Alina is amazing. Keep being nice to her."

Jay wasn't fazed by the underlying threat in that order. He appreciated that Alina had a true friend in Mandi. "I plan to for a long time."

Mandi raised an eyebrow at Alina.

Alina didn't comment, but the soft blush pinking her cheeks did his heart good.

"I'm glad you're back. Noel should be here any minute. I've filled several orders, but I need you to pull some information for me. I haven't had time to get to it."

Mandi went through the side door and joined Alina. "What information?"

"I'm doing some research for the prescription drug abuse talk I gave last week. I want to expand on the content and get more precise opioid prescription stats. Are most prescriptions a one-time thing? What's the average time a prescription is refilled? Based on the prescriptions' descriptions, can we determine if, considering the conditions they were ordered for, another drug could have been used instead with similar results? Did the person actually need such strong, addictive medication in the first place?"

Mandi's eyes lit up. "I'm on it. I love data mining."

Alina shook her head as Mandi ran for the computer and started typing. "Her boyfriend isn't the only computer geek in that relationship. If I tried to sort all that information from our database, it would take me days and a lot of hair pulling."

Jay shook his head. "I have a feeling you would have gotten through it just fine."

Exceptionally smart, Alina had graduated with honors in less time than the average student. He had no doubt anything she set her mind to, she accomplished in good form.

"Hello, ladies," a man said from the back. "What are you looking at there, Mandi?"

"Schedule II drug prescriptions. Alina asked me to pull some information for her. Oh, and her DEA guy is here."

Jay stood, ignoring the pinch of pain in his calf, and went to the counter. He wanted a look at the guy who'd been instrumental in helping Alina get established and seemed to think that gave him an excuse to make her uncomfortable. His behavior seemed kind but hinted at an obsession Jay didn't like. It was Jay's job to worry about Alina. His job to protect her.

Noel's gaze shot to him, the gun and badge at his waist, then to Alina. "What is the meaning of this? You can't give out confidential information without a warrant." He focused back on Jay, but didn't look him in the eye. "Do you have a warrant?"

"All I need is her say-so." Before Noel sputtered out

another protest as his anger spread red up his neck to his ears, Jay added, "To take her to lunch."

Alina tilted her head and studied her partner. "Noel, Jay is a friend. He's not here on official business."

"Boyfriend," he corrected, wanting to get that point across to Noel. He also felt Alina's suspicion that Noel completely overreacted to his presence.

Alina continued to watch Noel. "Mandi is looking up statistics I can use for my prescription drug speech."

Noel deflated with a heavy sigh, his head sinking between his slumped shoulders. "Oh. That's okay then."

"You ready to go, sweetheart?" Jay's hunger and need to spend time with Alina overrode his reservations about the way Noel had acted.

Alina dismissed Noel, too, with a slight shake of her head. "Let me grab my purse." She walked to a back office and disappeared.

Noel approached him. "So you and Alina are seeing each other?"

Jay nodded. "We have been for a while now."

"Funny, she never mentioned you."

Jay took the jab in stride. "I'm sure she wants to keep her business and private life separate." And she probably didn't say anything to Noel because she didn't share those kinds of personal things with him.

"Still, it's interesting she wouldn't mention dating a DEA agent. I mean, her brothers are agents as well."

"They're friends. I work with them all the time."

"Oh. And they're okay with you dating their sister."

Nosy asshole. "They appreciated that I was there for Alina after her so-called accident last week."

Noel paled. "I thought the police concluded it was random."

"We'll see."

Noel's eyes widened. "You're investigating."

"Her brothers and I don't think someone running her off the road after he'd followed her for some distance is an accident. It seems targeted, don't you think?"

"Maybe seeing you is dangerous," Noel shot back.

Jay went fishing. "We think there's something else going on."

Noel shrugged it off despite his earlier deep concern for Alina. "Strange things happen all the time."

If Noel had a thing for Alina, Jay expected him to be outraged someone would target her. He expected the guy to demand they find the culprit, put him in a cell, and throw away the key. Instead, Jay got *things happen.*

Alina appeared without her white coat, her purse over her shoulder, looking very pretty in black slacks and a pink top that made her gray eyes look more blue and her hair appear black as night.

Noel stared at the back of Mandi's head as she worked on the computer, then went to Alina. "After all that's happened, maybe you should let me take over the drug talks."

Alina narrowed her eyes. "You asked me to do it so you'd have more time with Lee."

"You're doing too much. You need time to heal."

"I'm fine," she assured him and stepped around him. "I don't mind doing the talks. In fact, it's become very important to me. The community needs the help. Now, I'll be back in about an hour."

Jay took her hand as she came out of the side door. Walking with the ice pack stuffed up his pant leg made his limp more pronounced.

"What happened to you?" Noel called after them.

"Someone tried to blow me up."

Noel's shock almost made Jay laugh as he held the door open for Alina. They stepped out onto the sidewalk outside the pharmacy.

"That wasn't nice," she scolded him.

"What? It's the truth."

"Yeah, but now I'm going to have to answer a million questions when I get back."

"Maybe you should ask him why he got so paranoid and agitated when he saw a DEA agent in the store."

"You noticed that?"

He cocked an eyebrow at her. "What do you make of it?" He led her to his SUV, held the door open for her, closed it once she settled in the seat, and made his way around the car to the driver's side, climbed in and started the car. He drove them out of the lot.

He glanced over and caught her pensive stare. "Well, what's up with Noel?"

"I'm not sure. He's under a lot of stress because of his wife's illness. His daughters are away at school, but they seem to be doing okay even though Noel worries about them being out on their own."

"None of that has to do with his freak-out that you were pulling records and a DEA agent was present."

"As you know, Schedule II drugs are strictly regulated and monitored. We face hefty penalties and fines for errors or not reporting who and how much we dispense the drugs to, loss, and theft. We have to account for every pill in stock. With all he's facing with his wife, maybe he panicked because the last thing he needs is an investigation when we are so diligent about keeping accurate records."

Sounded reasonable. "Maybe."

"Did you know home burglaries are on the rise in this area? The robbers are targeting people's medicine cabinets."

"Well, the DEA has seized a huge portion of the street drugs people use instead of those prescription pills because they're cheaper. This weekend, we seized two thousand pounds of cocaine and seven hundred pounds of heroin before it hit the streets. In the last year, Caden and Beck have closed down a couple of meth labs that had enough volume to supply most of the state. Because of that, dealers need to find another means to get their product and feed the demand of their customers. Prescription pills go for a high price on the streets."

"Drugs do so much more damage than just to the user. Two people lost their lives in those break-ins."

Jay pulled into a parking spot outside Mia's restaurant, Cream of the Crop.

"We can't eat here." Alina sank down in the seat.

"Why not?"

"My sister-in-law will tell my brother that she saw us together."

"Alina, I hate to tell you this, but your brothers are top-notch investigators and figured out you and I are together at the wedding."

"What?"

"Well, they suspected something was going on. Beck asked me about it after you left me at the hospital."

"I didn't leave you."

He chuckled at her incredulous tone. "You know what I mean."

"Well, you're still in one piece, so I guess he didn't try to kill you."

"No. But he did ask me my intentions."

Alina rolled her eyes and groaned. "Oh God, how embarrassing. They make me feel like I'm fifteen and incapable of running my own life."

"They don't think that. They want you to be happy. Which is why after my talk with Beck he promised that he and Caden would back off and let us do this without their interference."

"Really?" At his nod, she added, "Well, that's unexpected. What did you say to him?"

"That you and I want the same thing." He took her hand, brought it to his lips, and kissed her palm. "I told him, I need you. You make me smile and laugh and want all those things I put off for someday right now. When I'm not with you, all I want to do is be with you."

Tears gathered in her eyes. "Oh, Jay."

"No crying. Mia will see, she'll call Caden, and I will be dead."

"If the guys are going to stay out of this, let's keep them out of it, too."

"Deal." He opened the door and slid out. He meant to open the door for her, but she met him at the front of the car and walked right into his arms, went up on her toes, and kissed him. "What you said, it means everything to me." She kissed him again, then fell to her flat feet and smiled up at him. His chest swelled with emotion as he returned her smile.

"You guys are adorable." Mia stood between the parked cars, phone held up as she took their picture.

"What are you doing?" Alina asked.

"Sending this to Caden to show him his radiant sister with a caption that says, *The happy couple.*"

"You should mark it, *First official date.*"

Mia beamed. "And you chose my place. That's so sweet."

"Jay picked the place. And, yes, it is sweet."

Jay tried to hold back the sheepish grin. "They say they'll stay out of this, but they won't. Might as well embrace it. And eat. Please. I'm dying."

Alina pushed him toward the door. "Let's go. Two thick, grass-fed beef burgers, stat!"

"Do you want your usual fried zucchini?" Mia asked Alina.

"Please tell me you made that awesome ranch with the little bits of red onion."

Mia laughed at the pure desperation in Alina's voice. "Just the way you like it."

Alina sat across from him at the table near the kitchen. "Thick and creamy."

"As always. What can I get you to drink?"

"Iced tea," they said in unison with a laugh. "No lemon," they added at the same time.

"Jinx," Mia said for them. "Coming right up."

Jay reached across the table, took Alina's hand, and tugged her forward so he could kiss her palm and lay it against his cheek. Her smile set off a wave of flutters in his belly and made him wonder why he hadn't taken her to his place for something much more intimate and private. "I finally have you alone."

"Did you miss me?" The teasing tone didn't hide how much his answer meant to her.

"More than I can say."

"From all the drugs you seized, it sounds like you got a lot done."

"I did, but . . ."

"What?" She read something in the way he stared at her, hoping what he said next didn't frighten her off again. "Jay, you can say anything to me."

"I tried to stay busy, but it kept coming back to me at odd moments."

"The explosion?"

"Yeah. It came out of nowhere. All I could think was that I finally had a woman I wanted, more than anything, in my home and I wasn't going to make it back to her."

Alina squeezed his hand. "You made it. And I'm right here."

"In those moments, I wanted you to be there. I wanted to hold on to you and convince myself you're real. This is real." Jay never opened up like this with anyone. He and the guys joked, teased, told crude and inappropriate jokes to deal with the things they did and saw on the job. They held it in and coped with distraction. Some guys drank to dull the pain and blur the gruesome images in their heads. Others lost themselves in family life, ignoring the problem altogether. Some of the guys had become real adrenaline junkies. Others worked out, boxed, whatever to spend the excess energy and aggression that masked the pain they were in.

Jay usually found comfort at home on his ranch, riding his horse out on the open land where he could think and regroup. The last two days, he'd found he didn't want that ride, the solitude to brood and feel all the emotions he didn't share with others. He just wanted to be with Alina. She'd listen. She'd understand. She'd do what she was doing now and hold his hand and offer comfort. With her, he'd find a way to breathe through the bad.

Alina rose from her chair and came around the table. He sat back and she plopped right into his lap. Her arm hooked around his neck and drew him in for a hug. He wrapped his arms around her.

"Next time you need me, call me. You don't have to say anything, you don't have to give me all the details. I'll do all the talking if you want me to, or I can just be quiet with you."

That's exactly what he'd wanted. Someone there to fill the silence with their presence and understanding.

He held her closer and sat with her, ignoring the stares from the other customers. He inhaled her sweet citrus and honey scent, breathed, and reminded himself that bomb almost ended his life, but he had a damn good reason to live now.

"Everything okay?" Mia set their drinks on the table and eyed them warily.

Alina stared up at Mia. "I needed a hug. It's been a rough couple of days."

Jay silently thanked Alina with a squeeze for not out-ing him for being the one who needed the hug because some days his job was harder than others.

Mia nodded. "You two make a pair. Your bruises from the accident are fading and his are fresh. That gash on your head looks bad." Mia pointed to the line of stitches near his hairline.

Jay absently touched them. "They itch."

"The leg is worse, I take it. You're limping a lot."

Jay reached down, pulled his pant leg up, and pulled the warm ice pack out. "Mind dumping that in the trash?" He pushed his pant leg down.

Mia went back to the kitchen. Alina kissed him long and soft. Nothing too sexy because they were in the mid-dle of a crowded restaurant, but enough to let him know the heat between them hadn't dimmed. She slipped off his lap and took her seat again.

"So, we have an agreement?"

He liked that about her. She didn't let him get away with telling her he needed something without getting his promise that he'd follow through on it. "Yes. I'll call you."

"It's more than that, Jay. I want you to be honest when things are rough. I can take it. I want to be there for you. The last thing I want is to see that broken-soul look I saw in Beck all those months he worked one undercover case after another and suffered so many tragedies. You can't keep that all inside."

Jay didn't face the kinds of things Beck had faced undercover, but he did see some pretty bad shit. There always came a point where you just couldn't deal with any more of it. "I won't keep things from you."

Though it might be better. She'd been angry that he'd gotten hurt on the job. That wasn't what his father had done to his mother. He'd lost himself in work and the silence, isolating himself because he didn't want to burden Jay's mother with those terrible things. Maybe if his father had told her, not the gory details, but how his work affected him, they'd have grown closer. Maybe his mother would have felt needed instead of cast aside because of his father's demons.

Jay wanted to bring Alina into his world and give her a reason to stay.

Alina set her purse on the table, dug through it, and pulled out her bottle of pain meds. She twisted off the top and dumped a pill into her hand.

Concerned, he leaned forward on his arms and studied her. "I thought you were feeling better."

Alina stared across the table at him, her eyes going to the cut on his head, the bruises on his face, the stiffness he couldn't hide in his shoulders. "You need this more than I do."

Jay shook his head. "I took a couple ibuprofen before I picked you up. I'm good." Stiff, sore, but he didn't need the heavy-duty pain meds clouding his mind. Not when he might have to go back to work.

Alina dumped the pill back in the bottle and stuffed them into her purse. She leaned forward on her elbows, slid her fingers into her hair, and held her head as she stared at the table.

"Alina? What is it?"

"My ribs and shoulder are still sore, but nothing compared to what you must feel right now."

"Your accident was only a few days ago. You're still healing." He pointed out the obvious, not understanding the anger in her eyes.

"I don't need these meds."

"If you're in pain—"

"You're in pain. I've got what amounts to a dull ache. But because the doctor prescribed the meds, I simply pulled them out to take them without any thought to whether or not I needed something this powerful."

Jay placed his hand over hers. "Alina, it's okay. You're working on that drug talk, you're connected to the DEA, you see people come into the pharmacy in desperate need for these drugs. You're oversensitive to the issue and putting undo pressure on yourself."

She turned her hand under his and held on. "All true, but that doesn't discount the fact that just now I kind of felt an urge to take the pill before the last one truly wore off. Because I don't want to feel the pain? Or because I want to feel the way the pill makes me feel? That's different, Jay. That's how people get hooked."

"Not you. You're too smart for that."

"Drugs don't care if you're smart, or strong, or good, or bad. Nothing about who I am changes the fact I reached for a pill to make me feel better when I don't really need it."

Jay asked the hard question. "Can you stop taking them?"

She sighed and smiled at him. "Yes. Without a doubt. I just had a moment where it all became clear how some people can fall down that slippery slope without even thinking about it, or realizing it's happening. That's all. I don't need them. I'm not taking any more." She squeezed his hand, her eyes clear with intent and the truth. She was okay.

Mia delivered their thick burgers. "Are you two always this intense?"

Jay laughed with Alina and it did them both good and helped them ease back into enjoying their time together. "We're good together."

Alina nodded to reassure Mia.

"Enjoy, guys."

Jay dredged a hot French fry through Alina's ranch

dressing and stuffed it in his mouth. She was right about the dressing. "I know you have to go back to work after this, but will you come to my place tonight?"

"Want me to bring dinner?"

He shook his head. "I'll make you dinner."

"Even better." Her eyes filled with excitement and anticipation that had more to do with him than the fried zucchini she devoured.

"Will you stay over? I promise you'll be up early enough to get to work on time."

"But will I get any sleep?" A spark of devilment shone in her eyes.

He reached across the table and traced her arm, elbow to wrist, his fingers sliding over her soft, bare skin, making her shiver. "That, I can't promise."

CHAPTER TWENTY-FIVE

Alina walked into the house later that night to the soft glow of candlelight in the dining room casting the rest of the house in shadows. Red roses filled a crystal bowl on the table. Their heady scent filled the air, intoxicating her. He'd set two places with white dishes, antique silverware he'd mentioned his grandmother left him, crystal wineglasses, and a platter with grilled pork chops and potatoes and onions. Next to it sat a big bowl of salad.

"Jay, you did all this for me?"

"I told you I can't cook. But I can grill. I wanted to do something nice for you. And me," he admitted.

After they'd both been through traumatic ordeals, she understood his desire to indulge in something good. "It's lovely."

He took her hand and led her to the table and held out her chair so she could sit. She did. He took his seat at the head of the table and served her first, filling her plate with the garlicky potatoes and onions, then plopped one of the thick chops down in the center of her plate. She served herself the salad and added some to his plate.

He poured the wine and held up his glass to her. "Good food, better wine, and a beautiful woman by my side. The perfect night."

"You're sweet." She felt the same about spending a

quiet evening with him. She clinked her glass to his, then sipped the fruity, light rosé.

She didn't want to talk about work. His or hers. She wanted tonight to be about getting to know him better.

"Tell me something I don't know about you that you normally wouldn't tell anyone."

He stared at her for a long moment, then decided to play along. "You ready for this?"

She took another sip of wine and stared right back at him. "Lay it on me."

"I have like a thousand channels on my TV."

"Please don't tell me you're a die-hard Housewives of whatever fan. Seriously, this will be over. That's a deal breaker."

He chuckled. "Worse."

"Not *The Bachelor*. Please don't say *The Bachelor*."

"No. Not that either. The dog channel."

"The what? Huh?"

"There's a channel you can leave on for your dog. It's all these dogs doing different things. Chasing balls, wandering around outside, stuff like that. I like to watch it."

"Like cat videos." She sighed her relief that it wasn't some mindless train wreck where people did stupid things and were mean to each other for ratings.

Why can't people just be nice? The world needed more nice.

"Sometimes those dogs really crack me up."

She laughed under her breath and finished off another perfectly cooked and just the right amount of crunchy and soft potato. "Why don't you get a dog?"

"I'd love one, but leaving it alone for hours on end isn't fair to the dog. My horse doesn't seem to mind, but a dog is a social animal. They need their human friends."

"I am learning so much about you. Big, bad DEA tough guy is a softy."

"Because I don't want to abuse a dog?"

"Because you care about his feelings. That's so sweet." She laughed even harder at his incredulous frown.

"What do you like to watch?"

"Home and garden shows. I love how they take something old, worn, and neglected and make it functional and pretty again. Mostly, I like movies."

"Let me guess, romantic comedies."

She had no qualms about admitting that one. "Love is a part of life. I don't know why guys are always so down on a love story."

"I don't mind a love story as long as something blows up."

She propped her elbow on the table and planted her chin in her palm and stared at him. "Like our love story?"

He leaned in and kissed her softly, tasting of garlic and wine. "Now, that's my favorite story."

"Does it have a happy ending?"

"It does tonight because I get to spend it with you making love."

"My favorite part." She leaned back and took another sip of wine. "What about six months from now?"

He chewed and contemplated her for a good long moment that made her both nervous and anxious. "In six months? Well, by then you'll live here, have my ring on your finger, and the wedding will be no more than a few days away."

She gaped at him.

He leaned in to her again. "How does that sound to you?"

"Like there are still a lot of pages of this love story to be written to get there." She glanced around the candlelit room, the pretty table he'd set, the wonderful food they'd shared, and the man she loved more each day, though she still hadn't told him. She thought about their lunch earlier, how he'd opened up to her, dropped his walls, and let her into his world and his pain. She'd never felt closer to anyone. "If the days between now and then are like this, that's a reality I can't wait to see happen."

Jay held his glass out to hers. She clinked hers to his in a toast to the future they both wanted.

Jay yawned for the third time during dinner. "Sorry. I barely slept last night."

"Missing me?"

"Desperately."

They'd both done justice to the fine meal he'd prepared. She stood, took his hand, and tugged. "Come with me."

He stood and gave her a roguish smile. "Are we going to sleep?"

"Eventually." She blew out candles as they left the dining room and headed for bed. With every step, her heart beat faster, the warm flutter in her lower belly grew hotter, and every nerve sparked to life. And he hadn't even touched her yet.

She walked into the room ahead of him, but he stopped short, pulled her hand, and she swung around and rushed into his open arms as he leaned down for a searing kiss that turned the heat in her belly into a volcano of need.

"Are your neck and shoulder still bothering you?" he asked against her lips.

"Not much. You? How's your head, shoulder, and leg?"

"All I feel is drunk on you."

His hands slid down her sides, over her hips, and around to cup her bottom in both his hands. He pulled her up hard against his erection.

She rubbed against him, getting the growl of need she wanted.

Clothes fell off and went flying. Naked, Jay wrapped

an arm around her back, hauled her up so her chest pressed to his and she wrapped her legs around his waist, his thick cock pressed to her core. His big hand clamped onto her ass. He moved her up and down his length, driving them both crazy. He limped to the bed, though his strength never wavered. His steely arm around her, he laid her out on the bed and pressed her into the mattress with his warm, hard body. Hands free, she let them roam over every sculpted muscle down his arms, over his back, and up his rippled belly to his wide chest.

He left her mouth and headed south, nipping at her neck and over her chest. She arched up and he found one of the nipples she'd offered up to him. His mouth suckled softly, then hard, sending a lightning strike of fire to where she wanted him to touch her next. She didn't need to ask, his seeking hand slid down her side, over her hip, and dipped low between her legs. His fingers caressed her soft, slick folds. One, then two slid into her. She rocked into his hand, sliding her fingers through his dark hair and holding him to her breast as he drove her wild with need.

"Jay."

He reached for the bedside drawer and a condom without stopping the sweet torment, his fingers working deep inside her, bringing her up to the brink and holding her there. Just about to come apart, he withdrew his hand and thrust into her. Her whole body contracted, then let loose in a wave of ecstasy. He held still, jaw locked, as her body contracted around his. The second her body began to relax, he moved, sliding out, then filling her again. He leaned down and kissed her hard and deep, then wrapped his arm around her waist, held her hips locked to his, and rolled over, bringing her on top of him.

He kissed her again, then stared up at her. "That hurts my leg. Ride me, sweetheart."

She straddled him, rocked her hips forward and back. His eyes closed on a sigh. She slid her tongue along his bottom lip and nipped his chin. She sat up, raised herself up on her knees, sank back onto his hard shaft, and rolled her hips against his. His hands clamped onto her bottom, but he let her lead the dance. She found her rhythm and a kind of freedom she'd never felt in his arms. She let go, pleased him while she pleased herself, finding that perfect spot, just the right amount of friction and speed. He read her movements, her body's needs, and moved with her and against her until both of them were breathing hard, drawing out every stroke of their bodies moving in concert. She grabbed one of his hands and moved it to her swollen breast. He squeezed the soft globe and gently tugged her nipple between two fingers, setting off a wave of heat that had her grinding against him, her body locking around his. He thrust into her deep and they both let go and fell over the edge into blinding bliss.

She rode out the pulsing pump of his body and the contractions of hers until she collapsed on top of him in a puddle of contentment.

Somehow he found the strength to move and wrapped her in his arms and hugged her close. His chest heaved with every breath, but he planted a soft kiss on her head. She fell asleep on him, still connected and heart to heart and woke up snuggled against his side, his arm still around her. Dawn had barely broken through the dark on a new day when her mind formed one thought: *I want to stay right here forever.* And her heart agreed.

She needed to go home, work out, shower, and get ready for work. First, she wanted to do something as nice for Jay as he'd done for her last night.

She slipped from the bed and dressed quietly, then headed back to the kitchen, stopping in the dining room to gather the dirty dishes and wasted leftovers. She cleaned up the mess and went to the fridge, hoping to find what she needed. He might not cook much, but he did manage to stock eggs, cheese, and a jar of salsa. She could work with that. First, she found the coffee, scooped some into the machine, poured in the water, and hit the brew button. By the time it started dribbling into the pot, she had three eggs cracked and scrambled in a pan. A little salt and pepper, a dash of garlic powder and parsley flakes she found in the spice rack, and she flipped the eggs, added cheese and a healthy dollop of salsa, and folded the concoction in half to heat through and melt the cheese. One last flip and she turned off the burner. She poured a mug of coffee, plated the omelet, and took both with her back through the house and down the hall to Jay's bedroom. Their bedroom.

Thinking about this as their place got easier and more comfortable the longer she spent here. And it had only been a few days. Things were happening fast. And still felt not fast enough.

She set the plate and mug on the bedside table, planted her hands on the bed, and leaned down and kissed Jay on the forehead, brushing her fingers through his hair and down over his scruffy jaw. She absently played with the silver strands sprinkled just over his ears.

"I think I got a few more gray hairs when I heard about your accident."

She stared down at him and smiled. "Morning."

"Why aren't you in bed? Do I smell coffee?"

"Sit up."

"Hmm, first, this." He hooked his hand around her neck and drew her down for a soft kiss. "Morning."

She raked her fingers through his hair and ruffled it into an even messier array of sun-bleached, silver-threaded brown waves. "I have to go."

"I want you to stay."

"I know. But it's a long drive back and I can't be late for work. I open. Plus, I have some research to do on those printouts Mandi downloaded. But before I go, I made you this." She took the plate and mug from the table and held them out to him.

Jay sat up and bunched the pillows behind him all at once. His wide gaze met hers. "You made me breakfast."

"You probably have another long day ahead of you. You should eat a good breakfast before you head into work."

Jay took the plate and mug, sipped the coffee, and sighed. He stared down at the omelet like he'd never seen one.

"It's nothing much, just a little cheese and salsa."

Jay looked up at her, his eyes filled with wonder and gratitude. "Thank you, Alina. No one has ever made me breakfast in bed. I wish you could stay and enjoy this with me."

Her chest ached with that heartfelt thank-you. She leaned in, planted her hand on his bare chest over his heart, and kissed him one more time, holding back the happy tears glassing over her eyes. "I wish I could stay, too, but I'll see you soon."

"Uh, one of my other cases is heating up. I don't know how late I'll be."

She nodded, understanding all he couldn't say, because he didn't know how his day would go and what it would lead to later. "I'll see you soon." She headed for the door, but stopped and turned back when he called her.

"Alina." He paused, trying to find the words. "Last night, this morning"—he nodded to the plate in his lap—"it was really good, right?"

Obviously feeling like her, this thing they shared was

so intense and they both wanted it to be that thing they'd always wanted but never found. Until now. "It was perfect."

His soft, understanding smile knotted her belly.

"No woman should ever leave a man as sexy as you in bed alone."

The wolfish grin he gave her and the intensity of heat in his bourbon eyes sent a blast of heat low in her belly.

"I'm going to really regret this, but I have to go." She turned for the door before she gave in to the overwhelming pull and dove for him in that big bed.

"Alina."

She turned back again, caught in the intensity of his stare.

"I . . ."

She held her breath, waiting to see if he'd say those three words they'd expressed but never spoken aloud.

"I'll call you later."

The disappointment stunned her. In the past, she'd heard those words and so wanted to believe them. Other times, she prayed the other person wouldn't say them so she didn't have to let him down gently because she didn't feel the same. Now, she couldn't wait to hear them. From him.

Was she ready to tell him?

Soon. They were well on their way.

"Please be careful today. Keep your guard up. We still don't have a definitive answer on your car accident."

"I will. Promise. And I'd kind of like you back in one piece, so work on that today, too." This time when she turned away, his soft chuckle followed her out the door.

She glanced back, but kept walking down the hall, and stared at the man she never expected to show up and become such an important piece of her life in the blink of an eye.

One night.

One bad idea that had turned out to be so right.

She'd taken a risk and found everything she'd ever wanted in this unexpected man.

Temptation led her down this path and she'd found love. The real kind.

The kind that grows deeper every day.

The kind that lasts.

CHAPTER TWENTY-SIX

Alina felt so good she couldn't contain her smile all day. The hours at work flew by until it was almost time to go home. Jay, sweet Jay, sent her a text message this morning telling her he missed her. She'd only left him naked with breakfast in bed an hour before that. At lunchtime, he called just to say hi and let her know he probably didn't have to work late tonight.

She couldn't wait to see him.

"You get any happier, you're going to float like a helium balloon," Mandi teased.

She hadn't felt this light and happy in a long time.

Mandi leaned over Alina's shoulder and stared at the reports Alina had been sorting through for the last few minutes. "Did you see how long some of our customers have been taking those painkillers?"

"One of them has been on them for more than three years." Alina couldn't imagine being in that much pain that she'd need a steady dose of drugs for that long. And to live in that state of pain and numbing from drugs that had their own side effects.

Long-term use meant you needed a higher dose to achieve the same level of relief you got in the beginning. Not to mention the risk of damaging your liver, living with symptoms like nausea, bloating, constipation, and even more dangerous, respiratory depression, which could lead to hypoxia due to lack of oxygen.

"Some of these customers are on multiple drugs to counteract side effects. The longer the drug tries to hide the pain, the harder the body works to send the pain signal to the brain. They become more sensitive to the pain and need a higher dose to mask it. A few of these customers are taking Fentanyl. It's fifty times more powerful than heroin. Two milligrams can kill. The potential for overdose and death is so much greater than these other painkillers."

"Jeez." Mandi shook her head. "Makes you wonder if in a lot of these cases the underlying cause of the pain was ever really addressed in the first place."

Alina thought of her own situation. Did she really need such a powerful drug after her accident? Maybe for a day or two, but she'd had a real gut check at lunch with Jay when she found herself popping them when the pain had been a mere shadow of what she'd endured right after the accident.

Were others as aware as her of the dangers? Did they taper off when the pain subsided? Or did they take the meds as prescribed, not really thinking about it, then find themselves needing more? And more. How often did that scenario play out and ruin lives?

Mandi tapped the list with her silver-painted nail. "Mr. Woodward suffered a back injury in the winter shoveling snow. Maybe it was a pulled muscle, maybe something worse. But he's been taking those pills for months now. Maybe what he needs is physical therapy."

Alina pointed to another name. "This patient is seventy-three and she's been on them for fifteen months. Odd, looks like she had to renew the same prescription five months ago two days after she picked up her order. She must have lost her pills or something."

Mandi peeked over her shoulder. "Mrs. Green? She had a hip replacement last year. Never did feel right, she said. But what's even stranger is that she died three months ago in a home invasion burglary."

"Oh my God. That's awful. But if she passed away, who refilled her prescription the last two months?"

"I don't know. Someone in the family trying to get them for themselves?"

Alina pulled up her browser and did a quick search on Mrs. Green. Her obituary and a news article about the robbery and her death came up. "She suffered a major head injury after she was pistol-whipped by the burglar. You know, I listened to a podcast about burglaries like this on the rise. The burglars aren't looking for valuables, but prescription medications."

Mandi rolled her green eyes. "I don't doubt it. There's been a rise in teens having pill parties, too. They raid their parents' medicine cabinets, bring the pills to the party, and everyone picks pills from a pile. They don't even really know what they're taking."

"Or what could happen to them if they take too much or have an adverse effect to the drug. They're literally playing with their lives all for a high."

"Stupid, but that is the reality with the rise of painkillers being so widely prescribed."

Alina read the article and found the name of the other person killed during a similar robbery. Something nagged at her. She scanned the list of customers and found Mr. Ramos. "Mandi, look. Mr. Ramos died four months ago, but his prescription has been renewed every month since, too."

"That's weird. I remember him. He was a widow. His wife died of breast cancer last April. I forget what happened to him but a few months after that he got hurt on the job and ended up on disability."

Mandi found Mr. Ramos's wife in the files. "Amy Ramos. She's been renewing three different medications every month since last April when she passed."

Something didn't make sense.

She and Mandi both jumped at the sound of Noel's voice. "What are you guys working on?"

Alina put a hand on Mandi's arm to keep her quiet. "The research for my prescription drug talk. We were discussing how many customers have been on painkillers long-term."

Noel shrugged. "Sad, really. Long-term use of the drugs probably causes more problems than the reason they were originally prescribed them in the first place." Noel glanced down at his jacket covering his hands, then quickly back to her and Mandi.

His overt casual manner, hands clasped in front of him with his jacket draped over them, sparked her curiosity.

"I was prescribed ten days of Dilaudid after my car accident."

"You were severely injured." He studied the way she held herself without turning her neck too much. "You took the brace off your neck. You still look sore, but you heal quickly." Noel reached with one hand to touch her. The coat slipped, making something in his other hand crinkle. Noel snatched his hand back and buried it under the coat again.

What was he hiding?

"After a few days, a couple of Advil has been enough to see me through. I didn't need that many narcotics. Some people may think they need to continue to take the prescription even though a less addictive and milder medicine would work for them once the initial pain subsides."

"It's something the medical community is trying to address, but they still have a long way to go." Noel glanced over the reports in front of her and the article on her screen. "Looks like you're putting together a comprehensive class for your next talk. The community will benefit from your dedication."

"I'd like to talk to you about working with the DEA to do a take-back program here, so anyone with unused drugs in the home can bring them in for proper disposal. Mandi was telling me about the rise of teens stealing medications from their parents. Something like this could help educate parents and get deadly drugs out of children's hands."

Noel's lips pressed tight. "You know, when I gave you this project, I didn't think you'd take it this far."

Alina raised an eyebrow at the tone. "What do you mean?"

Noel shook his head. "You're still recovering. I never expected you to spend this much time and effort on this. I'll take it back and do the next talk. I'm sure you've got better things to do with your time."

"This is important, Noel. The epidemic in the state is growing."

"People are dying," Mandi added, her incredulous tone matching her narrowed, black-lined gaze.

Distracted, Noel didn't seem to hear them. He checked the time on the clock hanging on the back wall for the fourth time. "I'm late. I said I'll do it. Leave all this on my desk. I'll go through it later and use what's relevant. You're off the project." With that emphatic statement, he practically ran for the door. "I'll see you both tomorrow."

Did he really think she'd drop this?

"What is up with him?" Mandi shook her head, sending her purple hair swishing back and forth.

"I don't know." But Alina wanted to know what he had in the white paper bag he'd been hiding under his coat. She didn't want to believe it was filled with bottles of pills, but it sure did look like it.

Maybe they were prescriptions for his wife.

The bell over the front door dinged. Mandi went to help the customer. Alina had filled all the prescriptions for today's orders while Noel worked on orders that required phone calls to insurance companies and doctors. She hadn't seen anything for Lee, but that didn't mean Noel hadn't filled it himself.

She pulled up Lee's name on the computer. The last prescription refill had been two weeks ago. None of the prescriptions were due to be refilled for a few more weeks.

So, what was in the bag? Why hide it?

Maybe being hyperaware these last few days had made her paranoid and she was looking for things that didn't exist. But the knot in her gut and the little nagging voice in her head said she should pay attention. It wasn't nothing.

Noel had been kind, attentive, even overly protective of her the last few days. Something about her doing all this research made him uneasy. Why?

She stared at the article about Mrs. Green and thought about the prescriptions refilled after her death and Mr. and Mrs. Ramos's.

Why were dead customers getting prescription refills?

They weren't the same kind of painkillers, but in the same Schedule II class. If they died, why was the doctor still prescribing medicine for them? Who was picking it up? Did the doctors know the prescriptions were still being filled?

She pulled up Mrs. Green's information and called the doctor's number.

"Eastside Medical, this is Fran, how can I help you?"

"Hi, Fran, this is Dr. Cooke at Vista Pharmacy. I'm

calling regarding Mrs. Evelyn Green. Can you tell me the last time Dr. Mitchell prescribed her medication?"

"Oh dear. Mrs. Green shows as deceased in our system. Dr. Mitchell last prescribed her medicine over three months ago."

"Thank you, Fran. I'll update our records." Alina hung up, but didn't change the record in her system. Instead, she pulled up Mr. and Mrs. Ramos's files and called their doctors and got the same results: the doctors had not written prescriptions for them after their deaths.

So, the doctors weren't in on the scheme. But what exactly was happening? Before she accused Noel—she didn't suspect Mandi, who hadn't shown any reservation about pulling all the records—she needed to gather more evidence. Those drugs were highly regulated. If Noel found a way to game the system, make it look like doctors were prescribing medications when they weren't, then he'd put his life, hers, and their business in serious jeopardy.

The disturbing thought twisted her gut.

She needed to move fast. Noel wanted her to stop working on the project. He didn't want her to uncover his scheme. If Noel got caught before she went to the authorities herself, they may never believe she had nothing to do with this.

But was she right?

She hoped not. But she needed to keep digging. The business and her life were on the line. She didn't want to go to jail for something she didn't do.

"Alina, are you okay? You look a little green."

"Uh, I'm okay."

"It's really sad those people lost their lives during something as stupid as a burglary. Don't people have anything better to do than steal from old ladies and widowers? Seriously. Try not to let it bother you so much."

Mandi patted her shoulder and went to help another customer.

Alina wanted to dig deeper, but the bell over the door dinged again. Another customer. The start of people streaming in after work to pick up their prescriptions before closing.

By the time they locked the door for the night, Alina was tired and feeling the weight of her suspicions.

She went back to her desk, thinking about how best to tackle the problem, when her cell chimed with a text.

JAY: Meet me at Pizza Party on 7th St.
ALINA: When?

Jay and pizza sounded better than digging through data. And yes, she admitted, she feared what else she'd find and what that would mean to her future. And Noel's. Procrastination was just a form of hiding and not facing the hard truth. Maybe she should stay.

Her phone interrupted her swirling thoughts.

JAY: Now! I miss you.

So sweet. And a much better way to spend the evening than blowing up her life. She thought of Noel's sick and dying wife and her stomach dropped. Poor Lee. If what Alina thought was true, Lee would be devastated.

ALINA: Order me a beer. Bacon, tomato, green
onion pizza. Be there in 10.
JAY: You got it.
JAY: And me.

Alina smiled for the first time in the last two hours. He was hers.

She had a boyfriend and a date. A couple weeks ago, she didn't have either. She grabbed her purse, left her troubles for tomorrow stashed under some files in her desk drawer, and went to join the one person sure to keep a smile on her face.

CHAPTER TWENTY-SEVEN

Noel drove to the head of the hiking trail on the outskirts of town and parked in the dirt lot with his car facing out so he could leave in a rush. He didn't want to spend any more time with these guys than necessary. This late in the afternoon, only two other cars were in the lot. Their drivers probably still on the trail, but they'd return soon.

With the car off, the interior became stifling. He rolled down the front windows, hoping the soft breeze would cool him off and ease his frayed nerves. Sweat dripped down the side of his face. He wanted to believe it had only to do with the rising heat in the car, but anxiety held him in a state of turmoil.

Lee wanted him to spend more time at home. They'd had to hire a part-time nurse to care for her during the day. Another added expense to the growing number of bills. He wanted to be there for her, but he couldn't stand to see her wasting away each day, dying right before his eyes.

He wanted to end this bad business with Brian.

To top it off, he feared Alina might inadvertently stumble on his operation while researching for her pet project. He told her he'd take it back, but she wasn't the kind of person to easily let things go.

He should have never suggested she give the talk at

the community center. His reaction at the pharmacy sparked her suspicions. If he pushed any harder for her to let him take the project back, it would look even more like he was trying to hide something.

It had been so easy to hide from Mandi. She did her job, took her paycheck, and lived her life without questioning anything. Alina had a deep need to help people. She sympathized with customers. Her empathy for them shone through. They loved her. He loved her for it.

But if she kept digging and putting pieces together, he'd have to do something. What, he didn't know.

He couldn't fire her, she owned a piece of the business, but he'd made sure whatever they found on him, implicated her.

He hated to threaten her, but if it came to that . . . Desperate times . . .

He hoped she kept her nose out of his business and stuck to doing her job from now on.

The drug take-back program had nearly made him heave when she brought it up. That meant the DEA. But maybe he could use it to his advantage. Take in the pills, covertly hold some back for his side business, and come out looking like a community member who cared, an advocate for taking dangerous drugs off the street, and a friend of the DEA and their efforts. Maybe then, they wouldn't look too closely at him if a hint of what he was doing came to light.

Brian pulled into the lot and stopped in front of his car, blocking him in.

So much for a quick getaway if he needed one. Why had he ever thought it a good idea to partner with a drug dealer who enjoyed being a thug? He might be able to bend Alina to his will if need be, but he couldn't control Brian.

Brian and Davy climbed out of the truck. Brian came

to the driver's window. Davy leaned in the passenger side.

"What's up, Doc?"

Davy laughed at Brian's Bugs Bunny imitation. Both their eyes were dilated and red-rimmed. Higher than kites, they gave him dopey smiles. The smell of stale cigarette smoke and pungent marijuana wafted into the car. Strong as it was, he might get a contact high. The stench made him scrunch his nose and feel light-headed.

Brian held out his hand. "What do you have for me today?"

Noel handed over the white paper bag filled with bottles of pills.

Brian dug through the bag, moving the bottles around, and reading their labels. "A little light, but nice. Where's the list?"

"Not this time."

Brian narrowed his eyes. "We have a deal. I'll have this sold in the next day or two. We need more product."

"My partner has become aware of the rising number of break-ins in town."

"Nosy bitch," Davy spat out, then stared across him at Brian. "You should have killed her."

"If she can't keep her nose out of our business, I'll do just that."

The matter-of-fact tone sent chills up Noel's back a split second before fury ripped through his system as suspicion became truth. "It was you! You ran her off the road!"

Noel lost his head and shoved Brian's shoulder. He tried to open the car door, but Brian planted his hands on the edge and held it closed.

"Knock it off, Doc."

Brian held the door closed with one hand and pulled his phone out with the other. He thumbed the screen a couple times and held the phone up. "You don't want this to be you."

Noel gasped at the photo of Alina slumped in the front seat of her wrecked car, head bowed toward the deflated airbag.

Brian glanced at the picture. "She saw us together. She knows 'who.' Now she's looking for 'why.' Get her to back off, or else."

"She doesn't know anything, you idiot. You want me to cooperate and keep the supply coming, leave her alone. She's not looking for us, she's looking into prescription drug abuse."

"Do-gooder." Davy didn't sound impressed.

Noel fumed. "Leave her alone before you give her a reason to look harder into who tried to kill her. Stick to business. The DEA finally backed off the accident. Let's keep it that way. I'll keep an eye on my partner and handle her if she needs handling."

Brian tucked the phone away. "Told you it was a bad idea to bring someone else into your business."

"Yeah, well, I needed her money to keep it. You go after her again, her DEA boyfriend and brothers will either kill us or lock us up. So don't be stupid. Stick to business and steer clear of the pharmacy from now on." This time, Noel held out his hand to Brian.

Brian stood, dipped his hand deep into his front pocket, and pulled out a wad of cash. He leaned down by the window again, slapped the money into Noel's hand, then held tight. "Careful, Doc, you get caught by that sweet piece of ass you want to keep all to yourself, I'll cut you down before I let you rat me out."

Noel jerked his hand back, barely gave a glance to the thick bundle of money in his hand, and swung his gaze back to the man who'd just threatened him. Brian would kill him. If he tried to put a stop to the business, if he got caught, if there was any indication that Noel's existence meant jail for Brian, he was dead. He wouldn't be the first person to lose their life at Brian's hands. The deaths during the robberies weighed on Noel's heart.

Another fat bead of sweat ran down his face. He needed to leave before this meeting turned even more hostile. No telling what Brian and Davy would do when stoned.

"We'll meet again next week."

Brian frowned and shook his head. "That's too far away. I need that list. Business is picking up."

"You'll have to wait. It's too risky to get it right now."

"Because of your pretty partner?" Davy stared hard at him.

"We need to be smart. Give me a few days to be sure we're in the clear."

"Why wouldn't we be?" Brian grabbed his shirt. "Does she suspect something already?"

"After you ran her off the road and nearly killed her, she's cautious, looking for a reason it happened. That's on you."

"You said the cops don't have anything."

"They don't. At this point, I don't think they'll ever tie it to you."

Brian released him. "You're getting as paranoid as this one"—Brian pointed to Davy—"when he's high."

"You're probably right, but it's better to be cautious than reckless."

"Two days, Doc. We'll be in contact." Brian backed away from the car, pulled the cigarettes from his shirt pocket, shook one out, plucked it from the pack with his lips, then lit up, and exhaled smoke right into Noel's window.

Noel waved the smoke from his face and held his hand out to the truck blocking him.

"Two days, Doc." Brian and Davy jumped back into their truck and drove out of the lot so fast they sent up a cloud of dust that nearly choked him to death.

He rolled up his windows and blasted the AC. It didn't cool his rising temper. He didn't like them calling the shots.

"You'll get the list when I say," he shouted, finally finding his voice.

He had more to lose than them.

"I'm in control." He slammed his palm against the steering wheel. "Not them."

And if he wanted to keep things working the way they had for the last year, he needed to keep Alina out of his business.

CHAPTER TWENTY-EIGHT

Alina sat in the quiet office and took a deep breath. The last few days had been everything she'd ever wanted with Jay and she'd been busier than ever at work. Now that she had a minute to sit and think, pieces fell into place in her mind and amped her suspicions to a level that made her gut sour and tense.

Noel suddenly filled the doorway.

She stared up at him from behind the desk, feeling trapped. "I thought you left with Mandi."

"I locked up after her. I wanted to check in with you."

"Oh. What about?"

"Are you happy here?"

"Yes, of course."

"I thought so." His tone said he thought so before, but maybe not now. "Business is good. Customers love you."

"I enjoy the work. I've gotten to know several of our regular customers."

"You're excellent when it comes to compounding prescriptions. Parents love that you can make them the kids' favorite flavor."

"My favorite part of the job. Makes me feel like a mad scientist." She smiled, thinking how as a kid her favorite toy had been the chemistry set she'd begged her parents for when she was seven.

Noel glanced back out toward the pharmacy and storefront. "I love this place. It's provided everything I needed in my life. You've been such a help to me here. I count on you so much." His voice faded off at the end.

"Noel, is something wrong?"

"Everything seems out of my control sometimes. The girls are off living their lives. They speak to their mother all the time, but I feel like I've lost touch with them."

"They're spreading their wings, but they know you're home waiting for them to come back."

He nodded. "I miss my wife."

Alina didn't understand.

"The illness took her away from me. I see glimpses of her, but she's fading away before my eyes. She's still fighting, but every day it gets harder for her. We used to talk about the future. Empty nesters, we'd travel, go out to dinner on a school night, see a movie in the afternoon." His wistful smile faded to a deep frown. "Now she talks about what I need to do for the girls after she's gone. That I need to find a way to be happy again. She talks as if it's already over."

Alina, setting aside her suspicions about what Noel might be doing at the store, rose, and went to him, drawn by his grief. "Noel, it's going to be okay. There's still time for this round of treatment to work."

"I hope so, but I see the difference this time. She's tired. I'm tired. The doctor told us the worst thing we can do is lose hope. I find it hard to even offer her optimism when I feel so cast aside sometimes."

"Lee is a strong, practical woman. I'm sure she's fighting as hard as she can, but still wants to be sure that you and the girls will be okay if the worst happens. Her planning for that outcome doesn't mean she's given up or even believes it will end that way."

"She goes through the motions every day, but I feel the growing distance she puts between us."

Alina put her hand on the side of his arm. "You guys are in this together, Noel."

"Then why do I feel so alone?" He took her by the shoulders and pulled her into a hug she didn't expect. He held her close, his arms wrapped around her back, his cheek pressed to her forehead. "I miss the feel of her against me. I miss the way we used to make love. God, it's been forever since we did that."

A shiver of panic went through her the second she felt him harden against her belly. She gripped his sides and tried to push back and away from him, but he held firm. She raised her head to tell him to let her go, but he swooped in and pressed his lips to hers. She tried to turn her face away, but his hands came up and held her head still. That gave her the opening to move her body away from his, but he still had her in a lip-lock that made her cringe.

"Noel," she mumbled against his lips, which only gave him the opportunity to slide his tongue into her mouth, cutting off her protest. She socked him in the side.

Shocked by the blow, he jumped. His teeth grazed her lower lip and cut it.

She tasted blood.

She thought he'd end this ridiculous, inappropriate groping, but he had other plans and grabbed her to him again and went in for another sloppy, disgusting kiss. She had no choice. She kneed him right in the nuts just like her brothers taught her.

He dropped to his knees and grabbed his junk.

"What the fuck was that?" she yelled, her breath sawing in and out, a wash of panic and adrenaline racing through her veins. "Don't ever fucking touch me again!"

All of a sudden, Jay filled the doorway, gun in hand. He pointed it down at the floor, but trained it on Noel curled up in a ball at her feet with his hands on his nuts as he rocked his body and moaned. Jay glanced at her face, narrowed his gaze on the blood trickling down her lip and over her chin, then glared down at her partner. "Shoot him, or book him for assault?" The deadly tone said he'd do whichever one she wanted.

"I'm okay."

"You're bleeding." His words came out tight and as fierce as the look in his eyes.

"Put the gun away. He's no threat now."

Jay holstered his gun, bent to Noel, grabbed him by his shirtfront, hauled him up, and slammed him into the door so hard the handle went right through the Sheetrock wall. Jay held him against the door, Noel's feet dangling inches off the floor. "You ever touch her again, you won't have any balls left to kick."

"Let me go." Panic filled Noel's wide eyes. Sweat trickled down the side of his face. "You can't do anything to me."

"I can call the cops and have them arrest you."

Alina put her hand on Jay's rock-hard shoulder. Noel's weight didn't even faze him. Jay held him against the door like he weighed no more than a child. In his line of work, he probably tossed guys up against walls all the time. "Jay, honey, let him down." Jay didn't move a muscle. She slid her other hand up his shoulder and pressed her forehead to his back. "Please, honey. It's done. I need you to let him go."

Jay's muscles bunched for a split second, then he dropped Noel hard to his feet. Noel's legs might have buckled had Jay not held him up. He spun Noel and marched him out of the room and down the hall to the back door. Alina followed. Jay shoved the door wide and pushed Noel out of it. Noel stumbled a couple of steps before he caught himself.

"Get out of my sight before I forget I'm a cop and

there are rules and laws, both of which you broke tonight." Jay pulled the door closed, turned, and walked toward her.

Before the door closed, Noel yelled, "You don't deserve her."

Jay walked right to her, picked her up in his arms, and held her tight. "I may not deserve you, but I am trying damn hard to be the man *you* deserve."

Alina held him close, her arms wrapped around his head. "You're everything I need. I'm so glad you're here."

The door opened. Jay spun around, pulled his gun, and shoved her behind him all at once.

Noel stopped dead in his tracks, hands up. "I need my car keys," he growled and walked to his locker to grab them off the shelf. He slammed the door, dropped his head for a second, swore under his breath, then turned to her.

Jay still held her mostly behind him, his gun at his side.

"We'll talk about this tomorrow." Noel headed to the back door again.

"No. We won't."

That stopped him in his tracks. He slowly turned to stare at her.

"You will take tomorrow off and spend it with your *wife*. I don't want to see you at all tomorrow. When you return, we will not speak about what happened or why. You will treat me with respect and as a fellow colleague. Right now, we are nothing more. Maybe, given time, we'll find our way back to being friends."

"Alina, I never meant . . ."

"There's no excuse for what you did. To me. To your wife. I won't say anything if you drop this right now. If not . . ." She left the rest of the threat to tell Lee unsaid.

Noel stormed out, slamming the door behind him.

"I should have shot him."

The unexpected laugh bubbled up from her gut. She held her hands over her stomach and tried to stop, but couldn't.

Jay turned to her, his grim face morphing into a reluctant lopsided grin. "You think that's funny?"

She shook her head. "No. Not at all, but, yeah, kinda."

"Did he hit you in the head? You're not making sense." The grin disappeared the moment his thumb swept under her stinging lip. He went into the bathroom behind him and wet a paper towel at the sink. With soft strokes, he gently wiped her mouth, dabbed at the cut to stop the bleeding, and washed the stain off her chin. "Better?"

She took his hand and kissed the back of it. "You make me feel better."

Jay tossed the dirty paper towel into the trash and ushered her back toward the office.

She cocked her head to the side. "How did you get in?"

"The door was unlocked. I wish I'd come in sooner, but I got a call."

She tilted her head. "Did you see Noel let Mandi out?"

"Yeah. I figured you were closing out the register and locking up the drug cabinets. Instead you're fighting off an attempted rape."

She shook her head, her mind not wanting to believe Noel would have taken things that far. She needed to believe that, to stop the tremble of fear that shot through her again.

"Don't shake your head like that. You don't know what would have happened had you not taught his balls a lesson. Caden and Beck?"

"Ball busting and some self-defense moves," she confirmed, her Brother Boot Camp. They were always there for her, but they wanted her to be able to defend herself. She'd thought it silly. No one ever thinks they'll need those skills. But she'd enjoyed roughhousing with the boys. Now she appreciated their efforts despite her many protests. "If he'd gotten up, I'd have broken his nose with a nice uppercut with the heel of my hand."

Jay's mouth pressed into a frustrated grimace. He hooked his hand around her neck and pulled her into his chest. She turned her head so she didn't hit her swollen lip. Jay kissed the top of her head. "Damn, sweetheart, I'm sorry I was late."

An uneasy feeling twisted her belly. "I might be crazy, but I think Noel wanted you to catch us in that kiss."

He held her away by her shoulders. "What do you mean?"

"We never—never—leave the back door unlocked. With the drugs we have in here"—she shook her head—"that's just an invitation for someone to rob us. When Noel accepted me as a partner, he warned me that he'd been robbed twice in the past. That's why we've got the cameras, the roll-up security doors at the counter, the coded locks on the doors to the pharmacy area and back here, the extra heavy duty locks on the steel back door."

"Why would he want me to find the two of you together? He's married. He wouldn't want his wife to find out. Besides, I know you'd never cheat on me."

His trust in her made her heart melt. "I would never hurt you like that, Jay." The way his mother had hurt his father. And Jay. Heather's betrayal had broken up the family Jay knew, changed it, and not for the better. They'd all had to grieve the loss of what they'd had and find a way to live with a fractured family, Jay in the middle of his mother and father and his father's new family.

"You don't even need to say it." Jay kissed her cheek. "So why does Noel want me to think you're cheating on me? He can't possibly think he's got a shot with you."

"The whole thing seemed odd. We were talking about his wife."

"And then he tried to jump you?"

"Exactly." Alina had a feeling this had more to do with her suspicions about the discrepancy she found in the prescription refills and her research into their database. The more she thought about it, the more it made sense.

"What is that look on your face?"

She sighed and looked up at him. "I think he wants my *DEA* boyfriend to leave me."

Of course that raised Jay's suspicion meter to one hundred. "Why?"

She paced into the office, turned back to him, opened her mouth, but snapped it shut again.

"Alina? What aren't you telling me? Does this have to do with your accident?"

Her mind reeled at that thought. She tried to add that piece into the puzzle she still hadn't figured out and couldn't find where or why that would fit with the other things she knew.

"If you don't start talking, I'm going to go full-on interrogator on you."

She took his hand, pulled, and led him to the chair in front of her desk. "Sit."

He cocked his head. "Do I seriously need to sit for this?"

"Mostly so I don't get a crick in my neck staring up at you." That got her a slight smile.

Jay sat but leaned forward, forearms braced on his thighs. "Spill it, sweetheart."

"Okay, I need you to listen and understand that I can't tell you everything right now. If I do, you'll go all DEA super-agent on me and I really need more time before I know if there's really a reason for you . . ."

"To help," he finished for her.

She shook her head. "Blow up my whole life." She

dropped her head and stared at her feet. The magnitude of what might happen finally hit her. She'd been pushing it aside, trying to figure a way out of this, but once she knew about the dead people's refills without doctor's approval, she couldn't ignore it.

Noel had done a very good job of keeping her busy the last few days so she couldn't dig deeper, but she needed to do it. Even if it cost her the business. She wouldn't let it cost her career, too.

His eyes narrowed. "Sweetheart, I'm trying to be patient, but you need to start telling me something that makes sense right now. Does Noel have something to do with your accident?"

"I don't think so."

"You don't think so?" That question held a world of suspicion and concern for her safety.

"It doesn't fit in with the other thing I discovered. And I'm not even sure if it's more than the one thing I discovered because I haven't been able to look into it. But I think there's more. And if there is, then it's big, and I have a really huge, blow-up-my-life problem because I own half this business. I could be implicated. I could go to jail."

"Holy shit, Alina. Why didn't you come to me the minute you suspected something that could touch you?"

"Because I don't have all the facts. If I turn over the little bit I do know to the DEA—"

"I love you. I would protect you." He cut her off, stunning her into silence. "I would make sure you didn't go down for something he did." He stood and cupped her face. "I won't let anything happen to you. Don't you get it? I can't live without you."

Tears gathered in her eyes. One spilled over her lashes. Jay swept his thumb over her cheek, wiping it away.

"You love me?"

"You know I love you. Don't you? Haven't I showed you in every kiss?" He brushed his lips tenderly against hers. "In every touch?" He softly brushed his fingers through her hair. "In everything I say and do for you? You're everything to me. More than I expected. More than I deserve."

She shook her head. "That's not true. You're such a good man. You deserve everything good and wonderful this life has to offer. You see all the bad but you still have such a good heart. I wish I could bring so much more joy into your life."

"You do. Every time you smile at me. Every time you come into my arms and offer me every bit of yourself. You fill me up. You make me happy. You make me want to be a better man. Before you, I had work and nothing much else. Now I see a future with you and our kids and a life worth living to the fullest."

That, right there, tore open the floodgates on her heart and every bit of love she had rushed out.

He pressed his forehead to hers. "Sweetheart, I truly, deeply love you." His gruff voice reverberated with the emotion he put into his pledge.

Her heart swelled so big in her chest she thought it might burst free.

She stared into his gold-flecked brown eyes, put her hands to his face, and said the words she'd never said to another man. "I love you." The words echoed the deep feeling filling her heart and soul. Now that she'd said it, she felt light and free to love him without any restraint.

Jay's eyes filled with wonder and excitement, then heated with a passion unlike anything she'd seen in him. His mouth covered hers with a need that sparked her own passion. She matched the thrust of his tongue, not even feeling the sting of her lip. His hands went down her neck to her shoulders where he shoved her white coat down her arms, off, and tossed it aside.

He pressed his big body into hers. She rubbed her belly against his thick erection and sighed when his hands covered her aching breasts and squeezed hard, then rubbed softly over the mounds.

She attacked his belt before he hooked his hands under her arms, lifted her like a feather, and set her on the edge of her desk. His hands swept up her thighs, drawing her flouncy skirt up to her hips. She worked the button and zipper free on his jeans and tugged them down his hips, avoiding the badge and gun. She had other things to focus on, like his washboard abs and hard cock. She grabbed the thick column and rubbed her hand up and down the length. His groan set off a wave of heat low in her belly that dampened her panties. Those he attacked with both hands, one yanking one side down her hip as the other dipped inside, found her slick core, and thrust two fingers into her. She screamed out her orgasm. His dick jumped in her hand. She stroked him harder and made him growl. His grip tightened to the point her panties tore. He kissed her neck, jaw, and forehead and fumbled for something in his pocket. He used his teeth to tear open the condom.

Impatient for him to be inside her, she took the condom and rolled it on his hard length, then leaned back and wrapped her legs around his waist. He thrust into her as she pulled him close and locked her feet at his back. Jay cleared the way behind her with one sweep of his hand across the desk, sending papers, stapler, and phone to the floor. She didn't care. All she wanted was more of the man lying over her, kissing her like she was his every heartbeat, loving her with a passion and magic only they shared for each other.

The phone on the floor blared that annoying sound it makes when it's off the hook, Jay's cell phone rang, but they ignored both, lost in each other. Hell, the whole building could go up in flames. Nothing would stop them. She lost herself in the push and pull of his body over hers. Inside hers. But it was the look in his eyes when he stared down at her, thrust into her hard and deep again and again, and said without words that he was with her now and forever.

They hit the peak together in a shattering climax that slammed through both of them and left them breathless. Jay took her hands, threaded his fingers through hers, lay on top of her, his face in her hair, their arms above their heads, hands dangling off the other end of the desk.

"I love you," he whispered in her ear and ran his tongue along the edge of her earlobe, sending another wave of heat through her. Her body contracted around his again and she felt his smile against her cheek.

"I love you, too." She smiled up at the ceiling and giggled.

"What?" Jay let go of one of her hands and leaned on his forearm.

"I'm happy." The bright smile matched the joy in her declaration.

He rubbed his nose against hers. "Good. That's how I want you to be all the time."

"And I've never had sex anywhere but in a bedroom. This was fun. And sexy."

He raised an eyebrow and dropped his voice. "I hear a challenge in there somewhere."

Stunned, she stared up at him and saw the mischief dancing in his eyes. She wanted to say no, not going to happen. But then the idea of him making love to her in the wildflower-dappled field behind his house under the stars made her ache for him again.

"What's that face?"

"Will you make love to me in your backyard under the stars?"

"I'm sure I can manage that by the time we get home." He stood and pulled her up to sitting by their joined hands.

"I didn't mean tonight."

"One of the things I like most about you, Alina, is that you're always so willing to give, but you hardly ever ask for anything. You want to lie in my arms under the stars, there is nothing I want to give you more than your wish come true."

She smiled up at him, her heart overflowing.

He leaned down and kissed her softly. "Let's go, sweetheart." He plucked a tissue from the box on her desk, cleaned up, then dumped the garbage in the trash.

She pulled her torn panties off the one leg they were still tangled around, wadded them up, and stuffed them in her skirt pocket.

"Sorry about that." His sheepish tone made him even more adorable. "I'll buy you new ones."

She shrugged that off and helped him pick up the papers, stapler, and annoying phone.

"Didn't you get a call?"

Jay pulled his phone from his back pocket and picked up his open wallet from the floor where it landed after he'd gotten the condom out of it. "I'll listen to the voice mail while you make sure this place is secure."

She went to do just that, but turned back when Jay called her. A second ago, she'd been looking into the eyes of the man she loved. He was still there, but he'd gone into DEA mode. "You have forty-eight hours, then you need to tell me what is going on here whether you're ready or not. I trust you, Alina, but I already don't like this thing between you and Noel. If you think, even for a second, that he'll do something to you, you need to let me know immediately. Promise me."

"I promise, Jay. I'll pull what I know together tomorrow and look into the things I suspect. I'll have an answer for you the day after next." She hoped those answers didn't put her in jail. Jay, her brothers, they'd do everything they could to help her, but they couldn't change the law. And if Noel incriminated her, made it look like she was in on his activities, then even they couldn't save her from the inevitable.

Jay laid his hand on her shoulder. "I can help you, Alina. I'm good at research."

"I need to do this. I need to know what I'm facing."

He planted his hands on his hips. "I really don't like this."

"I know. That's why we're going home. Unless that phone call means you have to go to work, you promised me a night under the stars."

Jay hit the button on his phone for voice mail, put the phone to his ear, listened, then smiled broadly. "Looks like I get my wish tonight. That wasn't work, just my mom letting me know she fed the horses and left a cherry cobbler in my fridge."

"Have I told you how much I love your mom? Cherry cobbler is my favorite."

He smiled. "Mine, too."

"Then, let's go." Alina grabbed her purse, checked the front and back of the store, made sure everything was locked up tight, set the alarm system, then walked to her car with Jay right by her side. She followed him in her rental car out to his place, the anticipation growing with each mile closer to another night where they set work aside and could be alone together.

She parked next to Jay in the driveway, walked up the path to the front door with the welcoming light in the entry, went into the cozy house, and found herself kissed soundly right there in the entryway. "Wait here. I'll find a blanket."

"I'll plate up some cobbler."

Mischief lit Jay's eyes. "Double dessert tonight. Cobbler and you."

"This might turn out to be the perfect night."

Jay slid his hand over her hip and bottom and squeezed her ass. "I aim to please."

Alina handled the food in short order and met Jay in the dining room by the French doors. He'd found a thick quilt and a flashlight. They made their way out the back and away from the house into the field. Crickets chorused their progress and sang in the quiet night as Jay laid out the blanket. They sat close together under the stars and indulged in the closeness and amazing cobbler.

Alina lay back on the blanket and stared up at the stars.

Jay lay beside her and stretched out his arm. She lifted her head, lay in the crook of his shoulder, and snuggled close to him. "The sky is amazing."

A billion stars sparkled overhead. The quiet night enveloped them.

Surrounded by peace, Jay kissed her on the temple as she lost herself in the vast night sky. "If I didn't wait six months to ask you to marry me, would you?"

"Yes." Her heart pounded with excitement. A smile she couldn't stop if she tried spread across her face.

Jay rolled on top of her, his smile brilliant, the love in his eyes brighter than any of the stars sparkling overhead.

"Keep your eyes on the sky, sweetheart, I'll take you to heaven."

CHAPTER TWENTY-NINE

Jay walked out of the small office kitchen with his second cup of coffee. His mind replayed his and Alina's amazing night under the stars making love and reveling in the closeness that grew between them every day. It echoed through his mind and body. He'd never imagined a relationship like this. He'd never known he could feel this much.

Caden and Beck stepped in front of him in the middle of the rows of cubicles, blocking him from returning to his office.

Caden glanced at Beck, then back to him. "He's smiling again."

Beck shook his head. "You think he's high?"

Jay only smiled broader. "Don't you guys have something to do?"

"Deflecting," Caden pointed out.

"I've never seen it like this on him, but I think he's happy." Beck studied him with mock suspicion.

King, back from leave after the shooting, joined them. "What's going on?"

Caden tapped King on the chest with the back of his hand. "Notice anything different about our fearless leader?"

King studied him. "What the hell is that on your face?"

"He's smiling," Beck supplied.

Jay endured the ribbing. At least Caden and Beck were messing with him, not warning him away from Alina. Let them have their fun as long as they saw that he was happy with Alina. They had something great.

Something he didn't want to lose.

Something that required a ring and a promise.

The thought of buying a ring excited him. He'd never been one to buy gifts for women, but putting a ring, his ring, on Alina's finger seemed like the most natural next step. But getting her promise meant more to him than anything.

"I've been out of the loop, but I'm guessing this has something to do with Alina." King held perfectly still, waiting to see if Caden or Beck decked Jay.

"Don't worry, King. They know I'm seeing their sister." He meant to find a quiet moment to get Caden and Beck alone to talk to them about his plans. Why not now? "In fact, I'm going to marry her."

That wiped the grins off all of them and stopped the joking. Saying it out loud only solidified his resolve.

Beck found his voice first. "Are you serious?"

"I kind of asked her last night if she would accept if I proposed." He took a sip of his coffee, enjoying their discombobulation, and waited for their brains to catch up to the magnitude of what he'd confessed.

Beck got in his face. "Did you knock up my sister?"

"No!" Truthfully, he hadn't expected that assumption. But he loved the idea of kids with Alina.

Beck backed off, barely. He stood within punching distance and glared. Hard.

Caden pushed his shoulders back, chest out, and asked, "What did she say?"

"Yes." It still stunned and filled him to bursting with happiness.

"Holy shit." King took a step back just in case Caden and Beck went off.

They stood still as stone in front of him. Jay quit messing around and said what he'd thought about all night. "I love her. When I'm not with her, I can't stop thinking about her. When I am with her, I'm thinking about what we'll do the next day, and the next, until I see her in every day and a future I want more than anything. I want her life and my life to be our life. I want my house to be our home. Before her, all I had was work. Now, I feel like I have a life."

Beck shifted on his feet and took a more relaxed stance. "After all her reservations about your job, she wants this."

"That's become less important than holding on to what we have together and how we feel about each other. She wanted me to communicate with her more." He shrugged. "The not knowing where I am and what I'm doing scared her the most. So I call and text a couple times a day just to let her know all's good. She understands I can't share everything about the job, but I've found telling her about what I do and how it affects me helps. I kept a lot of shit bottled up. I feel better when I talk to her about it."

Beck nodded like he got it. After all, he and Ashley had shared their mutual pain and found a connection and deep bond Jay had envied. Until now, because he had Alina.

Caden tried to bring reason to something that already made perfect sense to Jay. "You barely know her. You've only been seeing each other a few weeks."

"I've known her a long time. All those little things about her past I'd discover over months I already knew because I know her through you and all the stories you tell about her. She gets me because I do what you guys do. I don't know what happened. I've seen her a hundred times, but only as your sister. At the wedding, I saw her as something more. Maybe seeing you guys happy and in love made me realize how much I wanted that. I had been looking for it before that day and when I saw her laughing with Mia and Ashley in the lobby, something clicked."

Beck's eyes narrowed. "So you guys are getting married?"

"Yes. Soon, I hope. But I still need to propose." Nerves fluttered in his stomach. "She deserves more than a hypothetical question." Was she ready for the real thing? God, he hoped so. "I want her to have the whole deal, whatever she wants. And I know that includes both of you giving your blessing. I know you want only the best for her. All I can say is that I will try every day to be that for her."

Beck's tense shoulders relaxed. "Alina has never been impulsive. She's smart and methodical about everything she does. If she wants to marry you, I know it's because she loves you and believes you'll have a happy future together. She isn't blind or ignorant to what life with you will be like. That will work in both your favors. More than anything, I want her to be happy. You're my friend, and I want you to be happy, too. And if she puts that stupid grin you wear every day now on your face, I can live with it."

Caden hugged him with a thump on the back. "Me, too."

Beck gave him another hug and hearty pat on the back and stepped back. "Welcome to the family."

It meant a lot to him to have their support. "When you talk to Alina, you might want to say something more than you can live with it." Jay smiled, letting them know he teased and understood they'd say something with more feeling to their sister. "And don't say anything yet. I still need to propose."

"When do you plan to do this?" Caden asked.

"Soon. I need to get a ring. I'm going out later today to do that."

Beck surprised him with a suggestion. "When she checked out Mia's and Ashley's rings at the wedding, she said she didn't want a set, but one gorgeous ring because she works with her hands all day. If that helps."

"I'd put a ring on every one of her fingers if that's what she wanted, but, yeah, that helps. I'll see what I can find."

"Want us to come with you?" Caden asked.

"I appreciate it, but I got this. I want her to know I picked it for her."

Beck grabbed his shoulder and squeezed. "She'll like that. She thinks we interfere in her life too much as it is. And since we're on Alina, I checked in with local PD about her accident. They've got nothing."

Jay didn't know what Alina had on Noel or if it was tied to the accident, but he needed to bring Caden and Beck in on whatever she was doing. "Alina is working on something today that may tie in, or it may not."

Caden and Beck both went on alert.

"What does she know?" Beck asked.

"I'm waiting to find out. I gave her until tomorrow night to tell me everything."

Caden shook his head. "If she's a target because of something she knows, she needs to tell us now."

"I tried to get her to open up, but it has to do with her partner."

"Noel?" Beck's mouth turned into a derisive frown. "What's he got to do with this?"

"I'm not sure, but last night he got real grabby with

her. She thinks, and I agree, that he was trying to split us up."

"What the fuck?" Beck raked his fingers through his hair. "Is she okay?"

"When I walked in, he was on the floor, busted balls in hand."

Caden smiled. "I taught her that."

Jay's flitting smile died when he thought of how upset she'd been last night. "Well, she shouldn't have to use it at work."

"The guy is married. Why does he want to break you two up?"

"I picked Alina up at the store the other day for lunch. He got real jumpy having a DEA agent there, especially one seeing Alina."

Caden's lips pressed tight. "And you say Alina found something. About him and the business?"

"That's what it sounds like. She wanted to gather more information. She's afraid whatever he's done could land her in jail."

"Shit." Beck fisted his hands. "She knows we'll protect her."

"She knows we'll try, but that we may not be able to get around the law."

"And you let her go into work today with him?" Caden took a step closer.

"He won't be there today. He doesn't know she knows anything. She's not even sure what she knows is anything more than an error, though that seems unlikely since she thinks they could be shut down and go to jail."

"We need to know what she knows now," Beck ordered.

"I tried but she wants to bring us facts. She doesn't want Noel to push all the blame on her. She left early this morning. She asked Mandi to meet her at the store two hours early so they could dig through the computer system. She's not alone there. I told her not to go anywhere alone until I pick her up tonight."

"I don't like this." Beck pulled out his phone.

"What are you doing?"

"Sending her a text, asking how she's doing. Don't worry, I do it all the time. She won't suspect anything." Beck smiled when his phone dinged with a text. He held the phone up to Jay.

> **ALINA:** Great. Best night EVER last night. Keep Jay safe for me. ♥

Jay found himself smiling like an idiot filled with joy and a warm heart that she wanted Beck to look out for him. Memories of last night made that glow in his chest turn into a fire for her. He'd wanted to give her something special for being so open and honest about what she wanted. They'd shared the "best night EVER." And he wanted a lifetime more.

"You guys and your happiness are starting to make me sick," King grumbled.

"Is Cara talking to you yet?"

"I need coffee." King walked away.

Jay felt sorry for King. "I'll take that as a no."

Beck nodded. "She'll come around. King's not the kind of guy who gives up."

Caden got them back on track. "So we're sure Noel isn't an immediate problem?"

Jay thought about it. "He doesn't seem the type to steal a car and try to kill her."

"He could have hired someone," Beck suggested.

Jay shook his head. "He thinks he's in love with her. His wife is sick. Alina is sweet to him, listens to his gripes, pats him on the back, and offers her support and comfort. She just found out, whatever she knows, so why go after her before she even discovered something?"

"Makes sense," Beck agreed. "Unless we're missing something."

"We'll know soon." Jay hoped he hadn't given Alina too much leeway.

"What are you doing right now?" Caden asked.

"I need to finish off the report on that drug lab we took down yesterday."

Beck smiled. "I bet you didn't tell Alina about that shot that missed you by an inch."

"I bet you didn't tell Ashley that scrawny kid got the drop on you and knocked you to the floor." Jay smiled at Beck's frown.

"He came out of the ceiling." Beck shook his head. "Stupid kid tried to hide in the rafters. It had to be a hundred and twenty up there at least. Kid got delirious and fell through the Sheetrock."

"Right on top of you." Caden smacked his brother on the back, then said to Jay, "I'll do the report. You go find my sister a ring."

Stunned, Jay smiled, because he hated paperwork, and Caden offering to do it so Jay could do something special for Alina touched him. "Thanks, man."

Jay didn't hesitate. He didn't want Caden to change his mind, and he couldn't wait to get the ring. One step closer to making Alina his wife.

Wow.

His stomach tightened and a surge of adrenaline shot through him and amped his excitement.

He was going to propose, get married, and have a wife. It kind of felt unreal and at the same time long overdue. He and Alina would be so happy together. They had so much to look forward to. The only dark cloud, this thing with Noel. But he'd get to the bottom of that soon and eliminate any threat to Alina's future. She'd worked hard to earn her degree and put all her money on the line to go into business. He wouldn't let her lose it all.

If Noel tried to take it from her, he'd put that smarmy bastard down.

CHAPTER THIRTY

"**M**other f-ing dumbshit." Alina bolted up from her seat in front of the computer, nearly toppling the chair. Rage and panic seized her heart and knotted her stomach.

Mandi took two quick steps back to avoid the fury Alina could barely contain. "It's bad, isn't it?"

Alina raked her fingers through her hair and tried to contain her frustration and the very real fear that this could ruin her life. "Bad would be accidentally refilling a prescription for a dead person because someone in their family is stealing the meds. This is fraud, theft, a violation of state and federal law. This is stealing Schedule II drugs to sell them on the street to addicts who could potentially overdose."

"You think he's dealing?"

"Or selling them to a buyer who is selling them on the street. He's discounted the purchases in the system and paid the very least he could get away with 'selling' them without alerting the feds that something is off in the accounting or purchase tracking. If we hadn't discovered that the two people who died are still our customers, I don't know that we would have ever found this."

Mandi winced. "Thirty-six people on the list of deceased."

"Thirty-six people refilling drugs at a hefty discount. Sixteen doctors who didn't prescribe those refills." They'd made one call after the next to confirm none of the doctors was involved. Noel was smart enough to refill on a schedule, so it didn't look like patients were abusing or selling. He never submitted them to the insurance companies, who would have known the patient died. He didn't refill all thirty-six at the same time. How he kept track, she didn't know, but he had a system and had been doing this for over a year, adding new people as they died and those prescriptions could fall into his refill plot.

She had another list of patients who reported drugs stolen, lost, or damaged who needed a replacement refill. Mandi called five out of the nine on the list and found only one legitimate.

Mandi also looked up local home robberies and discovered not only the two people who had died, but several others who were customers. She checked the records to see if those individuals came in the week of or before their home was broken into to refill a prescription and if it was a narcotic or stimulant. The news wasn't good.

"He's got to be working with someone who sells them on the street."

Alina sighed. "Okay, the pills are worth a lot of money, but Noel can only supply so much per month without raising suspicions. He's found a way to create a steady flow, but with demand rising, he needs another way to get more pills. So what does he do?" She thought about the pieces they had gathered. "He does what we did. He pulls a report for all Schedule II prescriptions filled that week or month. You can't steal from the same person twice, so he marks off the ones they've already hit. He finds a new prescription. He gives the names to his street dealer, who robs the person and steals the drugs. He sells drugs . . . burglary's not that big a leap. Noel plays the odds that most people keep their medication at home and only take a pill or two with them to work or whatever. Some people, like me, get a seven- or ten-day supply for an injury and probably don't take all of them. Even if they only score a small amount, it's still money in their pocket."

"That's a huge risk."

"Noel would know how many pills should be on hand based on the prescription. If he filled it and had the robbery take place a day or two later, the bulk of the pills would be there for the taking. His dealer sells them. A few pills sold at steep rates on the streets covers the cash cost here with the deep discount for the prescription refills on the deceased patients. The records look up-to-date and no money is missing from the accounting."

Mandi consulted her computer screen and the list of customers who had been robbed. Who knew how many other robberies had occurred and not been reported in a news article easy to find on the internet? They may have only hit the tip of the iceberg with their cursory research.

With the information they did gather, they'd created quite a few spreadsheets detailing how Noel worked. She'd be able to hand it over to the DEA or FBI, whoever took the case and shut Noel down and possibly the pharmacy. She hoped to be able to keep her license. It didn't seem likely. She might even have to serve time. Because, disturbingly, Noel started using her ID number on many of the refills over the last two months. On paper, or in megabytes, it looked like she was complicit.

"I've updated the robbery spreadsheet. You're right. Each of the robberies occurred a couple days after we filled the prescription."

"Right, so even if you or I filled the prescription, he would know about it by pulling the report."

Mandi nodded, her eyes sad and confused and angry. Noel's little side business put all of them at risk.

"I've never seen him with anyone who looks like a

drug dealer." Mandi hit Save on her updated spreadsheet.

"I saw him arguing with two guys out back a while
ago. They took off in a truck. I asked him about it. He said
you were arguing with your new boyfriend." Alina remembered something else. "But that wasn't right because
like twenty minutes later you came back from break and
your boyfriend came in to return your sweater."

"I remember that. You said you knew about our fight,
but I didn't know how you'd know since it happened at
home the night before."

"I remember thinking that Noel had lied to me, but
we got busy and I forgot about it."

"That's the night you got in your car accident."

Memories from that night hit her at odd moments. But
the foggy fragment right at the end before she passed out
had never been clear until now. "Oh shit. I saw him."

"Noel?"

She shook her head, trying to bring the image in her
mind into clearer focus. The guy in the other car didn't
have Noel's darker hair. But he had a tattoo on his arm.
"He had light shaggy hair. Like one of the guys I saw at
the back door arguing, not with you, but with Noel. And
the same snake tattoo circling up his arm."

Mandi fell back in her chair. "You don't think Noel
sent him after you?"

Her heart raced with the possibility. "If you asked me
that two hours ago, I'd have said no. But now, I don't
know." She didn't want to go there, but she had to accept
that the man she thought she knew yesterday was not the
same man revealed to her today in all she'd discovered.

"He seemed genuinely worried about me after it happened. In fact, his intense concern and questions made
me uncomfortable. I think he might have suspected it
had something to do with him." Her stomach soured.

"Oh God." Mandi pointed to Alina's face. "Are you going to tell me now how you got that cut and bruise on your lip? It was Noel, wasn't it?"

Someone knocked on the front door, startling them. Alina glanced at the clock on her computer. "We're a couple minutes late opening." Alina tossed Mandi her keys. "Go open the doors. I'll close this all up and transfer the files to a flash drive."

"Two."

"Why two?"

"Give one to me for safekeeping. Just in case." Mandi spun around, purple hair flaring out, and flew out the door to answer the knocking that had turned to all-out banging.

Alina took the clipped bundles of paperwork she'd printed out and stacked them in a file folder. She closed out the open windows on her computer and dragged the file folder to the thumb drive. It took a minute to transfer the files, but once done, she pulled the thumb drive out, replaced it with another she found in her drawer with the pharmacy name and logo on it. They handed them out as promotional items sometimes. Files flipped from the folder onto the thumb drive on her computer. While it finished, she went to Mandi's computer and transferred the folder she'd created with all her research on the accidents, the two deaths, the records for the refills for all the deceased, and the spreadsheets that showed when and for whom the refills were done.

They had a lot of information, but nothing that proved definitively that Noel was linked to the robberies and deaths. She wanted that proof.

Pharmacists consulted patients on the proper use of medications. Noel went against all they strived to do to help their customers. He was sending highly addictive drugs out into the streets where some kid looking for a high could take too much and die. She thought of the soccer mom Jay had busted driving with her toddler in the car.

Her heart couldn't take the horrible scenarios playing out in her head.

Mandi popped her head in the door as she pulled the second drive out of the computer. "I need you up front. Someone has a question about their medication and another customer wants a flu shot."

"Be right there." She stuffed one of the memory sticks in her pocket and held the other out to Mandi. "Put that somewhere no one will find it. No matter what, if Noel asks you if you know anything about what I've been doing, you say no. Can you do that?"

"I'm only a few years from being a teen. I think I can still lie with a straight face like I used to do when I told my mom that smell coming off me wasn't pot."

Alina sucked in a ragged breath and ran her fingers through her hair.

Mandi laid her hand on Alina's shoulder. "Are you going to tell Jay and your brothers now?"

"Yes. I'll hand this all over to them and hope they can save my ass."

Mandi squeezed her shoulder. "Jay won't let anything happen to you. He loves you."

"You think so?" She had no doubt, but wanted to hear what Mandi, someone who wasn't as close to her and Jay as everyone else in their lives, thought.

"It's so obvious every time he looks at you." Mandi glanced down the hall toward the counter. "Come on. Nothing we can do right now. The morning crowd is growing."

Alina switched gears from super sleuth to pharmacist. With Noel out today, she'd be busy until closing. She wouldn't even get out of here for lunch. No time to meet with Jay. She'd have to wait until tonight. If he didn't have to work late.

She hoped they talked soon. She didn't want to wait. Noel was not going to get away with any of this. She wanted the supply coming from her pharmacy shut down. Even if that meant she had to close the business to do it. The community needed them, but she'd do whatever was necessary to keep those drugs off the streets and out of the hands of people who could die from using them.

Two deaths were too much blood on Noel's hands.

God knew if anyone had overdosed because of him.

Those two thoughts weighed heavy in her heart. So much so, she could barely stand it.

No more. She loved her job, but it wasn't worth someone's life. She needed to stop him before anything else bad happened.

She put the thick folder in her messenger bag and hurried out to help Mandi through the morning rush.

CHAPTER THIRTY-ONE

Alina's troubles took a backseat to the busy morning and afternoon at the pharmacy. Understanding the dire circumstances and suspecting something happened between Alina and Noel the night before, Mandi hadn't left her alone all day. They ordered delivery for lunch and ate between customers during the lull.

Alina hated seeing the worry in Mandi's eyes.

The knot in Alina's stomach had turned into a lead ball. While most of the day she'd been able to focus on work, now that the steady stream of customers had slowed down, she fretted over what to do next. She liked to plan, be in control, and do things in a methodical way. It made her good at her job. But the moment she revealed Noel's nefarious activities, everything would be out of her hands.

She didn't want this to touch Mandi. She'd been a good and loyal employee.

It scared her to let go and trust that things would work out. Jay and her brothers would try to protect her, but with all Noel had done, she didn't delude herself into believing they could save her.

Alina put another order into the system and picked up the phone to call yet another doctor's office to get an alternative medication for the one not covered under the patient's plan when the back door opened and Noel stepped in, face grim, his eyes darkened by lack of sleep. He walked toward the door separating her from the back area, his gaze steady on her through the window. She waited for him to enter his code and come inside, but he veered off into the office instead.

"What's he doing here?" Mandi whispered.

"Stay here. I'm going to find out."

Mandi held her arm. "Don't. Let it go until you talk to Jay."

"I'm not going to say anything about what I know. But I do want to see what he's up to now. Every minute I don't turn him in gives him the opportunity to get me in deeper. I can't let that happen." Alina patted Mandi's hand, then went to the office.

Noel snagged the paper off the printer the second it spilled into the tray.

"What are you doing here? I asked you to take the day off."

"That's not how I remember it, Alina. Your boyfriend pulled a gun on me"—Noel jammed his finger into his chest—"while you ordered me out of *my* business."

"*Our* business," she snapped. "You seem to have forgotten we're partners. What you do affects me. That stunt you pulled last night—"

"Is that what you told him? I came on to *you*." Noel shook his head. "You've been playing this game since you arrived. Hot one minute, cold the next."

She couldn't believe he wanted to turn this back on her. "You're the one playing games."

"You made it pretty clear last night you wanted me to kiss you, standing close to me, putting your hand on my arm, drawing so close I could smell you with every breath I took. The second I give in to your invitation, you put up a fight because your boyfriend showed up and you didn't want to get caught."

She tried to contain the fiery fury raging through her, heating her face. "The only thing I offered was compassion for what you're going through with Lee. Your *wife*. Remember her? Because I do. I would never interfere in someone's relationship."

His voice dropped an octave as his eyes scanned her body. "Yet you flirt and walk around this place in those skintight pants and transparent tops."

A burst of laughter shot out of her at the ridiculous statement. Her slacks fit, but were far from skintight. If her blouses were ever transparent, she wore a matching tank underneath. She was always dressed professionally.

And she wore her white coat, which covered most of what she was wearing from shoulders to mid-thigh.

Maybe he believed the baseless accusation, or maybe he was deflecting and trying to get her to not dig into the business if she was stuck on their personal relationship. That wasn't as personal as he obviously thought.

She planted her hands on her hips. "You have some imagination. What I wear, how I act, doesn't give you the right to touch me. You acted inappropriately. You're married. That should mean something."

"My wife is dying." No hope filled those words, just a finality that brought out his anger. "She might as well be dead for all the attention I get from her." The bitter words stunned Alina. "So, yeah, I fell for your smarts, that killer body, all those smiles and pats you give me. I ate it up." Lust filled his eyes. "When you offered more, I took it."

She couldn't believe he'd complimented and insulted her all at the same time. "Noel, let me be clear. I never offered you anything but friendship. Jay and I are together."

"I'm sure you went out of your way to make up with your boyfriend last night." His eyes swept over her body in a lascivious gaze that made her want to take a shower.

She wouldn't let him taint what she and Jay shared or put the blame on her. "Why aren't you home with your wife? She needs you. That's why you wanted a partner, right? So you could be home with her and help her recover."

"You're not listening. She's not going to recover this time."

"Give the treatments a chance to work. Don't give up."

He rolled his eyes. "I came in to put the orders through because I didn't think you'd have time to do them today, but I see you already did it."

"We've been quite busy, but I did them as things slowed down."

"Yeah, business is great. The customers love you." The resentment in his voice turned the weight in her gut to a burning ball of unease.

"Noel, this isn't like you." She wanted to give him a chance to explain and make her understand. One last chance to tell her how he got to this place and that he wanted out. "Please, tell me what's going on. Maybe I can help."

His gaze locked on hers. In his, she saw all the worry, confusion, regret, and inevitability he couldn't hide behind his anger and resentment.

He opened his mouth to say something, but snapped it shut and shook his head. "You don't want to help me. You want to destroy me." He shot past her and headed for the back door, the paper he'd printed crushed in his hand.

Alina hit a few buttons on the printer for the log and reprinted the last job. She picked up the paper and stared at the list of customers, their addresses, and the prescriptions filled.

The paper fluttered to the floor at her feet. She couldn't believe he'd do this. If she hadn't seen all the evidence, she wouldn't believe it. She bent to pick up the paper to add it to the others in the file she'd compiled and noticed her messenger bag on the floor. With the flap against the side of the desk. The opposite way she'd put it there earlier.

She pulled her bag out and checked for the file. Still there, but the papers were off-kilter. Noel had not only moved her bag, he'd gone through it. He knew she knew.

She ran for the back door, stopped by her locker, and grabbed her purse and car keys. If she hurried, maybe she could follow him and find out whom he gave that list to, his accomplice. If she knew who, she could tell Jay and they could stop anyone else from getting robbed— and possibly killed.

She opened the back door an inch at a time, checking the lot for any sign of Noel. About to step out, she spotted him off to the right. She used the door for cover and spied on him writing something on the paper on the hood of the red-and-white truck she'd seen here when Noel argued with the two men at the back door. He tossed the paper through the passenger window to the blond driver she thought was the same man she'd seen all those weeks ago.

The driver said something to Noel. The devilish smile and Noel's deep scowl hinted that the driver teased him. Then he really did taunt Noel, holding out a rolled-up wad of what she guessed was money, then snatching it away when Noel tried to take it. The driver laughed and slapped it into Noel's outstretched hand.

Noel stepped back, stuffed his hands in his pockets, and yelled, "Just get it done!" Instead of looking in control, like that order implied, Noel walked away with his shoulders and head slumped, like a man defeated.

The last she saw of Noel, he had slipped into his car and stared straight ahead through the windshield, his face completely blank. She backed into the pharmacy, locked the door, walked back toward the office, and waved at Mandi to let her know she was okay, then sat behind the desk and took out her phone and called Jay.

"Hey, sweetheart, you caught me just in time. I only have a minute. Everything okay?"

She held back the tears clogging her throat. "No. No it's not."

"Alina, what's wrong?"

"That thing we talked about last night."

"What about it?"

"It's bad. I need to turn it over to you, or just call the police and give it to them. Someone has to stop him."

"Noel?" Jay growled out the name.

"Yes."

"We gotta go, Bennett. We're not set up soon, they'll see us coming and skip on us. We'll miss our shot at these guys again," someone yelled at Jay in the background.

"Sorry, sweetheart, there's this thing. I was about to text you that I'd be busy most of tonight."

She couldn't dump this on him when he was about to take down some bad guys and possibly face yet another life-and-death situation. Her bad guy could wait for the morning. All of the robberies took place during the day when most people were out of the house at work. She could only hope and pray the ones she hadn't found on the internet were also committed during the day and she had time to stop Noel's guys.

If she went to the police with what she knew, she wouldn't have Jay and her brothers' protection. If knowing them afforded her any in the first place.

"Are Caden and Beck with you?"

"They already left. I'm following them with my team."

None of them could help her right now. "Can I meet

you, Caden, and Beck at your office in the morning? I'll bring everything I have and we can decide what to do then."

"Are you in danger?" Urgency filled his voice.

If he was on the move to carry out some operation, she needed to keep this short and not distract him. The last thing she wanted to do was make Jay worry about her when he needed to be sharp and watch his back. So she put as much confidence as she could muster in her voice. "I'll be okay." She really hoped that was true. But just in case, she asked, "Would you mind if I stayed at your place tonight? Maybe you'll be done earlier than you think?"

"Alina, you can stay at my place any time you want. Just ask my mom to let you in. I'll text her that you're coming by later."

"I can't wait to see you. Please be careful."

"Always. And Alina . . ."

"Yeah."

"If you need me to come right now, all you have to do is say so."

She hesitated for a moment, but in the end didn't want to take him away from something important. "I know you mean that and it means so much to me."

She could give him all the information later tonight or in the morning. He'd have Noel and his accomplices arrested by lunch. Simple. Clean. Even if the aftermath would be a huge mess.

To be sure he didn't worry, she reminded him and herself what really mattered. "I'll miss you tonight. If I had nothing else but you, I'd have everything I need."

And tomorrow, she might only have him, and oddly enough, she was okay with that. He'd be there to support her as she picked up the pieces.

"Jay?" The connection didn't sound like it dropped.

"There aren't enough or the right words to tell you how much I love you. I bought you something today."

"You did?"

"Yes. And if I was there right now, I'd give it to you, knowing it would light up your whole face and make the blue in your eyes outshine all the gray. I can't wait to see your pretty smile. I'm sorry you have to wait. I don't want to wait either."

"You do your thing tonight. We'll sort out my thing when I see you. If you don't make it home tonight, text me when you get into the office, and I'll drive down."

"I'm going to miss you tonight. I won't be able to stop thinking about you in my bed." His gruff voice touched her heart.

"I'll miss you, too. Be safe."

They disconnected the call.

Her heart ached for him. She wanted to feel his arms around her and let that safe and protected feeling that came over her every time they were together wash away the worry and anger from today. She wanted another amazing night under the stars and to forget all her problems.

"What do I do if I can't be a pharmacist anymore?" She loved her job. She liked helping people. How would she pay her rent? All her money was tied up in the business.

What a nightmare. Before her mind spun out of control with worries not yet reality, she went back to the pharmacy to immerse herself in work so she didn't think about her problems, Jay out chasing bad guys, or Noel's warped mind.

Tomorrow, everything would be different.

Alina walked into the pharmacy and spotted Mandi in her boyfriend's arms. Mandi broke free and rushed to her. "Is everything okay? Did Noel leave?"

Alina nodded. "What's going on?"

"I called Robby just in case Noel tried to . . ." Mandi shrugged, unable to finish the sentence because neither of them could predict what Noel would do now.

Sweet that Robby rushed over to protect them. Jay would have done the same for her.

Mandi had found a really great guy. Alina had the best guy in Jay.

"Listen, Mandi, I think you should stay with Robby tonight."

"Do you really think Noel will come after you?" Robby wrapped his arm around Mandi's shoulders and held her close.

She wanted to say no. But the car crash came to mind and turned her insides cold. Noel left the dirty work to his other partners. "I don't know," she admitted. "Jay's working tonight, but I'm going to stay at his place just to be on the safe side. In the morning, I'll meet with the DEA and turn over the files. Once Noel and his accomplices are in custody, there won't be any reason to worry about what they might do."

Robby kissed Mandi and headed for the door. "You two stick together. Text me if you need me. I'll pick you up at closing."

"Thank you, sweet."

Robby beamed her a smile before darting out the door and off to the electronics store.

"If you want to stay with us tonight, we can totally make room for you. We'll pick up some barbecue, a bottle of wine, and teach you how to game like a champ." Mandi's easy smile didn't diminish the concern in her eyes.

"Thank you for the invitation, but I'll be fine at Jay's."

"You're hoping he'll get home early." Mandi's seductive eyebrow raise and smile made Alina laugh. "Seriously, I don't like leaving you alone."

"Don't worry. I'll be fine." Alina patted Mandi's hand on the counter. "Come on back. Let's get to work."

"Why? This place will probably be shut down tomorrow."

Alina hoped not, but knew that was a real possibility. She looked around the store and sighed. This had been her dream. Noel practically handed her everything she ever wanted for a career and stole it all away from her at the same time.

He needed to go down. And she planned to be the one who put him and his deadly cohorts behind bars.

She kind of felt a little like her brothers and Jay must feel taking down the bad guys.

CHAPTER THIRTY-TWO

Alina parked her car in the lot outside her apartment and blinked her tired, scratchy eyes. Hours staring at the information she'd gathered and typing out her notes on the computer gave her a serious case of eye strain. All she'd learned put her guard up, making her scan and check all the other cars around her looking for any sign of Noel or his buddies. Nothing. Worrying about what came next made her head pound despite the ibuprofen she'd downed after closing the store. Mandi and Robby escorted her to her car just to be on the safe side. Now, all she wanted to do was pick up some clothes from her place, maybe something to eat, and head over to Jay's and crash for the night.

She grabbed her purse and messenger bag off the passenger seat, checked her phone for a message from Jay, and headed to her door, disappointed he hadn't texted but still hopeful he got done early tonight.

She kept her eyes peeled as she approached her door and unlocked it. All the hyper-vigilance made her paranoid about every shadow and sound in her complex.

The darkness outside and in her apartment made her rush to flip the light switch as she walked through the door and shut and locked it behind her. She set her purse on the dining table and dropped her bag in the bottom drawer in the kitchen where she always hid her laptop when she got home. Autopilot took her to the cabinet for a cup to make her favorite tea. She filled it at the sink, placed it in the microwave, and grabbed her travel mug and a tea bag while the water heated. She went to the fridge to find something to eat in the car on her way to Jay's before she packed her bag and got on the road. She could hit a drive-thru on the way, but didn't want to take the time this late at night.

Since she spent so many nights out at Jay's place, she hadn't really stocked her fridge, but she did have the makings for a decent roast turkey sandwich. She set the lunch meat, tomato, and head of lettuce on the cutting board along with a knife she pulled from the block, then reached for the overhead cupboard for a loaf of bread and the bag of her favorite thin and crispy tortilla chips. The microwave buzzed. She abandoned her cold dinner, took the mug out of the microwave to finish making her tea, but set the cup on the counter and rushed to the table when her phone dinged to see if Jay had finally texted her. Maybe they could meet for a late dinner together.

Glass cracked and shattered, tinkling on the hardwood floor in the living room before she reached her phone. She gasped and turned toward the startling sound. Obscured by the kitchen lights reflecting her apartment in the glass windows, she didn't see the threat until it was too late.

One of the two men dressed head to toe in black tossed the fist-size rock he used to break the glass back into the garden and reached through the hole, unlocking the door. Her mind went to Crazy Town and mocked her for not listening to her brothers or Jay about getting an alarm system. She'd meant to make the call, but she'd been consumed with spending time with Jay after his near death-experience and getting the goods on Noel.

The lattice fence and bushes out back blocked anyone

from seeing into her apartment and concealed the two men walking right into her house, their eyes, the only thing she could see of their faces, locked on her.

"Get out." She lunged for the phone on the bar-top counter.

One of the guys ran through her living room and smacked the phone out of her hand, sending it flying across the room and into the wall. It landed on the hardwood and skittered across the floor. She backed up, knowing there was no place to go. The small space made it easy for them to block the routes to the front door, back slider, and hall to her bedroom where she should have run the second she saw them.

Fear froze her in place. It pounded through her veins now, making it hard to think straight.

The man stalked her, pulling a knife from his cargo pocket and holding it up, taunting her with the wicked sharp blade. "What you going to do now?"

She frantically glanced around and found the closest weapon. The hot mug stung her hand as she flung the steaming water into his face.

He bellowed out a curse and ripped off the scalding hot mask. She vaguely recognized him as the man Noel argued with at the pharmacy, though now his blond hair stood on end in disarray and his face burned bright red from fury and the hot water dripping from it.

"Stupid bitch." He slashed the knife down at her.

Alina put her left arm up to block the knife from plunging into her chest. The blade sliced through the underside of her forearm. She swung the mug and clocked the guy in the temple, sending him back a couple of steps.

Blood ran down her arm and hand and dripped on the floor. She had just enough time to throw the mug at the second guy as he rushed forward. The cup bounced off his shoulder and landed on the floor with a thunk. She stumbled back into the kitchen to grab the knife off the cutting board.

With both men coming at her, she'd maybe get one more chance to defend herself before they overpowered her. She didn't want to think about what they'd do to her once they had her subdued.

The guy with the knife backed her farther into the galley kitchen toward the wall at her back.

"That cut looks bad," he taunted, his voice amused. "You're going to bleed out, but not before I teach you a lesson about meddling into things that are none of your fucking business." His voice rose with his building anger.

Desperate for a way out of this, she snatched the knife off the cutting board and lunged at the taunting man. He blocked her attempt to stab him, pushed her sideways, and grabbed her around the throat, cutting off her air as he pulled her into his chest and squeezed. He held the knife with her blood on it at her shoulder. In one quick motion, he could slice it across her throat. His breath came hard and heavy at her ear. "Where are the files you took?"

Her immediate need to breathe overrode everything. Her bloody arm hurt too much to move. She scratched at the guy's arm ineffectually because the knife handle pressed between her hand and his arm, while the blade poked her chest a few times, pricking her skin and sending out little blasts of searing pain.

"I know you have them. Stupid fucking Doc was too weak to grab them when he had the chance. He thinks he can scare you into keeping quiet. But not you." He shook her in frustration. "You know he's got you dead to rights on the same charges he'll face. A girl who dates a cop, has cop brothers, you're hell-bent on fucking all this up. I can't let you do that."

She struggled to get free, but the sparkling lights in her eyes and lack of oxygen were taking a toll.

"You're a fighter. At least you'll know you didn't go down without a fight." He squeezed harder.

With a last-ditch effort, she found the strength and clarity of mind to stop trying to move his arm and swing the knife with what little strength she had left. The blade hit his thigh and sliced deep. His scream blasted her eardrum a second before he let her go.

The second guy rushed forward to grab her. The guy behind her shoved her toward him. The next thing she knew the knife in her hand plunged into the guy's chest, blood oozing out and over her fingers.

Time seemed to stop, then move in slow motion.

Hazel eyes stared at her through the ski mask filled with shock. His hands dropped to his sides. His knees buckled and he fell to the floor, the knife pulling free in her hand. He landed in a pile of loose limbs, blood pumping out of his chest as his body trembled, then went still. His eyes stared, void of anything anymore.

"Davy!"

Startled out of her shock, she spun toward her other attacker. Light-headed, unsteady on her feet, her throat aching as she tried to suck in air, she stumbled back as he came after her again, slicing the knife through the air. She tried to duck out of the way, but the blade caught her on the top of her head and cut across her forehead in a searing path of pain. The back of her head cracked against the granite countertop as she fell backward to the floor and crumpled, weak from blood loss and unable to fight. She did the only thing left to do and pretended to be dead, praying he didn't plunge the knife right through her heart like she'd done to his friend Davy.

"Fuck, fuck, fuck!" He kneeled beside her, grabbed

her by the shoulders and shook her hard. "Where are the fucking files?"

With her head splitting with pain, she couldn't answer even if she tried. The last thing she wanted to do was give him a chance to hurt her more if he thought she was still awake.

He tossed her back to the floor. Her head hit hard on the goose-egg swelling and nearly made her scream. She didn't have to pretend so much anymore as the darkness crowded into her mind. She tried to fight it off, to be sure he left so she could call for help.

She needed help fast.

Her arm lay in a pool of blood, more ran down her face from the long gash.

The contents from her purse rained down to the floor and over her face as he upended it. He searched through the bag, then everything on the floor, scattering the items all over the place. Her phone spun and smacked her in the neck. It dinged with another text message.

The guy bent and swiped the screen. "Lover boy won't get any more replies from you, bitch." He dropped the phone next to her.

So close. But she didn't dare try to use it. Not until he left. Waiting for him to make a move turned seconds into interminably long minutes. Or so it seemed.

He stood and moved away, tossing her place, looking for the files.

She faded in and out with the sounds of drawers in the living room and bedroom crashing to the floor. The whole time, she prayed she'd see Jay again.

The guy walked out of her bedroom and sent the items on the bar top sailing through the air to the floor with one swipe of his arm across the top. "Fucking bitch got what she deserved." She felt rather than heard him move closer. Maybe he stared down at his dead friend. Maybe he regretted the life they lived that led them here.

She regretted not asking Jay to meet her tonight like he said he'd do if she needed him.

Now it was too late, but not to make sure Noel and this guy paid for what they'd done.

She hadn't heard him leave. Maybe she'd faded out again. For how long, she didn't know, but she took a chance and opened her eyes a slit to scan the quiet room. Nothing. She didn't feel him here anymore either. She could barely feel anything anymore.

She turned to her side, fumbled for the phone, and swiped the screen. Jay's texts came up.

JAY: Done early I'm at the office Are you still at work?

JAY: Hey where are you

She tapped the phone icon and waited for Jay to answer, hoping she got through and had the strength left to tell him about Noel and everything in her heart before it was too late.

CHAPTER THIRTY-THREE

Jay rolled his tense shoulders. Between work and worrying about Alina he'd barely had a moment's peace. Tonight's simple surveillance and arrest had turned into a shit-storm. A low-level drug dealer turned informant tipped them off to a supply exchange that included two high-up dealers who supplied Bozeman and Missoula. They showed up early, along with a lieutenant from the cartel and six well-armed guards. When the DEA stormed in to make the arrests, the drug dealers scattered like cockroaches when you turn on the lights. In the ensuing gunfight, one agent got shot. In the vest, thank God. Another twisted an ankle running after a guy. And Jay got caught by the Bozeman drug dealer who hated cops and DEA most of all. He hadn't gone down easy, but Jay finally slapped the cuffs on him after the guy attacked him, thinking he could fight his way out despite them both having guns. Jay should have shot him, but they needed the information they could get from him.

Now they'd get it, but Jay was a bit worse for wear with a bruised jaw and a black-and-blue swollen eye. But he'd gotten the operation done a lot earlier than expected and couldn't wait to meet up with Alina at his place once he finished the last few details.

He walked out of his office, slower than normal from fatigue and sore muscles. He was getting too old for this shit. Alina was going to have his head when she saw him. Then she'd go all soft when the fear dissipated and turned to concern. They'd both be happy the incident was over and he came out on top again.

"Hey, man, put this on that eye." Beck handed him an ice pack from the kitchenette freezer.

He'd been headed for coffee and the first aid kit. He took the ice pack and pressed it to his face.

"Alina is going to kill you when she sees that."

"She'll be happy the other guy didn't kill me."

Beck held his hand out. "Take these, they'll help."

Jay accepted the two ibuprofen, popped them in his mouth, and swallowed them without any water.

The knot in his gut prodded him about Alina's unusual silence. She should have texted him back by now. Unless she'd left work later than normal and was on the road to his place. Still, he worried. "Have you talked to your sister?"

Beck shook his head. "No. Why?"

His cell rang. He pulled it from his back pocket and sighed. "It's her." He accepted the call and put the phone to his ear. Beck stayed at his side. "Hey, sweetheart, are you at my place?"

"I'm sorry." Her voice was so weak he barely heard her.

Alarms went off in his head. "Alina. What's wrong?"

Beck tapped his shoulder, then pointed to the phone, his mouth drawn in a grim line.

He put the phone on speaker, so Beck could listen.

"I really wanted that future we talked about. I'm . . . I'm sorry I have to leave you. Not . . . not much time."

"Alina, where are you?" He desperately needed to get to her. He didn't know what she was talking about, but the fatalistic tone and stilted words scared him to death.

"I'm so cold. Blood. Everywhere. Too much."

Jay grabbed Beck by the shirt before his knees buckled.

"He's dead. Me too. I love you so mu . . ."

"Alina!"

Beck shouted to another agent. "Start tracking this number." Beck rattled off Alina's cell number. "I want to know where that phone is right now."

Caden walked out of his office and saw them standing in the middle of the cubicles.

"Alina, please, baby, answer me." His voice shook.

Caden's face paled. Beck's mouth set in a tight, grim line.

Jay barely held it together.

A heavy, ragged sigh broke the silence. "Files. In the . . . kitchen drawer."

"Files? What files?" Beck asked.

"Mandi," Alina whispered. "Mandi knows everything. With Robby from electronics store. Save her. Too late . . . for me."

"No! It's not too late. We're coming, sweetheart."

The agent tracking the phone rattled off Alina's home address.

Beck yelled, "Call an ambulance, send it there. Now!"

Caden grabbed another agent. "Find Robby from this store." Caden wrote the name of the electronics store across the street from the pharmacy. "I want officers or an agent protecting him and his girlfriend, Mandi, right now."

The agent took the note and got to work.

Jay, Caden, and Beck ran from the building to the parking lot. Beck grabbed Jay's arm and pulled him to his Camaro, all the while Jay called Alina's name over and over again, hoping she'd answer him.

Halfway to her place, a shuddering breath came through the open line.

Relieved to hear any sign of life, he tried to reach her again. "Alina? Hold on, sweetheart, I'm almost there.

Please, baby. Don't leave me." Jay fell into the side of the car as Beck sped around another corner on what felt like two tires. "You can't leave me now. We're supposed to get married and have babies and live on the ranch together."

"Make. Love. Under. Stars." The words sounded far off with little enunciation.

He was losing her. "Yes. Every damn night if you want. Please hold on. You can do it. I know you can. I love you so damn much. There's nothing if I don't have you."

"Love. You." Another shuddering breath escaped her.

"Yes, you love me. I love you."

"Gift."

"Yes." He pulled the box out of his pocket. "I have it for you. You want it, don't you?"

"What?"

He pressed the velvet box to his forehead and tried to hold it together. "A ring. I'll give it to you, and you'll say yes. You said you'd say yes."

"Yes." The word came out on a heavy exhale, then nothing but terrorizing quiet.

Caden stared at him from the front seat, fear and the shine of tears in his eyes. He glanced at the velvet box, then back at Jay. "You'll get to put that on her finger."

But would she be alive or dead when he did?

That grim thought led to thoughts of his desolate future without her. The thought shattered his heart into a billion bits.

Desperate, he begged, "Sweetheart, come on, hold on, I'm coming."

Just when he thought he couldn't take any more, a loud bang and crash sounded. Shuffling sounds that made no sense until someone yelled, "Clear."

Then more movement and voices.

Jay's heart swelled with hope. Help had arrived.

"Jesus, that's a lot of blood."

Jay's heart dropped into his stomach.

"No pulse. This one's dead."

Jay's heart stopped.

"She's got a pulse."

Jay sucked in a ragged breath and thanked God she hadn't been taken from him.

"Barely."

His heart clenched again. He didn't know how much more he could take. He needed to be with her. Now.

"It's thready. Let's get an IV going. We need pressure on these wounds before she bleeds out."

Tears slid down his cheeks and he sat immobile, feeling useless, and overpowered with a need to get to her but stuck in this damn car instead of where he should be. With her.

He stared at the phone willing her to make one tiny sound. Anything.

But all he heard were the men working on her.

Beck skidded to a stop in the parking lot behind two patrol cars and the ambulance. Red-and-blue lights swirled against the dark building and bystanders on the sidewalk outside Alina's place. They jumped out of the car and ran into her house like a pack of wild dogs on the hunt.

Jay beat Caden and Beck into the living room. He glanced at the destruction, the broken back window, then turned to the kitchen, the dead man lying on the floor, the table and chairs pushed back against the wall, and the two men kneeling on the floor working on Alina, lying in a pool of blood, her face completely covered in it.

He'd seen a lot of bad shit in his line of work, but nothing as horrific as the woman he loved lying bloody and motionless.

The phone lay on the floor next to her head, blood pooled on top of it. A bloody knife lay on the floor by her side. His gaze went from it to the guy lying dead at his feet.

"What the hell is the DEA doing here?" an officer asked.

Beck waved the cop to him. "I'll fill you in."

Caden put his hand on Jay's shoulder to hold him back from going to Alina. "Let them work on her."

Jay crouched and stared at Alina's bloody face. "I'm here, sweetheart. You're going to be okay now."

The paramedics exchanged concerned looks that tightened the band around his chest to the point he could barely breathe.

The paramedics had placed a thick pad on her forehead and wound gauze around her head. Her arm was bound up so thick and tight he didn't know if she broke it or what. They had her blouse spread open, round pads with wires ran from her chest to a machine on the gurney at her head. The screen showed a steady beat. At least, he hoped so.

Small nicks and cuts left red marks just below her bra over her abdomen.

"What's the damage, guys?"

The paramedics glanced up at him for a second, saw the badge, then went back to work on Alina's arm.

One of them finally spoke up and pointed to her head. "Major head trauma to the back." He pointed to the blood smear on the edge of the counter. "Best guess, someone slashed her arm and face, then she hit there and fell to the floor."

"How bad are the cuts?"

"Both go down to the bone. Head wounds always bleed a lot. But most of what you see on the floor"—he pointed to the fat drops and small puddles—"came from the arm. She'll need surgery, if we can keep her stable. She's lost a lot of blood."

"What about this guy?"

"Stabbed once in the chest, right through the heart. When the knife came out, he died pretty quick."

Jay stared at the knife on the floor by Alina's bloody right hand. The left was bandaged.

Jay raked his fingers through his hair, chastising himself for letting this happen. "It looks like she stabbed him."

"That's my guess. Cops will bag the knife and print it. If she makes it, she can tell them what happened."

"*When* she makes it," he growled, unable to even consider the possibility he might lose her. He needed to believe. They all did. For her.

The paramedic exchanged another grim look with his buddy as they put the backboard in place, gently rolled Alina, laid her down, then strapped her down to transport her.

He gave them space to work because the kitchen was too small with a body on the floor, the two men, Alina, the gurney they put her on, and the tables and chairs pushed against the wall.

He turned to Caden. "What do you think happened here?"

"There were two of them. That guy doesn't have any blood on him other than the chest wound."

"If there had only been one of them, she'd have taken him down like she did this guy."

Beck joined them. "Cops thought this was just another break-in. I put them on to Noel. They're on their way to the pharmacy and Noel's home. I want that guy in cuffs."

"You think he did this?" Jay shook his head. "I've met the guy. Your sister practically kicked his ass. No way he came after her with a knife and tried to kill her. He's too pathetic to really stand up for himself in a physical fight."

"Who's that guy?" Beck gestured into the kitchen.

"Don't know. The cops will ID him, but this is a crime scene. As much as I want to rip that mask off and go through his pockets, we can't mess with the scene."

Caden glanced around the kitchen. "She said something about a file. The kitchen drawer. Mandi knows everything."

Jay stayed by Alina's side as the paramedics packed and loaded their equipment.

Beck carefully stepped over the dead guy and all the blood and went after the kitchen drawers, slamming them until he found her bag in the bottom one. He backtracked to the living room making sure he didn't disturb the scene.

Jay should have followed his gut and asked someone else to cover for him tonight. He'd let work interfere when he knew something was up with Noel.

This was his fault.

"Got it." Beck opened the computer and read the open file. "Noel refills deceased customers' prescriptions for Schedule II drugs. He gives them to someone else to sell."

"Probably this asshole on the floor," Jay guessed.

"Noel provides a list of customers who have new or recurring prescriptions and gives the list to someone who breaks into their houses to steal the pills."

"That explains these articles about local break-ins." Caden held up a stack of papers he'd pulled out of her bag. "I'll have to sort through these prescription records, but I'm guessing one bundle is deceased customers, the other customers with recent prescriptions."

Jay took Alina's hand as they moved her out of the kitchen toward the front door. "You guys figure it out. I'm going with her."

"We'll meet you there as soon as we confirm they've got Noel in custody." Beck answered his phone, listened for a minute, then sighed with relief. "Thanks." He hung up. "Our agent is with Mandi. She's safe. We'll have the story from her shortly. Keep in touch! We'll be there soon!" Beck shouted at him as Jay walked out the door with Alina's hand in his. He'd let Beck and Caden handle Noel and Mandi.

He didn't want to let Alina go. Not right now. "I'm here, sweetheart. You're going to be okay." He hoped she heard him. He hoped she believed like he needed to believe that she would make it through this.

Jay climbed in the ambulance behind one of the paramedics.

"How's she doing?"

He didn't give Jay a direct answer, just yelled up front, "Let's go. Time's critical."

Jay focused on Alina's bloodstained face, hoping for any sign that she knew he was there. Any twitch or movement. She lay still as death, and that thought stopped his heart.

"Come on, sweetheart, don't give up. We have a long and happy life ahead of us."

He had to believe that, because a future without her wasn't a future worth living.

By the time they rolled into the hospital emergency room, his nerves were shot and his prayers had whittled down to a single word: *live*.

CHAPTER THIRTY-FOUR

Distracted, on edge, Noel missed the turn for his street and swore as he drove around the block again. In the backseat, ice cream melted in one of the many bags of groceries he'd picked up for Lee. He couldn't concentrate, his focus was on Brian and Davy. He'd given them the list they demanded, but he'd asked for one simple thing in return. Get that damn file away from Alina. If she gave them to her boyfriend or brothers, he was a dead man. Or might as well be if he got caught and ended up in jail. His wife would kill him. His girls would never speak to him again.

He'd lose them, the business, everything.

And all for what? It seemed an easy way to make money. He never thought too much about the lives it affected. He'd told himself it was to keep his head above water on the medical bills. Now the money coming in far exceeded them. He'd tried to keep things small, but Brian pushed for more. And now the simple scheme had grown to hundreds of customers and orders.

And when Brian got caught in those two homes he should have walked away. But no, that punk had to go and be a badass and hit them.

Even Noel knew he was making excuses, the same way Brian did about what happened. Nothing but an accident. Hey, he got the pills, sold them, they all got paid. What the fuck did it matter?

It mattered to those people's family and friends. It mattered to Noel. But not enough to put an end to this. Because he'd seen in Brian's eyes that he'd never let Noel walk away clean. He'd threatened to go to his wife, to Alina.

Noel stopped at the stop sign on the street behind his, stared up at the star-speckled night, and tried to calm his nerves and racing mind.

Noel's phone vibrated in his pocket. He checked caller ID and picked up immediately. "Is it done?"

"Fucking bitch killed Davy. She sliced my leg clean open. I'm bleeding like a stuck pig. Fuck, fuck, fuck." Something pounded in the background again and again with each swear word.

Noel could only guess Brian was hitting something, but put that out of his mind and focused on what Brian said. "Davy is dead? How?"

"Your sweet-ass partner stabbed him dead center in the chest. He dropped like a zombie with his head cut off. She cut me. Fucking bitch. I put her ass down."

"You killed her!" Noel's heart stopped, then slammed into his rib cage like a jackhammer, threatening to break his ribs.

"If she wasn't dead, will be soon. I left her a bloody fucking mess."

"I told you to get the folder, not kill her!"

"If you'd had the balls to take the thing, none of this would have happened. This is on you, Doc."

"You were supposed to take it without her knowing."

"She didn't leave the bag at work or in her car. She took it home. I had no choice but to get it back. Besides, I thought you'd be happy about this. It eliminates her from the business. You own the whole thing again. Right?"

"No, you stupid . . . her share probably goes to her two *DEA* brothers. You've totally fucked us."

"I did what I had to do because you didn't take that shit away from her when you had the chance. Before I took off from her place, I saw the cops, the boyfriend, and two other guys show up. If they know anything, my guess, they'll be coming for you soon." Brian hissed in pain. "I can't get this thing to stop bleeding."

"Keep the pressure on until it stops. Clean it and bandage it. And for God's sake, don't call me again. This is done. I need to get out of here before the cops show up."

"We're not done, Doc. I'll be in touch." Brian hung up.

Noel didn't stop to think. Instead of turning right toward home, he turned left. A police cruiser sped toward him from behind, lights flashing, but siren off. Noel watched him turn down his street in the rearview mirror and tried to fight off another wave of panic.

Three blocks away, he breathed a sigh of relief that he'd escaped.

But where the hell was he going?

He thought of his poor, sick Lee. She'd be devastated. She'd blame herself, thinking he'd done all of this for her because of the doctor bills. His girls would blame themselves, too. He'd always told them how important it was for them to get the best education possible. He'd just never figured out how to pay for it all. He wanted them to have the best of everything. He wanted to make them happy.

And some part of him liked the danger of it all.

He'd been sinking deeper into debt until Alina came along. He'd already started with Brian, but the cash she put into the business gave him some much needed breathing room. Her smile and kindness brought sunshine into his increasingly dark world. He enjoyed going to work each day. Spending time with her made the day go by faster and made it enjoyable in a way it hadn't felt in a long time. He'd been in a rut. Stuck on the treadmill of life, every day the same.

Her youth and exuberance infused him with a renewed appreciation for his work and their customers. With his wife's future shrinking, he'd seen one with Alina spreading out in front of him.

He couldn't believe she was dead. A hole formed in his heart and bled with her loss. Missing her engulfed him with regret and remorse. He didn't like the way they'd left things. He wished he could make it up to her.

With his life turned to shit, he couldn't do anything but run and leave everyone he loved behind.

A wave of guilt and remorse swamped his heart.

He'd tried to do right by his family, but only ended up shaming himself and ruining their future.

He turned down a side street, not knowing where he was going, but understanding one thing for certain: those DEA guys would hunt him for the rest of his life to avenge Alina's death. He deserved it, and worse.

CHAPTER THIRTY-FIVE

Alina woke up by degrees, at first just aware of the quiet. The darkness that had claimed her time and again when the pain got too much to bear and sucked her back under receded this time so she knew she was lying in a bed. Her arm throbbed in time with the pulse in the back of her head. She opened her eyes a little at a time and found Jay sitting beside her, his head bowed, arms folded over his chest as he slept in a chair. Mussed hair, thick scruff along his jaw, and a fading bruise and swelling around his eye sent a bolt of confusion and concern through her.

She glanced around the room, not surprised to realize she was in the hospital, but shocked to see her two brothers on the other side of her bed with their wives asleep in their laps. She turned back to Jay. He sat so close to the bed, his arm pressed against the mattress. She reached down and touched his shoulder with her fingertips.

Jay's bloodshot eyes flew open and locked on her.

"Your lap's empty," she whispered.

He barely spared a glance to her brothers and sisters-in-law before he rose partway, turned to her, buried his face on her stomach, slipped one arm under her back, the other over her hips, and held her close. She rubbed her hand over his shoulders, careful of the IV line attached to it, then brushed her fingers over his hair.

His arms tightened around her. He wiped his face on the sheet covering her and rolled his head to the side and stared up at her, his eyelashes damp.

Shocked to see tears spilling from his eyes, she gasped, then laid her hand on his face. "Hey now. I'm okay. It's all right." Tears filled her eyes. She couldn't stand to see him upset like this. "What happened?" She softly touched her fingertips just outside the bruise around his eye. "Are you okay?" Her voice hitched with the emotion clogging her throat.

He slid his hand out from under her, rose up on his palms, leaned over, and kissed her softly, long and soft and filled with so much love her heart ached. He moved back an inch and stared into her eyes. "I've been waiting for you to come back to me for nearly three days. Don't ever scare me like that again." He kissed her again, this time adding a bit more punch as his relief washed over her.

It all came back to her in a burst of memory that swamped her system with a blast of adrenaline and fear. Her heart thrashed in her chest and the pain in her head went from an annoyance she could tolerate to splitting pain.

Jay leaned back and placed his big hand on her chest. "Breathe, baby. You're okay. You're safe."

"Did you get him? Did you find it? He has to be stopped."

"Shh." Jay tried to soothe her.

She tried to get up, but he gently held her down. She didn't know where she wanted to go, but the panic made her want to run and hide. "He sent them."

Jay's eyes went wide, then narrowed with fury.

A nurse appeared at her side with a syringe. Alina noticed her brothers and sisters were up and standing around her bed. She glanced at Jay, who didn't seem to know what to do with her in her frazzled state.

"I don't want that," she told the nurse. "I don't want to go back to sleep."

"It's for the pain."

Alina pressed her fingertips to the back of her head. It hurt like hell, but she needed to stay clear and find out what happened after she was attacked.

She sucked in a deep breath and tried to calm herself down. "I need to talk to him. Please, can you come back in a little while?" She sucked in another soothing breath. As her heart slowed, so did the pounding in her head.

Jay rubbed his hand over her arm. "Are you sure, sweetheart? You look like you could use that."

"I can wait. It's getting better."

The nurse set the tablet with Alina's medical information and syringe aside. She checked her IV line, took her blood pressure, then asked her a few simple questions to be sure she had her head screwed on straight. "I'll let your doctor know you're awake. He'll probably be here to check on you within the hour. If you want the pain meds before I come back, just hit the call button. I'll bring them right away."

Alina closed her eyes for a moment to give herself a chance to relax. Jay's hand slid into hers. He linked their fingers and held on. "That makes everything better." She squeezed his hand, then opened her eyes to the crowd around her bed. "You guys didn't have to stay here."

Ashley patted her thigh. "Nonsense. We love you. Jay's right, you gave us quite a scare."

Beck clamped his hand over her calf. "I sent Mom and Dad home to rest, but they'll be back later. I'll give them a call and let them know you're awake. They'll be beyond relieved."

Caden stood with Mia's back to his chest, his arm wrapped around her middle. Happiness and concern filled his eyes. "Mandi is safe and sound and helping one of our techs sort through the pharmacy database and all the information you uncovered. Noel got away. We've got the cops, FBI, and DEA all looking for him."

"What about the other guy? I stabbed him." Her hand trembled with the gruesome memory.

"He died in the kitchen, sweetheart."

Guilt and remorse filled her aching heart for Davy. She would never forget the empty look in his eyes when he died at her feet. She hated Noel for putting this all in motion and making her have to take a life to defend herself. She hated that it happened, hated that she'd done it. But she had survived and somehow she'd learn to live with it.

She shook off those thoughts and focused on the guy who tried to kill her. "There was another man."

Jay, Caden, and Beck exchanged a look, but Jay spoke for them. "We thought there might be someone else involved, but none of your neighbors saw anything. Mandi couldn't ID the guy we found dead on your floor. Without Noel, we had to wait for you to wake up." The gruffness in his voice told her that he'd had to face the real possibility she wouldn't wake up.

"I saw Noel with him twice at the pharmacy. They argued about something at the back door. Noel lied to me, said it was Mandi and her boyfriend, but then I met Mandi's new guy and it wasn't him. Then, the night I was attacked, Noel came to the pharmacy even though I'd told him to stay away that day. He printed something out. I had the copier print it for me again. It was a list of customers who had pain meds. I went after him. I was going to follow him to see who he was giving the pills and names to."

Jay's hand tightened on hers. "Damnit, Alina, why didn't you tell me? I would have helped you and kept you out of it."

She dismissed the anger in Jay's voice. He wanted to protect and keep her safe. She couldn't fault him for that. "I thought I had time. At least until I could deliver the files to you that night or the next morning. Noel cared about me. I never thought he'd hurt me."

"Two men tried to kill you," Jay snapped. "Do you have any idea how I felt when you made that call to me?"

"Like I felt when you texted me after you nearly got blown up." She gave him a soft smile, letting him know she got it.

He glared and growled out his frustration. "Alina." Just her name in warning to not push him. He'd been through a lot these last few days, so she backed off. Maybe now wasn't a great time to point out that he faced even more danger than she did on a regular basis.

"Noel sent those men to find the files. Once he had them back, I think he planned to blackmail me."

Beck nodded. "We went through the paperwork and your notes. He used your ID to refill orders to implicate you."

"Exactly. But the guys he's working with wanted to go back to just working with Noel with me out of the way and not nosing around in their business. So they tried to kill me again."

"Again?" Caden asked.

Jay swore. "They ran you off the road."

She nodded. "When I saw Noel give the guy the list of names, it triggered a fuzzy memory of the accident. I saw him sitting in the busted-up SUV before he drove away and left me there."

"I knew it wasn't an accident." Jay raked his fingers through his disheveled hair.

"I didn't really think so either, but I had nothing to back it up. We thought it was cartel related. It had to do with drugs, just not the way we thought. I wasn't targeted because you're DEA. I don't know who I killed, but the other guy is the one from the car accident, the one Noel seemed to deal with the most. The other guy was just in on it."

"So, the two leaders of the group are still at large." Caden glanced at Beck, some silent communication they'd get on it.

"I can give you a description of him and his truck."

Jay pulled a folder out of a bag on the floor. He laid it on her stomach, opened it, and rifled through the papers with his free hand so he didn't have to let go of her with the other. "The cops took the lead on the case with an assist from the FBI. The guy you killed had a couple speeding tickets and a petty theft arrest that got pled out to a slap on the wrist. They tracked down all his known associates and interviewed them all to see if they were at your place that day. Everyone alibied out, but they all said Davy spent most of his time with one guy." Jay held the photo up to her.

She lost herself in the nightmare. "They broke in through the slider. My first thought was that you guys were right about the alarm system and poor security." She couldn't even muster a self-deprecating grin. "He came after me, wanting the files." The same wash of fear she felt when it happened rushed through her again. "I was blocked in the kitchen, so I used whatever I could to fight him off. I was making tea and threw my hot water in his face and clocked him with the mug. It only made him mad. He pulled the knife and slashed my arm." She looked down at her bandaged arm and swollen fingers that tingled like her hand had fallen asleep.

Jay swept the hair from her forehead and tucked a lock behind her ear. "Seven hours in surgery to repair the muscle and ligaments. Doctor says you should regain full use of your hand with some physical therapy once it heals."

It hurt, but she wiggled her fingers just to see if she could. Relief shot through her on a wave of adrenaline.

"I grabbed the knife off the cutting board. He overpowered me and got his arm around my throat. He tried to strangle me. I tried to get free, but my cut arm was useless and I still had the knife in my hand." She touched her stomach.

"We wondered about the cuts."

"I kept poking myself as I tried to move his arm. I couldn't breathe. My mind wasn't working fast enough, but it finally dawned on me to use the knife. I sliced his leg." Disbelief filled her voice even as she remembered doing it. "It cut deep. He yelled. The other guy, Davy, rushed forward, but the guy behind me shoved me forward. I was holding the knife and it plunged right into Davy's chest." She lost herself in the unbelievable image and the surprise she'd felt in that moment. "I didn't mean to do it." Conviction filled her voice, because she'd give anything to take it back. "I just wanted to get away. He dropped to the floor. I couldn't seem to let go of the knife. Blood poured out of him. Everything in his eyes blinked out." She stared, seeing the poor young guy dead at her feet. "The rest happened so fast. I turned to the man still behind me. He tried to stab me, but I leaned back and he caught me on the head." She touched the bandage over her forehead.

"Twenty-nine stitches," Jay confirmed. "Another fifteen in the back of your head."

"I fell back against the counter and landed hard on the floor. I thought, play dead, but I think I was kind of in and out. There was a lot of noise and then nothing but quiet."

Beck rubbed her leg. "He ransacked your place looking for the files."

She looked up at Jay. "I thought it was over. I needed

to hear your voice one more time. I had to tell you I love you and how much it meant to me to have you in my life."

Jay turned to her family. "Mind giving us some time alone?"

Ashley smiled. "Mia and I will be back later. We'll bring you something sweet and decadent and some magazines to pass the time while you rest." Ashley tilted her head toward the door for Mia to come with her.

"Chocolate cupcakes with vanilla icing," Alina called to Mia.

"You got it." Mia smiled.

Jay released her hand and stood back, letting Caden in on his side.

Beck came to her on the other and leaned down and kissed her cheek. "You're one tough lady, sis." He hugged her close.

She held on to him and whispered, "I learned it from my badass brother."

Caden brushed his fingers over her hair, then tugged a lock of it like he used to do when she was little and being a brat. "The worst I thought I had to worry about was some guy not treating you like the princess you loved to play when we were kids when you made Beck and me your valiant knights. I never thought you'd have to go through something like this. I'm so proud of you, sis. You fought hard. Don't dwell on what happened. You won. You came back to us. That's all that matters." Caden leaned down and kissed her cheek. "I love you, sis."

"I love you, too." She glanced over at Beck. "You, too."

Beck smiled and gave her thigh a pat, then walked around the bed and wrapped Jay in a bear hug. He stepped back and looked Jay in the eye. "Take care of her, brother."

Caden gave Jay a hug, too, then gave him a smack

on the shoulder. "Thank you, brother, for making her happy."

It touched her deeply to see her brothers say so much to her and Jay with those few words that conveyed their trust and gratitude.

They walked toward the door to leave her and Jay alone, so they could talk privately.

"Hey," she called. When they turned to her, she smiled and hoped they understood how much it meant to her that they accepted Jay. "You're still my knights."

They came back, kissed her cheeks, and hugged her again before walking out the door, leaving her heart filled to overflowing with love.

"You know what them calling you brother means, don't you?"

Jay nodded, rubbing a hand over his chest. His heart had some bad moments these last few days, but his partners and soon-to-be brothers-for-real had touched him deeply. "Yeah. I know." He wanted to crawl in bed beside her and hold her close, but opted to sit on the edge of the bed and take her hand because he didn't want to hurt her and they wouldn't fit. "I thought it might take a while for them to really accept and be comfortable with you and me, but all it took was me going crazy at your bedside for them to see how much I love you."

"Jay . . ."

"I'm sorry I let you down." He'd known something was wrong, had even offered to drop everything and go to her. He should have listened to his instincts and done it. His instincts had kept him alive more than once. This time, his not listening nearly cost him the love of his life.

"You did not let me down. I believed Noel would never hurt me. I didn't take into account his partners. It's my fault. I told you it could wait. I should have driven straight to your house instead of stopping by mine to grab some food and clothes."

He didn't want to dwell on it anymore. "The DEA shut down the pharmacy."

Her mouth tilted in a half frown. "I figured they would."

"You'll be the key witness against Noel. You'll need to testify."

"Wait. What? I'm not being prosecuted?"

"Technically, you turned him in. Your records and notes were specific and detailed. With your background, and having so many DEA agents in your life, the ones in charge of the investigation, along with the FBI, believe you'd have done a much better job covering your tracks if you were involved. The whole thing was blatant but contained to the pharmacy. If Noel hadn't taken you on as a partner and exposed himself to you discovering what he was doing, then he'd have probably gotten away with it for a long time."

"So I get to keep my license?"

"Yes."

"And how much of the DEA and FBI understanding that I had nothing to do with this had to do with you making them believe that?"

"You can thank your brothers for the major part of that, but I backed them up when the FBI came to question me."

Emotion clogged her throat. "You never left my side."

"Hell, no. I hoped that if you could hear me, know I was here waiting for you, you'd fight even harder to come back."

"Was I really that bad?" Fear laced her words.

"The cuts and surgery were nothing compared to that head injury." He closed his eyes on a sigh. The weariness sapping his energy and letting all his doubts and concerns flood back. He had to open his eyes to reassure himself she was awake and talking and even with the bandages and pale skin she was the most beautiful woman he'd ever seen.

"I'm tired and sore, but I'm okay." She squeezed his hand. "Go home. Sleep. I'm not going anywhere."

Jay shook his head all through those words. "I'm not leaving here without you."

The gun and badge at his waist told her why. A flash of fear shot through her eyes. "You're afraid he'll come to finish me off."

"I'm not giving anyone a chance to try. I catch that guy before the cops do, he'll wish he was dead." He meant every word.

She smiled, appreciating the sentiment. "You're sweet."

He felt surly and ready to beat that guy into the ground. Six feet under would make him happy. "About you leaving with me."

She settled deeper into the pillow, sleep creeping in as her eyes fluttered. She rubbed her thumb against his palm, the motion growing slower. "I don't want to go back to my place. I can't stop thinking about it." A shiver ran through her, raising goose bumps on her arms.

He ran his hand over her skin to smooth them away and comfort her. "Stay with me."

"Hmm. That sounds nice." She began to really drift.

He wanted to get this settled now. "Move in with me."

Her eyes flew open. "What?"

"Say yes."

"Jay," she sighed. "You're upset about what happened." She didn't believe he meant it.

"Either you move in with me, or I move in with you. Either way, I'm not spending another night without you. So what's it going to be? Your place or mine?"

She studied him for a minute. He didn't back down from his resolve. This was the least of what he wanted, but he'd get to the rest soon enough. He wasn't proposing to her while she lay in a hospital bed. She deserved special. She deserved everything wonderful that asshole tried to steal away from her and Jay when he almost killed her.

"How about we make your place *our* place?"

He let out the breath that lodged in his chest when she didn't answer him immediately.

"Deal." He practically fell down to her and kissed her softly.

The door opened behind them. He pressed up on his hands and whipped his head around to see who was there, keeping his body over Alina to protect her.

Her hand slid up his chest to his scruffy jaw. "It's just the nurse. I really need those meds now."

He nodded down at her. "Sleep. I'll be here when you wake up."

The nurse checked the band on Alina's arm, the chart, and the syringe to verify they all had the same code. "This will have some kick and work quickly." She shot the drugs into the IV line.

It took a second, but then Alina's eyes went wide. "Wow. That's got some punch."

The nurse smiled and retreated.

Jay rubbed her arm up and down as her eyes drifted shut again. He'd settle back into his chair and quiet vigil once she was out again.

Alina sighed and adjusted her position, trying not to move her bandaged arm. "Did you tell me you bought me a present?" Her drug-groggy voice faded with every word.

He smiled and pulled the velvet box from his hip pocket. "I did. I'll give it to you when we get home."

"'Kay," she whispered.

He flipped the box open and stared at the diamond ring he wanted more than anything to slip on her hand. But one glimpse of her swollen fingers and he prayed the doctor was right and she'd regain full use of her hand. They wouldn't know until it healed and she started using it. No matter what, he intended to keep her safe, marry her, and have a long and happy life with her by his side. Forever was a start.

First, he needed to find the men who hurt her and make them pay.

CHAPTER THIRTY-SIX

Jay approached the abandoned house with the other officers from the local PD and the two FBI agents overseeing the multi-jurisdictional case. The tip came in an hour ago and Jay hoped the neighbor who spotted a man limping badly going into the slanting building with the sagging porch panned out. Noel wasn't the threat Brian posed, and Jay wanted that bastard locked up or six feet under immediately.

Overgrown bushes crowded around the house. Most of the windows were boarded over or missing. The approach left them in the open, but Jay hoped they kept the element of surprise.

One of the officers held the battering ram, but they didn't need it. The front door hung open six inches from one hinge. Jay and the team members held their breaths, listening for any sound inside. Jay had done this more than a hundred times, but he found it hard to hold back the adrenaline rush and need to shoot on sight. He sucked in a breath and focused on the job. He wanted to go back to Alina and tell her he'd found the bastard who hurt her and she was safe.

She'd woken him in the night, caught in a nightmare that had her thrashing in the bed and screaming in her sleep. It took him ten minutes to calm her down enough so the nurse didn't have to sedate her. That chilling scene alone made him want to put a bullet in the stupid prick who should have known better than to go after a DEA agent's family, his girlfriend, and the most important person in Jay's world.

The fucker had to pay.

The officer ahead of him shouldered the door open and against the wall, allowing Jay and the other agents and officers to enter, guns drawn.

Jay met Caden in the open living area as his team came through the back. Jay stared down at the bloody rags on the broken wooden table. The other officers and agents fanned out and checked the single bedroom and bathroom. They had more people than they needed, but everyone in law enforcement wanted this guy because Alina was tied to Jay and her brothers. Law enforcement looked out for their own. He'd put his life on the line for any one of them if it was someone in their family.

"Clear," rang out several times, a note of disappointment in all their voices.

"He's not here, but I think this is our guy." Jay swore. "He's bleeding badly. Did the neighbor spot a red-and-white truck?"

"No," one of the officers who'd covered the back said. "But there are tracks in the dirt. If he parked out there by the tree, no one would have seen it unless they went around the back of this dump."

Jay swore again. "The call came in an hour ago. He couldn't have gotten far."

The FBI agent—Jay couldn't remember any of their names, he was so tired—answered. "We set up roadblocks in conjunction with coordinating this. We hoped to arrest him here, but made contingency plans just in case he left before we got here or he escaped. I'll check in with the teams, see if they've spotted the truck or our guy."

Jay walked around the living room and kitchen, looking for any clue to tell him where this guy had been or was going.

Aside from wrappers from two frozen burritos and a small chip bag, they didn't find anything else.

"Do you think he ate them frozen?" Caden asked.

"Gas station grab and go. He nuked them there, then found this place to lie low for the night." Jay slammed his fist on the scarred and sticky counter. A mouse ran out from under it and skittered across his boot and the dusty wood floor. "I can't believe we missed him."

"I'll have Agent Williams coordinate with the local PD to check out all the convenience stores in the area to see if our guy stopped for gas and food."

"That will tell us where he was. I want to know where he is right now."

Caden clamped his hand on Jay's shoulder. "So do I. I want this guy as bad as you do." Caden slapped him on the back. "You better get back to the hospital. I'll keep you posted. Alina needs you right now."

Jay needed her. Tired to the bone, he wanted to take her home and get her settled. He wanted to hold her in his arms and reassure her everything would be okay.

More than anything, he wanted to tell her this was over.

But this cabin was only fifteen miles out of town. If the dumbshit hadn't run and gotten as far away as possible by now, it could only mean one thing: he wanted to finish what he started.

CHAPTER THIRTY-SEVEN

Alina held both hands on the tray table over her bed while Ashley painted her nails a pretty, soft lavender. Beck sat in the chair beside her, staring at all the people walking by staring at his famous wife, but she knew better. He was watching out for her because they'd finally coaxed Jay to go home this morning to shower, eat a proper meal, and, she hoped, get some sleep.

Or so they'd told her.

Beck checked another text and grumbled under his breath and typed out a reply.

"So they didn't get him, huh?"

"No." Beck stopped typing and swore. "I need to go back undercover. I'm losing my touch."

"Where is Jay, really?"

"We got a tip that someone matching Brian's description was squatting in an abandoned shack." Beck looked up at her. "Don't tell him I told you."

"I take it Caden is with him."

Beck didn't look at her. Ashley nodded confirmation.

"Jay was supposed to go home and rest. He's barely slept the last four days."

Beck tilted his head and met her annoyed glare. "He wants to catch these guys before they hurt you again. I've never seen him like this. He's always driven, but for you, he's a man on a mission. Even from here, he kept track of the investigation and hunt for these guys."

"Do you know how Lee is doing?"

Beck's eyes grew troubled. "She was here yesterday for her treatment. I spoke to her briefly. She's devastated."

"I can only imagine. One day her husband goes to work, then doesn't come home and the cops show up, you think the worst, but you discover there's more than one kind of worst and your husband is a drug supplier—and not the kind you thought."

"He's more than that. He's implicated in those two home invasion deaths and your attempted murder." Beck read another text that only made him frown harder.

"Don't mind him. He's just mad he's not out there with the guys." Ashley blew on Alina's wet nails and screwed the lid back on the nail polish bottle. "Done. So pretty."

Alina admired her perfect nails. "You know, if the whole acting thing doesn't work out, you could open your own nail salon."

She and Ashley laughed together. Ashley was used to having people fuss over her on a movie set. It made Alina feel a bit strange to have Ashley fuss over her. With two older brothers, she'd grown up more tomboy than girly-girl. But the distraction helped keep boredom at bay and the nightmare of what happened from swamping her mind and sending her into a full-blown panic attack. Her hands shook when she thought about it. That one image of her holding the knife in Davy's chest and him slipping to the floor sent chills up her spine.

"Alina!" Jay snapped to get her attention.

Davy's dead eyes vanished from her mind. She shook free of the fear clawing at her insides and stared up at Jay standing next to her. "Hi."

Jay cupped her face. "You okay?"

"Yeah, fine. How was your shower and nap?" She eyed his still scruffy face and bloodshot eyes.

He rubbed his hand over his thickening beard. "The thing is—"

"You lied to me."

Jay glanced at Beck and Ashley, their avid audience. His gaze turned frosty on Beck. "I didn't want to worry you."

"Don't blame him. You said you were going home. You need to sleep."

"I need to find those bastards," he snapped, his frustration getting the better of him.

She leaned into his hand. "Okay. But you don't need to lie to me about it."

"After what you went through, the way you looked when I walked in here . . . I don't ever want to see that kind of fear in you. I need you to be safe. And more than anything I want you to feel safe."

"I do, when I'm with you. So take me home. Be with me."

Jay cocked his head. "They discharged you already?"

"Half an hour ago. Beck refused to take me by my place to pack some things. He said I had to wait for you."

Jay and Beck exchanged a look only they understood.

Ashley headed for the door. "I'll go tell the nurse you're ready to go home."

"Great, she'll probably start a riot in the halls." Beck went after his famous wife. No fewer than fifty people had traipsed past Alina's hospital room, trying to get a peek at Ashley.

Jay brushed his hand over her hair. "Are you feeling well enough to leave? How's your head?"

They'd removed the massive bandages around her head and on her arm to allow her a quick shower this morning. She felt clean and almost human again. But the sight of all those stitches across her forehead and over her arm made her heart sink and stomach ache. She didn't want to be reminded of what happened every time she looked in the mirror. The doctor assured her the scarring would be minimal and would fade over time. He said the same about the punch the memories had when they came, too.

"The headache is gone." She held up her arm. "They wrapped it but said I could take it off in a day or two." She touched just under the line of stitches on her head.

Jay read her upset. "It's okay, sweetheart. In a couple of days when the swelling subsides and the bruising fades, it won't be so bad." To distract her, he held up her good hand. "This is nice."

"Ashley painted them while we waited for you to get back from hunting bad guys."

"I'm sorry, sweetheart." He yawned and covered his mouth with his hand.

"You can't keep me in the dark on this, Jay. If I know what's happening, then I won't let my mind spin out on all the what-ifs." She could control the overwhelming fear and anticipate the consequences.

Jay yawned again and reluctantly said, "I'll keep you in the loop."

"What did the cops say after they interviewed me this morning?" She'd recounted her story for them with minimal elaboration on the gruesome details. She'd just wanted it to be over.

"Alina."

She stared at her lap. "Yeah."

"Look at me."

She did what he said, though it was hard to see the depth of his concern. "You are not in trouble for what happened."

"You mean for killing that guy." Her heart throbbed with a punch of regret again.

"You did what you had to do to save yourself, Alina. They were going to kill you. It was self-defense and everyone knows it."

Guilt made her want to fix it. "I feel like I should do something for his family." She desperately wanted to tell them how sorry she was for taking him from them.

"He was there to kill you," Jay snapped.

She knew that, but it didn't lessen the depth of her remorse.

Jay brushed his hand over her hair. "You need to try to accept that you did what you had to do. The guy was no saint. His family knew what he was and, though they hoped it wouldn't end this way, knew the possibility existed because of the way he lived his life. Let them grieve, Alina. I know you're used to taking care of everyone. You have such a big heart. But right now, you need to take care of you."

"I need to take care of you, too." Which meant getting him home before he fell asleep on his feet.

She slid off the bed when the nurse came in with the wheelchair followed by Beck and Ashley. She slipped her bare feet into the sandals Ashley brought from her apartment along with her favorite pair of leggings and the super soft French terry pink tunic made for lounging on the couch. Ashley had also grabbed a few other outfits and toiletries since Alina had no idea how long it would take her to be able to go back to her place.

"Put the sling on," Beck ordered.

She wiggled her fingers. "I don't need it."

"Doc said to give that arm time to heal. Don't overdo it. You don't want to mess up what they fixed." Beck held the sling up.

She slipped it over her head and tucked her arm inside, letting her hand rest without pulling on the muscles and tendons. Jay kissed her on the side of the head and smiled his thanks for not being stubborn. She rolled her eyes and sat in the wheelchair. Jay took her hand as they left her room. Beck and Ashley carried her belongings. Her hand tightened on Jay's as they went down the hallway and people stared. She knew it was because of Ashley, but her heart raced as she checked every face to be sure it wasn't Noel or Brian.

By the time they got downstairs to the patient pickup, her nerves were shot. Jay had parked his SUV by the doors. He opened the passenger side and helped her out of the wheelchair. Before she got in, she spotted the boxes filling the entire back of his SUV. "What's all this?"

Jay ran his hand down her hair. "You agreed to live with me at our house, so I had Beck take my car last night. He and Ashley went by your place this morning to get you some clothes for today, but they also packed up the rest of your clothes and things they thought you'd need until we officially move you out of your apartment. Beck also had a professional cleaning crew go in and clean your place and fix the broken window."

She turned to her brother. "Thank you."

He hugged her close. "You'll be much happier at Jay's place. Caden and Mia drove your rental car out there this morning, too. You don't have to go back to your place until you're ready. Or never. Caden and I can pack it up for you if that's what you want."

"We can decide that later." Jay nudged her to get in the car, knowing making those decisions was beyond her at the moment.

She waved to Ashley and Beck through the side window as Jay drove them out of the hospital lot. Three blocks away, she realized why his head looked like it was on a swivel. "Are we being followed?"

"Only by Beck four cars back."

"Is he going to follow us all the way home?"

"No. Just to the edge of town where he'd split off to his place. The rest of the way to our place is wide open. I'll see anyone coming."

"Jay?"

"Yeah?"

"How many guards do you have at *our* place?" She liked that he already thought of it that way.

He finally looked at her. "Uh, just one. A sniper on the roof."

"What does your mother think of that?"

"I think she has the hots for King, but he's stuck on Cara, so my mom is shit out of luck."

"Isn't King a bit young for your mom?"

"I pointed that out and got the whole, 'what's good for the goose' crap. Am I really that old and you're that young that we don't make sense to anyone but us?"

"All anyone has to do is see the way you look at me and they'd get it."

He glared at her. "How do I look at you?"

"Always with love. Even earlier when you snapped at me, I saw the frustration because you didn't get Brian, and you want him because you love me. But, Jay, when we get home, you're going to set this aside for a few hours and get some sleep. I'm worried about you."

"I can sleep when he's dead."

"Okay, tough guy, how about you take me to bed and I'll distract you."

"Sweetheart, that's a great idea, but you are in no condition—"

"Jay, I need the distraction and you right now, so please, just say yes." Her throat ached with the emotions she'd been holding back for too long.

Jay went to grab her hand, but bypassed her arm in the sling and laid his hand on her thigh. He gently squeezed, then rubbed his big hand up and down. "Yes, sweetheart. Whatever you want."

The drive seemed longer because she wanted to be there, alone with Jay. She made him leave her things in the back, except for the bag Ashley had packed her. They went inside. Alina waved with Jay up to King on the roof as he gave Jay the all clear.

Jay plucked out the note stuck in the front door, read it, then handed it to her.

Alina,

Your favorite cherry cobbler and vanilla bean ice cream are in the fridge. Pop the lasagna in the oven at 350 for about 30 minutes. Garlic bread under the broiler for 5 minutes. Feel better, honey. My monkey lost his mind these last few days without you. I'm so glad you're home where you belong.

"Did you tell your mom we're moving in together?"

Jay led her into the house. "No. She knows me. When I called her from the hospital . . . I wasn't in a good place. I guess she figured when you came around, so would I, and I'd beg you to stay with me."

"You ordered me to move in." At his eyebrow raise, she smiled. "No begging necessary. I'm here. Where I belong." She echoed his mother's words. They touched her deeply. She didn't want to be a new conflict between Jay and Heather. She wanted them to be a family.

If the sweet note and lovely meal left for them meant Heather finally saw how happy and in love Jay was with her, and Alina was with Jay, and accepted it, then it looked like they'd have a much more peaceful future together here on the ranch. Together.

She turned, grabbed the strap on her bag over Jay's shoulder, then pulled him toward her as she backed up down the hall to *their* room.

"Do you want to eat?"

She shook her head.

"Is it time to take your meds?"

She shook her head again. "It's time to get naked and show me how much you missed me."

Jay's gaze took her all in. "I don't want to hurt you." The softly spoken words touched her, but didn't override her need for him to wrap her in his arms.

"You won't. You're going to make me feel everything good until there's no room for the bad anymore."

Jay dropped the bag inside the bedroom door and kept coming toward her. In the quiet, he stripped the sling and all her clothes away one article at a time like he had all the time in the world. Here, they did. He didn't touch her. Not the way she wanted him to with his rough hands and greedy mouth.

Naked, she stood before him filled with anticipation and need. She vibrated with it, but held still, letting him lead. He took her hand and led her around the bed, pulled back the sheets and blankets, and gently nudged her to lie down.

He grabbed a spare pillow from the chair by the window and placed it under her injured arm. "This arm stays here." He hooked his hand over his head and grabbed his shirt between his shoulders and pulled it off, revealing a wall of rippling muscles.

Her body quivered at the sight of all that contained strength and sculpted perfection. "I've missed you."

He leaned down, planted his hands on either side of her shoulders, and gazed into her eyes, his filled with longing and heat. "I nearly lost you. God, Alina, do you know how much I love you?"

"Show me."

The gleam in his eyes should have warned her. "This might take a while." In the same leisurely fashion he'd stripped her, he rid himself of the rest of his clothes and casually grabbed a condom from the bedside drawer, tore it open but didn't take it out, and put it down within easy reach. "For later."

Before she could ask him what he meant by that, he went to the end of the bed, laid his chest between her thighs, hooked her legs over his shoulders, and pressed his tongue flat against her soft folds and licked his way up over her clit in one long, slow glide that nearly sent her to pieces. He kept her right on the edge, circling her clit with the tip of his tongue, then sinking it inside of her and gently sucking until her hips came off the bed and she begged him to be inside her.

He slithered up her body with soft, wet kisses to her breasts. He circled one hard tip with his tongue and then the other before taking it into his mouth and suckling hard. Her hips rocked against his hard cock, but he took his time, lavishing attention on both her breasts before trailing kisses up her neck to her mouth. The kiss was sultry and deep, his tongue gliding along hers to that sultry, sweet tempo he'd kept, loving her slow and easy and oh so thoroughly.

His mouth never left hers as he rolled on the condom and rubbed the head of his cock against her slick folds, teasing and tempting her to take him in. She pushed down on him and he thrust into her in one long glide, then backed out almost all the way. She whimpered her disapproval and he sank deep again. She matched his rhythm as he pulled back. She circled her hips to tease the head as he groaned and sank into her again.

He broke the kiss, held her close, his mouth right next to hers, their breath whispering over each other's cheeks. She held him with one arm, her hand splayed wide over his shoulder as their bodies moved together.

She lost herself in the feel of his weight, the friction of their bodies moving against each other, the feathering of his breath against her skin, the beat of his heart against hers. He filled her with love so warm and bright and wonderful, it burst from her as he thrust into her hard and deep and held himself there as he joined her in paradise.

His mouth found hers for another of those soft, long kisses that made her body pulse.

Jay ended the sweet kiss, stared down at her, brushed his thumb over her cheek, and wove his fingers into her hair. "Welcome home. I'm so glad you're here."

Tears gathered in her eyes. "Me, too." She rubbed her hand up his scruffy jaw, the brush of his whiskers soft against her palm. "This is forever, right?"

"Yes." He kissed her softly, then rolled to his side and gently snuggled against her and held her close. "Get some sleep, sweetheart."

The hospital hadn't been all that quiet and relaxing. She found herself drifting off, then remembered something he'd told her. "Didn't you get me a present?"

His chest rose and fell steady and even. His words came out slow and sleepy. "Yes. Later."

They woke up hours later and instead of waiting for the lasagna to cook, they ate cobbler and ice cream in bed. They made love again and slept in each other's arms. He held her through another nightmare, whispering sweet things in her ear until she slept again, safe and protected with him.

In the morning, she woke feeling the need to do something. "I want to go and check on Lee."

Jay glanced over at her lying beside him. "It's not safe to go out until we find Noel and Brian."

"I have to go see her. I wasn't the only one affected by what happened. She's suffering, too, without the man she loves beside her to help her through the nightmare."

Jay swore, but couldn't stand up to her resolve. She stared him down until he swore again and got out of bed to take her, though he grumbled the whole way.

CHAPTER THIRTY-EIGHT

Noel grimaced at the stale stench coming out of the ancient refrigerator at his grandfather's old cabin. His mother still owned the place and one day it should come to him if he wasn't in jail or dead. But once his mother found out what he'd done, she'd disown him. Maybe she'd leave the place to his girls.

He slammed the fridge door, too upset to eat or drink anything.

He used to bring Lee and the girls here all the time. He should be home with Lee now. She must be devastated after he abandoned her. He'd like nothing more than to turn back the clock and be home with her.

What would she tell the girls? What would happen to them now? How would Lee make it through her treatments? Would his girls leave school to take care of their mother? Would they go back and finish their degrees and have the bright future he wanted for them because they didn't have money for tuition?

His cell dinged with a text. Not the one in his name that he'd destroyed so he couldn't be tracked. The one his wife and kids had probably left several messages on trying to find him.

He pulled the burner cell out of his coat to shut it off. He should have done so any one of the dozen times Brian tried to contact him. The picture brightened his screen and darkened his world. He gaped and nearly fell to his knees. His sweet girl sat with a gag in her mouth, her hands taped together in front of her in the front seat of Brian's truck.

He jumped when the phone rang. "What the hell did you do?"

"Daddy? He won't let me go."

His heart dropped at her trembling voice so filled with fear he felt it rush through him. "Heidi?"

Another familiar voice came on the line. "Hey, Doc. Miss me?" Brian tried to pull off light and friendly, but an edge sharpened his voice. From the reports Noel had seen on TV, Alina lived through the brutal attack. His relief was so great, it couldn't be measured. Noel wished she'd ended Brian the way she'd killed Davy.

Thinking about her hurt. He'd never wanted her to find out or get involved. But when he couldn't get out, he'd dragged her in without her even knowing it.

"What have you done?"

"You wouldn't answer the phone. I figured you'd answer for your precious baby."

Noel hated that his actions had brought his daughter home to care for her mother and put her in danger. "Let her go. She's got nothing to do with this."

"Maybe not, but you seem to think you can just disappear and leave me hanging."

"Why haven't you disappeared yet?"

"The cops raided my place before I got to my stash. But I'll bet you've got just what I need. Now you're going to help me escape the fucking mess you made." Brian tried to lay the blame on Noel, but if he'd stayed away from Alina in the first place, none of this would be happening.

Guilt sent a sharp pain through his heart. Of course, it all started with Noel. If not for him, none of this would be happening.

"Kidnapping my daughter only makes this worse. Let her go. Please. Drive out of the state before they find you."

"That bitch partner of yours killed Davy. I'm not leaving until she pays for what she did."

"Be smart. You go after her, you'll have the full weight of the DEA after you."

"They already are! And that's your fault. You brought her into this. I'm taking her out."

"Don't be stupid. I can't get her alone. She's protected by her boyfriend and her brothers."

"Figure it out. You've got an hour before I arrive."

"How do you—"

"Grandpa's cabin. Heidi has fond memories of how much you used to love that isolated, wide-open space. Who's the stupid one? How long before your wife gives up that place to the cops, dumbshit? Let's hope it's long enough for us to finish our business."

"Please, Brian. Let this go before it's too late."

"If your partner's not there, your daughter is dead. And so are you."

Heidi whimpered in the background. Brian hung up on those ominous words. Noel had no choice. He needed to save his baby, even if that meant dragging Alina back into this mess.

CHAPTER THIRTY-NINE

Alina knocked on the door. Jay stood right behind her, his back to her as he scanned the street outside the ranch-style home looking for any sign of Noel and Brian. Alina had to admit, this might not have been her best idea. Nerves fluttered in her stomach. Fear made her think any second Brian would attack.

She tried to relax, but the second the door flew open and she saw the worry in Lee's eyes, alarms went off that had her backing into Jay.

"You're not Heidi." Lee pressed her hand to her chest.

"Lee, what's wrong?"

"She went to the grocery store and hasn't returned. She won't answer her phone."

"How long ago did she leave?" Jay pushed Alina into the house, even though Lee hadn't invited them in. He slammed the door and waited for Lee to catch her breath.

"Almost two hours ago." Lee placed her hand on the table by the door for support.

Alina took Lee's arm and led her into the living room and into a leather chair. "Did she have any other errands to run? Maybe her phone battery died."

Lee shook her head. "We only needed a few things and she checked her phone before she left just in case I needed her. Something's wrong."

"Do you think she could be with your husband?" Jay asked.

Lee's eyes shone bright with unshed tears. "We haven't heard from him at all. But . . . but I guess it's possible." For the first time, Lee focused on Alina and the stitches across her forehead. "Are you okay? That man, the one police say is working with Noel, he hurt you."

"He tried to kill her. And he *is* working with your husband." Jay couldn't hide the temper in his voice. "I'm sorry. I know this is a difficult time for you."

"Yes. And now my daughter is missing."

Alina sat on the ottoman and placed her hand on Lee's knee. "We don't know that yet. Maybe she met some friends while she was out and lost track of time."

Lee shook her head again. "She wouldn't leave me alone this long. Not without calling to let me know."

Jay pulled out his phone. "What's her number? I'll put a trace on it, see if we can locate her."

Before Lee rattled off the number, Alina's cell rang. She pulled it out to silence it, figuring one of her brothers was calling to check on her, but saw the unknown number. For a second she thought to disregard the call, but something compelled her to answer.

"Hello."

"Don't hang up on me." The desperation in Noel's voice sent a cold chill up her back.

Alina put the phone on speaker. "Noel, where are you?"

"I need you to listen. He's got my daughter."

Lee gasped. "No. Not Heidi. How could you let this happen?"

"Lee. Oh God, I'm so sorry. I never meant—we don't have time for this. Alina, I need your help. We don't have much time. If you're at my house and you drive really fast, you may make it in time to save my daughter.

Please, you have to come to the cabin. It's the only way to end this."

"I'll have Jay and the DEA come. They'll get her back."

"If you don't come, he'll kill her. You have to leave right now." His desperation made her want to act fast.

Jay pulled her hand close so he could speak to Noel. "He's not going to kill her until he gets what he wants. She's his leverage. So what exactly does he want?"

"He's smart enough to know I have money and a stash of drugs. He's dumb enough to think he can get them and kill Alina and get away."

Lee covered a gasp and anguished sob. Noel had finally admitted to his part in the illegal activities. Others had told Lee the horrible truth, but she'd never heard it from her husband's lips and the impact hit her hard.

"He's pissed she killed his friend and ruined your business," Jay guessed.

"If he'd left well enough alone and let me handle it, none of this would have happened."

"Because you'd have blackmailed Alina to keep her quiet, right? Even though you had your side business up and running before she became your partner, you made sure to make it look like she joined both businesses. You made her look guilty so you could use it against her and keep her quiet."

"I thought she'd see the benefits and the future it would give us."

Lee sat up straighter and stared at Alina, past suspicions taking on a new reality.

Alina gave her a sad smile.

Jay cleared things up. "Alina turned you down flat and turned her back on you and you sent that thug after her."

"I just wanted the files back."

"You wanted to keep the cash flowing."

"I wanted to give my family everything." Those earnest words belied the reality he'd put himself and his family in danger.

"All the while trying to seduce Alina even after she and I got together so you wouldn't be alone."

Alina put her hand on Jay's arm. "Stop. She gets it." Alina didn't like Jay's tactic of letting Lee in on all the dirty secrets her husband kept.

Lee needed to face the truth about her husband, but enough was enough.

Overwhelmed, Lee sank back into the chair, tears spilling down her face. "He's completely lost his way."

"I never meant to hurt anyone. I feel like I've already lost you, and I needed someone—"

"Shut up. I don't want to hear any more excuses. I want my daughter. You get her back, or I swear to God, jail will feel like a picnic compared to what I'll do to you." The strength and conviction in Lee's voice made even Jay raise an eyebrow in admiration.

"I've hurt everyone I love, I know that. I want to make it right. I want Heidi safe. So please, Alina, you have to hurry. I'm sure Jay has already started forming a plan. I can help. I want to help because I don't want anyone else to get hurt."

Jay's mouth drew into a tight line. "How do I know you're not setting this up to get back at Alina?"

"I think you know the answer to that," Noel admitted. "You're right. I got greedy. I reached for far more than I deserved at the same time I had everything I ever wanted."

Alina and Lee shared a poignant look. Noel thought he wanted Alina, but what he really wanted was his wife back after the cancer stole her from him.

Alina pulled a small notebook and pen from her purse and handed them to Lee. "Write down the address." She spoke into the phone. "We're on our way."

Noel's heavy sigh along with his relief came through the phone loud and clear.

Jay swore, went to the front door, walked out, then walked back in with the cops behind him.

"Where did they come from?" Lee asked, surprised they appeared so quickly.

"They've been watching your house since Alina was attacked in case your husband decided to come home. They'll stay with you until we get your daughter back." Jay held his hand out to Alina. "Let's go."

Alina leaned down and hugged Lee. "I'm sorry."

"This is all his fault." Lee glanced up at Jay. "You've got a good man. Hold on to him."

Alina took Jay's hand. "I'll never let go."

She and Jay ran out of the house. Alina held on to the cell phone with Noel still on the line. They jumped into Jay's SUV. He handed her his cell before he sped down the road. "Call Caden and Beck. Get them on the move. We'll fill in details as we set up this plan on the fly." The sarcasm and frustration in his voice let them both know he didn't like this one bit. "And there's no way in hell I'm letting you go in there," he bit out.

"She has to or he'll kill my daughter."

"He won't, not when what he really wants is Alina."

"You don't know that. This guy is out of his fucking mind thinking she'll come here without you guys coming with her."

"You know why criminals get caught?" Jay asked Noel. "Because they're stupid. They always do something that gets them caught or killed."

"I don't want my daughter to be collateral damage."

Alina got Beck on the line. "It's me. I'm on the phone with Noel. Brian has his daughter and wants me. We're headed to Noel's cabin now. I need you and Caden on the move ASAP."

Jay took over talking to both Noel and Beck at the same time, while Beck used Ashley's phone to get Caden involved. Alina listened to them go over the cabin and property layout. They laid out a tactical plan with several contingencies. Brian had chosen a good place to try to tie up loose ends and escape. The cabin was wide open on all sides. He'd see a SWAT team moving in. With Noel helping them, they'd work around that problem and hopefully end this before it became a hostage situation that ended in a standoff.

Jay, her brothers, none of them wanted her involved, but this didn't work without her. The longer she listened to them coordinate, the more at ease she became. Yes, she was scared, but with them backing her up, she found the courage to face this head-on.

They kicked in doors and took down drug dealers much more organized and deadly than Brian and his crazy plan for revenge. He didn't know what he'd gotten himself into, asking her to come. But he'd find out, because Jay was smart and cunning and organized her brothers and the rest of the team who'd be on standby near the cabin for backup.

Brian would walk into the cabin, but he wouldn't walk away.

Jay understood criminals like him, feeding off their greed and vengeance. They thought they could play with fire and not get burned. Brian had no idea the kind of man he'd faced off with, but he would soon.

Alina wouldn't want to be in his shoes when Jay's plan played out.

She'd always worry about Jay on a case, but this up-close view of how he thought, how he worked, proved what she already knew but needed to see to ease her mind: her boyfriend was a badass.

CHAPTER FORTY

Beck held up the bulletproof vest. "Take your shirt off, sis."

Alina raised one eyebrow. "It's creepy when you say that to me."

Jay couldn't even find a smile for the absurdity of the situation. He took the vest from Beck, turned Alina so her back was to her brothers, and helped her put the vest on and pull her shirt over it. She'd taken the sling off her arm in case she needed to use both hands to defend herself.

That thought led to a dozen more of how this thing could go wrong and it knotted his stomach and twisted his heart.

"You keep him in front of you at all times. Never turn your back on him. Stay out of his reach. He's not really interested in killing Heidi. He wants you. Remember that. Don't give him an opportunity to do it."

"I got it. We've gone over this ten times."

"It's second nature to us," Beck pointed out.

"It's only been five days since this guy tried to kill you." Jay took her trembling hand. "Fear can do funny things to people. I don't want you to freeze. I want you thinking about what I'm drilling into you. Always protect yourself. Trust us to keep you safe."

She stared up at him, her gaze direct and resolute.

"I trust you. I want this over and done. This is the only way to do it. You storm in there without me, he will kill her." She'd made that argument the whole way here every time he and her brothers tried to come up with a plan that didn't involve her. All those plans had a slim chance of ending with Heidi's death because Brian had nothing left to lose. None of them wanted to take the chance with Heidi's life.

As much as Jay wanted to kill the bastard for hurting Alina, he'd never put an innocent person in jeopardy.

"Where the fuck is she?" Brian yelled at Noel again.

"She'll be here. You don't need to point that gun at Heidi."

Yeah, the gun hadn't exactly been a surprise thanks to Alina tying the burglaries and pistol-whipped murder victims together with Brian and Davy. Thank God Brian only used his knife on Alina. Bad as that was, he could have killed her with one bullet.

That wouldn't happen today. Jay would make sure of it.

They'd kept Noel's phone hidden from Brian but still live so they knew where everyone was in the cabin, what they were walking into, and if Brian said anything that meant they needed to alter their plan. They muted Alina's phone so Noel and Brian couldn't hear them. If Noel tried to double-cross them, they'd know about it. But with his daughter's life on the line, that seemed highly unlikely.

Still, Jay didn't trust Noel or Brian when it came to Alina's safety.

Caden slid another rifle into the back of the SUV. "Ready to go?"

Jay stared down at Alina as her brothers backed off. "I'm not happy about this."

"I'll do exactly as we planned. I'm scared but I'm not

stupid. You promised me forever and that doesn't end today." She tapped her index finger against his chest. "You
got that?"

Jay nodded. She worried about him, too, and it did
his heart good. He'd be even better if she was a million
miles away from here right now. "I'll be there with you
even if you can't see me." He kissed her hard and fast,
no time for anything else. "I love you." When this was
done, he planned to hold on to her and never let go.

"I love you, too."

ALINA DROVE THE SUV with Jay and her brothers lying
down in the back with several guns and rifles. Packed
tight as sardines, she bet they couldn't wait to get out.

Her hands shook, so she tightened her grip on the
steering wheel. Odd time to notice, but her left hand remained weak and tingling, but responsive. She'd feared
that asshole had left her disabled. Hope grew that with
more time to heal and physical therapy, she'd be back
to normal. She hoped her mind would heal, too. A car
crash, an explosion, a knife fight followed by this trag-
edy in the making had her adrenaline working overtime
and fraying her nerves.

She took a deep breath and spoke to the guys in back
without moving her mouth. "Pulling in now." She didn't
want Brian to look out the window and see her talking
to anyone.

She parked just as they planned with the car parallel
to the cabin, front end close to the door, back end at the
side of the cabin where the bedroom was located away
from the living room space where Brian held Heidi and
Noel as his captive audience. Once she distracted Brian
inside, they'd slide out the back and take up positions
around the house.

"Make sure that bitch is alone," Brian ordered.

The cabin door opened and Noel stood in the opening, his face grim. "She's alone."

"You've got this, sweetheart. We're right here with you. We won't let anything happen to you." Jay's faith in her and assurance that he'd protect her, they all would, gave her the strength to step out of the vehicle, hands raised, and walk into the lion's den.

"About damn time." Brian stood in the corner of the room, a gun pointed at Heidi. She sat in a chair in front of the window. Brian had tucked himself into the corner, making it impossible for anyone to shoot him through the windows without potentially hitting Heidi. "Check her for a weapon."

Noel did a cursory search, sweeping his hands down her sides and up her legs. He didn't reveal the small pack at her back for the wire she wore under her loose shirt so the guys and the team waiting could hear everything. "Nothing."

"Damn bitch, your face is all fucked up. You're not so pretty anymore, are you?" Brian's proud smile pissed her off.

She took in his gray pallor, the sweat beaded on his forehead, and the bandage wrapped around his leg over his torn, dirty jeans. An open medical kit and discarded bloody, pussy, disgusting bandages sat on the table beside a large plastic bag filled with money and several bottles of pills. Noel's stash. "You think I look bad? You look like shit. How's the leg? Infected? Rotting? Poisoning your blood?"

"Fuck you." Spittle dripped onto his chin. He wiped it away with the back of one shaking hand.

"What are you doing, Brian? You should be in a hospital, not frightening young girls."

"Don't pretend you care one fuck about me. You'd

have killed me just like you did Davy if you'd gotten the chance."

"You shoved me into Davy. You made me stab him. You came into my home to kill me."

Brian cocked the gun and pointed it at Heidi's head. "Shut the fuck up or I'll blow her head off."

Heidi whimpered behind the gag, tears falling from her eyes.

"What's the plan here, Brian? You shoot me, take the money, and make a run for it? Do you really think you'll get away now that you've brought me here?"

Brian moved the gun away from Heidi and pointed it straight at Alina. "I bet lover boy is close by along with your fucking brothers. Doc went and got himself a partner tied to the damn DEA. Stupidest fucking thing ever."

"Stupid? You've put yourself up against well-trained agents who are master tacticians. They take down thugs like you all day, every day. My brother, they call him Trigger."

Brian's eyes went wide at that piece of disturbing news. He should be scared.

"He's the best sniper the DEA has ever had. But all I need is Jay." Reminded of the intensity in Jay's eyes before they drove to the cabin, she knew to her soul he'd lay down his life for her. "You really fucked up there, coming after me. You think he'll let you get away with hurting me, you stupid fool?"

"Shut up," Brian raged, fisting his free hand and punching his thigh.

Alina signaled Heidi to run to the bedroom. Instead, she jumped up and slammed her shoulder into Brian's. The gun went off, hitting the back window. Glass shattered to the floor. Heidi ran for the bedroom where Jay waited to get her to safety.

Brian swung the gun back to Alina and fired, hitting

Noel in the shoulder as he stepped in front of her. Noel dropped to the floor, blood pouring out of his wound as he pressed his hand over the hole. Blood oozed over his hand.

Heidi screamed for her father from somewhere outside.

Alina dropped to her knees and pressed her hand over Noel's. She couldn't believe he took a bullet for her. Brian ran forward, grabbed her by the hair, hauled her up in front of him, and jammed the gun into the underside of her jaw as her scalp stung and her hair pulled in his fierce grasp.

She waited to see if Caden rushed in the back and Jay came out of the room. Due to the circumstances, she expected them to alter their plan and take Brian down in here. But they held back and she could only imagine their fear that this thing hadn't exactly gone to plan.

With the gun pointed at her head, they wouldn't risk her life.

She needed to get Brian outside in the open.

Idiot accommodated her. "Grab the bag, we're out of here. Your boyfriend or brothers make a move on me, I'll kill you."

"Then they'll kill you." She pointed out the obvious.

"Maybe I'll just shoot you in the side and let you bleed out for hours while I get away."

Okay, score one for the bad guy.

She grabbed the bag with her left hand and tried to hold on to it but her grip wasn't that strong, especially with his hand gripped around her upper arm. He moved her to the door, his chest pressed against her back, the gun digging into the soft underside of her chin. She desperately wanted to look into the bedroom at her left, but headed straight for the door, opened it, walked out onto the porch, and down the single step toward his truck parked by a tree.

Her heart thrashed in her chest, fear squeezed her throat tight, but she pushed the fear away and did what she needed to do to save herself and end this once and for all.

She dropped the bag on the path and stopped short, making Brian stumble into her back. Off balance, Brian tried to keep from falling. She took advantage of his misstep, twisted toward the left, away from the gun in Brian's right hand, and fell to her knees.

Jay stood on the porch, his hands in front of him, gun pointed at Brian behind her.

She covered her head and closed her eyes tight.

The second Alina hit her knees, Jay fired. Three shots rang out. Two shots hit Brian dead center in the chest, his and Caden's. Beck fired from the roof, hitting Brian right between the eyes. He dropped to his knees and fell forward onto his face, dead in the dirt.

Jay was by Alina's side in one leap from the porch. He took her gently by the shoulders and pulled her into his chest and wrapped his arms around her. "Are you okay? You're not hit, right?" He didn't think so, but his brain and heart weren't working in reality at the moment.

He needed her to be okay.

"I'm fine." Her voice quivered and her body trembled against his. "Have we concluded the Take Your Girlfriend to Work day? Because I'm done. I want to go home now."

He held her tighter. "You're okay. You did so good."

"She okay?" Beck called down from the roof.

"I've got her," Jay assured him. "She doesn't want to join the DEA."

"Thank God, I don't think my heart can take it." Beck tossed his rifle to one of the agents who closed in on the cabin as the ambulance rolled into the driveway, then jumped down from the roof, landing hard on the porch path.

"Mine either," he whispered into Alina's ear. "You scared me again, sweetheart. You gotta stop doing that."

"Oh, I'm done. I'll leave the bad guys to you from now on." She finally extracted her face from his shoulder and looked up at him. "You saved me."

"We're even. You saved me first." He never knew how lost he'd been until she came into his life and made it brighter and better and so filled with happiness and love he didn't know what to do with all of it. Except hold on to her forever.

CHAPTER FORTY-ONE

Jay had been waiting for this moment for more than a month. That's how long it took to conclude the internal investigation into Brian's shooting and close the cases on the kidnapping, Noel and Brian's drug operation, the home invasions and the two deaths that resulted from them, and to clear Alina of any involvement in all of it.

Noel would spend the next ten to twenty years behind bars. With the help of her family, Lee sold their house and moved closer to her girls. She continued her treatment and was doing better with her daughters' love and care. Somehow she found the strength to start over.

Alina moved into his home and settled in like she'd always lived there. He came home each night to her smiling face, but he'd sensed her growing restlessness. She feared the business and her investment in the pharmacy were lost and she'd have to start all over.

If anyone would hire her after what happened.

Today, he got the best news and couldn't wait to share it with her.

Because of all that happened and their whirlwind relationship, he'd decided to take her on a much-needed vacation so they could spend some time alone together. He surprised her with the trip to Hawaii and the secluded house he rented on the beach.

He stepped out the back door, walked across the patio

and down the path to where she lay on the double lounge chair staring at the rolling tide, the moon just inches over the sea, and the brilliant stars overhead.

Postcard perfect.

And the beautiful woman waiting for him, AMAZ-ING! In all caps with the exclamation point. She blew him away with her sweetness and warmth, the way she always thought of others, and especially the way she loved him.

He'd nearly lost her twice. Now, he wanted her to promise forever.

"I can't believe this place, Jay. How did you find it?"

He stood behind the double patio lounge and stared down at her. "One of Ashley's friends owns it. He rents it out when he's not using it, but only to people he knows, or friends of friends."

"One of Ashley's famous friends?"

"Danny Radford."

"Uh, wow. I can't believe you did this."

"I wanted something special." He leaned over and kissed her bare shoulder. "We deserve special."

Alina's off-the-shoulder sundress gently fluttered at mid-thigh. Her hair blew back from her beautiful face. The stitches were long gone, the scar on her forehead nothing but a thin pink line that would fade even more over time. She'd regained most of her mobility in her left hand. What she lost was mostly unnoticeable.

Alina stared out at the rolling ocean more at ease than he'd seen her these last weeks.

He hoped to put whatever worries she still harbored to rest so they could both enjoy these next few island days finally at peace, the past behind them. "I have good news."

"We get to stay here more than a week."

"If you want, I can take a few more days off work, but that will also delay you reopening the pharmacy."

Her head whipped to the side. Shock widened her eyes a split second before they filled with hope. "What?"

"Beck left me a message. The entire case is officially closed. You're completely exonerated. Lee agreed to the payout you and I talked about—"

"Wait, I can't afford—"

"I'll put up the money."

Her gaze narrowed. "You want to buy into the pharmacy?"

"No. Well, yes." Jay took her hand and gently tugged her up with him to walk down to the water.

"Jay, honey, I don't understand what you mean."

He stopped a couple of feet from the water's lapping edge and took a deep breath, letting his nerves settle. He'd been up against some scary dudes in his line of work, but one woman scared him more than all of them. She had the power to destroy him with one word: *no*.

But she'd already said yes. She moved in with him. This was nothing but a formality.

But it was everything.

A lifetime of her smiling face and open arms when he got home and walked in the door. A friend to confide in and share his hopes, his dreams, his secrets, the good, the bad, the normal, everyday stuff.

"Jay, are you okay? You seem nervous."

He took both her hands and stared down into her up-turned face. "The worst is over. This past month, we've had a taste of the life I want with you."

Alina's head tilted. "Jay, honey, you have to know how happy I am, how much I love you."

He touched her cheek and brushed his thumb over her soft skin. "I love you, too. More than I can say. We found each other unexpectedly, or maybe it was always meant to be and I just didn't see it until I saw you laughing in the hotel lobby and you smiled at me at the bar. You were apprehensive about my job. For good reason."

"Mine turned out to be just as dangerous," she pointed out, teasing, but not.

"And I want you to go back to doing the job you love, which is why I'm happy to put up the money you need in order to keep the pharmacy. As your partner, and your husband."

She covered a gasp with her fingertips.

He dropped to one knee, her other hand still in his. He pulled the ring he'd had far too long out of his pocket and held it up to her.

Tears glistened in her eyes, her free hand went to her chest, and she gave him one of those sweet smiles he loved. "My present."

"A symbol of my promise to you. We share a house, a friendship I've never had with anyone else, a bond I feel every second of the day. My heart is yours. This ring is yours. And if you want it, my name."

She didn't speak, but her head bobbed up and down.

"What we've been through these last months shows I can't promise a carefree future, but I can promise that I will be by your side through the good times, bad times, every up and down." He squeezed her hand. "I will never let go. I love you. Will you marry me?"

Her head hadn't stopped going up and down, but he'd wanted to get it all out and give her the proposal she deserved.

"Say something," he coaxed, anticipation making his heart flutter.

"Yes!"

He stood just in time to catch her in his arms as she launched herself into his chest and kissed him hard. He took over, slowed her down, and took the kiss deeper, then pressed his forehead to hers and stared into her bright, beautiful eyes. "You said yes." The wonder of it filled him up.

"It was yes the second you sat down beside me in the bar. I just didn't know it, and then it was the one thing I knew for sure."

He kissed her again, long and deep. Remembering the ring, he stepped back and took her left hand. He slipped the diamond ring on her finger, stared at it there where it belonged, and his heart swelled. "You're going to be my wife." He couldn't believe his luck and couldn't wait to marry her. Soon. They'd do it at the lodge Caden and Beck got married at—where he and Alina found each other.

A bright smile bloomed on her lips. She flipped her hand around to show him the ring and stomped her feet in the sand, smiling and laughing, excitement bubbling out of her in waves of joy. "I can't wait to tell my parents and brothers. Everyone."

It dawned on him then. He wrapped his arm around her, pulled her to his side, and made her look back up toward the house. "Wave." He did so toward the camera he'd set up with a live stream for their families. "They're all watching."

Alina got over her initial shock and waved. "We're getting married!" She held up her hand to show them his ring on her finger. Right where it would stay for the rest of their lives.

He led her back up to the house, stopped for a second to wave one last time before he turned the camera off, and walked her into the house and straight to the rose-petal-strewn bed where he made love to his fiancée with the waves crashing outside and his heart overflowing with love for the woman in his arms, a woman he'd once told himself to walk away from, she wasn't for him, but had been tempted by a love so strong it brought them together. Forever.

MANDI FLIPPED HER purple hair over her shoulder and leaned into Robby. "Ah, sweet, I knew those two were destined for each other. Nothing will ever tear them apart."

Robby continued to battle in the Howling Abyss, her champion standing immobile while she watched Alina and Jay get engaged, but Robby took a moment to stare at her. "We're Kog'Maw and Lulu." The perfect League of Legends battle pair.

Mandi melted, kissed him, then picked up her controller to fight alongside her man.

HEATHER BLEW A kiss to her son, Jay, a split second before he cut the feed. "Of course she said yes, monkey. That girl is smart. I liked her from the beginning. You'll do right by her. And soon I'll have beautiful grandbabies."

ASHLEY LAY BESIDE Beck in their bed, watching the video, tears in her eyes. "I've never seen her that happy."

Beck clicked off the screen and set the tablet on the bedside table and held her close with his other arm. He turned to her and wiped the tears from her cheeks with the pad of his thumb. "Me either. It's why I backed off. I saw it in her eyes. She loves him. He'll make her happy."

Ashley smiled. "How about you make your wife happy?"

Beck nuzzled his nose against her soft skin. "My favorite thing to do."

CADEN KISSED MIA on the side of the head and rolled on top of her.

"You're happy for her." Mia smiled up at him.

"She always wanted a husband and family. I wanted her to be happy. With Jay, she'll have it all."

"We have it all."

"How about we work on that baby some more?" He softly kissed her neck.

"We don't need to."

It took him a second to figure out what she meant. He rose up on his hands and stared down at her. "You're pregnant?"

She smiled and nodded. "I didn't want anything to overshadow their engagement."

Caden slid down and kissed her belly with reverence and wonder. He stared back up at her. "We'll tell everyone when they get back." He kissed his way back up to her mouth and poured everything he felt into the kiss. They were going to have a baby. His chest couldn't contain all the love bursting out of his heart. "Tonight, we celebrate."

"CAN YOU BELIEVE this all started with a blind date between Caden and Mia? I knew they'd hit it off." Aunt Taffy wiped a tear from her soft cheek, her lips tilted in a satisfied grin.

Aunt Nancy snuggled closer. "They've all been through some rough times, but it only brought them closer together."

Aunt Taffy sighed and held Aunt Nancy close. "None of them believed there was someone out there for them. I'm so glad they found their soul mate, just like I did."

"Everyone deserves to be as happy and in love as we are."

Continue reading for a sneak peek at the first book
in Jennifer Ryan's Wild Rose Ranch series,

DIRTY LITTLE SECRET

Coming March 2019!

PROLOGUE

Six years ago
Clark County Fair and Rodeo, Nevada

Roxy leapt off her horse, landed in the dirt, and tried to contain the smile that spread across her face for the man sitting in the stands staring right at her. His smile, the pride in his eyes, made her heart swell with joy and drown in sorrow all at the same time.

John came, but he wouldn't speak to her. Not here where others could see them together and possibly connect the dots that she was his daughter. A child no one knew about. A child he'd never expected and didn't want.

Her mother made sure of that.

Roxy had been doomed to be an outcast before she was ever born.

John came today to watch her barrel race on one of the horses he secretly sent to her. It's why she practiced every day and rode so hard in competition. The little girl inside her wanted to make him proud. She wanted him to like and admire her.

She wanted him to stand up and say, "That's my girl!"

But in eighteen years, he'd never even come close to admitting that to anyone.

These little glimpses of him and what could have

been lashed at her heart and made it bleed. As much as Roxy wanted her father to love her enough to keep her, she wanted him to stay away.

"You won!" Sonya wrapped her in a hug.

"Again!" Juliana scrunched her mouth into a pretty pout. As much as she wanted Roxy to win, she wanted to beat her, too. Little sisters were like that.

Adria hugged her, then held her at arm's length. "He came." She glanced over at John. "And so did your sexy stepbrother."

"He's not my brother." But still John raised him as his own.

The son he always wanted.

Noah, the man sitting beside him, who got to call him Dad, who knew John as a good and decent man, knew nothing about her. Noah and Annabelle, his adopted children, got his love and devotion every day. They grew up with the life she could have had if only John had fought for her and revealed his dirty little secret.

"Noah's got the best ass in denim in this whole damn place."

"Don't swear," Roxy scolded Juliana, though she couldn't disagree with the statement.

The girl was growing up way too fast. At fifteen, she looked twenty-one. And men noticed.

Here, everyone stared at the notorious Wild Rose girls. If they hadn't entered their first rodeo in Nevada and won in spectacular fashion, maybe no one would have linked them to the infamous Wild Rose Ranch brothel located in a little town outside of Las Vegas—where prostitution was legal and their mothers worked.

It didn't matter that Roxy and her sisters *didn't* work there.

When Roxy and her sisters showed up at a rodeo, every eye in the place turned to them. The buzz of whispers spread, letting everyone know the girls from the Wild Rose Ranch had arrived to ride.

Many a cowboy had mistaken *what* they came to ride.

When they went to a rodeo, it was for the competition and winning.

It didn't seem to matter that they were in their teens. Their *Wild Rose Ranch—We Ride Hard* T-shirts sparked all kinds of cowboy fantasies.

Yes, they used the provocative name. They wanted to make it their own and be proud of it. They wanted where they came from to mean something more.

They wanted their little legitimate piece of the Ranch.

They were the best. She and her sisters had proven that again today. After all, Roxy may have just won the grand prize, but her sisters were in second, third, and fourth place right behind her.

They dominated.

A man whistled out to them. No matter how many wins, they were still perceived as *those* girls from the Wild Rose Ranch.

Which is why her father remained in the stands, a safe distance from her and any chance of rumors.

"Why don't you just walk up to Noah and tell him who you are?" Juliana nudged her with her elbow.

"He stares at you just like your father," Adria pointed out.

"Noah stares because he thinks we're prostitutes."

Sonya laid her hand on Roxy's shoulder. "Introduce yourself. Not as John's daughter, but just you."

"Why? What will that change? 'Hi, I'm Roxy.' Then what?"

"See what happens." Adria smiled. "Ask about him. You know you want to know what his life is like living with your father."

"I know what his life is like with John. Everything my

life wasn't." John always sent the checks, but when she was really young her mother used the money to support her habit before she remembered to take care of Roxy.

She bet Noah was never ridiculed for being on the free lunch program at school. She bet he never had to root through trash in the cafeteria to scrounge up extra food for the weekend because there was no food in the house. He didn't grow up with cocaine dusting the table where he did his homework, or have to step over trash and used needles to get to the couch that smelled of stale cigarette smoke and pot. He probably never had to wear shoes a size too small and pants three inches too short because there wasn't any money for new clothes.

Noah didn't know what it was like to hide in a cupboard or closet when strange men came over. He didn't know how creepy and scary it was to have a strange man grab you and make you sit on his lap, his hold too tight, his face too close.

No, he didn't know that kind of fear.

He didn't know how it felt to have a mother named Candy, who had a body made for sin and used it to make a living. Only Roxy's sisters knew how it felt for people to look at you and think the worst because of who and what your mother was, because their mothers worked there, too.

Noah didn't know anything. He lived his perfect life free of scandal and of being ostracized.

And that's how John wanted to keep it.

"It's time to go. Let's collect our prize money, load up the horses, and get the hell out of here."

Roxy led her horse away and kept her back to her father and Noah. She didn't want to think about what might have been anymore. She'd spent countless hours and sleepless nights doing that.

Her life hadn't been all that bad the last ten years.

Not since Candy had moved them out of the last grungy apartment to the Wild Rose Ranch.

Roxy liked the cozy house away from the big mansion.

She didn't mind being on her own with the girls who had become her sisters.

She didn't mind being alone in the world.

She didn't, she told herself again.

But just once she'd like one of her parents to choose her. She'd like someone to choose her.

CHAPTER ONE

Six years later
Whitefall, Montana, Speckled Horse Ranch

John slumped in the saddle, fell off his horse, and landed in a heap in the dirt and tall grass as the horse danced away.

Shocked, Noah jumped off his horse and kneeled beside his stepdad. "John? John, are you okay?"

John moaned and rolled to his side. Pale, a fine sheen of sweat covered his rugged face. His unfocused eyes filled with pain. "I have to tell you . . ."

"Is anything broken? Where do you hurt?"

John grabbed Noah's arm. "I'm okay. Need to tell you . . ." John closed his eyes and tried to catch his breath.

Noah tamped down his panic and worries. A moment ago, they'd been sitting atop their horses on the overlook, staring at the long expanse of Speckled Horse Ranch spread out before them. Now, Noah grabbed John's hands and pulled him up to sitting, hoping the weakness he felt in John didn't mean something serious. "I need to get you home and to a hospital." Noah's mind went to a stroke or heart attack, neither of which Noah wanted to be true.

John's limbs remained limp, his body unsteady. Noah went around to John's back, squatted, wrapped his arms around John's middle, and lifted him up to his feet. "Come on, old man, help me out."

John reached for the saddle pommel.

Noah held John in place with his shoulder, reached down, grabbed John's jean-clad leg, and helped him put his boot in the stirrup. It took all Noah's strength to lift and push John into the saddle. Before John could topple down again, Noah swung up behind him.

Lucky for him, the horse took both their weight without bucking or rearing up and throwing them off.

Noah grabbed the reins and hooked one hand around John to keep him steady. "You okay?"

"This is damn embarrassing."

He'd get over it.

Noah nudged the horse to head home and kept their pace brisk, even though he wanted to gallop. "Hold tight. We'll be there soon."

John placed his hand over Noah's on his stomach. "You run this place well." A man of few words, John didn't say things he didn't mean.

The praise stunned Noah. "I learned from the best." Noah tried to pull John up, but John slumped forward again.

"I'm a difficult man, set in my ways. Rode you harder than any of the ranch hands."

That he did. No sense arguing with the truth. Not at a time like this.

Noah resented John's relentless drive when he was young. He had more than a few moments where he thought John thought he couldn't do anything right. But John sprinkled just enough praise and encouragement along the way to remind Noah that John wanted him to be the best and a partner he could count on.

Noah owed John so much, so he'd worked hard to earn his place at John's side on Speckled Horse Ranch.

"Your mother was a good woman. She loved you. Loved me, even though I never made it easy."

"She was happy here." Thinking about his mother always made him sad. She married John when Noah was two. Four years later, she died from complications due to an ectopic pregnancy. "I don't remember her well, but I still miss her." The admission didn't come easy.

John's big body trembled with the effort to stay upright in the saddle. His skin turned a sickly gray. Noah wondered if all this talk about the ranch and his mother meant John wanted to join her in heaven.

The thought stopped his heart. They couldn't cover the ride down the hill and across the wide pasture fast enough.

"Beth was happy here. I was happy with her," John confided.

When Noah's mother died, John sat him down in his study and told him straight out that no matter what, he'd stay on the ranch. From that day on, even though he was only a boy of six, John had taught him how to run the ranch, working day in and day out side by side. Noah had no other family. He couldn't lose the only father he'd ever known.

"After I lost Beth . . . well, no one could replace her. I tried but never found that kind of connection. So I settled. Lisa played to my ego. She made me feel young and alive again. But that all changed almost the minute we got married."

Noah hadn't liked Lisa from the second he'd met her. The feel of the house changed the instant she'd moved in, and he'd never gotten that sense of his mother and home back. Lisa's presence, the way she changed this and redecorated that, sucked out the last reminders of Noah's mom.

He resented Lisa for that and the dismissive way she treated John and their marriage. It left John even more closed off and disheartened.

Noah still didn't understand why they married when they both carried on a string of affairs neither of them spoke about and tried to hide despite the other knowing.

Noah would never forget the look in John's eyes when they stood outside the hospital nursery window looking in at Annabelle. He'd never seen anyone look so disappointed, and even more unbelievable, hurt. John never let it show that anything got through his thick skin, but seeing that squalling blond-haired, blue-eyed baby put that hurt in his golden eyes like Noah had never seen. To this day, although John always treated Annabelle with nothing but kindness, Noah sometimes caught him looking at her with that same hurt in his eyes.

Noah, young and uncertain about having a stepsister, hadn't understood the look until days later when they brought Annabelle home and he'd overheard John and Lisa's heated argument in their room that night. One look at Annabelle had told John what all of Lisa's protests to the contrary didn't. Annabelle wasn't his daughter, but the product of one of the many affairs Lisa kept quiet but hadn't managed to keep secret.

While John accepted Annabelle, even loved her in his own way, he'd never forgiven Lisa. Not for the affair, but for the undeniable proof that he'd been unable to get her pregnant himself after years of trying.

Noah remained silent on the subject. He focused on the ride, wishing for one of the guys from the stables to come out, see them coming, and help him with John.

"I don't know why I married her. After your mother

and the baby . . ." John ran his hand over his black hair that had grown more salt and pepper these last years. His Stetson still lay on the grass where he'd fallen. "I wanted another child." John squeezed his hand hard. "Don't get me wrong, you were a good son. I'm the only son to parents who had little family when I was born. Don't know if any of them are still around. I just wanted my name, my blood, to be here long after I'm gone."

Noah, still reeling from hearing John say he was a good son, high praise from a man who doled out very few compliments or niceties, understood the man's need for a legacy.

At thirty-one, Noah had been contemplating his lonely-looking future and wondering if it wasn't time to find a wife, have some kids, and make a family of his own. Without any good examples of a happy marriage and with a string of flings under his belt, he often wondered if he could make a relationship work.

Hell, who was he kidding, he'd learned from John, never let a woman get under your skin. He ended his last relationship because Cheryl wanted more than he was willing to give. Judging by the number of voicemails and text messages Cheryl had left on his cell phone, she wasn't ready to give up on him.

John expected some kind of answer, so Noah said, "I understand. You took care of me, sent me to college, and gave me a job and a life here on the ranch, even though I'm not your son. I appreciate everything you've done. A lot of men, my father included, would have dumped an unwanted child." He knew little about his own father, who cheated on his mother while she was pregnant with him. She divorced him, and his father took his freedom and never looked back.

"You were never unwanted," John replied, his voice gruff. "No matter my shortcomings as a parent, never think I didn't want you here. You reminded me of my-self at your age. You love ranching, the horses, the life. I enjoyed teaching you, seeing you discover new things. You wanted to follow in my footsteps. You put that college degree to work, changed things here and there, and helped make this place what it is today."

A lump formed in Noah's throat.

John broke the silence that settled between them. "I'm not proud of some of the things I've done. Most you know about, but some, well, I've kept a few things to myself. I have lots of regrets. One that is too late to make right. I hurt her because I was a coward, concerned about my reputation instead of protecting her."

Noah had no idea who or what John was talking about.

"Listen, son, what I'm trying to say is that soon this will belong to you."

Noah's heart sank. He hoped that day wasn't today, but feared John's heavy weight against his chest meant something dire.

"I have things I want to say." John sucked in several quick breaths. "Things. I. Need to tell you." He strug-gled to get the words out.

"John, please, stop talking. We're almost there. I'll get you to a doctor."

John winced in pain and leaned heavily to the side. It was all Noah could do to hold him up and against his chest.

"I need to get this out. You run this ranch, but you don't know . . . everything. Promise you'll take care of her. She's never had anyone."

"I promise. Annabelle will be fine."

John's head bobbed forward and up several times. "No. I need to tell you about . . ." John's words trailed off and his whole body went lax.

Noah swore. Hoping he was close enough to the stables for someone to hear him, he whistled. The high-pitched sound carried and Robby rushed out and spotted them. Noah reined in next to the ranch foreman.

"What happened?"

"He collapsed. Help me get him in the truck."

Robby took John by the shoulders. Noah swung down from the horse and caught John's legs.

Annabelle ran out of the house. "Oh my God!"

"Get the truck door, Sprite."

Noah and Robby muscled John into the front seat and buckled him in. No time to wait for an ambulance to drive all the way out here, they'd drive him to the hospital and get him the help he needed.

Noah hoped they would be in time.

THE HOSPITAL WAITING room walls closed in on Noah as he paced, his long stride eating up the stained carpet. He rolled his shoulders, but nothing eased the ache that had taken hold and wouldn't let go. Wild thoughts raced through his mind.

He hung on to only one: John Cordero was the strongest, most stubborn man he'd ever met. He wouldn't dare die of something as stupid as falling off his horse.

But John hadn't been in the saddle in more than two months. He'd made excuses and complained of getting old and aching joints and too much damn paperwork.

The usual John complaints Noah heard so often, he didn't think anything of it.

"Mr. Cordero?"

The doctor's voice brought back the panic he'd felt seeing John unconscious in the truck.

"Yes. It's just Noah. How is he?"

Annabelle stood and wrapped her arms around Noah's middle. He hugged her close, needing her support as much as she needed his.

"Your father is in the ICU. He's critical."

"What happened?" Tears streaked down Annabelle's pale cheeks.

"His condition has deteriorated over the last several months . . ."

"What condition?" Noah didn't understand what the doctor meant. "John's as healthy as a horse."

"I'm sorry, I thought Mr. Cordero informed his family about his diagnosis."

"Please, just tell us what's wrong with him," Annabelle pleaded.

"I've been treating Mr. Cordero for the past eight months. He has a rare brain tumor."

"The trip to Chicago two months ago." Noah put the pieces together.

"I sent him for some specialized treatment in hopes of shrinking the tumor and prolonging his life. Unfortunately, it wasn't as successful as we hoped. Frankly, it was a long shot, but Mr. Cordero was willing to endure the treatment."

"He's been so tired lately." Annabelle pressed closer to Noah's side. At fifteen, she'd endured enough loss in her short life. Her mother, Lisa, fed up with raising a baby and John's increasing disinterest in anything his wife did, walked out when Annabelle was just three.

Again, John lost the woman, but kept the child. He and John had done their best raising Annabelle on their own.

"Last I saw him a week ago, he was having difficulty with his balance, his vision was blurry, and his motor functions were deteriorating."

If Noah had known he'd have never let John on a horse. The thought of what could have happened if he'd fallen while they galloped across the fields shuddered through Noah's body.

"The tumor has caused some bleeding deep in the brain. It's only a matter of time."

"Are you saying he's dying?" Annabelle couldn't seem to comprehend the doctor's implausible words.

"I'm sorry, miss, but yes."

"How long?" A strange gruffness filled his voice, and Noah choked back the emotions welling up inside him.

Annabelle's nails dug into his side, her grip tightening along with the band around his chest, but he didn't feel the pain. Everything inside him went numb.

"Hours. Maybe a day or two." The doctor waited a moment while they absorbed the devastating news. "Mr. Cordero left instructions detailing his wishes. I've contacted his lawyer, letting him know we've invoked the living will. We've made John comfortable. He slips in and out of consciousness with varying degrees of alertness. This may continue for a while. You're welcome to stay with him in the room. If there is anyone you need to contact, I suggest you do it immediately."

"Mary and Robby, our foreman, are at the house. They'll want to come and say goodbye," Annabelle stammered. "What about Mom?" she asked, uncertain.

"You can call her on my cell, Sprite."

"She probably won't care."

Probably not, Noah agreed, but didn't voice his opinion. "Try her. No matter what she says or does, at least you know you tried." He dug his cell out of his dusty jeans pocket and handed it to her.

He waited for her to take a seat in the corner before he spoke to the doctor again. "Is there anything you need me to do? Decisions have to be made."

The doctor clapped a hand on Noah's shoulder and squeezed, offering what little comfort he could under the circumstances. "Eight months ago, I told Mr. Cordero to get his affairs in order. The living will he set up takes care of all the decisions needed in this situation. Spend time with him. Say goodbye."

The doctor left with that damn sympathetic look on his face. Noah turned to Annabelle, worried about the call to her rattlesnake of a mother. Not surprising, Annabelle looked worse for talking to her instead of better.

"She's not coming," his sister mumbled, and dropped the phone in his hand.

He bent in front of her and put his hands on her knees. "I'm sorry, Sprite. You tried."

"Fat lot of good it did me. She hates me."

"She doesn't hate you. She doesn't even know you."

"Isn't that worse?" Sometimes Annabelle was too damn smart for her own good.

Noah cocked up one side of his mouth. "Do you think she'll ever change?"

Annabelle folded her arms over her chest. "No."

"Then quit expecting her to do what you *hope* she'll do, instead of the thing you *know* she'll do."

Annabelle's head fell forward. "What's going to happen to me?"

"What do you mean, Sprite?" He brushed a strand of wet hair off her tear-stained cheek. He wasn't prone to tender gestures, but her eyes were still bright with unshed tears, the blue depths filled with nothing but sadness and a fear he understood all too well. No one liked to be left behind.

"I'm a minor. If Dad dies, I'll have to go stay with my mother. She doesn't want me. She'll leave me again and I'll be alone."

"Never." Absolute certainty filled his voice, though he wasn't sure he spoke the truth. If John died and Lisa wanted Annabelle, he'd have a hell of a time gaining custody. "I'll never let her take you."

He hoped Lisa didn't get some wild bug up her ass and make him a liar.

"Can we see him now?"

He held his hand out to her. "Come on, Sprite. Stop worrying. No matter what, it's you and me."

"You swear?"

Noah understood her fear. Where she still held hope that her mother would come around and want to be with her again, Noah had erected a shield to keep people out and his feelings in.

Much like John, he'd learned that no one could hurt you if they didn't know you cared.

"I swear. No one will ever come between us."